BREAKFAST AT SLIMOTHY'S

MIRANDA OSBORN

Published by: The Bright Wild Company, LLC

ISBN-13: 979-8-9939241-3-7

If you find yourself lost,
follow the slime trail.
Results may vary.

the great forest

dwarf chenille

dwarf chenille

butterfly bush

Roger's house

scorpion's-tail

Distance: Slimes
A garden bed = 3 slimes

To the fence = 6 slimes

To mild regret = 1 slime

To enlightenment = infinity slimes

1 slime = the average length of Slimothy's nightly slime trail before he gets distracted (about 8 feet)

Acknowledgments

In no particular order, because order is for spreadsheets, not slugs:

JS once had a plant so perfect I immediately committed light botanical espionage and brought home its twin. Our inside joke still blooms—immigration will always be the best form of flattery. Thank you for the late-night talks, the sage wisdom, and enough friendship and wine to irrigate an emotional vineyard.

JR—Director of Slug Sanity, keeper of calm, and spark of wonder. You opened the gates to the Bright Wild, mapped its corners, named its inhabitants and danced through every milestone since. Without you, none of this would exist, and Slimothy would still be ranting to a basil plant with poor listening skills.

EL lent me "Dracula," her ear, and an entire constellation of cosmic wisdom—and taught me, without trying, that the universe listens best to those who manifest their destiny loudly, and with snacks.

My mom, first and forever storyteller, favorite author in the sky—you set the bar for magic, mischief, and metaphors. I'm still here, scribbling from the ground, glancing upward, hoping my words find you among the stars (or at least make decent company on the way).

MS—the inaugural "Planter of Plants"—thank you for whispering "that's amazing" to every sprout until the hesitant turned into harvest and the garden grew legs, leaves, and laughter.

To my husband—Slimothy's dad—strong enough to lift the heavy things, kind enough to read the origin stories, and patient enough to live with both a slug and his human mother. You've been the steady roots beneath everything we've grown. Thank you for letting me follow my dreams and for keeping us caffeinated; with you, even Tuesdays feel possible.

Slimothy and I bow our antennae to you all—forever in debt, forever in gratitude, and forever wandering through the Bright, weird pages of the Wild.

Dream Interpretations for Emergency Use Only

"Hello, and welcome to *Viruses You Didn't Ask For,*" Slimothy declared with the manic cheer of someone who had absolutely not rehearsed.

He peered over the lectern like a very damp professor who'd slept in a compost bin and woken up certain he had tenure—despite being a slug with the kind of misplaced confidence that should disqualify him from handling data entirely.

"Tonight's episode: Cucurbit Leaf Crumple Virus—CuLCrV if you're in a hurry and already emotionally exhausted, which is the only correct way to experience plant pathology."

He clicked the remote. The slide looming overhead erupted in huge, judgmental letters: "SELECT RESISTANT CULTIVARS," delivering agricultural shame in 72-point font.

Slimothy nodded solemnly, trying not to take the aggressive typography as a personal attack.

"*Right. Moving on.* Anyway, you may know its close associate, the silverleaf whitefly ..."

A little animated arrow on the slide scooted across the screen, mocking him with unnecessary enthusiasm. It kept moving, circling labels it had no business highlighting, behaving like a toddler with a laser pointer.

"—*Bemisia tabaci*—or as I like to call it, 'Nope With Wings,'" Slimothy went on, pretending not to notice the arrow's tragic performance. "It's small, it's rude ..." he drew in whatever dignity-laden air he could muster—no easy feat with a scarf wrapped around him like a panicked sea creature—"... and it's turning perfectly respectable leaves into crumpled salad confetti and single-handedly ruining the garden's quarterly performance metrics," he finished in one heroic exhale.

He gave himself a tiny shake—his version of hitting "refresh"—and barreled ahead.

"In an ideal world," he continued, "we'd select crops with actual tolerance ratings. In *this* world, someone plants pumpkins in the fall and then files a complaint when the garden immediately catches the flu."

Slimothy took this last part personally, as a creature who had only recently discovered that pollen could, in fact, hold a grudge.

"That means if you are a squash, melon, cucumber, or pumpkin, congratulations: you are basically an all-inclusive resort for tiny sap thieves with commitment issues—complete with a poorly managed buffet."

He tapped the clicker with his scarf, as if to illustrate his point. The remote, displaying excellent boundaries, did absolutely nothing. Slimothy cleared his throat in the universal tone of a slug pretending the technology wasn't winning.

"They don't just pop in for a quick sip of phloem. They bring friends. CYSDV. CCYV. A disturbing portion of the viral alphabet—each one showing up with a mystery casserole nobody asked for."

The spotlight burned hotter—unreasonably, illegally hot. Slimothy blinked into it, briefly convinced he had wandered into a TED Talk hosted inside a malfunctioning Easy-Bake Oven.

"This is where integrated pest management—IPM—comes in," he added, trying to sound authoritative while slowly broiling. "Step one: pick resistant crops. Step two: accept that yellow squash has the constitution of a Victorian fainting couch. Step three: plant cucumbers and butternut, who—unlike pumpkins— don't immediately swoon at the sight of a virus."

He attempted a dramatic gesture toward the screen behind him—a feat made difficult by the fact that he had no arms and was now being dive-bombed by a gnat that kept strafing his eye stalk. The slide blared: "CROPS: HIGHLY APPROPRIATE / MODERATELY APPROPRIATE / DOOMED."

"In conclusion," he announced, trying to ignore the gnat's seventh pass, "know your host range, choose your cultivars wisely, and remember: somewhere out there, a silverleaf whitefly is planning its next move. Probably on your kale."

A cluster of ornamental onions immediately fainted, collapsing in a dramatic heap as if someone had whispered "sauté."

It was, unfortunately, at that exact moment that Slimothy—finally fed up—swatted at the gnat, missed spectacularly, and delivered a full-body slug-impact event to the remote instead. The clicker rebelled instantly, snapping downward like a mousetrap designed specifically for the uncoordinated. The spotlight flared hotter, sizzling him like a damp canapé left under a broiler for one unforgiving second too long.

He attempted a tactical retreat, but his entire underside slid onto a pedal—why was there a pedal?—sending the stage lurching like it had personal grievances.

Suddenly he was no longer on stage at all. He was in the rear passenger compartment of something questionable rolling backward down a hill, and before he could question the physics of it, he found himself mashing pedals with no feet—an arrangement as useless as it sounded, as if hoping sheer panic could substitute for limbs. Naturally, that's when the world opted to veer sharply onto another route—a lane full of judgmental vegetables, disapproving snails, and one deeply disappointed frog wearing a headset.

He did not have time for rationality.

All he could register was the kaleidoscope of produce shrieking around him and the existential wrongness of automotive infrastructure inside a motivational garden seminar.

"WHY ARE THERE LANES?" Slimothy broadcast in sheer panic as an entire row of horticultural bystanders screamed in chorus.

Internally, he made a mental note to file a complaint with whoever was in charge of dream transportation safety—because clearly no one here had passed an inspection since 1998.

Externally, the universe denied him processing time entirely. A leafy voice from the front row erupted: "WHICH ONE OF US WOULD YOU SAVE IN A

FIRE?"

Slimothy opened his mouth to answer—despite having absolutely no evacuation plan—and woke up tangled in the kale patch, wheezing like someone who'd just tried to outrun a hose timer while the humidity wrapped around him in a clingy, atmospheric handshake.

He blinked, took stock, and conducted a one-slug emergency briefing:

Moisture levels: catastrophic.
Mind: scrambled.
Scarf: knotted like a tragic pretzel.
Clipboard: gone.

It took a few extra seconds for the most alarming fact to register: his clipboard never migrated. It never wandered. It was the only object in the Bright Wild that respected order, protocol, and basic decency. If it had vanished, something was wrong on a level that required forms. Many forms. Possibly a subcommittee.

Which meant one thing: action.

Slimothy extricated himself from the kale and fumbled in earnest for the small, battered notebook he kept tucked beneath a basil leaf—hoping it hadn't grown legs too. It was his field guide—his self-authored, self-edited opus, rendered increasingly unreadable by layers of cucumber pulp and what he insisted were "field-appropriate revisions"—but essential nonetheless. If a dream woke him at this level of sweat, he considered it a prophecy. Especially when machinery was involved. Along with data, Slimothy had no business interpreting vehicles of any kind—which made them, in his mind, mystical objects entirely above his pay grade.

This was already shaping up to be a multi-sweat event, the sort that absolutely required documentation—because if a nightmare wasn't logged in sweat units, was it even real?

He swallowed, braced himself, and flipped to the sweat-unit appendix of the garden handbook no one asked him to annotate—a section he generally avoided unless things were extremely dire or unexpectedly damp.

Temporal Shmooing + Other Catastrophes

One sweat = the amount of moisture Slimothy collects in the time it takes to say "humidity clung like polyester."
A cool night = -10 sweats.
A muggy July = 1,000 sweats.
A rave under aggressively enthusiastic lights = off the chart sweats.

Slimothy pushed a trembling leaf aside and took inventory.

Pulse: frantic.
Scarf: aggressively knotted.
Mind: disheveled.
Clipboard = still gone. Not misplaced. Not "under a leaf somewhere." Gone in the specific, catastrophic way important objects vanish right before cosmic doom.

He navigated to a fresh page to analyze his dream state—because if the universe insisted on sending him chaos, he might as well categorize it while he was at it.

Vehicle rolling backward = clearly a sign the garden gods are reversing time. Not as a warning—likely because they probably forgot their pruning shears and needed a redo.
Backward motion = unfinished business, unpulled weeds, the universe immediately undoing itself the moment organization tries to come to the shed.
Official-sounding label generated impulsively = "Temporal Shmooing."
Definition = not provided, and almost certainly unhelpful.

Being in the backseat = deeply ominous; universe-issued demotion.
Something sticky underfoot = snacks within reach but socially forbidden.
Someone else driving the narrative arc = unacceptable.
Field note = never trust a dream where the starring role has been

reassigned.

Pedals that didn't work = cosmic sabotage. "Trying to water the plants, but someone forgot to turn on the spigot of destiny."

Also see broken pedals: dried watering cans, squirrel interference, meetings without snacks, temperatures under 40 degrees.

Conclusion = this is what happens when basil course is skipped.

Veering onto the other side of the road = the lane of chaos, inhabited freely by those who don't value stability.

Drifting across lines = temptation by forbidden produce; boundaries shifting without proper documentation; fate nudging toward unauthorized subplot.

Summary = sometimes life swerves. Refusal protocol: become slime.

He shut the notebook, nodding like a seasoned expert in nonsense. "Overall meaning," he declared to the entirely imaginary basil-leaf stenographer, "Greatness imminent. Snacks inevitable. Vehicle moving backward? Abandon mission immediately. Works for wheelbarrows too."

Slimothy puffed up, convinced he had just made a major breakthrough in dream science, sweat metrics, and possibly metaphysics. The dream fog began to lift—only for a passing leaf to drop as if it had been waiting all morning to hit him specifically.

A sound drifted across the garden—delicate, papery, wrong. A soft rustle. A slow crumple. A whisper of curling, chlorotic misery straight out of the nightmare lecture he'd just given. Slimothy's mind performed a rapid, panicked cartwheel. Something was out there. Something real. Something meddling.

With the gravity of a slug chronicling his last known moments, Slimothy scribbled one final line, painfully aware that his garden-issue writing surface was still unaccounted for and possibly in enemy hands.

Field note = danger unknown; panic confirmed; approach from the left, snacks recommended.

CHAPTER ONE

No Beans, Only Magic

Slimothy liked to call himself a philosopher of the garden, though most of his life lessons came from staring up at things much taller than he was. That happened to be almost everything. His world sparkled with secrets: vines twisting into riddles the soil refused to solve, punctuation even the compost pile wouldn't edit, and flowers glowing faintly like diaries of the sun that always ended on a cliffhanger. To Slimothy, the Bright Wild was less a patch of plants and more a stage, where he had happily cast himself as its smallest thinker, delivering soliloquies from the world's tiniest soapbox to an audience of snails who reviewed him harshly on Garden Yelp.

One late summer afternoon, midway through one such imagined performance, he craned his tiny slug neck so far back he nearly toppled over. Looming above him were the eggplants. No longer cute sprouts but full-grown giants, six feet tall and swaying like skyscrapers in a wind tunnel, looking down at him like they owned the block. Slimothy almost expected the snails to file another one-star review: *"Views obstructed. Too much eggplant. Would not recommend."*

They looked magnificent. Slimothy's stomach rumbled. Four and a bit months ago, they were seedlings. Now they towered above him, inkish black helmets glinting in the sun, completely out of reach. Worst of all, they tasted amazing—

the kind of feast you brag about on leaf forums for weeks, dangling just beyond his slime trail.

At barely 1.5 to 3 grams, depending on hydration, mood, and basil intake, Slimothy was a thumbprint-sized TED Talk enthusiast with oversized ideas. Forever dreaming big, forever too short to reach dinner.

One of the biggest mysteries of all was his nose, twitching at pollen, sighing at dust, staging its own private operas in the moss. Some mornings it seemed less like a nose and more like a broken compass, unhelpfully directing Slimothy toward trouble he couldn't identify but was probably allergic to. It made him wonder about scale, about size, about whether the world was really so tall or if he was just built inconveniently close to the ground.

That train of thought inevitably brought him to Jack. Slimothy blinked slowly and wondered if Jack's legendary beanstalk had really been all that special—or if maybe Jack was just unusually short. Perhaps they all belonged in the League of Vertically Challenged Visionaries, where the membership dues were paid in sighs and unreachable vegetables. Their motto was simple enough: *"Looking up since forever."* Perspective, after all, was everything.

The irony of it all was that there wasn't a single bean in sight. No beans simmering for dinner, no green stalks climbing poles, not even a sad can of baked beans rolling by. This was an eggplant patch—stubborn, midnight violet, and proud. Still, Slimothy, ever the poet, declared it a land of magic beans—because sometimes magic wasn't in fairy tales but in the ridiculous reality of six-foot produce that tasted like steak and blocked his view of the mailbox.

Magic beans of patience, sprouting every morning when Slimothy waited for blossoms to open as if watching paint dry on salad.

Magic beans of mystery, because how exactly had these things grown taller than the garden shed without anyone noticing?

Magic beans of comedy, when one toppled and nearly flattened the watering can, instantly winning Best Physical Comedy at the Bright Wild Awards.

Magic beans of possibility, whispering that the Bright Wild followed rules so strange they probably required a notary and a turnip to enforce them.

Slimothy, postage-stamp-sized armchair theorist with kale-colored glasses, craned his neck, sighed, and accepted that life was stranger than fairy tales anyway. Jack could keep his beanstalk—Slimothy had eggplants. Eggplants that stubbornly acted like VIPs in a garden where Slimothy was still waiting for his wristband. He'd probably been bumped for someone with better foliage.

As the wind swayed the violet-crowned towers, he entertained a few possibilities about what might wait at the top. A grumpy giant? A chicken laying golden eggs? Or maybe just a very confused volunteer from the county extension office, waving a pamphlet titled "Bean Problems Only" and muttering at the eggplants, *"Peas, I can handle. Beans, no problem. You, however? You're unsanctioned vegetation."*

For Slimothy, though, the sight was proof that the garden was more than food. It was magic disguised as edible foliage, wonder hidden in stems and leaves. Right on cue, his stomach growled again, undercutting the poetry, and Slimothy, staring up at the aubergines, sighed, *"Fine, be giants. I'll just starve poetically."*

No beans, perhaps. Still plenty of magic. Also plenty of culinary yearning. A slug resigned to starve theatrically, notebook in slime at the ready, scrawling his memoirs in cucumber juice and radish pulp, hoping someone would quote him later as the garden's smallest and hungriest lettuce laureate. In his more theatrical moments, he even dramatically foresaw his last words etched into the side of a compost bin: *"He dreamed of eggplants ..."* though, knowing the Bright Wild, an earthworm would probably carve it in crooked and spell it *"eggpants."*

CHAPTER TWO

Slimothy and the Mystery of the Half-Eaten Tomatoes

The night Slimothy first spotted the figure, it crouched at the edge of the garden—quiet, patient, unsettlingly statue-like. Slimothy, perched on the stoop after one too many glasses of wine, surveyed the scene like royalty who had misplaced both the crown and the throne and was now embracing the anarchy of it all. His almost-drained glass caught the moonlight as he raised it skyward, as if to toast the compost pile itself.

For a moment, Slimothy thought he might be witnessing the opening act of some strange backyard opera starring one slightly tipsy gardener, a questionable supporting cast of tomato plants, and—judging by the apparition's dramatic timing—an understudy character who had clearly not rehearsed his lines.

The performance got underway when the stage lights of moon and cloud shuffled into place. Out of the wings emerged a shape that could have doubled as a petrified sandwich from a miner's lunchbox—if that sandwich had legs and opinions. It hopped into view with prehistoric dignity, as though the Cretaceous had RSVP'd late.

The stranger didn't walk so much as perform an interpretive hop routine—

pause for 3.142 minutes, hop, pause again. Like a tiny archaeologist testing ancient stone slabs, the frog moved with slow, ceremonial precision. Slimothy remembered the number clearly because it was the same as pi—not the math kind, the dessert kind—and Slimothy never forgot pie. At last, the lone amphibian delegate stopped beneath a towering pink mushroom and stared at it for what felt like forever, as if casting his vote in a very tense garden gnome union election.

Night after night, the after-hours loiterer returned. Sometimes he looked like a museum prop that had wandered off at closing time. Other nights, a partially collapsed beanbag chair that had clearly failed its audition for furniture. Slimothy, armed with sarcasm and free time, christened him with names to fit the look of the day: General Wartsworth. Sir Hop-a-Lot. Mayor of Awkward Pauses.

Whatever his identity, they developed an odd sort of politeness—a silent exchange of, *"Pardon me, sir … after you, sir … mind the tomato plants, sir."*

Slimothy had questions. Was this the culprit behind the tomatoes with suspicious bite marks he woke up to every morning, gnawed just enough to ruin them for everyone else? Or was he the kind of neighbor who "just borrowed" your hose, forgot to return it, and then tried to smooth things over by leaving a suspiciously self-satisfied garden gnome on your porch as a peace offering? Slimothy couldn't shake the feeling there might be a secret frog-gnome alliance at work, plotting midnight raids and cover-ups beneath the society garlic.

He didn't rush mysteries—he let them ripen. Slimothy was built for wonder, and wonder made him linger. To him, every leaf might hide a secret, eggplants could grow into skyscrapers, and radishes, with their little shoulders peeking from the soil, were proof that nature had a sense of humor. Which is why Slimothy watched with the kind of focus he usually saved for fresh basil. Naturally, this new character in the Bright Wild had him hooked. Soon, the mystery deepened—because of course it did. His life never chose normal when chaos was available.

In the northwest corner of the garden, a picture-perfect white picket fence rose up, complete with a toadstool terrace that looked like it was auditioning for a role on "Extreme Makeover: Amphibian Edition."

At the center sat the frog's throne: a chipped terracotta pot tucked beneath a mushroom roof, its rim worn smooth by countless evenings of silent judgment. At its base, a supporting leaf pile swelled like a shadow—layers upon layers of mulch and hushed whispers. It seemed less like comfort and more like a hoarded secret, a living mound breathing softly in the night, marked with an unspoken command: *"Do Not Disturb."*

Slimothy could have sworn the discarded foliage shifted when he glanced away, edging nearer, creeping along on the power of dramatic timing alone.

A strawberry pole stood sentinel, the ruby fruit gleaming like a blood-red beacon—equal parts warning and invitation—its stillness a little too intentional to trust. Yet when Slimothy looked back after rubbing his eye stalks, the fruit seemed angled differently, tilted toward him in quiet accusation. Beyond it, a small gate, two mailboxes, and a scatter of garden tools arranged themselves with uncanny precision. They felt less like clutter and more like props set carefully for a ritual whose meaning Slimothy could not decipher. He narrowed his eyes at the letter boxes, uneasy, almost convinced one hid his missing tomato cages and just as certain he didn't want to know what else might be inside. Towering above it all was the crown jewel: a storybook keep with layered walls rising so high they seemed to tiptoe into the edge of night. Its minarets shimmered beneath the starlight, their pointed tops glowing like lanterns hung by ancient hands, casting a gentle enchantment over the dark.

To Slimothy, they looked less like simple spires and more like watchful lighthouses, each one leaning inward ever so slightly, as if trading secrets only the night could hear. Shadows pooled along the layered parapets in soft currents, giving the entire stronghold the dreamy illusion that it might shift or sigh or subtly rearrange itself when the world blinked.

Framed by a canopy of red flowers and blazing stars, the whole structure appeared both regal and faintly theatrical—a fortress doubling as a stage set. Some stars dutifully twinkled in the sky; others had the audacity to bloom on stalks, stretching taller and taller like contestants in a pageant for Most Overly Dramatic Plant. Slimothy wouldn't have been surprised if one waved, tossed a sash over its leaves, and thanked the judges.

From his mound of earth beside the moat, snugly tucked beneath a draped leaf, the frog ruled with quiet authority. Sometimes he semi-buried himself there, as if the garden itself had raised him like a statue of living soil. He presided with the air of a monarch—issuing silent decrees Slimothy suspected were less about grandeur and more about practical matters—curfews for crickets, speed limits for slugs, and zoning restrictions on society garlic, which was forever trying to expand its territory without filing the proper paperwork.

Slimothy couldn't help himself. Watching the frog was like tuning into a reality show no one asked for, and in his head, he became the narrator. Lord Mudfoot, touring swamps with "character." "The Croaker Clan," experts in dramatic silence and passive-aggressive ribbits. Plus his personal favorite, "Tadpole Makeover Challenge," where contestants tried to glam up a pond using nothing but soggy driftwood and lost flip-flops.

Every stakeout came with its own soundtrack. Slimothy tried to stay silent, but his nose had other plans—erupting into squeaks and honks, part broken accordion, part off-key recorder recital, until he resembled a middle school marching band trapped in a rain barrel. A one-slug orchestra entirely beyond his control. He worried the frog thought he was mocking him with nose music.

Misunderstandings tended to follow Slimothy; he was no ordinary slug. Small in size but brimming with oversized ideas, Slimothy had always carried a strange sort of gravity, as if he'd simply wandered out of a dream and forgotten to go back. No one knew exactly where he'd come from, only that one day he was there—polished outer layer gleaming faintly, eye stalks bright with impossible ambition.

When he first arrived in the Bright Wild, he felt unstoppable. New leaves to nibble, new pebbles to conquer, endless radishes to admire. Yet almost as soon as he settled in, the forever sniffles arrived like an unwelcome roommate—the kind that never paid rent, left tissues everywhere, and refused to move out no matter how many hints you dropped.

To solve the mystery, Slimothy had been making frequent trips to the doctor. He insisted on second, third, and even fourth opinions, because surely someone must know how to cure a slug with sinuses that sound like a balloon deflating in slow motion. Was it the humidity, the pollen, or cosmic payback for every basil leaf he'd ever stolen under cover of darkness? Either way, the sniffles became the soundtrack to his surveillance.

The more Slimothy watched, the more names he invented. Wartlock Holmes. Sir Amphibius the Stoic. Baron Ribbitstein. Whatever the name, one thing was clear—this frog wasn't just passing through. He was setting down roots.

Slimothy told himself it was just neighborly curiosity, but in reality it had turned into a full-blown stakeout. Every night he rehearsed possible introductions like he was auditioning for a community theater play called "Meet the Frog Next Door." Should he start with a casual, *"Evening, sir,"* or go dramatic with, *"State your business in these tomatoes?"* His sinuses, of course, sabotaged the entire production by providing a nose solo that sounded like a goose stuck in a trombone.

Slimothy, naturally, overthought the etiquette. Should he bring a welcome basket? A sprig of driveway basil? Or would that be bribery if the tomato theft rumors proved true?

For now, Slimothy waited—patient, watchful, sniffling. Every night he perched in the shadows, equal parts neighbor, detective, and unwilling brass section, workshopping opening lines that never made it past his sinuses. The frog never wavered, always pausing like he was in the middle of a dramatic soliloquy Slimothy wasn't invited to hear.

Slimothy matched him beat for beat. The stalemate continued: frog squatting beneath his mushroom like the world's least enthusiastic gargoyle, and Slimothy crouched nearby, his sinuses providing a soundtrack of damp discontent— somewhere between jazz and plumbing.

Even Slimothy knew this couldn't last forever. One night, someone would speak first—and when it happened, the Bright Wild would never be the same.

Until then, he waited—steadfast, congested, and mildly dramatic—ready for the day when the Mayor of Awkward Pauses finally revealed his true identity as that one neighbor who never waves but mysteriously knows everyone's Wi-Fi password.

CHAPTER THREE

Ancestry-Dot-Compost: The Slimothy Files

Ask five residents of the Bright Wild where Slimothy came from, and you'd get six different answers. Some said he was hatched from an especially ambitious compost pile. Others swore he'd arrived by mail—part of a short-lived live garden mascot subscription service. No one really knew where Slimothy got his start, least of all Slimothy.

He preferred the theory that he'd simply emerged, fully formed, slightly damp, and mildly confused on a Tuesday morning that already felt like it had too much responsibility.

By all accounts, he was unremarkable in size but oddly memorable in color: a soft green with a faint golden sheen, as though he'd been dipped partially into optimism. Under strong light, an opalescent shimmer rippled across his back like sunlight on pond water—though, depending on the day, it might've just been residual coffee grounds.

A gastropod with grandiose plans, garden riddles to unravel, and a suspicious number of artistically nibbled tomatoes to his name, Slimothy wore his trademark orange scarf at all times. Not for warmth (he was, at best, temperature-indifferent), but for identity. Wearing the scarf said *distinguished garden figure*, and, more practically, made him easier to spot after rainstorms or during poorly timed sprinkler incidents.

In terms of lineage, Slimothy claimed descent from the Myrtle Slugs of Lower Bed Three—a noble line, allegedly—though the claim was unverified and possibly invented during an overly confident garden council meeting. Others whispered he might be partially banana slug, citing his dramatic tendencies and the faint citrus scent he gave off when startled.

What was known, however, was that Slimothy had inherited a certain philosophical streak—passed down, he insisted—from his great-great-grandslug—a compost scholar who once attempted to write a memoir titled "Slime and Punishment." Only two pages survived, one of which had been laminated for posterity and now served as a coaster beneath Slimothy's tea jar.

Questionable ancestry aside, he carried himself with purpose. He wasn't just a slug—he was a founder, a thinker, and, according to his self-awarded title plaque, "Head of Supportive Vegetation Management."

He believed the Bright Wild was more than a garden. It was a civilization—one that required vision, leadership, and, from time to time, snack breaks.

CHAPTER FOUR

Slimothy and the Case of Sourdough or Chickens

S omewhere between the hairy asters and the dwarf chenille, the Bright Wild looked like it had been designed by a botanist on their third energy drink and a dare. A plant flopped dramatically across the bed, its fuzzy red catkin-like flowers trailing behind it like an octopus getting a pedicure, serrated green leaves bristling with attitude while bright red flower spikes stuck up like a punk band having a bad hair day.

Slimothy squinted at the name tag. Dwarf chenille. Honestly, who came up with this stuff? At this rate, he dimly expected to stumble across an anxious arugula or a passive-aggressive thistle. Somewhere out there, a botanist was getting paid real money to mash random adjectives and body parts together. Slimothy, meanwhile, was working for lettuce.

When Slimothy first dipped his antennae into gardening, he had no idea the world was hiding such wonders. Radishes had shoulders? Gardens could float in mismatched pots of concrete and clay like some avant-garde fairy kingdom? Apparently yes. Every day brought a new phrase to stumble over—*tender perennials, cut-and-come-again salad bars, overwintering.* Slimothy wrote them down like spells in a grimoire, certain he was unlocking secrets mortals weren't meant to know.

At first, he was simply proud to keep a few green friends alive. Naturally, in classic Slimothy fashion, a modest collection quickly grew into a multi-level urban jungle with roughly 284 varietals and a sitemap he updated more often than his calendar. A friend warned him this was how it always started: *first gardening, then cooking, and before you knew it, sourdough starters and backyard chickens priced like luxury sedans.* Slimothy brushed it off with dramatic indifference, but secretly he was already wondering if there was a chicken model that paired well with kale.

The kale fixation began at a Fourth of July party. Not because of the fireworks or the patriotic bunting, or even the questionable potato salad sweating in the sun. No, Slimothy's life turned upside down with a single bite of lemon poppyseed sweet kale salad.

It was crunchy. It was tangy. It had tiny red specks scattered across the leaves like edible fireworks frozen mid-burst. To Slimothy, it wasn't seasoning—it was destiny sprinkled from the heavens. In that instant, as sparklers fizzled and the night sky bloomed with light, Slimothy had a revelation.

He could grow this himself.

Goodbye bagged greens suffocating in 10 layers of clingy plastic, each one rustling louder than an enthusiastic kazoo convention when you tried to sneak them open at midnight. Sayonara limp leaves that tasted of disappointment and smelled faintly of refrigerator regret.

Hello, homegrown obsession—equal parts leafy greens and pure delusion. By the time the grand finale boomed overhead, Slimothy wasn't watching the sky. He was staring at the salad bowl as if it were a crystal ball. He saw rows of kale stretching out before him, shimmering in morning dew, a kingdom of curls and crunch.

From that moment on, he wasn't just a gardener. He was a prophet—a kale evangelist with dirt under his feelers and destiny in his slime trail. Neighbors spoke of fireworks that night; Slimothy remembered only the holy crunch that changed his life.

Somewhere in the background, as smoke drifted across the sky, Slimothy whispered his first true prayer to the soil: *"Let there be kale."*

The very next morning, Slimothy began his crusade. He declared the south corner of the garden his personal kale kingdom and immediately set to work, convinced destiny would handle the details. Because when you believed kale was destiny, failure wasn't failure—it was just character development.

Slimothy's patch was more than a garden. It was a crossroads, a stage, and on certain nights, a buffet. At 9 p.m. sharp—or closer to 11 if they were feeling frisky—five deer floated in like clockwork. They crossed the street, vaulted the neighbor's six-foot fence, and lined up at the mulberry bushes as if auditioning for "Swan Lake"—graceful on their hind legs, nibbling leaves in perfect unison, utterly unaware the audience hadn't paid for tickets.

Lizards shot up concrete walls like thrill-seekers in a climbing gym, while beetles, ants, and nameless crawlers marched the pint-sized steps Slimothy had laid out for them, transforming his mismatched beds into a transit hub disguised as a yard. Buses of bees, flights of butterflies, and the occasional drunk moth all arrived according to a questionable timetable.

In the middle of it all, Slimothy slid proudly, convinced this wasn't just a patch of dirt. It was destiny under construction—the kind of grand vision only he could see and only weeds seemed eager to support, equal parts theater, cafeteria, and civic disaster.

Every performance needed an audience, and every circus needed one critic who thought they could run it better. Slimothy had his. He appeared habitually—black, silent, unimpressed. Amid the nightly parade of deer, lizards, and beetles was the mysterious new neighbor: Mr. Frog, whom Slimothy eventually decided to call Roger. Why Roger? Maybe because of the way he hopped like he was late for work, maybe because Slimothy once stumbled across a soggy envelope addressed to Roger, Esq., or maybe because the name just fit. Whatever the reason, he slipped into the Bright Wild cast list as part sidekick, part referee—applauding Slimothy's small victories with a silent blink and sighing dramatically whenever chaos broke out.

If the garden needed a voice of reason, Roger was it—though he preferred quietly devastating judgment over actual advice. His sighs could flatten entire evenings, the kind of exhale that made Slimothy feel like a disappointing group project.

If Roger was the Bright Wild's resident judge, then Allison the hummingbird was its tax collector, health inspector, and over-caffeinated security drone all rolled into one. Where Roger ruled by silence and stares, Allison governed by velocity. She appeared without warning, a jeweled blur slicing the air, showing up 23 times a day to audit every flower for nectar compliance. She could remember every sugary stop she'd ever made, down to how long it took each one to refill, as though she kept ledgers in the air.

She was awake all day, diurnal and relentless, and ate with the urgency of someone who knew she could not store much for later—nectar by the beakful, five to eight doses an hour—zooming from bloom to bloom like a winged espresso addict. By sunset she had visited what felt like every single blossom in the Bright Wild and probably a few Slimothy had never even noticed. He sometimes wondered how much of her was feather and how much was caffeine. Eventually, he decided the answer was neither. It was brain—nothing but heavy brain, crammed into a head that looked three sizes too big for the body carrying it around. Which explained a lot, in his opinion, since auditors always had the biggest heads.

Slimothy knew she had a thing for red. The shrimp plant, the red hot poker, even the garden hose nozzle—all irresistible. She wasn't picky. Any bloom would do, as long as it poured sugar on tap. Quick as lightning, with a beak like spring-loaded chopsticks, she could also snatch protein snacks out of thin air between sips. To Slimothy, she wasn't just a bird. She was a glucose accountant with wings, balancing the books one flower at a time.

Of course, the audits came with enforcement. She checked the paperwork before dive-bombing the *Justicia brandegeeana*—a broadleaf evergreen with rosy-pink flowers that, to Slimothy, was far too serious a name for something that looked like a shrimp auditioning for a role in a seafood parade. She came at it like Slimothy was trying to smuggle spinach without a visa, wings buzzing with bureaucratic fury. Meanwhile, her invisible clipboard ticked with the satisfaction of a tax auditor who had just found an unreported cucumber.

Sometimes she hovered with violent intensity, circling above Slimothy's head like a ceiling fan with a grudge, eyes bright with suspicion. He could've sworn she was muttering: *"Shrimp plant—borderline. Basil—excessive leaning. Skyflower— show-offs. Slug—still suspicious."* Then, just as suddenly, she would vanish to clock in at the neighbor's dahlias as though they offered better dental.

Allison's throat shimmered red in one moment and green in the next, which left Slimothy 63% convinced she had a doppelgänger. Science might've explained it, but Slimothy preferred the crime-drama version. To him, it was a disguise—vivid neck hues shifting with light levels, moisture, the angle of viewing, and even a little wear and tear. Slimothy just called it what it was: bird-based trickery. A two-bird racket. One handled inspections, the other handled collections, and together they ran the nectar beat like mobsters in feathers.

With her ultraviolet vision, Allison probably saw him glowing like overripe lettuce under a blacklight—the perfect mark in a sting operation he hadn't agreed to. Either way, she was loyal to the red shrimp plant, never the yellow. Yellow shrimp weren't even real in Slimothy's opinion, and if they were, the plant naming department had clearly been day drinking and daring each other to sneak bad jokes past the greenhouse manager.

She tolerated the purple skyflower, but only barely, eyeing it the way a detective eyes a suspect who's far too pleased with their own alibi. Its petals were too showy, too eager to be admired, and therefore undeserving of her attention. In Allison's book, that made it guilty. Guilty of wasting her time. Guilty as charged. Sentence: zero nectar.

Across the garden, Roger was drafting his own list of grievances.

Slimothy, watching them both, couldn't help but wonder if they were really just the Bright Wild's HOA. Roger played the role of bored vice president; Allison the hyperactive compliance officer, buzzing around issuing violations for unruly vines, suspiciously tall eggplants, and failure to register a decorative flamingo. Together they ran the world's tiniest but strictest subdivision. Slimothy wasn't sure what the HOA fees were, but he suspected he'd been paying in kale leaves all along.

A strange setup, given Slimothy held the mayor's sash, yet he was still treated like the clueless homeowner who had missed every single meeting. Perhaps it was also proof he was creeping toward the sourdough-and-chickens phase of life, forever dodging citations for disturbing the peace with his midnight nose solos. Knowing Allison, she was probably already drafting one in ultraviolet ink.

CHAPTER FIVE

The Potting Bench Predicament

How many potting benches does one slug need? Slimothy would argue at least three. Possibly four if you counted the one he kept "just browsing" in his online cart.

The first was purchased in a moment of weakness. It was sleek, beautiful, and promised to change his gardening life. Unfortunately, patience had never been Slimothy's strongest virtue, and when two-day shipping stretched into what felt like an eternity, Slimothy canceled it in dramatic fashion, declaring himself done with false promises and broken dreams.

The second was panic-ordered the very next morning. He demanded something faster—something that would arrive before the previous one—never mind that he'd already canceled it. Fate, of course, laughed in his slimy face. Instead of a refund, the company rewarded his impulsiveness with expedited shipping. Slimothy now had two potting benches racing to his doorstep like rival suitors in a bad rom-com.

Enter potting bench number three.

For as long as he could remember, Slimothy had lived peacefully in his urban manor, blissfully unaware of the joys of the great outdoors—or that his shed would someday house one of the greatest treasures he had ever seen. The tiny outbuilding itself had always been a world of wonder he never ventured into—a shadowy kingdom of cobwebs stretching like banners across the beams, cardboard boxes sagging under the weight of forgotten seasons, and broken windows that fractured the light into shards of silver and gold. Rusted tools slouched in the corners like weary guards, and the air carried the perfume of dust, damp wood, and faintly remembered summers.

Waiting among them was a potting bench the color of sunbeams set on fire, its orange frame glowing with a rusted, molten brilliance that made the shadows recoil. The wood across its top had weathered into a deep moss-green patina, streaked and scarred like an ancient map—as though time itself had pressed its fingerprints into the grain. It looked denser than memory, heavier than fate—a relic that might anchor the whole shed to the earth. To Slimothy, it was less furniture than altar—a flaming shrine of metal and wood, dripping with mid-century modern charm, every slat and screw whispering promises of gardening greatness.

As if that weren't enough, the sacred little setup came with offerings. A chipped terracotta pot, its bite-sized nick making it feel storied, chosen, almost fated. Beside it, a folded paper leaf container rested like a forgotten scroll case, creased edges softening into fragile wings, the faint smell of damp pulp lingering in the air. Slimothy circled them reverently, convinced he had stumbled upon the Ark of the Covenant for hobbyists—a holy trinity of pot, bench, and vessel. The planter radiated the aura of an unopened invitation just waiting to be RSVP'd, while the paper container hummed with the delicate patience of something not built to last but determined to endure anyway. It was as though the universe itself were daring him to say yes.

From that moment forward, the orange bench wasn't just furniture—it was destiny, hauled out of the shadows in a slow, solemn procession and enthroned in the garden, where sun and soil crowned it as relic returned, ruler restored, altar revealed.

The floodgates opened. Slimothy was now the proud, slightly panicked owner of three potting benches. The first stayed unopened in its box, repurposed as a coat rack and occasional snack table. The second lurked in the corner, smugly reminding him of expedited shipping every time he passed it. The third—the firelit jewel—became his pride and joy, the dais upon which his gardening dreams would rise.

Destiny, however, had other plans. Within days, Roger had claimed the little clay vessel for himself. Somehow the chipped container migrated across the yard and ended up tucked beneath his mushroom overlook—a throne repurposed by a frog entirely unburdened by shame. Roger lounged in it daily, legs origami-ed into the most self-satisfied amphibian pose imaginable, the picture of unbothered superiority. Slimothy pretended not to notice, but every time he saw Roger basking in what should have been his treasure, he felt like a landlord who had accidentally rented out the penthouse for free.

Which, in Slimothy logic, meant the obvious solution was ... another potting bench. This one had wheels—a cup holder, of all things—and shipping that promised to arrive before he even clicked "place order." Slimothy wasn't fooled, but he was tempted.

CHAPTER SIX

Slug vs. Scorpion's-tail: Roger's Overgrown Dilemma

At the farthest corner of the garden, Roger had set up his office. Not a house, not even a throne, but what Slimothy had quietly declared the Bright Wild Courthouse. From this worn earthen seat of justice, Roger carried out his self-appointed duties as Chief Justice of the Hopreme Court—long blinks that passed for rulings, strategic hops that doubled as zoning decisions, and the occasional throat-clearing that could only be interpreted as "overruled."

Naturally, his jurisdiction extended to the surrounding grounds. Roger's castle estate was guarded by towering mushrooms that looked suspiciously like umbrella rentals gone rogue, with a single colossal plant rising above them all, stretching skyward as if it had every intention of annexing the entire neighborhood—complete with its own zoning board.

Slimothy remained the duly elected mayor, sash and all. Still, he bristled that Roger had snagged the gavel, the prestige, and possibly the better office perks. The Bright Wild now had both a mayor and a judge, and neither seemed entirely sure who was really in charge.

Their rivalry played out in mock city council meetings where decisions were made by vote. Slimothy pushed for more basil rations, Roger demanded stricter zoning for puddles, and the mushrooms abstained every time. In the end, most motions passed only if snacks were involved.

No amount of snacking could distract from the real problem towering over the council, however: Roger's hedge. Slimothy had never seen anything grow so fast in his life. One week it was an innocent sprout, the next it was looming like a leafy skyscraper—dwarfing the picket fence and blocking sightlines so badly it turned the neighborhood into pea soup with attitude. It definitely needed a haircut, but every time Slimothy trimmed it, the Hydra grew back in triplicate, as if it had a personal vendetta against lawn care.

At first, Slimothy thought it was just one modest little thing tucked into the corner of the garden—a polite background plant, maybe. The deeper he looked, the clearer it became: this wasn't a plant at all. This was a full-blown identity crisis wrapped in greenery. Was it a bush? A vine? A hedge moonlighting as an air-traffic controller? Nobody knew.

Officially, it was called scorpion's-tail. Yet the instant you introduced yourself, it was also sore bush, rooster comb, cat tongue, bright eye bush, butterfly heliotrope, dog's tail, alacrancillo, white clary, and wild clary. Slimothy didn't know whether to ask for an autograph or a driver's license. One thing was certain—this plant had more stage names than a rock band on tour.

Whatever its name this week, it was busy producing the daintiest little white whips of flowers, perched on top of a lily-like explosion of stems. They multiplied faster than Slimothy could keep up, sprouting like over-caffeinated rabbits. No matter how many times he hacked them back, the plant returned the next week in multiples, glowingly self-congratulatory and flourishing, as if to say, *"Nice try, slug."*

Roger may or may not have appreciated this foliage frenzy. On scorpion's-tail mowing day, the northern flank of Slimothy's kingdom briefly cleared, letting mushrooms bask in the sun—until the problem regrew 15 new heads to replace the ones just lobbed off. From his terracotta pot, Roger did nothing but blink slowly, the amphibian equivalent of a sigh, as if to say, *"You're losing control of the neighborhood again."*

Slimothy considered nibbling one of the leaves. It wasn't his fault—hunger was persuasive. Unfortunately they tasted like bitter lawn furniture. Another wasted opportunity. He sighed, stomach growling, and slid off to find a mushroom snack instead. Behind him, Roger shifted ever so slightly, delivering his signature silent judgment. It was less a look and more a full-time occupation—his way of reminding Slimothy that someone, somewhere, was keeping score.

CHAPTER SEVEN

Local Slug Loses to Weather

Living in the South, Slimothy discovered, required a few concessions. Chief among them: hurricane-rated garden accoutrements. Greenhouses, potting benches, patio furniture, Slimothy himself—everything was considered liable to take flight in a solid 40–60 mph gust.

The trickledown effect extended to his plants as well. When wind kicked up, wisteria clung for dear life, the birdhouse condos rocked like storm-tossed hotels, and the garden hose had developed a reputation as the neighborhood's most unpredictable whip.

Still, Slimothy liked his garden equal parts chaos and elegant eccentricity. He told himself this was intentional design, not disaster with dianthus. That, of course, meant any expectation of things being hurricane-rated—or even resistant to crumpling if a leaf so much as sneezed nearby—was never going to be met.

None of the trellises in the entire world would do for his prize achievement: a glorious, creamy-orange, stalwart summer squash. A vegetable so noble it deserved its own anthem, possibly a parade float, and definitely a stronger support system than anything Slimothy had cobbled together with twine and optimism.

The day the "storm" hit, Slimothy stood guard like a knight sworn to protect a very lumpy, orange monarch. The squash gleamed in the afternoon sun, noble and oblivious, while the trellis Slimothy had "engineered" (read: lashed together from leftover tomato stakes and reckless optimism) trembled in the wind.

Except it wasn't really wind. It was a summer breeze—a polite whoosh that barely tousled the wisteria and made the birdhouses sway like they were at a garden party.

Regardless, he saw the wind coming and did his best to save the sad metal structure. Slimothy hurled himself across the trellis like a one-slug sandbag operation, slime spreading in desperate reinforcement. He clung there in total silence, his tiny body vibrating with determination, while the trellis groaned back at him as if it had already given up.

With one final creak, the structure folded inward, collapsing under the crushing weight of despair and squash it had never truly been built to bear. Thus ended a valiant battle that lasted all of three seconds—Trellis vs. Slight Breeze. Slimothy rode the wreckage to the ground like a stuntman in a low-budget disaster film, landing flat in a heap of twisted metal and every bad decision that had ever been made with zip ties.

The squash didn't even wobble. It sat there radiant and victorious, as if it had personally orchestrated the collapse and was now waiting for its trophy. In Slimothy's mind, the headlines were already rolling in:

"Heroic Squash Defies Storm, Local Slug Defeated in Three-Second Upset."

Then the commentary started its usual routine:

"Welcome back to the Garden Games! Today's marquee event: Trellis vs. Slight Breeze. Ohhh, folks, it's over before it even starts! Three seconds on the clock—the trellis folds like a lawn chair at a family reunion! The squash is still standing, proud as ever, while our underdog Slimothy is … yes, currently face-planting into the soil. That's a dirt sandwich with extra shame for Team Slug. Rough night for the little guy."

Slimothy groaned. Even in his own imagination, he couldn't buy a win.

CHAPTER EIGHT

Operation *Libérez l'Escargot*

Not much in the garden moved slower than Slimothy, and he preferred not to discuss the few things that did. Except one.

Escargot—edible land snails in theory, but never in practice. Still, he had to admit: the word was delightful to say, like rolling marbles across your tongue. Whenever he stumbled across this so-called delicacy, he made it his solemn duty to liberate it from whatever ridiculous captivity it had been sentenced to.

The very first of these missions began one sunny afternoon on an outing to his favorite store. Slimothy had hitched a ride, as he often did, in what he liked to call *his* car. In reality, it was a human's hatchback, with Slimothy tucked into a reusable grocery bag like a first-class passenger on Slug Airlines. Off they went, jetting toward town, Slimothy tagging along, ready to glide down polished aisles with the easy leisure of someone with absolutely no errands to run.

That's when he saw it. A masterpiece. An homage to snailhood. One giant, ceramic cobalt-blue *Helix pomatia* perched like royalty between the garden gnomes and the lawn flamingos.

Though nobility it was not surrounded by. To its left: a six-foot inflatable cactus wearing cowboy boots. To its right: a stack of glow-in-the-dark toilet plungers marketed as yard art. Just behind it, for reasons no one could explain, a life-sized cardboard cutout of Abraham Lincoln holding a tiki torch.

Slimothy's eye stalks recoiled. This was no aisle—this was a hostage situation.

Operation *Libérez l'Escargot* had become a moral imperative.

Slimothy flattened against a bag of fake grass, humming the "Mission: Impossible" theme in his head. His slime trail doubled as a laser tripwire in his imagination, and every wobble of the ceramic snail was a coded signal: *free me.* He adjusted his non-existent headset and prepared for extraction.

The plan was simple. Step one: distract the flamingo with the martini glass. Step two: avoid eye contact with Lincoln. Step three: secure the package.

He inched forward, feelers twitching like radar. The inflatable cactus loomed, boots squeaking faintly whenever the store's AC kicked on. Slimothy halted, then rolled dramatically onto his side as though dodging sniper fire.

At last, he reached the base of the shelf. He gazed up at the deep-blue shell titan, majestic and tragic, like an emperor exiled to the clearance section with nothing but markdown stickers for company. "Hang tight," Slimothy whispered. "This is what I was born for."

With a mighty shove, Slimothy rocked the porcelain slowpoke free. Time hiccuped. The blow-up cactus trembled in awe. A raccoon with a welcome sign respectfully tipped his hat. Moments later—success. Monsieur Bleu tumbled into an inexplicable kiddie pool full of unsold rubber ducks, splashing down in a sea of squeaks before coming to rest in perfect safety.

From that day forward, the ducks became part of his story. In every daydream of daring escapes, Slimothy summoned the image of the squeaky flotilla waiting faithfully below—a yellow-and-orange safety net of beaks and grins. They weren't just clearance rubber toys anymore. They were the Duck Brigade, his unlikely parachute team.

Slimothy slithered down after his quarry, chest heaving as if he had lungs— technically he didn't—but theatrics were everything in a pursuit this important. He patted the cool ceramic shell like a coach congratulating the star player. "You're free now," he whispered, as the ducks squeaked their approval. In that moment, under the flicker of fluorescent lights and the faint perfume of pumpkin spice, Slimothy felt what few slugs ever do—victory, with a side of clearance pricing.

CHAPTER NINE

Will Roger Fall in Love?

Slimothy often wondered about Roger's heart. Did frogs even have those, or were they powered entirely by cattails and bad moods? Was Roger destined for love, or doomed to spend his days croaking at mushrooms and fairy castles alone? Slimothy didn't have the answer—and frankly, he wasn't sure Roger did either.

What he did know was that pondering amphibian romance was exhausting work for a slug of his size. So, in need of a mental palate cleanser, he turned his thoughts to something easier: shopping.

Today's adventure had taken him to an off-brand garden center, the kind of place where price tags curled at the edges and every aisle whispered of forgotten plants waiting for rescue. Slimothy hitched along for the ride, eager for the promise of new green-leafed friends.

Not long after the third exit, it became clear he wasn't traveling solo. A tiny four-legged stowaway clung to the back window like an amphibious daredevil. Froglet? Tree frog? Freeloading cousin of Roger? Whatever it was, the little hitchhiker had the grip strength of a rock climber and the determination of a garden slug chasing lettuce. Slimothy briefly considered charging it fare, but decided instead to mark the moment as "suspicious passengers" in his mental travelogue.

Naturally, Slimothy did what any responsible slug would do. He demanded an emergency stop to stage a dramatic rescue. Only when the car pulled over and Slimothy peeked around, the frog was gone. Launched into the unknown—completely, utterly, and without warning—swept away by 60 mph of adventure. Slimothy stared at the empty glass, his body heavy with disbelief. For all his questions about Roger's heart, here was proof that frogs did not linger. They leapt.

Slimothy was crushed. He had planned to offer the brave traveler a cozy new habitat—perhaps even introduce it to Roger as a potential soulmate. Instead he was left with questions. Had the frog found freedom, flung into some brighter destiny beyond the highway's edge? Or was this simply a missed love story, a fleeting connection gone with the wind, leaving behind nothing but a slug's sigh and an empty pane of glass?

What if that little stowaway had been Roger's girlfriend, off to see the world beyond fairy lights and gnomes? What if she had hitched a ride just to taste freedom, her scarf fluttering, her tiny froggy heart beating fast, her destiny calling from a ditch somewhere near Exit 112?

What if, one day, she came hopping back, rain-soaked and dramatic, whispering, *"It was always you, Roger?"*

Slimothy couldn't help but wonder if he had just witnessed Roger's missed chance at love.

Back in the garden, Roger seemed entirely unbothered. He croaked and hopped among his favorite things: the mushrooms, the castles, the fairies, the gnomes. Did he feel the absence of someone to share his terracotta pot and white picket fence with through the long winter? Or was Roger secretly a bachelor by choice, independent, mysterious, content to live his best amphibian life?

Could frogs fall in love? Did Roger dream of tadpoles and family ponds, or was he the kind of soul who belonged only to the Bright Wild itself? Slimothy didn't know. If life worked anything like the fairy tales, or the rom-coms humans binged on rainy nights, then Roger's story wasn't finished. Maybe the froglet would return. Maybe another love was already on its way.

Until then, Slimothy was left to wonder if frogs really needed romance, or if mushrooms, mischievous fairies, and scandal-prone gnomes were love enough.

CHAPTER TEN

Slimothy's Great Pond Caper

In a world where you could be anything, being a slug didn't sound too bad. Patience, persistence, and quiet strength were the vibe. Move slow, act smart, thrive in your own way.

Unless, of course, you were two inches long, named Slimothy, and suddenly convinced that building a pond was the only way to help your friend Roger find true love. After all, how else were tadpoles supposed to show up if someone didn't provide the starter home?

What did one need for a pond? Inspiration. A rabbit hole of never-ending garden ideas. Endless scrolling. Slimothy digitally wandered, daydreaming of metal tubs, fairy fountains, and garden oases—until at last, the vision appeared: a 44-gallon oval tank. Overnight shipping. Thank you, big orange box store.

Hours later, or maybe just moments—time was slippery in the Bright Wild—a giant cardboard delivery appeared at Slimothy's doorstep, humming with destiny as though it had traveled from the far corners of the kingdom just for him. He circled it slowly, antennae twitching, the way knights once approached treasure chests in stories that never ended well.

With great ceremony, the fortress of corrugated destiny was breached, and out came the prize: an oval vessel, gleaming with promise. Spray paint cans stood at attention like royal guards. Slate gathered in quiet formation. The grand plan had begun—because if Roger was ever going to find love, he'd need more than suspicious fungi and a nicked orange pot. He needed ambiance. He needed tadpoles. He needed a pond. Possibly a tiny waterfall, a few twinkling fairy lights, and at least one motivational snail waving a tiny banner. Slimothy jotted mental notes with grim determination, fully aware that true romance demanded logistical precision.

The only question was where to put it. In-ground or above-ground? Slimothy had no patience to wait for the eggplants to die back at season's end—and the squash bed was already spoken for. Which left only the island, better known as The Banana Republic, population: two. Home to Spaulding the pineapple and his long-suffering roommate, Wilson the banana tree.

Slimothy plotted the pond's future with all the precision of a slug managing international diplomacy. The terrain presented a challenge—tree roots. Everywhere. Persistent. Entirely uncooperative. Above ground it would have to be. He considered splash zones, tadpole traffic, and the optimal positioning for fairy fountains and lily pads. Ambitious? Absolutely. Necessary for romance? Without a doubt.

Spaulding did not take the news well. He leaned into his role like a one-hit wonder on a farewell tour, tossing out one last burst of spiky attitude before Slimothy gave him a gentle nudge and declared him history. The pond had claimed the stage.

Wilson, ever the chill one, just shrugged—already daydreaming about a hammock somewhere sunnier.

Slimothy wasted no time. Spray paint, check. Pavers for leveling—or pretend leveling, since nothing in this garden was ever truly level—check. Six heavy bags of river pebbles landed at the gate, and the delivery crew left shaking their heads, muttering about the slug with too many projects.

Rocks. So many rocks. Rock washing, rock stacking, rock regret. By the third bag, Slimothy started questioning his life choices. By the fifth, he was sure he'd accidentally enrolled in some kind of punishment-based fitness program.

Then came the plants. Who knew you could only buy aquatic plants from the smile store in pairs? The buddy system, apparently. Quiet companions of chlorophyll. Four soggy bundles soon arrived, wrapped in damp brown paper, reeking faintly of cross-country truck air. Slimothy grumbled. He liked odd numbers. He planted them anyway, muttering about forced symmetry.

Water followed—the magic elixir of life, beloved by slugs, snails, frogs, and any creature wandering through suburban garden kingdoms. The pond flickered with aquatic ambition, the surface catching bits of sky, promising that maybe this was worth all the rock regret.

Next came the fountain. Too loud. Way too loud. Slimothy flinched like he'd been dropped into the front row of a rock concert without earplugs. This was less peaceful pond and more tsunami in surround sound. He swapped nozzles. Once. Twice. Three times. Four. By the fifth attempt, victory at last: gentle ripples, soft splashes—finally downgraded from disaster movie to garden lullaby.

Then came illumination. Underwater lights. Which, as he would later note with great bitterness, would have been far easier to install before he committed six bags of rock to permanent residency. Slimothy dug, shifted, adjusted, cursed, and moved them no less than 14 times. Which brought him to his next foe: the conduit box. The packaging claimed it was waterproof. Slimothy claimed liar. Still, the lights glowed, wavering beneath the surface like stars captured in a puddle.

At last, the new potted residents were arranged around the edges, each in its own little container, ready for Slimothy's entirely unnecessary roll call. Rocks had been shifted, stacked, and re-shifted until they found their resting places— at least for now. The pond was alive: gurgling, glowing, reflecting whatever illumination the evening could scrounge up, like a liquid mirror. Slimothy slid to the edge and stared. It was perfect. His very own splash pad. A sanctuary for Roger. An oasis for passing wanderers. A crown jewel for his garden kingdom.

The plant companions bobbed politely in their pots, swaying in the ripples. The slate shimmered. The fountain whispered. Slimothy leaned in, wondering if one of those new aquatic plants might taste like lettuce. He took a cautious nibble. Chewy. Decorative. Not dinner.

Still, he was proud. Hungry, but proud. It had been worth every pebble. In Slimothy's mind, a project of this scale demanded an unveiling. A ribbon-cutting, if you will. The problem, of course, was that ribbons were notoriously slippery in the slug world. Slimothy settled for a limp piece of garden twine and a ceremonious nod to no one in particular—since he had scared the rest of the garden off with all the racket.

Yet, as the faint garden glow hit the surface, glinting off every ridiculous rock, Slimothy realized that maybe this was exactly what a pond was meant to be: messy, loud, alive. A tiny amphibian amusement park, a food court, and—hopefully someday—a tadpole nursery.

Slimothy smiled in his own sluggy way. The pond was more than water. It was a promise. A dream made real, one rock at a time.

So many rocks. Too many rocks. An absolutely unreasonable, backbreaking, garden-redecorating number of rocks.

True love was going to take a lot more rocks.

Slimothy sighed. *Why did it always have to be rocks?*

CHAPTER ELEVEN

Big Butthole Energy: Aisle 12

Life often gave Slimothy pause. Sometimes it was delightful, like finding a forgotten piece of spinach under a leaf. Other times it was dreadful, like realizing midway through writing his gratitude list that he was sitting in fertilizer.

Today's pause was supposed to be easy and routine—just a quick trip to his favorite shopping location, the discount maze where you go in for socks and come out with a kayak—for a browse, maybe a basket of snacks, and back home in time to check on the radishes.

Instead, he found himself trapped in the most unlikely battlefield of all: Aisle 12.

Twice now, on two separate visits to different branches of the same bargain jungle, Slimothy had been ambushed—once at checkout and once deep in an aisle, while minding his own slimy business. Out of nowhere came outbursts, flaring attitude, and people who acted like their carts required diplomatic immunity.

Admittedly, Slimothy's first shopping incident might have been partly on him. Being a slug meant he was late to everything, especially mealtimes. The lady in front of him, instead of going to the cashier, stopped mid-stride to do who knows what. Maybe she was checking her horoscope, maybe inventing a new TikTok, maybe having a full-blown decision crisis over cheap fake jewelry. Slimothy knew it had to be fake because if you buy the real stuff they make you check out at the jewelry counter—which, in a twist of cosmic retail justice, would have spared him all this exasperation.

Anything except checkout.

Slimothy, stomach growling, finally inched past the bedsheets, dog sweaters, and tubs of cheese balls, and took the open spot.

The result was outrage. Gasps. Angry words poured out like Shakespeare in a food court, complete with finger wagging and tragic monologues about "tripping over karma." One woman clutched her pearls by the bath mats, and someone else muttered about civilization collapsing, but Slimothy couldn't hear a thing over the chaos in his own head. It was like a mall PA system blaring, *"Attention shoppers: Slimothy is doomed."*

Slimothy tried to retaliate with a calm explanation, but all he got back was the hissed phrase, "You know what you did." That's when he muttered under his breath, "I hope your skin turns green from the fake bronze." After a few more sentences thrown his way, he realized he was hopelessly outmatched. In a panic, he grabbed the nearest item—a mini chicken coop he absolutely did not need—and slimed toward the exit. Back in the garden he would later stare at it, wondering if he was supposed to get chickens, rent them, or just sleep in it himself.

So of course the next time stung even worse. Maybe this was his karma, forever doomed to face Karens in the Aisle of Eternal Clearance, where spatulas go to die. This time he was innocent, patiently waiting, when an Aisle Hogger staked her claim with cart, attitude, and a platter so long it could double as a runway, blocking both left and right flanks as if she'd been crowned Queen of Housewares.

The prize cow of aisle warfare, earpiece in, jaw working like she was chewing cud, she parked her cart diagonally across the aisle like she was building a roadblock for Homeland Security. The buggy itself was loaded with nonsense: a non-descript statue, a vat-sized tub of applesauce, and what looked suspiciously like a pool noodle. Even Slimothy, who understood slow better than anyone, could not shimmy past this blockade.

After a respectful pause, Slimothy tried the classic slug detour. When he looped back, there she was again, anchored at the other end of the aisle as if leading a masterclass in Advanced Aisle Obstruction. Finally, in his gentlest yet slightly aggravated slug voice, he said, "Alright, I just need to get behind you."

The response was nuclear. She demanded, again and again, that Slimothy say *"excuse me,"* but not just say it—sing it, project it, maybe even curtsy while doing it. When he didn't, she escalated to yelling, finger-pointing, and wild accusations that he had committed the ultimate crime: not delivering the phrase in the exact theatrical tone she required.

In an instant, the aisle became a courtroom. Suddenly he was on trial in the Court of Aisle Manners, with Judge Judy presiding, a jury of throw pillows casting accusatory glances, and the sentence: solitary confinement in the scented candle aisle with no escape from pumpkin spice.

Slimothy hated confrontation. If given the choice between a showdown and sliding away, he would ooze toward the exit every time. What was a slug to do? His head pounded, his stomach growled for the snack aisle he never reached, and he decided enough was enough. He didn't really need to see anything in his favorite decor aisle after all.

With great dramatic flair, he abandoned his cart and flung himself through the automatic doors like a slug in a telenovela finale, leaving a trail of indignation and slime behind him.

Back in the blessed safety of his people-free garden, Slimothy buried himself in basil leaves like a weighted blanket and tried to reboot his brain. The absurdity of it all buzzed louder than cicadas hosting karaoke on a summer night.

Later, still restless, he heard the familiar mantra of his Director of Slug Sanity drifting through his thoughts: *"People are grumpy. Don't let strangers dictate the amazingness of your day."* To Slimothy, everything she said felt like being handed the meaning of life in a gift bag.

Translation: *"Don't be a butthole."*

Slimothy tried to take it to heart. After that first debacle, he whispered a prayer to the universe, replayed witty comebacks he had never said, even let another shopper cut in line the next day, which he considered slug sainthood.

His spiritual progress lasted roughly 24 hours. Enlightenment, it turned out, had a short shelf life.

He thought about what therapists are forever recommending: *put your thoughts in a box, shelve it, and move on.* If Slimothy actually did that, he would need a warehouse the size of a minor continent, full of boxes labeled, "Woman Who Declared War in Aisle 12," "Unfinished Business With Romaine," and "Neighbor's Lawn Gnome That Definitely Moves at Night."

Later, to soothe his nerves, Slimothy planted spinach, picked his very first radishes, and immediately ate three. Crispy, crunchy, peppery little miracles. Until this afternoon, he didn't know radishes grew shoulders that popped out of the dirt when they were ready to pick. Nature was fascinating. Slimothy, who had no shoulders of his own, felt personally attacked.

He licked his lips, or would have if he had them, and remembered his friend's wisdom: *"Don't let buttholes ruin your day."*

Thus began Big Butthole Energy—the motto Slimothy would carry in every aisle, garden, and pantry patch.

"Excuse you, ma'am."

CHAPTER TWELVE

The Frog With a Shiv

The chances of being taken out by a frog with a shiv in your own backyard? Low. Yet with Slimothy around—never zero.

He had been minding his own business one evening, dragging a leaf across the garden like it was a victory parade float. The pond glowed in the fading light, crickets tuned up like an orchestra in the pit, and for a moment all seemed calm. Almost too calm.

Then he saw Roger.

Slimothy had seen Roger on plenty of evenings before, part of the usual hop-around-the-garden routine. Perfect pathway symmetry, nothing out of the ordinary. He hopped through his domain like a land surveyor, inspecting new arrivals and taking mental notes about border disputes. Tonight was different.

Roger was not just hopping. He was advancing, one deliberate step at a time. Watching. Measuring. Closing the distance with a purpose Slimothy did not like one bit.

Then Slimothy saw something—a glint. In Roger's ... hand—if frogs even had hands—was something long, thin, and sharp. A cattail? A twig? Or was it the unmistakable outline of a shiv? In the questionable lighting of the moment it gleamed with menace, and Slimothy's stomach dropped.

The air thickened. The pond stilled. Even the crickets cut their soundtrack short. Slimothy's every nerve jangling, slime pooling beneath him like a chalk outline already drawn. His feelers twitched, betraying him.

"Easy now," he rationalized in his inner monologue. Should he raise his leaf like a white flag, a peace treaty, an offering? The standoff stretched on, every second as heavy as wet soil. Roger's eyes flicked once, then twice. A slow blink. Nothing more. He didn't need words to make his point.

Slow blinks in cats meant affection. In frogs, Slimothy could only hazard a guess. *Approval? Threat? Boredom? Debt collection? "I know what you did to that basil. Meet me by the pond at midnight. Bring snacks."*

Did this mean he needed to start packing emergency rations in a handkerchief, ready to flee across the plains like an outlaw hobbit? How bad could that be? Much like Slimothy, hobbits treated second breakfast as a sacred, non-negotiable life principle. Was this retribution for accusing Roger, even in thought, of being the tomato thief? Or was this a warning—the kind that came before something hopped out of the shadows and changed everything?

Just as suddenly as he had appeared, Roger slipped back beyond the pond, leaving Slimothy trembling in the grass, vaguely relieved and partially convinced the frog was only biding his time.

He forced himself forward, doing a terrible job of pretending not to notice, but in his head scenarios multiplied with unhelpful enthusiasm: a berry rolling across the path like a tripwire, a line of twigs stacked just so, even an overturned flowerpot balanced precariously above the pond's edge—absurd little traps that could've been Roger's ... or his own overactive imagination. Classic deterrents. Classic confusion.

Did he really believe Roger had sharpened a cattail into a weapon? Maybe not. Could he rule it out? Never. The Bright Wild was unpredictable. Especially with amphibians around, anything was possible.

Slimothy adjusted his leaf, cleared his throat, and kept moving. Just a peaceful stroll, nothing suspicious at all. Still, he couldn't help glancing back behind him, just in case.

Roger was no longer there. He hadn't hopped or croaked, hadn't even stirred a blade of grass. He had simply melted into the shadows, swallowed whole by the night as if he had never existed at all. Only villains left a scene that clean.

CHAPTER THIRTEEN

Slimothy vs. Dirt Mold: A Love Story

Slimothy's week had been a bit of a disaster. It began with the looming horror of allergy testing, which to a thumbprint-sized slug meant one thing: needles. He had spent days working himself into a slime about it, convinced that the prick would be the size of a javelin and that his entire life would flash before his eye stalks the moment it struck. The night before, he even practiced fainting dramatically in the moss, just in case he needed to sell the performance.

The preparation was no better. No basil for breakfast, no oregano to calm his pounding head, no mint leaves to settle his nerves, no parsley sprigs to crunch when he needed courage. Five long days of abstaining, each one dragging by like a season in exile. He lay on his grassy knoll writing mental elegies for himself, glaring at thyme for existing when he could not have it, and bargaining with the universe for just one leaf of sage. By day three he was so desperate he began imagining shady herb deals in the compost pile, seeing himself in a trench coat made of lettuce, whispering, *"Psst, got any rosemary?"* to a beetle that clearly knew too much.

On the fifth dawn, stripped of every herb and ounce of dignity, he slithered toward the clinic like a wilted salad in search of answers. Today was reckoning day: 42 tiny stabs stood between him and enlightenment.

Flat on his stomach, Slimothy endured each prick of destiny—tiny needles introducing him to everything he'd ever sneezed at: trees, dogs, grasses, bed bugs, and, insultingly, dust. It felt less like a test and more like a betrayal, each jab a reminder that even nature had notes on him. Then came the waiting—15 eternal minutes of absolute stillness, forbidden to move, itch, or so much as breathe too enthusiastically, lest he ruin the masterpiece of welts blossoming across his back.

When the verdict came, it was worse than he could have dreamed: dirt mold. Imagine telling a slug he could not roll around in the very soil that brought him joy. It was like telling a fish to avoid water, or a cat to quit judging people. Impossible. Cruel. Unthinkable.

The doctor, at least, had been lovely. She leaned over the chart with the kind of enthusiasm usually reserved for carnival rides and told him his allergies were some of the worst she had ever seen. *"Off the charts,"* she chirped, as though Slimothy had just set a new high score. Allergy shots appeared to be in his future, which she announced with the cheerful certainty of a waitress suggesting dessert. There was no escape.

His head throbbed like a tiny bass drum, his slime felt sluggish, and his favorite shady patch was officially off limits. Slimothy was adrift, untethered, a slug without a stage. What was a garden-loving gastropod to do when banished from the very dirt that defined him?

Retail therapy, obviously.

So off he slid, mucus trail shining like determination in the morning light, to the garden center in search of solace. Not seeds, not herbs, not anything remotely practical. He craved drama. He craved danger. He craved something that screamed *treat yourself,* preferably with thorns.

Enter the diva of the plant aisle. She stood like a star on the red carpet, petals layered in couture, thorns gleaming like jewelry no one dared to touch. The air around her practically shimmered with perfume and self-importance, as if she had hired the wind itself to be her personal hype machine. Other plants leaned politely in their plastic pots, but this drift of flowers demanded space, demanded reverence, demanded paparazzi.

The garden rose, after all, had a long and complicated history. Love, beauty, war, politics—she'd seen it all and survived it in style. This particular varietal, *Rosa gallica* 'Empress Joséphine,' was impossible to miss beneath the fluorescent lights, radiant and ethereal, a motivational garden specimen headlining her own Vegas show. (Fitting, Slimothy thought, given that the real Joséphine once collected roses with the dedication most reserved for grudges.)

Slimothy was altogether overwhelmed. She had eluded him all season, dodging his gaze every trip until now.

This time, she didn't flinch.

Slimothy froze mid-slime, awestruck. This wasn't gardening. This was destiny in a three-gallon container.

She locked eyes with him across the aisle.

"Pick me," she demanded. *"I dare you."*

Slimothy's feelers twitched. He wasn't sure if he was buying a plant or entering into a binding contract with a starlet who had clearly been preparing her big entrance for weeks. Either way, he knew one thing—resistance was futile.

Slimothy, overcome, scooped her up in the only way a slug could: awkwardly and reverently, leaving behind a trail of commitment and questionable impulse control. Every ounce of his attention was locked on her, radiant and thorned, as if the rest of the aisle had faded into shadow. She was the prize, the crown jewel, the headline act—and Slimothy knew it.

However no queen can reign without a throne. Thus began the quest for the perfect pot. Three different stores. Rows upon rows of pottery. Too tall. Too squat. Too plastic. Too neon. Decision fatigue set in—a cruel irony for a creature without hands to wring in despair. By the end, Slimothy was whispering apologies to his thorny new companion, swearing she would not be homeless for long.

Then it hit him. Destiny had been waiting all along. Back in the garden by the carrots sat an inky-black planter that stood out like a secret, panic-bought weeks ago and left without purpose. Four-cornered, sturdy, weathered enough to suggest gravitas—a castle waiting for its queen. A singular, defiant presence in a garden otherwise packed with concrete pots.

It felt inevitable, then, when Queen Joséphine settled in like the royalty she was, taking her throne. Her roots pressed down with authority, gripping the soil as if signing a decree. Leaves unfurled one by one in self-contented triumph, the slow wave of a queen greeting her subjects. Even the air seemed to pause, heavy with weight and authority, as though the garden itself had agreed to stand at attention. Slimothy watched, spellbound, as if he'd just witnessed a coronation in a clearance castle—regal vibes, bargain price.

He sighed with relief, his slime trail loosening with the weight lifted from his mind. Happy rose, happy life. Cottage-core level unlocked. He could practically hear a lute somewhere, strumming the opening notes of a medieval ballad in her honor.

Of course, no new arrival in the Bright Wild escaped inspection. Allison the hummingbird swooped in within minutes, circling the queen with the scrutiny of a jeweler hunting for flaws. Her audit was impossible to ignore. She hovered, she judged, her chest fluttering like a drumroll—each tiny breath, one after another, 150 of them every minute—puffing with the urgency of a creature who lived entirely on deadlines. At last she gave one final circle, dipped low as if signing her name in the air, and vanished in a glittering blur. To Slimothy it felt like she had stamped the rose with an invisible seal of approval, complete with the sound of a tiny gavel bang and a muttered *"case closed."* Slimothy was left both relieved and slightly insulted, realizing that in his own garden he was never the final authority. The bloom was clearly the star. He was just the stagehand setting the scene.

Still, Slimothy beamed. Order had been temporarily restored, the rose ruled, and his allergies had been briefly outwitted. *Take that, dirt mold.* Even if 60% of his kingdom made him sneeze, love—thorny, dramatic, and high-maintenance— still found a way to bloom.

CHAPTER FOURTEEN

Resting Bug Face: Slimothy's Field Guide to Bad Attitudes

D o slugs smile? Slimothy wasn't sure. Sliding in lazy loops across his garden kingdom, he had been pondering this for days—maybe weeks. It was the kind of deep philosophical question only a slug with forever sniffles and too much free time could obsess over. Humans had resting bitch face. Was that really a species-exclusive affliction? Slimothy thought not. The garden was practically crawling with proof.

Take the possums. They always looked like they had just discovered their coupon expired yesterday and were fully prepared to escalate the issue to corporate. No manager in sight? No problem. They would take it straight to the mayor. Slimothy wore the sash, after all, and he had zero training for possum complaints.

Then there were the lizards. They draped themselves across the sidewalk like minor royals reclining on a chaise lounge. Their eyes declared, *"I own this slab of concrete, and you, peasant, may step around."* They sunbathed with such entitlement

Slimothy partway expected them to start handing out glossy pamphlets for timeshares in Miami no one could afford.

Frogs were worse—the smirkers of the kingdom. Every time one snapped up a fly, it was never just business. No, they had to pause, savor, and beam as if they had just won Wimbledon. Slimothy burned with envy. He had never radiated that level of protein confidence. Lettuce did not lend itself to smugness.

Cats, well, they were untouchable. Not only had they invented resting "This Is Beneath Me" face—they'd trademarked it, franchised it, and opened a luxury spa where others could learn to perfect it. Even in their sleep, they managed to look like they were silently judging Slimothy's entire life, from his mucus trail to his questionable potting bench investments.

The deer, meanwhile, were a paradox. Always wide-eyed, always startled, as if they could not believe they were deer. Every night they leapt fences like ballerinas sneaking snacks backstage—stunned at their own existence, stunned again when they landed. Slimothy sometimes wondered if they needed a support group devoted entirely to being startled.

Then, of course, there were the gnomes. Technically not alive, but the judgment radiating from their painted eyes could curdle milk. Slimothy was convinced they held nightly gossip sessions, whispering about his questionable life choices with porcelain smiles that never cracked.

By the time his survey was complete, Slimothy's stomach rumbled. He glared at a neighborly cat, who narrowed its eyes back—a quiet little showdown of cross-species judgment. Even in hunger, Slimothy wondered: did disdain taste like chicken? If so, cats were basically walking rotisserie ovens.

The real trouble, Slimothy decided, was that slugs lacked the equipment for expressions. No lips. No Instagram filters. His whole face was one damp circle of possibility. Did that mean he was doomed to neutrality? Or did his glittery slime trail count as his smile? Because honestly, if leaving a sparkly line of goo across the patio wasn't the gastropod version of grinning ear to ear, what was?

Still, Slimothy practiced. He leaned over a rain puddle like Narcissus's sluggish cousin, stretching, tilting, wiggling his eye stalks at different angles. Did this one look self-assured? Did that one say mysterious? Could he manage a flirty look— or did it just come across as congested?

In the end, his reflection revealed the truth: his best smile looked hungry, mildly triumphant, and a little slimy. A face that said, *"Yes, I just ate your lettuce, and yes, I would do it again."*

Honestly, Slimothy thought, that was perfect.

CHAPTER FIFTEEN

Roger and the Case of the Darkened Lights

I n one breath, the solar lights lining the perimeter of Roger's castle estate glowed in their usual steady row—tiny beacons marking order, security, and the frog's questionable taste in lawn décor. The next, darkness. Every last one of them.

It wasn't the casual kind of darkness either. This was a statement—the kind of blackout that suggested intent, rebellion, maybe even crime. The air felt different too, thicker, as if the night itself was holding a secret. Slimothy crept closer, antennae raised, scanning for signs of foul play: bite marks, drag trails, suspicious puddles. Nothing. Just the faint smell of damp plastic and Roger's royal aura fading by the second.

He lingered there for a long moment, considering possibilities. A power conspiracy? Solar mutiny? Or perhaps, he thought grimly, the frog had finally discovered the off switch.

A malfunction was possible—a cloudy day, a sulking sun, or a leaf with terrible timing blocking the solar panel. Yet his instincts twitched. This didn't smell like bad luck. It smelled like planning. Slimothy remembered the story of an octopus in an aquarium who grew so annoyed by bright tank lights that he squirted a perfect stream of water at the control box until the system shorted out. Darkness. Silence. Peace.

He admired that squid—visionary, bold, clearly operating on a higher frequency of spite. Slimothy understood that kind of motivation. After all, how many nights had he lain awake wishing the motion sensor near Roger's office would stop blinking like an impatient star? Maybe, just maybe, someone in the Bright Wild had finally taken justice into their own—technically non-hands—appendages.

Slimothy gazed across the garden at Roger's stronghold, encircled by the suspiciously precise border Roger called defenses, tucked beneath the shadow of the scorpion's-tail, its curling stems arched overhead like a green cathedral. It was a strange blend of suburban charm and medieval paranoia. Roger sat motionless within, eyes weighted with the wisdom of too many late nights, croaking softly to himself.

"Coincidence," Slimothy whispered, "or sabotage?"

The evidence nagged. Roger had always been … unusual. Slimothy hadn't forgotten the time he spotted Roger clutching a shiv in his damp little limb—for what purpose, no one knew. Now the lights, extinguished in one fell swoop, just as the moon brightened the garden—pointing toward a plan he wasn't meant to understand.

Was Roger planning something nefarious? Slimothy dreamed up mushrooms arranged like blueprints, a full garden takeover drafted in spore and slime. Was he trying to trip unaware travelers, plunging them into lawsuits and settlement claims? Did Roger have a lawyer on retainer? Slimothy could already see it: a snapping turtle in spectacles, briefcase balanced on a log, billing by the hour in lily pads.

Or perhaps it was simpler. Maybe Roger preferred mood lighting—the fairy lights twinkling overhead, the soft glow of fireflies at the pond's edge. Maybe Roger wanted romance, not revolution. Perhaps the darkened path was nothing more than a backdrop for evenings with Mrs. Roger, if such a Mrs. Roger existed.

From his vantage point near the radishes, Slimothy studied the strange quiet draped over Roger's domain. The earthen rise, the weathered gate, the citadel, the spire of stone—everything cast in shadow. Roger blinked once, slow and deliberate, a gesture that revealed nothing and promised less. The lights stayed dark. The mystery deepened.

"Inquiring Slimothys want to know," he muttered, sliding back into the shadows himself.

The case remained unsolved.

CHAPTER SIXTEEN

Slimothy and the Balloon He'll Never Board

The wisteria tree stretched out like a purple blanket, its delicate leaves draping like lace curtains while spiraling tendrils climbed ever upward, clearly aiming for a penthouse suite in the clouds. The pond stirred in reply, bubbles puffing into crystal castles no bigger than teacups, lily pads drifting across the surface like bumper cars in slow motion.

Meanwhile, the cucumber had burst free of the trellis on three sides—now competing for the title of tallest vegetable of the season and eyeing the end-of-summer clearance rack. Fairy lights twinkled—347 of them to be exact—because even magic had an inventory. A breeze shuffled the leaves like a distracted percussionist, while the crickets wrapped up Symphony No. 913 with an encore that sounded suspiciously like Symphony No. 912.

Slimothy's favorite spot was near the hot-air balloon. To him it was a glowing beacon of adventure, whispering, *"Come fly, tiny slug, see the world."* Would there be beans at the top? Could he finally settle the Jack debate once and for all? The firelight inside the balloon flared and flickered across the basket. It was exactly Slimothy-sized, as if made for him.

Yet Slimothy was, regrettably, a scaredy slug. Heights made him queasy—or so he assumed. Being as vertically limited as he was, he had never gotten high enough to test the theory. The closest he had come was the top shelf of the housewares emporium, and that was only because a kind employee left a step stool. Truth be told, he preferred solid ground beneath his belly—preferably sprinkled with breadcrumbs or basil leaves.

Life at his level was dreamy enough. Bees bustled around him like caffeinated accountants, hurrying to balance their honey budgets before winter closed the books. Did the garden's winged workforce sense their short timelines? Did the hive queen feel any guilt? Slimothy sometimes entertained the notion of being royalty himself—tucked away through winter, honey-stuffed and cozy. Then he realized he would be lonely. What if Roger hibernated too? Who would he complain to about cucumbers with no sense of personal space?

He wondered if hibernation was like a vacation. He had never taken one but heard they were fashionable. Allison went on them all the time, gallivanting to faraway places. Maybe he should branch out too.

In typical Slimothy fashion, he stayed where he was, however—curled in his corner of the yard, keeping watch over the leaves and the bugs while the neighborhood moths crash-landed into the fairy lights like tipsy pilots. To Slimothy it looked exactly like a circus, minus the popcorn. He even thought about charging admission: two basil leaves a ticket, kids under one gram free.

The headliner was about to begin—the deer show—complete with dramatic pauses and synchronized leaf-nibbling. They were better at telling time than a cuckoo-clock convention in Zurich.

If vacations were really better than this, they must come with unlimited snacks and a souvenir cup. Otherwise, he wasn't interested. In his mind's eye he could already see the glossy brochure: *"Visit anywhere. Leave with crumbs on your shirt and a free cup."*

CHAPTER SEVENTEEN

Slimothy vs. The Slime Mold

A neighborhood cat sauntered by on the outskirts of town, pausing at one of the portable refilling stations as if it were a five-star lounge. The Bright Wild had its own landmarks now: the corner of Cactus Ave and Pineapple Alley, Citronella Lane, The Leaf District. Even Spaulding, the pineapple with personality, was listed on the town register. Slimothy—of course, as its self-proclaimed mayor—swiped a bright orange credit card that matched his scarf and an alarming amount of garden décor every time the potting soil ran out.

After a shuffle over to check his tomatoes, Slimothy mulled over the latest gardening "wisdom" that insisted watering should only happen at the base. If leaves didn't need water, then why had rain been falling from the top for a few million years? Was Mother Nature just a rookie gardener with bad aim, or was Slimothy once again spiraling? Either way, the catmint wasn't helping— especially now that he was considering writing a sternly worded letter to the rain.

Naturally, the universe had decided he needed fresh chaos at that moment. Something else nefarious was afoot—literally. Slimothy rounded the corner by pineapple junior, Marty McFly, and froze mid-slime. "What the heck is that?" he exclaimed, antennae quivering.

There it was: a blotch so garish it looked as if a jar of saffron had detonated in the baking aisle and splattered across his kale. A crime scene in highlighter yellow.

Perched dead-center in the chaos, looking far too pleased with himself, was a tiny green tree frog. Slimothy couldn't decide if the creature was bravely standing guard, staging a coup, or simply squatting rent-free in the neighborhood's newest hazard zone. Either way, it was grossly adorable and very inconvenient—the exact kind of amphibian Roger would probably start a two-frog comedy tour with, leaving Slimothy stuck selling basil at the merch table.

Dog vomit fungus—aka slime mold—was the verdict after three hours of late-night "research," which involved exactly two facts and a heroic amount of ceiling-staring. Nature's cruel punchline. Slimothy had to admit it was a painfully accurate spirit animal. Honestly, if he ever needed a rebrand, "Slime Mold with Antennae" had a certain ring to it. He just hoped the tree frog wasn't already drafting the press release.

That's when the fluorescent freeloader seemed to sneer at him from its neon blotch, like a conceited yellow roommate. *"Thanks for the moisture, slug. I couldn't have done this without you."*

Slimothy groaned. He hadn't just overwatered—he had personally sponsored the mold's grand debut.

The watering debate had already been raging for weeks, an endless online war of base versus leaves. Too much water, too little, or none at all. Every article promised enlightenment and delivered only chaos. Slimothy had even tried timing raindrops with a stopwatch, convinced he'd crack the code. The trouble was, every "expert" contradicted the next, and his stress was pooling faster than the yellow goo around his kale.

By that point, the debate had worn him down to a damp nub of confusion. His notes were soggy, his confidence wilted, and the vomit mold was thriving like it had tenure. To escape, he flipped through his Flower of the Week subscription. A scintillating issue awaited him: "53 Articles Featuring Different Flowers, Each Expected to Bloom During the Week it is Labeled."

For a while, Slimothy lost himself in the pages. Petal portraits, soil tips, and flowers with names that sounded like they could request tea service at any moment. The world beyond his garden shrank to a whisper. Even the slime mold seemed to behave, as if momentarily impressed by his commitment to floral literacy.

For a moment, even the Bright Wild felt orderly, quiet, balanced, almost civilized.

Until, of course, Slimothy leaned back into the catmint patch, triggered the solar lights, flattened three seedlings, and reset the chaos.

He sighed. Balance, it seemed, was a limited-time offer.

CHAPTER EIGHTEEN

Spanx, Spurge, and Sleepless Nights

The garden was asleep. Everyone tucked into their leafy beds, the moon sliding slow across the Bright Wild. Everyone, that is, except Slimothy. Night was his favorite time to philosophize. He thought about the mosquitoes (who really should have hibernated like respectable creatures), about Roger's midnight meals, and about the mysteriously vanished lights around the citadel he called home. Naturally, his internal monologue took a detour toward carnivorous slugs. Were there any? Or were they all gentle omnivores like him?

If carnivorous slugs were real, Slimothy was convinced they would resemble the dog's vomit mold he discovered last night—something between a science fair project gone wrong and pudding with trust issues. Kale never looked so trustworthy.

By morning, his thoughts lingered like dew, spilling across his kale-adjacent lemongrass—now puffed up as the yellow menace had migrated overnight, stuffing itself into the stalks like sunshine-colored spray-foam insulation squeezed into Spanx two-sizes-too-small.

The problem with staying up so late was that mayoral duties still came early, and spinach still needed guarding.

Coffee was supposed to be a deterrent for slugs—something about caffeine's toxicity and the abrasive texture of the grounds. In theory, it killed or repelled those of his kind. In practice, Slimothy found it invigorating. Coffee was his only salvation. The smell alone could revive him from a near-death overwatering episode.

By noon, he'd usually had enough to stun a lesser creature. By two, he was unstoppable and slightly vibrating. He often wondered whether he should place orders from Allison's supplier—or if she simply mainlined the stuff straight into her bloodstream. Either way, he respected her methods. His ambitions, however, went beyond basic alertness.

Caffeine kept him going—legacy kept him dreaming. He wanted a glass fortress in the middle of the garden: part plant nursery, part pillow fort, part winter palace. Potting bench number one had tempted him with its tiny starter dome, but it was hardly big enough to contain his ambition. He had spent hours scrolling garden catalogs, mourning the financial reality of it all, and wondering where exactly he'd put such a marvel in the ever-shrinking Bright Wild.

Meanwhile, arrivals continued. Slimothy's favorite so far was a lemon tree planted in a white terracotta pot with curly handles that looked suspiciously like they had their own passport and came from somewhere that smelled faintly of salt air and secrets. He considered setting it beside the olive tree—but would they get along?

Research told him plants needed companions, but Slimothy wasn't buying it. What if friends fought? Did they want opposites or cliques sprouting up in matching pots? One corner of the yard had gone yellow with drama, the lemongrass whispering to the lemon slime mold, both clearly trying to impress the new lemon tree, who was basking like a celebrity in her bright ceramic planter. The air practically smelled of citrus-tension. Was that jealousy? Was this a garden or a soap opera? Slimothy sighed, realizing his future might involve less gardening and more couples therapy for plants.

Then there were the care instructions: prune after each bloom cycle or give the tree a hard haircut in the spring. A haircut? What was he supposed to do—roll out a barbershop chair, drape the plant in a cape, and ask it about its weekend plans while he snipped away? He could already hear himself muttering,

"So, traveling anywhere this summer?" before the plant awkwardly tried to tip him a quarter out of sheer politeness.

A strange little vision formed: him with a clipboard, running weekly mediation sessions between jealous perennials. Roll call would be a disaster. *"Dwarf chenille, please stop interrupting. Dwarf peanut, no one is laughing at you. Yellow spurge, we've talked about boundaries."*

The whole thing sounded less like a garden and more like reality TV. Slimothy was convinced the plant-naming department didn't even try anymore—just pulling random junk out of a desk drawer when the vowels ran out and meshing the unrelated bits together in a last-minute act of botanical naming chaos at 4:59 p.m. on a Friday. Probably the same jokers who also named candle scents like "Wednesday Laundry," crayon colors such as "Sunburnt Salmon," and ice cream flavors like "Mystery Raisin."

Still, he wasn't above experimenting either. His sweet kale salad was nearly perfect, and the missing masterpiece ingredient? Poppy seeds. Getting those into the garden would be no problem. The only concern was whether his "mayoral" duties might come with random drug tests. He could already imagine Roger convening the Hopreme Court, croaking out, "Case number 42: Slimothy v. Salad," before sentencing him to probation on cilantro rations only.

One thing was certain: the yellow spurge was here to stay, immovable as a bad in-law who showed up with luggage. Or maybe it was just lemongrass trying on a winter coat. Slimothy had no idea. He had never gardened before, and if there was a manual, Roger was probably using it to level his patio furniture.

That might've been why he hadn't yet confessed the missing spinach situation. Mostly denial, partly trauma. It was supposed to be the crown jewel of the Bright Wild's winter greens, protected by every contraption he could rig short of motion sensors and a moat. Yet, for all his efforts, there was no spinach. None.

He squinted at the evidence like a seasoned investigator—or at least like someone who'd almost finished a true-crime documentary once before falling asleep. The scene was grim: partially-chewed stems and suspicious slime trails—enough to make even the bravest vegetable uneasy. Whoever did this wanted him to know they could do it again.

He dragged a stick through the dirt, outlining the crime scene with dramatic flair. "Perimeter secured," he muttered. "Victim identified. Time of death: probably around snack o'clock."

There was a whole lineup of suspects to rule out first. Roger was out—he'd never eat spinach voluntarily. The butterflies were too flighty, the ants too busy unionizing, and the worms were generally pacifists. That left the usual suspects: snails. Always snails. The proud-as-a-peacock cousins of slugs who thought a shell made them sophisticated.

Slimothy wasn't opposed to family, but these ones? Repeat offenders. He'd caught one last week loitering by the compost, pretending to admire the view while clearly casing the lettuce. "Classic diversion tactic," he declared to no one in particular.

He stared at the empty patch, dramatic music swelling in his mind—the kind that played when the detective realized the call was coming from inside the house. Then, as the morning dew sparkled like forensic evidence, he saw it: a faint glimmer of green just beyond the coffee cup. One lone spinach sprout, trembling but alive.

Slimothy, curled in the damp grass with his lukewarm life elixir nearby, knew one thing for sure—something was eating his spinach. Somewhere, a dramatic narrator was almost certainly gearing up to announce, "Tonight on Spinach Crimes."

He filed it under "Unsolved Cases: The Great Spinach Betrayal," "Attack of the Midnight Snails," and "Who Framed Baby Kale."

He took one last sip, looked back at the fragile sprout, and nodded solemnly. "Survivor," he whispered. "We'll protect you."

Justice would have to wait until after coffee. Slimothy solved crimes, not mornings.

CHAPTER NINETEEN

Celebrity Slimposters

It started innocently enough. Back in the day, there was just Slimothy. Just him, his plants, and the comforting illusion that he might be lonely. He wasn't, of course. He had schedules, paperwork, and several thriving one-sided friendships with ferns.

Then came the garden slugs.

A whole extended family of slime cousins he had never met, showing up uninvited, eating his reputation one leaf at a time, and leaving trails everywhere like cheap knockoffs.

Fine. He could live with that. Imitation was, after all, the sincerest form of low-budget admiration.

Except it didn't stop there. They started sliding across his favorite rocks, posing under his lighting, and worst of all, recreating his famous "thinking beside the potting bench" photo. One even had the audacity to caption it "original content."

Slimothy tried to ignore it. He really did. Even so, it was hard to stay humble when your likeness started trending under #Mood, #SlugLife, and #DirtButMakeItFashion.

Then it spread. Suddenly there were Halloween slugs, wrapped in toilet paper like discount mummies and parading around as if they were starring in horror films—most notably "Night of the Living Moist."

Then came the "SpongeBob" situation. Slimothy squinted at the TV more than once, deeply suspicious. Gary, that suspiciously charming "snail," had merchandising deals, theme songs, and a house. A *house!* Meanwhile, Slimothy was out here negotiating rent with mushrooms.

Don't even get him started on Slim from "Sesame Street," the so-called skateboard prodigy. Really? A slug who could ollie? Show-off. Slimothy could barely climb a lettuce leaf without losing traction, and this guy was out there defying gravity and copyright law.

It was all getting a little too close for comfort. The line between fame and fraud was starting to look as slippery as his own reflection.

Still, none of that compared to what he saw next. One morning, during an innocent bout of garden-influencer doom-scrolling, Slimothy stumbled upon something more horrifying than plagiarism: merch.

Little did he know the algorithm was only the opening act. The real villain was waiting in retail. On a perfectly unnecessary adventure through yet another off-brand home store, Slimothy stumbled across the most heinous impostor yet. There, plastered across a shiny endcap display, was … Bob.

Bob the slug. Smiling. Winking. Selling biscuits. Or possibly fruit roll-ups—it was hard to tell—but either way, it was deeply offensive.

His shiny cartoon body was splashed across every box, mid-slide, leaving a trail of artificial strawberry glaze in his wake. *"Stick With Sweetness!"* the tagline chirped.

Slimothy stared in horror. It wasn't inspiration anymore—it was character assassination by marketing. A slug, selling sugar. The sheer irresponsibility!

He looked closer. Bob even had his same tilt. His same little self-assured eye stalk angle. The resemblance was criminal.

"Et tu, Bob?" Slimothy whispered. *"Et chew?"*

A likeness so brazen it stopped him mid-slime. The audacity.

These slugs were all rich! Merch deals, cereal boxes, Saturday morning cartoons. Whole empires built on the backs of fake slugs with suspiciously glossy finishes.

As for Slimothy? He was hungry. Hungry and exasperated.

Where was his golden ticket? His licensing deal? His collectible figurine? He was objectively more handsome than that mealy-faced green creature peddling "healthy snackage," with an entourage to prove it. Roger, Allison, the fairies, the fungi folk, the radishes—an all-star ensemble. No skateboarder, no cartoon snail, no Halloween gag could compete with that lineup.

Frankly, if the Bright Wild ever got a TV deal, a majority of the cast was already camera-ready.

Slimothy sighed, stomach growling. He had always believed he was an only child—a rare jewel among thorns, a one-slug show in a world of background extras. The problem was lately, everywhere he turned, the universe seemed determined to mass-produce him.

He glared at Bob's box of "healthy snacks," his reflection warped in the glossy packaging. Bob grinned smugly, holding his wares like a trophy. One day, Slimothy decided he was going to eat the competition. Literally. Paired with a nice compost reduction and a sprinkle of pettiness. Out of spite and curiosity, in that order.

CHAPTER TWENTY

Slimothy vs. The Ethics of Salad

Slimothy poured himself another glass of Cabernet Franc, leaned back, and thought with great satisfaction: gardening was wonderful.

Of course, that was before the moral dilemmas set in—an age in which strawberries required eulogies, tomatoes demanded prize ribbons, and squash loomed like ethical landmines. It wasn't just gardening anymore. It was philosophy. It was politics. It was the constitution of coleslaw.

Like any good law, it came with loopholes. Which is how Slimothy found himself staring at Swiss chard, wondering what crime it had committed to deserve such a confusing name. What did Switzerland have to do with chard? What in the slime trail did chard even mean? It wasn't rhubarb, it wasn't kale, it wasn't celery. So what exactly was it good for? Until he came to the Bright Wild, he'd never even heard of such a thing. It certainly looked wonderful—stalks glowing in shades of red, green, even umber, holding up big leafy flags to the sky. Still, the questions gnawed at him.

Slimothy decided that was a mystery for another day, because right then his attention fixed on a tomato so spectacular it seemed ready to give an acceptance speech. Firm, red, glistening with late-morning dew. It was the personification of perfection—the biggest tomato he had ever grown, worthy of a prize ribbon at the fair. *"I'd like to thank the garden, the sunshine, and Slimothy,"* it might have said. Slimothy was chuffed to tears.

Not that he had always been so bold. In the early days the idea of picking anything sent him spiraling into a full existential crisis—which was impressive, considering he already had a smaller one scheduled daily.

When his first plants arrived many moons ago, he treated them like priceless antiques. He polished leaves with imaginary gloves, he measured their growth like a scientist with too much free time, and he practically built a velvet rope around them. Despite that, he could barely bring himself to pick the fruits of his labor.

The first tiny miracle he harvested was one perfectly beautiful strawberry. Slimothy did not want to sacrifice it. He thought it might hurt his plant—or worse, hurt its feelings. The strawberry itself sat quietly, glowing red and innocent, perfectly content to do its job. Slimothy, meanwhile, was tying himself into knots, staging imaginary ceremonies and rehearsing farewell speeches. Which raised the question: what was the point of having a kitchen garden if he could not bear to harvest from it?

Slimothy fretted for days. He drafted invitations in his head, wondered if Roger could be persuaded to officiate, and even considered writing a hymn in the strawberry's honor. He felt morally obligated to hold a ceremony—a eulogy, some kind of thanksgiving service for the fruit. After many conversations, a few too many cups of coffee, and a lecture or two from his friends, he finally heard the logic: *"The fruit wants you to pick it. That's what it's designed to do. If you don't pick it, it will hurt the plant."*

That was a hard concept for Slimothy's thumbnail-sized brain to grasp. Picking helps plants? Leaving hurts them? It was gardening turned upside down. Flowers stay on stalks, leaves stay on trees, strawberries stay on plants—that was the natural order of things. Slimothy paced circles in the grass, weighed the moral cost, and even considered writing a pros and cons list on a damp leaf. In the end he caved. One evening, with no ceremony at all, he plucked the strawberry, muttered a quick thank-you to the universe, and sank his teeth into it.

It was delicious. Sweet, bright, everything a tiny red miracle ought to be. Surprisingly, the guilt was much lighter than he'd expected. In fact, he felt oddly triumphant, like he had just solved gardening itself. One berry down, a lifetime of produce to go. He briefly considered giving an acceptance speech of his own before realizing he was still chewing.

Of course, the problem came roaring back when his championship-sized squashes appeared—hulking brutes that looked like they could enter the county fair's demolition derby. Paint them neon, slap a number on the side, and they would roll right in between the funnel cake stand and the prize pig barn. He decided that too was a dilemma for another day.

By the time the eggplants arrived, Slimothy was an old pro. He hacked away with the confidence of a salad surgeon—cut and cut and kept cutting—until there were eggplants on the potting bench, eggplants in the wheelbarrow, even eggplants squatting in flowerpots. The first batch alone weighed 7.4 pounds, the equivalent of 2,000 Slimothys nervously crowding onto a bathroom scale. Worse still, the 9.2 pounds of squash hadn't been tallied yet, largely because it refused to stop growing—another 3,000 Slimothys of impending chaos.

Slimothy started to think the garden was less a patch of soil and more a union hall. Membership: vegetables. Dues: measured in wheelbarrow space. Agenda: overthrow the slug and enforce mandatory crop rotation breaks. Were they holding secret meetings when he wasn't looking? In his mind's eye he could see them gathered in a circle under the fairy lights, glossy heads nodding gravely. One would clear its throat. *"Motion to overtake the wheelbarrow?"* Another would second it. Minutes would be scribbled in compost with a stick of chalky limestone, filed neatly under Top Secret Root Business.

Before adjournment, a final vote would be cast on which eggplant deserved the blue ribbon that week. By dawn they would return to their posts, innocent as ever, pretending nothing had happened—except, perhaps, a faint whiff of funnel cake in the air.

CHAPTER TWENTY-ONE

How to Accidentally Open a Portal

Slimothy's pond lights were on the fritz.

They blinked in Morse code at each other. First one went out completely—so much for navigation beacons. Then another flickered like it was whispering, *"Stay strong, brother."* Slimothy squinted, the betrayal unfolding one lumen at a time. Were his pond lights unionizing? It sure looked like a walkout—one bulb at a time. He half-anticipated a tiny picket sign to bob to the surface reading: *"Fair wattage for all!"* Another light sputtered like it was delivering a closing argument, and Slimothy braced for chanting. He didn't speak Morse, but he was fairly certain they were demanding dental benefits.

It was maddening, especially after all the hours Slimothy had spent relocating rocks just to get them positioned perfectly. Now the lights were treating him like management. Rock Relocation Expert was a thankless job—and apparently one that came with strikes.

Either way, he was starting to sympathize with that octopus at the aquarium who had sprayed water across the wiring system until it all fizzled out. Honestly, Slimothy thought, if he had eight arms he'd probably be out there staging a full electrical coup too—maybe even forming a rival union of his own.

Meanwhile, where was the wildlife he had practically built this pond for? Roger hadn't so much as hopped by for a visit. Slimothy had designed the whole setup with frog romance in mind—moonlit reflections, strategically placed lily pads—yet not even a single hopeful croak. Did frogs even like water, or had he been lied to his whole life? Did hummingbirds ever sleep, or were they tiny caffeine addicts flapping 24 hours a day? Did lilies get to pick which part of themselves floated above the surface like a snorkel while the rest sulked underwater, wrinkled and pruney? What happened if one particular leaf just wanted a day off—did the whole plant hold a vote, or did it sneak below the surface like an employee calling in sick?

The cucumber, at least, wasn't taking a break. It had staged a full-scale escape, crawling over the fourth side of its trellis like a drunk pilgrim determined to discover new lands he had no map for. Slimothy strung up another crooked rope path, only to watch his view vanish under wave after wave of green ambition. The problem was he didn't even really like cucumbers. Pickles, though—those were his personal religion. Crisp, briny treasures that lived in jars. The tragedy was Slimothy had no clue how to make his own. Still, he was determined to learn, if only to give meaning to the relentless quest of a vegetable that seemed hell-bent on manifesting destiny. Maybe the cucumber just needed rest to calm down, Slimothy thought—before immediately wondering if rest came in dill or bread-and-butter flavor.

Bulb season was another thing on the horizon. Dozens of bulbs sat tucked away in the fridge, under the sink, even wedged into the furthest corners of the couch like little botanical time bombs waiting for the signal. Which way was up? Bulb side up, bulb side down, bulb sideways for variety? Gardening had far too many rules. Slimothy briefly considered drawing tiny arrows on each one, then panicked at the thought of them launching a coordinated revolt against him for micromanagement.

At least his Flower of the Week subscription was rolling in with daffodils. Slimothy was especially excited—they were the first flowers to wake after winter, lifting bright faces like sleepy eyes blinking at the spring sky. No wonder they were called the Eye of the Garden. With more than 32,000 registered varieties, Slimothy figured he'd be entertained for quite a while. Then again, who really needed 32,000 versions of the same flower? Was there a variety called "Looks Exactly Like the Other One #47"? He figured the bulb companies were just renaming them at random—"Daffodil Supreme Deluxe Ultra Gold"—to keep gardeners feeling fancy.

Of course, he had to pause over the myths. The story of Narcissus—staring at his reflection until he became a daffodil—felt uncomfortably close to Slimothy's own habit of gazing into pond water and practicing his "mysterious slug" look. As for Persephone being snatched into the underworld while picking blooms? That was downright unsettling—and raised some logistical questions, like how the whole "till death" clause was supposed to work below ground. Daffodils were sacred to Hades and his wife. Slimothy wasn't sure whether to be reassured or worried that the Greek ruler of the underworld and his bride were so intrinsically connected with this usually bright yellow flower. On one hand, his new favorite bloom came with serious ancient street cred. On the other, he now imagined Roger in a little black cloak, offering ferry rides across the pond for two acorns and a daffodil. He wondered if planting them in his yard meant accidentally opening a portal.

Daffodils, according to the experts, were easy. Tuck them into the soil a couple of weeks before the ground froze, and they'd handle the rest like tiny botanical professionals. *Rest, relax, enjoy.* That was the advice. Slimothy, however, had never trusted anything that claimed to be easy—especially now that portals were on the table. Should he plant them in a circle? Was that summoning? What if the bulbs arranged themselves into some kind of ancient sigil while he slept? He began drafting a mental checklist of "portal-proof" gardening steps: no circles, no triangles, and absolutely no chanting while watering.

Slimothy had never not done anything in his life. Relaxing sounded lovely in theory—until it turned into boredom. That particular restlessness was just hunger in disguise. Rest itself began to sound almost edible … the way his mind circled it like a snack. Yet hunger was a greased slide straight into chaos. Boredom led to hunger, hunger led to mischief, and mischief usually ended with twine, painter's tape, and regret.

Maybe it was safer to stay busy after all.

CHAPTER TWENTY-TWO

Waiting on Rain

Slimothy didn't relish bringing plants inside for the winter. What if they all hogged his Wi-Fi connection at the same time? His mind stitched together a strange scene—mosses streaming garden podcasts at full volume, succulents trapped in an endless group chat about who's too moist, and the foxtail fern eating up bandwidth binge-watching "Lawns & Order."

It hadn't rained in 14 days—a flash drought. No precipitation since Slimothy installed an electric pump and lights in his pond. Nor had there been any since his friend and confidant put up gutters on her dwelling on the other side of town—so elaborate they looked like they were siphoning rainfall from three counties over just to water her begonias. The rain was MIA. Very unusual, since the month prior had been the wettest in history for his corner of the world. He wondered what rain did when it was bored.

He couldn't give his plants the same nutrients they got from a proper soaking—the type that dripped from above, the kind all the gardening authorities claimed was bad for the leaves. Slimothy wasn't so sure. After all, dog-vomit slime mold had staged a full blockade in his garden for three straight days, and it didn't seem worried about following the rules.

Still, he waited, hoping. Rain wouldn't solve the mold menace, but it would at least give him a break from the endless cycle of work all day, try to relax, then water the garden. Only, the garden was getting big. Too big. Practically overnight, Slimothy had gone from hobbyist to mayor of a sprawling botanical metropolis. The squash demanded better roads, the peas lobbied for taller trellises, and the basil kept filing noise complaints about the peppers. Slimothy had not officially run for office, but here he was—writing bylaws, managing scandals, and wondering if he'd ever get a day off from city-hall watering duty.

The radio taunted him daily. "No rain, no flowers," it sang in a maddeningly catchy jingle, the kind that stuck in your head until you wanted to compost yourself. Slimothy caught himself humming it while hauling water—the world's saddest backup singer in a band he never joined. Even the eggplants seemed to bob along, smoky-violet groupies swaying at the driest concert in existence. Slimothy scowled. He didn't need backup dancers. He needed rain.

By the third verse, Slimothy was the unwilling front man of the drought-themed garden spectacle. The peas started chanting, "RAIN, RAIN, RAIN" between lyrics, and the basil pretended to faint dramatically in the front row. Slimothy dragged the watering can behind him like a roadie past his prime, muttering, "This isn't a tour—it's a hostage situation."

Meanwhile, the lavender wanted nothing to do with the show. Most had already walked off the job and gone to the plant rainbow bridge. The few holdouts sat off to the side with tiny clipboards and folding chairs, looking like they were preparing for arbitration. Slimothy could practically hear them muttering about bylaws, dues, and electing a treasurer who actually meant business.

It wasn't long before the rest of the garden joined in. The lavender wanted less water—naturally—demanding better drainage and hazard pay for soggy roots. The kale, on the other hand, staged a hunger strike for moisture, flopping over dramatically and refusing to photosynthesize until Slimothy intervened. At one point it even wheezed out slogans like, *"No justice, no juice,"* and *"Photosynthesis is a right, not a privilege."* The cucumbers tried to restore order—but mostly just blocked the path like a picket line—blowing their tiny whistles and scribbling grievances on oversized cabbage leaves, the ink smudging green across the margins, threatening to take Slimothy to Garden Court for crimes against irrigation.

Slimothy sighed. His garden wasn't wilting—it was negotiating. Which left him stuck between factions, a one-slug management team who had somehow become responsible for collective bargaining.

The wind picked up. Could inclement weather finally be on the horizon? Slimothy didn't even know why he wished for it. He hated being cooped up, staring out the window while rain smacked every surface like it was trying to break in. He had never seen a hurricane, but he lived where they were common. That left him wondering: if one did arrive, what exactly was going to happen to his kale? His brain, never helpful in a crisis, immediately jumped tracks. Would he need a designated tornado shelter in the garden? How many snacks would that require?

Still, beneath the worry, Slimothy itched for a good puddle jump—his favorite rainy-day activity. That and the delicious relief of a day off from watering. Though knowing his luck, the minute he jumped into a puddle, the lavender union would fine him for reckless splashing.

CHAPTER TWENTY-THREE

Day Planners are for Deer: Chaos is for Slugs

Along with the missing rain, Slimothy hadn't seen the daily deer procession in a while either. Was there a greater mystery linking the two? He couldn't say, but in his quiet hours he often thought of them as colleagues in a grander office. Without watches or alarms they still managed to keep impeccable schedules, which Slimothy found both impressive and vaguely annoying.

He remembered their traits as if he were writing them down in a secret notebook. Antlers looked less like ceremonial hats than protest banners waiting to be raised. Their ears were satellite dishes tuned to channels he could never access. Their eyes carried a permanent "don't bother me" expression—the sort of look that made you reconsider all your life choices with a single glance. Legs were four-wheel-drive suspension, equally suited to leaping fences or intimidating vegetables, while tails served as emergency flags—one flick meant "meeting adjourned, scatter immediately."

At dawn, the deer clocked in for breakfast as though reporting for duty. Fields and hedges became their buffet line, every mouthful accounted for. Their chants might as well have been echoing across the grass: *"No justice, no juice!"* and *"Photosynthesis is a right, not a privilege!"* Kale, of course, had supplied those slogans, but the woodland herd seemed happy to adopt them. By midmorning they retired to cover, slipping into wellness breaks that looked suspiciously like corporate nap time. Chewing cud seemed to be their way of taking minutes, each munch logged neatly in stomach compartments. Slimothy envied the order. His own digestion couldn't keep a schedule if it tried.

Twilight was their gala. They emerged again, silhouettes sharp against the fading light, dining with the formality of guests at a banquet where shadows were the dress code. Later, in the deep night, they transformed into socialites. Bucks wandered like politicians at a mixer, pausing here, nodding there, radiating antlered charm. Slimothy thought how different it must be to have a crowd to mingle with instead of his usual company of sniffles and soil mold.

After midnight came the digestive conference. The nighttime salad bandits withdrew to hidden spots, reclaimed their places, and ruminated with the gravity of a board meeting. Every chew felt like a line item entered into the record. Somewhere between bites Slimothy swore he heard a muffled chant carried on the night air: *"What do we want? Better cud! When do we want it? Now!"*

Then came the closing session before dawn. A final snack in low fields, a flick of white tails, and the meadow troupe was gone—planner reset for another day. Slimothy liked to imagine them fading into first light with the solemnity of a committee meeting pausing for snacks until further notice, chanting as they disappeared: *"Hey hey, ho ho, soggy roots have got to go!"* He sighed, took a grounding whiff of rosemary sprigs, and admitted that chaos suited him better anyway. Order was for deer. Even without a planner, he always managed to find the snacks.

CHAPTER TWENTY-FOUR

The Scan and the Storm

Slimothy had never had a CT scan before. Heck, he didn't even know what sinuses were—he just knew his face hurt, and he'd do just about anything to make it stop.

He was great at sitting still, so that part was no problem. In fact, he was looking forward to sneaking in a catnap between watching the slime mold settle in for fall and waiting for the infuriatingly late rain.

Would it hurt? What would they find? He was practically buzzing with anticipation. Plus, it was a nice break from the yard and all his duties.

The waiting room was packed with plants, so he felt right at home among the mismatched chairs and glossy, catalog-perfect office greenery. Oversized abstract flowers floated across the walls, looking suspiciously like someone had described "eggplant-colored art" to a printer who lost interest somewhere around the magenta stage.

The weatherman droned on from the little black TV box—possible rain here, hot spells there—but Slimothy quickly lost interest. The tulips on the wall caught his eye instead. He couldn't wait to grow his own, the real kind that lived in the ground, not trapped in postmodern glass. White and yellow with lush green stems, the bulb packets had promised. For now, though, his tulips were doing time in solitary confinement in the fridge crisper, awaiting parole.

The fluorescent lights pressed down on his mood, but nothing could shake his hope that he might finally get answers and send his forever sniffles on permanent vacation. He wondered what it would be like to feel "normal." Did he even remember what normal was? Probably boring. He secretly liked his own brand of chaos, even if it came with too much cortisol from all the steroids.

When it was finally his turn, the machine hummed and buzzed like a supercollider. He was fairly sure this was what tornado debris felt like—spinning through the air. It was fascinating and terrifying, and over far too fast. He hadn't even managed to close his eyes.

By the time he slimed back outside, the heavens had opened. Slimothy tilted his face up into the downpour, wondering if he ought to buy a lottery ticket after all the miracles that had lined up for him lately. Somewhere across town, he was sure his friend's new gutter system was either performing beautifully or already mid-insurrection courtesy of her own full-scale yellow slime mold rebellion—water gushing through the brand-new tunnel irrigation system with more entrances than exits, an underground drama Slimothy could only compare to the sewer system of a bustling city.

In his mind's eye, he was suddenly a tour guide, pointing out "historic attractions" to mildly puzzled but very polite visitors. *"On your left, centuries of questionable drainage decisions. On your right, a slime mold blockade holding firm since Tuesday. Please keep your hands and roots inside the walkway at all times. Tickets are five acorns each—complimentary poncho if you survive."*

Before he had a chance to ask her how the grand opening was going, the weather episode—much like the blissful nap he had not really gotten to enjoy—was over as quickly as it had begun. Gutters everywhere fell silent, the puddles stilled, and Slimothy was left with nothing but daylight and the prospect of arduous yard duties after all.

He trudged back toward the garden, torn between dread and the expectation of finding the cucumbers stretched across the rope path like a living speed bump, the lavender leaning in suspicious unison. The rain had been far too short to satisfy anyone. If he knew his plants, they were already deep in another closed-door session without him—drafting bylaws for new plant members only and arguing over whether compost breaks should be every hour or every 30 minutes.

Out on the horizon, twin hurricanes spun off the coast, circling each other like bickering siblings. Slimothy couldn't tell if they were bringing the rain with them or just fighting over who got to hog it. Maybe storms needed weather support buddies too.

CHAPTER TWENTY-FIVE

Remote Control, Remote Chaos

S limothy was irritated. He had just moved rocks in and out of the pond for what felt like the 400th time this week and cleaned the pump—which he hadn't even known was clogged. The eggplant was overachieving again, cheerfully producing more than anyone asked for, and Slimothy was sick to death of the rocks.

The purge had finally tested his patience. He had unceremoniously ripped out the poor, drowning English thyme in the corner of the garden where the dog-vomit slime had claimed territory. It probably scattered spores with every tug, seeding little yellow rebellions in all directions—but Slimothy didn't care. The garden was his domain, and he wasn't about to let the highlighter-colored spray foam beat him in a game of stalemate. Stubbornness was one of his strongest core competencies.

The rocks, however, seemed to be in on the game. Every time he hauled them out, they multiplied like they were cloning themselves behind his back. He could have sworn some of them were the same ones he'd moved yesterday, smirking at him from slightly different angles.

It was still unbearably muggy outside. Mother Nature hadn't gotten the memo that her autumn collection was in season and her summer wardrobe was out.

Humidity clung like polyester in July.

Still, Slimothy thought, it was glorious.

Glorious—except for the part where he had to remove all 407 of those rocks to replace the pond lights. One was flickering at the edge of his vision like an industrial lamp after a tornado, and another had given up entirely. The garden deserved better than bargain-bin brightness. The old string had done its time, buzzing and sputtering like it was auditioning for a horror movie, but the effect was less cozy ambiance and more a haunted warehouse. The new lights, however, were everything the old ones weren't: unblinking, obedient, and straight out of the box smelling faintly of victory.

The best part? They came with a remote. Slimothy admired it like a magic wand he had no business operating, convinced he now commanded both illumination and destiny—assuming, of course, the batteries hadn't already given up. With great ceremony he pressed the first button, bracing for thunder or applause. Instead, the pond erupted in flashing neon like an underwater rave, pulsing magentas and electric limes that could have summoned a school of glowstick-wielding minnows.

It took Slimothy 14 frantic button presses before the chaos finally subsided and the lights agreed to shine in a single, civilized color. In that time, he fully envisioned Roger hopping in wearing tiny sunglasses and demanding a cover charge, while the cucumbers formed a conga line. The lilies, meanwhile, would probably start a limbo contest with their own stems.

He couldn't help imagining what else the remote might work on. Maybe he could mute the peas when they got too ambitious, or dim the lavender when they leaned into overdramatics. Perhaps even hit "power off" on the slime mold and watch it vanish in a puff of smoke.

He aimed it at the pond, then at the garden, then at himself—just in case there was a secret nap mode waiting to be discovered. If there was, Slimothy figured he might finally have found the greatest invention of all time.

He clicked the button and held perfectly still. Was this it? Was he asleep? He cracked one eye open. The bugleweed was still tooting along like a brass section warming up, the cape leadwort was still draping itself dramatically over anything that would hold still long enough, and the dog vomit slime mold was still pulsing with unbearable self-satisfaction in its corner. Nope. No nap mode.

Unless ... maybe it was delayed.

He clicked again. Suddenly he sneezed. Was that reset? He tried another. Now he had hiccups. Volume up? Another click, and he swore his slime trail sparkled faintly in the sun. Brightness setting. By the seventh button press, he was convinced he'd found disco mode—and honestly, he wasn't even mad about it.

If his pond was destined to turn into Studio 54, at least he'd finally have mood lighting for when the eggplant staged another dramatic performance. Besides, a sparkling slime trail gave him main-character energy he hadn't felt since the day he mistook Miracle-Gro for a sports drink.

CHAPTER TWENTY-SIX

All-You-Can-Eat Milkweed & the One Slug Pyramid

Turns out Monarch butterfly babies are even pickier than Slimothy at an all-you-can-eat buffet. Tropical milkweed? Too ordinary. They'll turn their antennae up at that. The real chef's special was swamp milkweed—the five-star entrée of the Bright Wild—served fresh with excellent egg-laying conditions and a side of superior caterpillar survival rates. Reservations recommended.

On his morning stroll, Slimothy came face to face with one of these royal diners: a big, chubby future butterfly-in-training clinging to the milkweed like it was saving him a seat. Yellow, black, and impossibly squishy, it was one of the most beautiful things Slimothy had ever seen. He wondered if he should set out a dessert menu.

Monarch butterflies apparently migrate twice a year, which, frankly, sounded exhausting. Each fall, a special "super generation" packs up and heads south from August to November, flying thousands of miles to overwinter in Mexico or along the California coast. In spring, they head back north again to breed, their offspring finishing the journey over several generations—like a relay team that forgets where the finish line is but keeps running anyway.

Slimothy admired them but also felt a little vain. Sure, Monarchs traveled thousands of miles—but had any of them ever moved the same rock 400 times in one week? Probably not. If he were a Monarch, he suspected he'd quit migrating after the first snack break anyway. Preferably somewhere with pickles.

The thought made him hungry, which was dangerous. Hunger always led to projects. Last time it had inspired him to start playing with concrete—his new favorite love language. This week, he'd gone bigger.

The Bright Wild had new residents: passionfruit. Their winding vines carried a kind of swagger, curling around anything they pleased. Slimothy felt they deserved an upgrade worthy of their vibe, so he set about crafting a trellis straight out of his structural fantasies—a semi-circle, sun-shaped marvel, heavy, immovable, and allegedly hurricane-proof. It rose from the soil like a monument, equal parts garden structure and medieval fortress.

Slimothy's creation weighed in at about 200 pounds—the equivalent of roughly 54,054 Slimothys. He did the math himself, slowly and carefully, like a slug accountant with a very tiny abacus. His trellis didn't just feel colossal—it was basically a one-slug wonder of the world.

No wonder he felt superior standing next to it. The passionfruit had a horticultural palace, the cucumbers had no excuse, and Slimothy—well, Slimothy was clearly operating on a super-generation level of his own.

Then another thought crept in. If Monarchs had "super generations," then surely slugs ought to as well. What would a Super Slimothy even look like? Twice the slime? Four times the patience? Or maybe just one slug clever enough to stop moving rocks.

CHAPTER TWENTY-SEVEN

Merlot in the Mailbox

Birdhouses hung from every angle—more than 24 by last count—plus countless other miniature dwellings scattered across the garden. Hundreds of tiny homes, each with a door you could technically crawl through yourself if you found the right angle—or after a boldly enthusiastic cocktail hour.

Add to that a solid dozen more tucked into the pond edges, vegetable beds, and concrete planters, and the Bright Wild was no longer just a garden. It was a village.

Slimothy adored it. He loved birdhouses. He loved birds. He loved nests. Mostly, he loved the idea of home. The Bright Wild was all of it at once—safe and secure, a little avant-garde, a little contemporary, and undeniably his. Wine flowed freely here, matched only by a sense of awe—as though the world were unveiling itself brand-new just for his little slug life.

Slimothy was good at wonder. He always stopped to smell the roses—partly because wonder was what propelled him forward, and partly because, well, it took him a while to get there. Tonight's wonder, however, required a fresh bottle of wine.

Slimothy picked wine for the labels. Sure, he skimmed the occasional biopic on the back, but if there was a bird, a bee, or a flower on the front, the decision was already made. His favorite, of course, was anything with a feathered friend.

Slimothy uncorked the evening's bottle, admired the little sparrow etched on the label, and let his imagination wander. If the Bright Wild was a village, then surely each birdhouse was its own vineyard cottage. The tall, narrow one tucked into the oak branch? That was Château Cardinal—specializing in bold reds that stained your lips and your dignity. The squat round one near the cucumbers? Obviously Bluebird Blush—light, fruity, and guaranteed to give you a headache by the second glass.

He constructed a little internal vignette: a tasting room run by the robins, where you had to pay in earthworms instead of cash. The wrens, of course, would be the sommeliers, swirling dewdrops in acorn caps and telling you your slime trail had "excellent minerality."

By the time Slimothy poured a second glass, the entire birdhouse row had turned into an upscale vineyard strip. All that was missing was live music. He glanced at the Egyptian star cluster, expecting a celestial symphony, but it only managed a faint twinkle, like a toddler mashing piano keys. The finger lime tried to save the moment by rattling its citrus pearls like maracas, but the result was less "romantic vineyard evening" and more "drunk produce attempting karaoke."

Slimothy sighed happily. Even if the music was questionable, the night was undeniably his—messy, magical, and just tipsy enough to sparkle.

CHAPTER TWENTY-EIGHT

Lettuce Celebrate

It was a big day in the Bright Wild—a huge day. The inaugural cut-and-come-again salad bar had officially opened for business, and Slimothy was first in line. The bees were buzzing, the birds were bickering—about wake-up calls or seed distribution or whatever else kept them busy—and low, promising clouds hung overhead like a slow-moving buffet of rain.

Slimothy heard none of it. He was too busy smacking his lips, thinking about the fruits of his very first lettuce harvest—and, most important of all, his first homegrown kale. He had waited weeks for this moment, whispering encouragements to his plants daily. *"Grow faster. Grow greener. Be leafier. Believe in yourselves."*

Baby cucumbers were popping up left and right, and a purple flower Slimothy had never seen before exploded into the world, petals sticking out like messy morning hair after a slug nap gone wrong.

Then came the moment he'd been waiting for: the salad. The *salad!* He carefully plucked leaves from each bunch—not too much, not too little—only the outer layer. Each one was magical, curly, colorful, glowing in hues from deep green to neon chartreuse, erupting into magenta and everything in between. They were perfection incarnate, and Slimothy's stomach growled so loud a nearby wren paused mid-argument.

After much cutting, he found himself with a giant bowl of fresh-picked greens he could hardly wait to dive into. He'd made a solemn vow that when the first harvest came, he would start eating better. Too many snacks lately had left him looking suspiciously like a queen bee—round, well-fed, and ready to live off fat stores all winter. Slimothy knew it was time to rein it in. Today was that day.

Not one to garnish his food with unnecessary accessories, he decided this auspicious moment deserved a little ceremony. Sea salt, a little olive oil, and a heartfelt thank-you whispered to the buffet of plants that had made it all possible.

Slimothy took his first bite and chewed slowly, savoring the crisp crunch, the earthy sweetness, the triumph of growing his own food. With each mouthful he was transported to wherever salad dreams come from—a leafy-green paradise where the sun always filtered gently through lettuce ruffles, every nibble echoed like music, and where he could almost believe croutons rained from the skies above like golden, toasty meteors—light showers in the morning, heavy sourdough storms by afternoon.

He blinked, fully prepared for a breadstorm to roll in. Instead, his eyes landed on the garden itself, alive with its own kind of theater. The other benefit of being up early was seeing creatures he normally wouldn't, like the beautiful red, blue, and green painted bunting that waltzed into the birdbath with a tiny towel over its shoulder, splashed around like it had booked a spa package, and preened under the clouds as if waiting for cucumber slices to be delivered.

Slimothy couldn't help but think it was comical that the bird matched the lettuce he had just collected almost impeccably. Salad and bird, twin jewels of the morning. The garden, he realized, was full of small luxuries.

His gaze drifted back to the rows of baby cucumbers staging their own slow-motion parade. The salad had been worth the wait, he decided, and now he had something new to look forward to. Pickles. However they were made—through strange vinegar spells or dill incantations—he fantasized about them arriving like a weather system all their own: briny fronts rolling in, herby showers sweeping through, maybe even the occasional thunderclap from the secret Pickle Guild that only met on Tuesdays.

CHAPTER TWENTY-NINE

Spinach Witness Protection

I t was 11:03 p.m.—late enough to count as "at night" in his book. Why on earth were birds chirping?

Only one light remained on in the garden—a sure sign it was past everyone's bedtime—except for Slimothy, who never seemed to want to go to bed. There was just too much excitement, too much he didn't want to miss. He couldn't even say what he might be missing, only that the garden never slept, so why should he?

Every time he turned around, there was something new in the Bright Wild—neat little row-house subdivisions appearing here and there, newcomers settling quietly at the periphery. Gardens were full of a secret, underground commerce. Things just grew, literally beneath your nose, but you never saw it happen, even if you were watching very closely.

Which is why the Spinach Witness Protection Program was weighing heavily on his mind.

His spinach had gone missing before. Leaves nibbled down to skeletons. Entire plants vanishing in the night. No suspects, no leads—just the gnawing paranoia that something, or someone, was eating away at his green empire.

Had the baby Monarchs decided to up their leafy game? Slimothy pictured them forming a tiny gang, leather jackets fashioned from milkweed, antennae slicked back, swaggering into the spinach patch with no regard for garden laws. He all but heard them muttering, *"Kale today, spinach tomorrow."*

Still, he shook his head. The Monarchs were messy eaters. If they'd been involved, there'd be shredded evidence everywhere. No, the thief was cleaner than that. Smarter. More deliberate.

The only solution, he decided, was relocation.

So he moved them. One by one, spinach plants were smuggled under cover of darkness into "safe houses" across the Bright Wild. Some went into clay pots tucked discreetly behind hedges. Others were hidden under the wide leaves of the banana tree. One particularly nervous plant was disguised with a marigold "hat" and instructed not to talk to strangers.

For the high-risk cases, Slimothy set up elaborate cover stories. Each spinach got a new identity: false names, fake backstories, even relocation papers scrawled on damp napkins. *"You're not spinach anymore,"* he whispered to one trembling leaf, *"you're sage. Keep your head down."*

He arranged decoys—empty pots stuffed with parsley clippings meant to lure the thief away from the real targets. He murmured passwords to the plants as he tucked them into their hiding spots, though he'd never remember them later. *"The code is leaf-litter tango,"* he said solemnly to one cluster. *"Repeat it back to me."* The spinach, predictably, said nothing.

By dawn, he was exhausted. The Bright Wild was dotted with hidden spinach, each tucked away like a secret agent awaiting extraction. Slimothy surveyed his work with pride. The thief might strike again, but not without a challenge.

Of course, there was one small problem: Slimothy had forgotten where most of them were. Days later, he'd stumble across wilted "witnesses" in the oddest places—behind Roger's terracotta courthouse, perched mid-potting bench in quiet defiance, even one stuffed in the overturned wheelbarrow like it were awaiting trial.

The thief might have been foiled, but Slimothy had a sinking suspicion: he was his own worst suspect.

Still, he couldn't let his guard down. Each creak of the garden gate was a threat. Each flutter of wings could be an informant. The birds chirping at midnight weren't just birds anymore—they were lookouts, posting coded warnings to the unseen menace.

Slimothy raised his feelers to the wind like a detective sniffing out a lead. Somewhere out there, the spinach thief was watching. Until Slimothy cracked the case, every head of spinach would have to live under deep cover.

The Witness Protection Program was in place. The only question was who would crack first—the thief or Slimothy? Either way, someone was going to wilt.

CHAPTER THIRTY

All Petals, No Subtlety

Slimothy's rose wasn't merely blooming—she was detonating. Petals erupted in a cascade of peach ruffles like confetti at the end of the world, as if the universe had given her one final night to flaunt everything she had before the curtain fell. This wasn't gardening; this was theater. A floral apocalypse in silk and perfume, a finale so grand it made the rest of the Bright Wild look like unpaid extras.

She stood in her black planter like it was a throne, every blossom a declaration, every thorn a carefully worded legal disclaimer. The air itself seemed to pause around her, heavy with reverence and fragrance—fragrance Slimothy, thanks to his chronic sinus congestion, could only imagine. Probably something fancy, he thought. Maybe like morning dew and destiny. Or possibly salad dressing and bread. He'd never know for sure.

He could only stare. Some plants grew. This one performed. Some blossoms opened. These unfurled—dramatically, purposefully—like an aria in slow motion.

Queen Joséphine ruled accordingly. She had no doubts about her place in the world: front and center, perfectly lit, framed by the golden hour. Her blush-pink blooms didn't just open; they made an entrance, each peeling back with the patience of a leading lady who knew the audience would wait.

She was refined. She was demanding. She was, without question, convinced the entire garden had been landscaped purely for her convenience.

There was something delightfully over-the-top about it all—the kind of flourish Empress Joséphine, long celebrated as a purveyor of fine roses, would have deemed "proper floral conduct."

The myth of Joséphine roses said this kind of behavior ran in the lineage. Empress Joséphine—arguably the first patron saint of plant drama—had once supposedly filled her château with every rose she could find. She brought in elite gardeners, imported rare species, even enlisted her powerful—vertically challenged—husband to intercept ships at sea so their cargo could be searched for rose specimens. Wars were raging, empires collapsing, and somewhere in the chaos a bewildered soldier was probably guarding a potted flower because the Empress had a collection to complete.

Slimothy wondered if he, too, ought to appoint a royal painter. After all, if Empress Joséphine had hers, who somehow managed to spend the French Revolution quietly painting petals instead of dodging guillotines, it only seemed fair that Queen Joséphine of the Bright Wild should have her own court artist. Someone to immortalize every ruffle and thorn in watercolor glory.

He briefly considered applying for the position himself, but the logistics were … complicated. He lacked both hands and artistic restraint, and his last attempt at "creative expression" had ended with an art materials accident involving compost tea and regret. Still, he thought, glancing back at her blazing blooms, maybe some flowers really did deserve a portrait—or at the very least, a flattering filter.

Her planter was her stage, her petals were wardrobe changes. Every passing breeze was an encore. Of course, if Slimothy ever thought the salad bar was his crowning achievement, the queen was here to remind him otherwise. She was the achievement—everything else was garnish.

If anyone dared to question it, she had only one reply, delivered in the tone of someone who had never known doubt, humility, or an off-season: *"I don't compete with the garden. I am the garden. You may applaud now."*

It wasn't so much a statement as a decree—one that should have been engraved on marble, possibly accompanied by faint harp music.

Slimothy stared. She was holding so perfectly still she could've passed for a statue already.

"Show-off," he muttered, giving her planter a suspicious side-eye before shuffling off toward the last known whereabouts of the spinach.

Glamour was overrated anyway—especially when the missing spinach was a case file still very much open.

CHAPTER THIRTY-ONE

The First National Spinach Bank

H e had seen her only once—rust-colored and radiant, tail tipped white like the edge of the garden's planter boxes. She appeared as if conjured, and for a moment Slimothy thought he was staring at a dream. He mistook her for a baby deer until he saw the breeze ripple through her fur. She drifted across the street like a flame searching for air—and then she was gone.

What was she? A vision? A trick of the wine? Had he eaten too much catmint again? The last time that happened he became absolutely convinced the lamb's ears had organized a clandestine swingers' club, complete with velvet ropes, coded knocks, and bylaws written in dew drops. He wasn't sure what the dress code was, but he suspected it involved more sequins than strictly necessary. Another time he decided the compost pile was running an underground movement—worm lawyers, beetle bodyguards, secret messages rising in steam from rotting melon rinds. He even swore it was recruiting agents, whispering assignments to mushrooms when it thought no one was listening.

Or maybe, just maybe, she was a fox.

She was his mirage, his kryptonite, the kind of vision that made the rest of the Bright Wild blur into background noise—allegedly all 40 USDA-certified varieties of sounds she could produce. Slimothy was beginning to suspect she was personally responsible for every racket after dark. The midnight shriek by the lettuce bed? Probably her. The ominous rustling near the compost? Definitely her. Even the cough that sounded suspiciously like a raccoon with stage fright—he was starting to pin that on her too.

Maybe she was everywhere—not just a fox at all, but the Bright Wild itself moving through fur and flame, stitched into the night like a myth come to life.

Had she even been real? Or had too much evening wine spun illusions in the dark, painting shadows into shapes he wanted to see? Slimothy could not be sure. All he knew was that he longed for another glimpse—one more chance to prove she wasn't just a trick of the night but something dazzling and untouchable that had chosen, however briefly, to pass through his garden.

So he waited. Night after night he planted himself at the edge of the yard, eyes trained on the spot where she'd disappeared. Hours passed in deep, unbroken quiet. Only the shadows dared to move.

Yet Slimothy held fast. Slow and steady, he told himself, was how wonder revealed itself. The kale would grow, new garden friends would sprout, and maybe—if the night was kind—the fox would return. Until then, she remained what she had always been: a dream Slimothy refused to wake from, a secret folded into the hush of the wild.

Still, Slimothy's mind would not rest. Her white-tipped brush of a tail haunted him. To Slimothy it wasn't just a tail—it was a banner unfurling through the night, a signal flag, a semaphore, a whole alphabet of flicks and flourishes. A balance beam, a fur coat, a smoke signal. It was everything at once. One twitch could mean *danger.* Another might mean *snack secured.* A sharp whip could very well have been her way of declaring dominion over the lettuce bed. Slimothy was positively convinced she could spell entire messages in the air if she wanted to—dispatches no one else could read.

Which, naturally, left him with no choice but to try. He spent an evening in front of a puddle practicing signals with a lettuce leaf balanced like a makeshift tail. Flick left: *Hello.* Flick right: *Where have you been all my life?* A dramatic swish: *This spinach is mine.* The reflection was less than convincing, but Slimothy told himself all great linguists had to start somewhere.

Slimothy had a sudden realization. Foxes were expert diggers, stashing food in hidden caches they remembered later. What if his missing spinach wasn't gone at all, but tucked neatly under a pile of leaves in some secret location?

The thought of his greens sitting in some kind of fox-run spinach savings account, accruing interest in dirt, was almost worse than losing them outright—especially if she planned on charging withdrawal fees. Slimothy imagined her behind a desk in a tiny vest, spectacles perched on her nose, stamping his spinach with an official seal before sliding it into a vault under the mulch. Kale accepted as collateral. Interest rates subject to change without notice.

Slimothy decided the true nightmare wasn't losing spinach—it was owing it to a fox banker. He wasn't about to be in spinach debt—though if she showed up tomorrow carrying his greens in her mouth like a love offering, he'd sign up for monthly payments on the spot.

CHAPTER THIRTY-TWO

Cone of Uncertainty, Cup of Snacks

Slimothy was bored tracking his first impending-ish hurricane. It was moving slower than a slug on a Sunday morning—outwitting him at his own game of low speed.

Winds gusted, and though the yellow dog's-vomit slime was finally on its way out, it left behind a far less appealing relative: algae. His pristine white rocks, moved and rearranged no fewer than 409 times, were now turning the color of kale on a night out at the club—limp, brown, and trying too hard under bad lights.

First step: the pond pump. Obviously broken.

Second step: barley straw in a neat little pond solution package. Somehow, Slimothy was almost certain it made things worse. His water, once cloudy, now had the vibe of backyard bisque.

What was next? Wait for the hurricane rains to flush the system? Introduce fish? Add plants? Bribe a passing heron? He didn't know the first thing about ponds, gardens, or hurricanes, but he knew he had to learn fast. Which, for Slimothy, was the exact opposite of his life motto: slow down, do less, maybe take a nap.

Every forecast he'd seen swirled in his head in a noisy mess of cones and spaghetti, like a pile of worms in lines all wriggling straight toward his zip code—though he wasn't entirely sure worms even had zip codes, or tiny post offices where they shuffled forward one slime-length at a time to send soggy letters.

Yet, for all the noise and predictions, Slimothy wasn't worried about the storm itself. Wind and rain didn't scare him—he had the structural integrity of a jellybean. What concerned him was his pond. His masterpiece. His algae cauldron. Would it overflow and sweep his carefully curated rocks all the way to the purple gromwell patch—or worse, into the frogfruit—leaving him pondless and disgraced?

He was not a licensed pond professional. He was no landscape specialist. As for hurricanes? Forget it. With days still to go before the first fat drops arrived, Slimothy began to batten down the hatches—no small task, considering the Bright Wild was basically 87% hatches, huts, burrows, and questionable lean-tos.

The most urgent were on Pebbleton, a mysterious little mound that had appeared in summer when the water dropped. It had become prime real estate—crowded with cliff homes built without engineering permits, a hollow reed condo development, and an old toy boat that had washed in long before Slimothy kept records and was now zoned as a duplex for whoever was bold enough to move in. Slimothy inspected each one, taking notes only he could read.

Structural integrity? questionable.
Curb appeal? excellent.
Insurance premiums? don't ask.

He nodded gravely as though FEMA had dispatched him personally.

By the time he'd circled Pebbleton twice, the storm hadn't budged an inch closer, but Slimothy had convinced himself he was mayor of a very damp municipality. It was a heavy responsibility—one that called for wise decisions, firm leadership, and possibly a ribbon-cutting ceremony at the hollow reed condos. He even drafted a campaign slogan in his head: *"Cleaner water, more lily pads, brighter tomorrow."*

He eyed his emergency snacks, then remembered he was supposed to be dieting. The storm outside was still circling far away, but the one inside had already made landfall: he could eat the snacks now, of course, or attempt the nearly mythical feat of slug restraint. For now, Slimothy hunkered down—equal parts hero and snack-deprived slug—bracing for the squall. Outside, the sky grumbled. Inside, so did his stomach.

CHAPTER THIRTY-THREE

Bright Wild Winter Wear

The looming weather front had turned out to be a dud. Good for those in its projected path, bad for Slimothy—who now had a large pile of snacks asking to be eaten.

Even so, the rain had come steadily for a while, sheeting gusts, batting at the windows, begging to be let in. Slimothy was grateful—thankful the weatherman had been right for a change, tickled he didn't have to water his plants for the third day in a row—but also worried he might need to have an emergency raft on standby. Hopeful the pond was finally getting the much-needed water change it had been sulking about.

If it came to that, he decided, at least he'd float away in style. While he waited, Slimothy nursed a particularly delicious wine—one with a name as absurd as anything produced by the Department of Plants and Interiors: 689. What kind of title was that supposed to be? Like three raccoons with a spreadsheet had just pointed at random numbers on a page and someone stamped it on a bottle. The logo was equally bad—like the graphic designer had gone on holiday and left the keys to the squirrels. That's what Slimothy got for branching out of his usual bird-themed vino-buying habits.

Not that the plants were much better. Most of them sounded like secret passwords or spells: *Echinacea purpurea, Scaevola aemula, Foeniculum vulgare*—all tongue-twisting messes that made 689 look positively elegant. At least the bottle wasn't called Foxtail Fern 689 or Dwarf Chenille Reserve. Not unlike wine, his plants demanded perfect soil, water just right, too much light or not enough, and turned into divas of another dimension at the first hint of neglect.

They were needy—every last one of them. Yet for all their drama, Slimothy adored them. Sunset hung low and red across the horizon, bathing the garden in an afternoon glow while the tree above flicked defiant water drops onto him as he rocked in his favorite spot—his swing—cushions squishy beneath him.

He'd proudly built it himself, of course, from the big-box in the sky store—a delivery that arrived three days late and one existential crisis early. The assembly instructions were laughably unhelpful, so he'd resorted to watching "How To Tie Your Own Rope" videos for hours on end—a heroic effort considering his complete lack of opposable thumbs.

Chains, cushions, and questionable ladder balance were all involved in the process—but somehow, against every known law of physics and slug safety, he'd managed it. Now here it was—the perfect perch from which to watch the Bright Wild—home to chaos, compost, and one rare, untouched tomato growing with all its might. Perfection—temporarily.

Which meant only one thing: trouble was on the horizon. Winter was coming, and perfection wouldn't last. Slimothy already had a mental clipboard of plants that would keep him up at night. Basil was top of the list—the ultimate high-maintenance herb icon—with mint and lemon balm not far behind. Rosemary and sage might swagger through a mild snap, but even they made him nervous. Dwarf chenille, shrimp plants, Siam tulips, tropical milkweed, Mexican heather, the butterfly bush—he might as well start knitting sweaters now.

Meanwhile, Spaulding and Marty McFly—his pineapples—along with the finger lime and olive tree were firmly in the cover-me-or-lose-me category.

The medium-worry crowd wasn't much better. Lavender, coneflowers, dianthus, gaura, balloon flower, stokes aster, wild coffee—sometimes they toughed it out, sometimes they sulked like teenagers. Foxglove, bleeding-heart vine, wisteria—they put on a brave face but would need Slimothy hovering like a helicopter parent. The nearby foxtail fern, society garlic, coastal buckwheat, woodland sage—hardy-ish, but a hard freeze would send them crying to

Slimothy for hot cocoa.

At least he didn't have to worry about kale. Kale was no fussbud. Kale had common sense. Sweeter after a freeze, it practically strutted under frost—showing off greener, more tender leaves while everyone else fainted. Slimothy relished the thought of snacking on it beneath a white, icy blanket, sunlight glinting on the crisp edges. Kale didn't demand sweaters, hot cocoa, or heated scarves—it just did its job.

He had months yet before supplies would run low, and in typical Slimothy fashion, he decided he would worry about that later.

By the time Slimothy had finished fretting about the actual problems at hand, he had designed a full winter wardrobe catalog in his head. He named it The Frost-Bite Line: Fall/Winter Edition. Scarves for the coneflowers, obviously. A puffy jacket for the rosemary. Earmuffs for Spaulding, with Marty McFly in a matching set. Shrimp plants in woolly socks, dwarf chenille in a cashmere wrap, and lavender tucked into thermal underwear.

He even produced a mental catwalk clip in which the foxglove strutted down a frosty runway—cape billowing—while the society garlic demanded a heated scarf with pearl buttons.

Of course Slimothy was the announcer. *"Ladies, gentlemen, and gastropods of distinction,"* he whispered to himself, *"next up on the runway, we have wisteria in a dramatic floor-length coat, perfect for resisting both frostbite and judgment."*

He added a little throat-clearing hum. *"Coming in hot (or rather, staying warm), please welcome the dianthus in a sequined parka—dazzling the frost right off its petals."*

Then his focus slipped. The sequins blurred into thoughts of sugar crystals—the parka puffed itself into a dinner roll—and suddenly the whole runway looked suspiciously edible. Foxglove's cape? Cotton candy. Rosemary's jacket? A flaky croissant. Even Spaulding kept winking at him like, *"you know I'm actually food, right?"*

The Bright Wild fashion show had been hijacked by his appetite.

He sighed. That tomato might make it to the kitchen—but the rest of the Bright Wild? It was going to be a long winter of worrying, watching, and wondering if slugs could learn how to crochet plant blankets—or at the very least, stop imagining couture as a buffet.

CHAPTER THIRTY-FOUR

Scoreboard of Smells

S limothy could smell the inside of his sinuses—and the air outside matched it note for note. Dank and musty, like a wet throw blanket that hadn't seen a wash in 13.5 years and then been flattened by three shopping carts for good measure. It was as though the weather had peeked inside his nostrils, stolen the scent, and filed a copyright to use it freely across the Bright Wild.

He anticipated a bill to arrive any moment—royalties charged per sniffle, cough, or dramatic sigh. The air was brazen like that, shamelessly bottling his misery and selling it back to him in bulk. Slimothy snorted once, experimentally, and swore the breeze winked and whispered, *"Complimentary sample, first one's free."* He couldn't escape it—inside or out, his sinuses and the clouds had clearly signed a licensing deal, launching Eau de Congestion™ as the Bright Wild's newest seasonal fragrance.

The sky brimmed overcast, heavy and swollen—gloomy like his mood and as dire as the last of his summer basil rations. The plants were thinning, their leaves curling in on themselves, and Slimothy knew he was staring down the end of the season. He measured his happiness in sprigs and lately there weren't many left to count.

The foreshadowing of winter hung over him like a wet tarp—sagging in the middle, dripping at the edges, and flapping just enough to be annoying. Slimothy was convinced it had a personal vendetta—waiting for the perfect gust of wind to smack him in the face just when he'd gotten comfortable. It whispered of gray mornings and empty planters. It stressed him out—the way endings always did. In his head he was already stockpiling emergency supplies: scarves, candles, six backup thermometers, and possibly a shovel with his name etched into the handle. If winter was coming, Slimothy intended to greet it like the apocalypse—armed with tissues and snacks.

In the beginning, the Bright Wild was pinks and whites and yellows—a rainbow of color fighting to outshine itself. Now fall curled its fingers around the garden, coaxing things into dormancy. Slimothy missed the kaleidoscopic chaos and was in a desperate fight not to let the season end—as if sheer willpower, plus maybe an emergency snack bribe, could convince autumn to turn back.

Soon it would be time to rotate to his Fall/Winter scarf from the Bright Wild lineup. It wasn't exactly practical—knitted three sizes too long, patterned like a traffic cone, and trailing behind him dramatically whenever he took a corner too fast—but Slimothy liked the statement. It said, *"I may be cold, but I am also fabulous."*

There was promise ahead, though—twinkling lights strung like constellations, giant evergreens muscling their way into every corner, and a crispness sharp enough to sting his nose in an entirely new way. The kind of sting that said, *"yes, you are alive—and also slightly underdressed."* Slimothy briefly considered bubble wrap as a winter accessory—practical insulation and an endless source of entertainment when things got dull. He let a ridiculous self-portrait form in his mind—him waddling through the Bright Wild, every step punctuated by a chorus of pops, the first Michelin-slug in recorded history. Fashion-forward, fully insulated, and perfectly suited for effortless naps wherever he happened to plop down.

With the season's change, came a to-do list—but it shrank quickly. The welfare of his kingdom's wildlife came first. *"Don't cut back the plants until spring,"* the annals declared. *"Leave the seed heads. Save the birds, the Rogers, and all the other critters who burrow under leaves, tuck into brush piles, and nibble dried husks through the cold months."*

Slimothy perked up. No yard maintenance for three whole months? That sounded less like a responsibility and more like a coupon for laziness. He fully expected to find himself proudly explaining to anyone who asked that the weeds were "for biodiversity," the untrimmed shrubs were "ecological infrastructure," and the pile of questionably folded garden cushions was "critical amphibian habitat." Even the snacks he left lying around could now be justified as "foraging opportunities."

By the time he was done rebranding his mess, Slimothy had promoted himself from sluggish gardener to world-class conservationist—single-handedly saving the Bright Wild, one unwashed blanket and forgotten cracker at a time.

However, the lack of projects left him restless. Sluggish by nature, sure—but this was different. He thought about vacations (of which he'd had none) and wondered if it was finally time to explore the looming jungle just beyond the Bright Wild's manicured edges—a grand adventure waiting to happen. It called to him like a drumbeat—mysterious, perilous, irresistible.

Slimothy paused, listening harder. Was it destiny—or just his stomach grumbling again? Either way, the beat was steady, insistent, and getting louder. Adventure or snacks was calling—and Slimothy had never been good at ignoring either.

If he were going to answer that call, though, he'd need to be prepared. The Bright Wild was one thing—the wild beyond was another. No neatly lined stones, no carefully curated shrubs, no neighbors watering basil at suspicious hours. Out there were mysteries, predators, and possibly (he shuddered) chores he had not yet invented names for.

So he began a list of supplies. First came a hatchet. Then tissues—because you never know when the weather might turn tragic. Next, snacks, obviously. After that—an emergency scarf, a blanket, a whistle, two flashlights, a spare notebook for cartography, and maybe a kazoo in case he needed to establish dominance. By the end of it, his list looked less like survival gear and more like packing for an extremely confused field trip. Still, he told himself, preparation was key.

After all, how dangerous could it be, really? The deer traversed through the jungle daily and survived. Allison crossed the divide 400 times every 24 hours racking up the equivalent of 500 miles in wingbeats. Slimothy mentally tallied a scoreboard in his head—deer, undefeated. Allison, record-breaking. Slimothy, zero attempts, zero wins, zero injuries—for now. He picked up his supply list and awarded himself five points just for preparation. If he ever actually set one eyestalk across the border, surely that would be worth at least 10.

His first challenge loomed ahead. The great beyond was guarded at the northwestern border by a giant butterfly bush—towering stories high, with red spiked flowers bursting like fireworks, feeding who-knows-what. To Slimothy, it looked less like a plant and more like a final boss level—bristly, unyielding, and absolutely the type to yell, *"YOU SHALL NOT PASS,"* if approached too quickly. Slimothy had never seen anything so big—and that was saying something. He wondered how the birds even located their snacks in the chaos without earning themselves at least three bonus lives.

He logged the butterfly bush on his imaginary scoreboard. If this was only the entrance, what in the world waited inside? The Bright Wild might have been his kingdom—but out here every step was borrowed time and questionable courage.

Then the wind shifted, and Slimothy paused again. Between the towering spikes and restless leaves, he saw it—lights flickering in the distance. They shimmered like enchanted lanterns strung across an invisible garden fairground, a secret carnival calling only to him. Or maybe, he thought with a gulp, they were just porch lights from a rival homeowners' association. Either way, they twinkled with promise and mischief.

Maybe that was where the spinach thief hailed from. Slimothy conjured a shadowy figure slipping in under cover of night—clad in black, rolling silent wheels of greens like getaway cars, leaving chalk marks on the rocks to taunt him. A whole heist crew of garden bandits—armed with trowels and disguises—vanishing before dawn without a trace. The idea made him shiver—caught somewhere between fear and admiration.

Outside the Bright Wild's safety was pure wilderness—alluring, visceral, untamed. The kind of place people in stories traveled weeks or years to reach—chasing treasures or the unknown.

Slimothy the Explorer. It had a nice ring to it. He tried it aloud, testing the weight of the title, then let a whole cover spread form behind his eyes—

"Slimothy the Explorer and the Secret of the Spinach Thieves" splashed across it. A whole series could follow—action figures with removable scarves, a movie adaptation where he'd be voiced by someone dramatic but just nasal enough, maybe even a theme park ride with suspiciously wet seats.

The branding opportunities were endless—if slightly questionable. A logo with crossed kale leaves and maybe a compass that only pointed toward snacks. Collector's mugs printed with his serious explorer face—though the image would inevitably warp in the dishwasher until he looked like a soggy raisin. Scarves in every color, marketed as "limited edition" but restocked weekly. Even tissues, sold as "field gear."

He mentally arranged it all on shelves under a giant banner: *"Slimothy the Explorer: Adventure You Can Wipe Your Nose On."*

He bet nothing needed watering over there. A paradise. Dangerous, sure—but free from chores, pruning schedules, and the constant guilt of forgetting to fertilize. The sheer relief of it set him off. First a snort, then a laugh—loud enough to scare a passing moth. The sound fizzled almost immediately, though, leaving him with the uneasy sense that the Bright Wild was suddenly too small—like a playpen he'd outgrown. The wilderness beyond wasn't just a backdrop anymore—it was a giant, crumpled map waiting to be unfolded—probably upside down, missing a corner—but begging to be read anyway.

To the north, stretched impenetrable jungles. To the south, deer, foxes, and neighborhood cats wandered freely. To the east, greenery spread for miles. He'd never thought much about directions before—but now it felt like a choice. It reminded him of those fairy tales where paths promised adventure—except in his version the candy house would be out of snacks, the witch would squint at him and mutter, "close enough to a newt," and he'd find himself bobbing in her cauldron like an overcooked dumpling.

He could practically hear her debating whether to season him with rosemary—or just toss in a handful of croutons for texture. Slimothy shook his head hard. Whatever way that wasn't—that was the way he'd go.

It was like a choose-your-own-adventure book—where every turn rewrote the story. Mystery in one direction. Familiar beasts in another—though in his imagination they weren't just grazing or prowling but running a bed-and-breakfast, offering turn-down service with acorns and complimentary howls at midnight.

The air hung thick—carrying that same musty sinus-smell that had dogged him all season—only now it seemed to drift out of the wilderness itself, daring him to follow. Slimothy wrinkled what passed for his nose. Was this the call of adventure—or just mildew with good timing? Either way—it reeked of commitment. In fact, it smelled suspiciously like a sales pitch: *"Adventure: now available in musty sinus-scent, only for a limited time."*

Slimothy decided destiny could wait until the wilderness came out with a fresher fragrance—maybe something citrus. For now, he turned back toward the Bright Wild, muttering that even explorers had to carb-load before greatness—and that the crackers in his emergency stash weren't going to eat themselves. He awarded himself five more points on the scoreboard—one for bravery, four for snacking—and called it a draw with destiny, at least for tonight.

Behind him, the wind rustled the leaves and carried one last musty whiff after him—as if the wilderness had started keeping score too.

CHAPTER THIRTY-FIVE

20,000 Wildflowers (Some Restrictions Apply)

2*0,000 wildflowers guaranteed to bloom—or your money back.* Slimothy counted six. Seven if you included the weed squatting where the other blooms should have been.

Where were they then? Late to the party? Late bloomers? Late for supper? Slimothy had decided that waiting for vegetables to "hatch" was already a test of patience. Flowers? Flowers were downright absurd.

Every day he played the "Is this a flower or a weed?" game—and every day the answers blurred together. He poured himself another glass of wine. What were weeds good for anyway?

Naturally, that led to research.

"Many common weeds are edible, providing nutritious greens, seeds, or even a coffee substitute, such as dandelions and lambsquarters."

Slimothy had never heard of lambsquarters before—but he sure wasn't ready to swap his double-shot oat milk espresso for something named after a livestock body part. Mild, spinach-like flavor or not.

Then there were the aliases! Lambsquarters was also white goosefoot.

Slimothy had questions. Could the plant-naming department please pick one animal per leafy green? Who, in the history of taste-testing, looked at a waxy, diamond-shaped leaf and thought: *"That goose's foot looks tasty. Let's eat that,"* then dragged a lamb into the branding? Slimothy was almost afraid to ask.

Weeds weren't funny in the garden—they were a problem. Pick them, pluck them, smother them, destroy them. Repeat. Gardening was exhausting.

It was hard enough keeping track of the carrots' due date and when the peas would need their trellis extended. The vine contingent had already staged a coup—annexing a quarter of the yard into their creeping jungle.

After directing 20,000 wildflowers in a full-blown floral symphony, the rest of the garden read more like background actors. No choreography, no solos—just cabbage. Ordinary green and red cabbage. Ornamental leaves in white, pink, purple. The possibilities were endless. Apparently, cabbage could even "bolt."

"Bolting usually occurs in cabbage when temperatures get too hot."

If it bolted, it flowered. If it flowered, it looked fabulous—but its career as food was over. Decorative versus edible, edible versus decorative—Slimothy tried to keep it all straight.

"Regular cabbage is for eating, flowering cabbage is for looking," he repeated like a mantra. The truth was, he didn't care. Flowered, unflowered, green, purple, neon blue—if it popped up in the Bright Wild, Slimothy was ready to cheer it on.

Questions of delicious or decorative could wait until tomorrow. Tonight, all that mattered was another glass of wine—and the six wildflowers he was proud enough to claim (seven, if you counted the weed). If anyone asked about the other 19,993 missing blooms, well ... he already had his refund letter drafted:

"Dear Sir or Madam, I regret to inform you that my meadow resembles a patchy comb-over. Kindly process my refund in the form of wine. As proof of purchase, I am mailing you the weed currently pretending to be wildflower number seven. Please handle with care—it has developed an inflated sense of self-worth."

CHAPTER THIRTY-SIX

Kaleopolis Rising

It was Oct. 1, the day the world turned a little greener. National Kale Day. A marked occasion with recipe swaps, bright shirts, and hashtags—as if kale needed more publicity than it already had. One day? Just one? Slimothy thought it insulting. Kale deserved at least a month, maybe its own calendar, possibly its own religion complete with hymns like "Amazing Leaf" and a holy text printed on biodegradable seed paper. To Slimothy, kale wasn't a passing holiday. It was a 401(k), a personality test, and his emergency contact.

Draped in his natural green, Slimothy slid proudly through his kale patch like a one-slug parade float, radiating unearned enthusiasm—a walking billboard. A marketing department, PR firm, and unpaid intern all rolled into one, whispering at every leaf he passed: *"eat your vegetables."* He didn't need confetti or cooking shows. His entire existence was advertising—sponsored by kale, powered by kale, starring kale.

Of course, not every plant could keep up that level of drama. Spinach—soft and polite, like the kind of neighbor who waters your plants but then judges you for forgetting. Romaine—as exciting as damp printer paper. Collards—sturdy but exhausting, the heavyweight champion you respect but don't invite to brunch. Nothing could compete with the rugged curls and rich, stubborn flavor of his chosen leaf.

Kale wasn't just food. Kale was personality. Bold. Crunchy. Slightly bitter in a way that made you respect it.

He laughed whenever he saw the so-called "world's healthiest vegetable" list. Some scientist with too much free time had handed the gold medal to watercress. Watercress! Slimothy snorted (if slugs could snort). It tasted like something that should stay in the creek—sulking with the minnows. Let watercress keep its medal. Kale didn't need trophies. In Slimothy's Garden Olympics, kale was the gymnast, the sprinter, the opening ceremony, and the fireworks.

Besides, Slimothy wasn't fussy. He called himself a generalist eater—a connoisseur of whatever grew within sliding distance. Still, there was strategy to his choices. Without a shell, his body was a soft, vulnerable thing—basically a pudding cup with opinions. Every leaf was more than a meal. It was structure, scaffolding, armor.

Kale in particular was calcium dressed as flavor—a daily defense against the crueler corners of the Bright Wild. He chewed it with the solemnity of a knight donning chainmail, convinced every bite made him less squishable. Each curly leaf was a shield. Each crunchy stem, a lance. In his mind's eye, Slimothy marched into battle gleaming in leafy plate armor—unstoppable until someone introduced vinegar.

So while others clapped for kale on a single autumn morning, Slimothy kept his quiet faith in it year-round. Where they saw a garnish, he saw strength. Where they saw health trends, he saw survival. For him, the celebration never ended. It wasn't a holiday—it was life. Honestly, it should have come with a parade, complete with banners of green, marching bands crunching in unison, and Slimothy himself rolling proudly at the front, Grand Marshal of the Leaf.

Still, life had a way of interrupting even the best kale crusades. That afternoon Slimothy had gotten disappointing news from his doctor, which cut short his deep dive into 2025's Fat Bear Week winner—a mountain of fur and glory named 32 Chunk. Slimothy found himself wondering, if a bear weighed 32 chunks, how many chunks was he? Two? One? Maybe half a chunk if he really sucked in his gut. He did the math, tapping his feelers like an accountant on deadline, and landed on 0.0007 Chunks, generously rounded up to one slimy crumb of Chunk for confidence. On the official Bear Scale, he wouldn't even make the footnotes.

A rock Slimothy regretted moving—half a chunk. A bottle of wine—precisely 0.05 chunks, though it could feel like three after a generous pour. Roger's patience was measured exclusively in negative chunks—a black hole of chunks sucking optimism straight out of the garden.

Before he could finish calculating the garden's worth in fractions of Chunk, a leaf blower shattered the peace—rattling the sanctuary like a freight train through a teacup. Slimothy flinched. According to the doctor, there was nothing wrong with him. No infection, no mystery ailment. Just ... his head. Maybe pollen? Maybe nerves? Maybe the universe playing tricks? It wasn't a diagnosis at all—only a vague suggestion to keep muddling forward, like being handed a map with *"good luck"* scribbled across it.

Slimothy scowled, his temples throbbing. Allergies be damned. Kale could carry him only so far. Tonight he didn't want wine—he needed something stronger.

To find it, he would have to go beyond. Beyond the familiar patch, past the safe vegetal rows, and straight into the unknown. The jungle loomed before him—not just a tangle of leaves but an impenetrable fortress of leafy matter, bristling with shadows and secrets. To Slimothy, it was no mere garden bed—it was a rainforest, dripping with menace, where cucumbers coiled like pythons and squash sprawled like ancient ruins. Vines hung heavy overhead like ropes in a forgotten temple, and every rustle of a beetle's wing was surely the battle cry of some hidden tribe.

Doctor number three had told him he couldn't eat his favorite fruits and vegetables during their corresponding pollen seasons—but they had also said there was nothing wrong with him. So who was he to believe? Give up his favorite veggie nosh, start his own apothecary, or set off on his own adventure? The answer lay somewhere past that green barricade. If nobody believed he was sick, then nobody would miss him when he disappeared into the undergrowth—chasing not just relief but the promise of something far stronger than wine.

Slimothy thought through his journey attempt from the safety of his comfortable patch beside his championship kale. Kale would miss him, he decided. The leaves would wilt in despair, composing tragic ballads in chlorophyll minor. The stems would hold tiny vigils, whispering, *"Come back to us, Slimothy.*" He considered leaving behind a framed photo of himself in a rain puddle—so the kale could remember his face while he was gone.

Then came the math. The fastest recorded slug was pretty pacey—apparently 17.6 meters per hour—which translated to 693 inches per hour, or 11 ½ inches per minute. Math gave him a headache worse than the one he already had, but he pressed on. If the edge of his patch was, say, 2,000 inches away, that meant … well, a really, really long time. He projected the journey taking 47 years, three heroic snack breaks, at least two midlife crises, and one epic showdown with a leaf blower. By the time he got there, the pollen season would be over, kale would have gone out of fashion, and his obituary would read: *"Made it to the fence. Died immediately of math."*

Still, the numbers didn't lie. One inch at a time. 11 ½ inches per minute if he was feeling athletic—which in his mind was basically the pace of an Olympian, and they always start with a dramatic sendoff.

The first inch would be glorious. Raised feelers like a marathon champion crossing the finish line—even though technically he would have just left the starting line. By inch four, he would already be winded, demanding a water break from a dewdrop clinging to a blade of grass. By inch seven, he would need a motivational speech.

At inch 10, Slimothy mentally staged a dramatic collapse onto a pebble— declaring it "base camp" and promising to continue his expedition in the morning.

By the time he slid past inch 12 in his mind's eye, Slimothy was convinced the Olympic Committee would be calling any minute. Yet—even the legends kept records of their training. Naturally, so would he. Thus began the official log of his Great Inch-by-Inch Expedition.

Day One, Inch 10
Distance covered: 10 inches. Distance remaining: 1,990. Morale: heroic. Knees: nonexistent. Supplies: one dewdrop, a partially eaten kale leaf, and a pebble now called Base Camp Alpha.

Day Two, Inch 19
Progress slow. Encountered hostile ant traffic. Negotiated safe

passage by surrendering one crumb of kale. Spirits remain high—though patience reserves from Roger measured in negative chunks.

Day Three, Inch 37
Morale slipping. Snack supply questionable. Dewdrop rationing underway. Motivation provided by a particularly dramatic sigh from Roger— interpreted as applause.

Day Five, Inch 62
Weather: unbearably muggy. Trail conditions: slippery. Accidentally circled back to Base Camp Alpha—declared it a victory lap. Confidence restored.

Day Nine, Inch 120
Confidence gone. Tripped over the fallen garden hose, rolled backwards two inches, and pretended it was part of the training regimen. Renamed the site Hose Mountain.

Day 12, Inch 225
Spirits lifted by discovery of wine bottle cork. Declared it holy relic. Morale once again heroic.

Day 17, Inch 400
Supplies low. Faith in kale the only thing propelling mission forward. Roger's sighs now sound like funeral hymns.
Projected arrival: inch 2,000—sometime in the next geological era.
Obituary draft updated: "made it to the fence. Died immediately of math, dehydration, and poor time management."

Day 20, Inch 500
Navigation concerns.

Slimothy considered his slime trail a built-in compass—a shining breadcrumb path guiding him home. Foolproof, glowing, flawless … in theory. In practice, he promptly ignored it, wandered off, and got lost anyway—circling himself like a tourist trapped in a corn maze. After rounding his own slime signature three times, he declared it a newly discovered continent and immediately began drafting maps no one had requested. The loop was christened the Great Goo Divide. A nearby puddle was elevated to Slimefjord. A particularly shiny pebble was promoted to the capital city of Kaleopolis, population: one slug, two wine stains, and a questionable sense of grandeur. History, he decided, would thank him for rewriting itself in mucus.

Science claimed slugs weighed an ounce and could hit 1,500 feet per second—packing the punch of 3,000 foot-pounds of energy with a range of 100 yards. Obviously, this referred to him. Slimothy ran an internal highlight reel of himself breaking the sound barrier somewhere over the cucumbers—a silver streak of destiny tearing across the Bright Wild, broadcast live on ESPN:

"Unbelievable, Jim, he's clearing the mulch pile at Mach 2. His slime trail's sparkling, his eye stalks are flapping like car dealership balloons, and the cucumbers may never recover!"

Obituary draft amended: "made it to the fence. Died immediately of math, dehydration, and the complete misunderstanding of basic ballistics."

Before collapsing, Slimothy raised his feelers high and proclaimed, *"Let it be known that I, Slimothy the First, claim dominion over all that glistens!"* Then he flopped face-first onto the pebble—declaring it both throne and bed—and entered the slug version of sleep: 22 minutes of absolute nothingness, followed by the likelihood of 41 hours of wandering in circles. Depending on humidity, this nap could also escalate into a months-long hibernation—a dark age in which Kaleopolis would be ruled solely by weeds.

The Bright Wild's greatest explorer ended the day not with triumph, but with a nap squarely across his own slime trail, as if marking it "under construction"—the only record book entry being:

Proclaimed empire. Immediately abdicated in favor of sleep.

CHAPTER THIRTY-SEVEN

Paperwork and Petty Crimes

Where in the world was Roger? Slimothy hadn't seen him in days. He missed the silence of his unlikely companion—even if they stayed worlds apart when the rest of the garden was awake. He counted another wildflower this morning on his daily stroll, bringing the running total down to a missing 19,992—assuming the weed still counted, which it absolutely did.

Roger's sudden absence, paired with the endless rotation of chores, left Slimothy's already overactive mind spiraling in every direction—like the cucumber vine that, having run out of trellis, decided that down and through were clearly the next best directions. He even checked beneath the hedge of the scorpion's-tail for any sign of Roger, which had, of course, grown back in full stately glory—blocking all views of the skyline like a green wall of defiance.

Perhaps Roger had retreated to his summer estate near Allison's. Slimothy fancied it had a white fence draped in extra moist moss, overlooking the water. Yes, that sounded like Roger: tasteful, understated, probably furnished with an antique lily pad chaise. Slimothy decided he too was verdant, lush, green, and technically composed of water. A hydrostatic spatchcocked skeleton, really—like a balloon held up by pressure. The trouble was, that pressure was worried.

Worry, as it always did, slid him right back into panic mode—specifically his pre-winter panic kind—piling new cortisol on top of the already questionable stack his pint-sized body carried daily.

"It's a great time to jot down the successes and shortcomings of this garden season and start developing goals for next year," he read aloud, quoting from the gardening magazine someone had left by the compost bin. *"Take out your garden journal and walk around the yard. Check back to your gardening wish list for any items."*

Slimothy squinted, translated, and rewrote the command in his own head: *Continue harvesting.* Check. *Gather herbs for drying or freezing to use throughout the year.* Double check. All of which, in Slimothy's translation system, meant only one thing—eat all the remaining basil immediately.

He made a lukewarm attempt at the "journal" part by dragging his slime across a pebble in looping cursive. It looked less like reflective prose and more like someone had sneezed on granite. "Progress," he declared.

Two basil leaves later, he began sketching out chapters in his mind. Chapter one: "A Slug is Born." Chapter two: "Kale and Other Religions." Chapter three: "Radish Shoulders, a Love Story."

By the time he hit Chapter seven: "The Mystery of the Half-Eaten Tomato," he was certain this would become a classic. He envisioned scholars in little gloves unveiling his "Collected Works," whispering reverently about the punctuation blobs. Was this an Oxford comma—or an existential crisis?

His dedication came easily: *"For the basil, who never gave up on me."*

He paused, dramatically signed his pebble manuscript with an extra flourish of slime, and let his mind offer up the glowing review: *"'Garden Memoirs' by Slimothy the Slug, a groundbreaking exploration of chlorophyll, mucus, and ambition. Four stars. Would read again."*

Alas, even celebrated authors had chores to face: harvesting vegetables was supposed to be simple—but how did one actually know when carrots were ready? Slimothy had tossed an entire packet of seeds in the dirt months ago and watched the feathery green tops climb skyward at a maddeningly slow pace. Truth be told, that was how most of his gardening worked—by pure chaos. A sprinkle here, a scatter there, and months later he couldn't tell artichoke from beets, driveway weeds from asparagus, or asparagus from the asparagus fern.

In fact, he'd been so busy doting on kale, he forgot he'd planted a whole contingent of seeds somewhere along the way. Now they were popping up like an herbal ambush—unsolicited, unwatered, and entirely too pleased with themselves. Parsley lurked in the corner like it was hiding state secrets. Thyme was scribbling notes in tiny invisible notebooks, obviously keeping track of everyone else's whereabouts. Meanwhile mint ... mint was everywhere— spreading like it had bought the deed to the Bright Wild and was three spreadsheets into subdividing it, trying to colonize the whole block.

All of them demanding water, sunlight, and attention he clearly did not have to give.

Still in his "calculating era," with rain falling for the fourth day in a row, Slimothy tried to do the math. How many gallons of water did it actually take to keep the Bright Wild alive? Why did water measurements sound like bad nicknames? Hogheads, butts, firkins. Hogwash, indeed. Meanwhile, tomato number two was swelling into suspicious ripeness. Was this finally proof Roger was the tomato thief after all—or was it just the timing that made the whole thing feel like an inside job?

Everyone was a suspect. Allison hadn't been seen in days either. Had everyone absconded to a secret garden retreat—one Slimothy had most definitely not been invited to? Guilty until proven innocent, he decided.

Except the eggplants. They were blameless. Loudly, aggressively multiplying, they had no time for conspiracies. Their only crime was existing in obscene abundance. So many, in fact, Slimothy was beginning to suspect they were trying to start their own breakaway nation.

Then came the latest disaster—new HOA rules. Reclassification, en masse. What even counted as a "house" anymore? The Bright Wild already had villages, subdivisions, even a tiny book-borrowing library that might still be holding Slimothy's overdue copy of Snails Illustrated. Sidewalks were up for debate. Crossing attendants were being threatened, and to make matters worse, a zoning meeting had been scheduled: three weeks away.

In slug time that was practically a century of waiting for someone to decide whether a hollow acorn counted as a single-family dwelling. Slimothy was no closer to solving Roger's disappearance, the mysteriously nibbled tomatoes, or the vanishing spinach. Now he also had to worry about right of way at garden intersections. Did lettuce yield to parsley, did bees stop for slugs, and was he about to get ticketed for jay-slugging across the street without a permit?

The rumors didn't help. Word was the HOA planned to install tiny stop signs made from popsicle sticks and red construction paper. Speed limits would be enforced—which sounded fine until Slimothy learned that mint had been clocked at "reckless spread" in a zucchini zone. Worst of all, there was talk of roundabouts—tiny, infinite loop intersections where slugs, beetles, and frogs would be forced to circle each other indefinitely, doomed to eternal politeness until someone finally yielded.

Slimothy shuddered. If Roger had vanished into the vegetables to escape all this, he couldn't entirely blame him.

The bees, naturally, had ignored the whole hibernation memo, and were still buzzing like it was midsummer. They hovered over the cauliflower like tiny helicopter parents—micromanaging every floret-to-be. Slimothy sighed. He worried he'd double-booked the zoning meeting day. Was it the hearing on whether moss could legally count as a front lawn—or had he scheduled a cross-examination of parsley?

Either way, his calendar looked less like a plan and more like a ransom note written by dandelions. If the weeds were already sending threats, it was only a matter of time before the rest of the garden turned on him too.

Clearly, this called for paperwork—or at least a damp leaf with suspect names scribbled on it. Roger. Allison. The bees. Possibly even the kale, though it seemed far too self-absorbed to stage a conspiracy.

He'd been ready to launch a full-blown slimy investigation when the HOA struck. Overnight, the Bright Wild was suddenly subject to "reclassification." Entire snail shells, wicker baskets, and suspiciously ornamental pottery had to be reevaluated to determine whether they counted as "houses" or "accessory units." Slimothy's own lettuce-leaf lean-to was in zoning limbo. Was it a temporary structure? An illegal subdivision? Would he be fined for not having a tiny mailbox—or worse, forced to check it twice a day for junk leaves addressed to "Current Resident"?

The new bylaws were endless. A rule about "maximum gnome density per square foot." Another dictating "proper stewardship of driveways, gutters, and all sewage-facing façades." By the time he'd slogged through the paperwork, the mystery of the disappearing Roger had grown colder than leftover pumpkin soup forgotten in the back of the fridge behind the pickles.

Still, the evidence nagged at him. The tomato ripening like it had somewhere important to be. Spinach gnawed down to the nub—like a midnight snack gone horribly unsupervised. Roger missing in action. The bees, meanwhile, zipped around sipping nectar lattes like they'd already signed book deals about the trial. By next week, Slimothy was sure they'd launch a true-crime podcast about it— complete with dramatic reenactments and theme music stolen from cicadas.

The zoning meeting was looming on the horizon—but Slimothy wasn't sure he'd survive the wait. Was the Bright Wild about to be paved over with red tape before he cracked the case? He couldn't decide what was worse—Roger vanishing without a trace, or being forced to grind to a halt every few feet while an insufferably pleased crossing guard waved parsley across the path like it had the right of way.

One thing was certain—everyone was a suspect. Now the HOA wasn't just on the list, it was the mob boss of the Bright Wild, running protection rackets in the name of "property values." Some called it the garden mafia—laundering sunshine through soil samples and shaking down residents for unpaid leaf fees.

It was all adding up—and none of it smelled like compost anymore.

CHAPTER THIRTY-EIGHT

Live, Laugh, Slug

Slimothy awoke to yet another plot twist he never requested. He had been catnapping undisturbed—dreaming of motorcars rolling by with flags of Kaleopolis snapping smartly from their antennas—when a passing crow dropped what appeared to be part of a Pop-Tart directly onto his head.

It wasn't exactly the kind of omen he'd been hoping for. If destiny was going to give him a head-bop, he'd at least expected tiramisu. Instead, he brushed off the crumbs, poured himself a wine from 2013—practically old enough to be his therapist, his ex, his landlord, and a substitute teacher on the side—and started wondering about heritage, time capsules, and who would even inherit his legacy when he eventually abdicated.

Someone had just unearthed a car from 1949—still with a partially eaten sandwich in the glovebox and the radio tuned to a station that hadn't existed for decades. The headlights flickered on like it had just been waiting for its cue. If a tuna melt and big band swing could last 75 years, surely his story deserved at least a few centuries.

Moreover, who would he even leave it to? The kale was too vain, the parsley too jumpy, and the mint would just spread it everywhere until the whole garden was overrun. The basil was a contender—but even basil had its limits. Which left … the deer. Slimothy shuddered. The deer would eat his legacy before the ribbon-cutting ceremony. Maybe, in the end, that was the point—to be remembered as delicious and important enough to chew twice.

Still, he took comfort in one fact—slug slime carried anesthetic properties. Anything that tried to eat him would end up with a numb mouth, a blank stare, and second thoughts. Maybe that was its own kind of legacy—less a flavor profile, more a garden experience.

Perhaps he should commission a statue of himself—a concrete bust that truly honored his gleaming, slightly damp heroism. A slug immortalized forever, not in slime, but in stone. He could see it already: children on school trips tossing pennies at his base, pigeons perching on his noble brow, even the occasional beetle tour guide pointing up and whispering, *"There he is. The one who changed everything."* Preferably displayed somewhere with good lighting and a plaque that read, *"Visionary. Gardener. Local legend."*

Of course, the statue would need to be accurate. Tasteful. Dignified. He briefly considered commissioning the ants—they had strong work ethic and an eye for detail—but they always bit him, and he didn't trust artists who snacked on their clients. The beetles, on the other hand, were creative but unpredictable. His last collaboration with them had ended with a "modern interpretation" made entirely out of damp bark and despair.

Maybe he'd just sculpt it himself. How hard could it be? A bit of clay, a steady slide, and a healthy disregard for proportion. Besides—who better to capture his essence than the slug himself?

He'd already envisioned the full experience: the statue, the guided audio tour, even a small gift shop at the exit. Posters, magnets, commemorative slime jars—the works. *"Live, Laugh, Slug,"* printed across limited-edition tote bags.

The tour narration was already forming in his head: *"Slimothy began his work here, at the Bright Wild, where he revolutionized compost philosophy and supportive vegetation management."*

He smiled at the thought. Legacy wasn't about what you left behind, he decided—it was about who got the merchandising rights.

He raised his glass and toasted the idea. "To immortality," he murmured, "and to finding a base wide enough for dramatic lighting."

Then he took another sip—and promptly fell back asleep on the blueprint.

CHAPTER THIRTY-NINE

A Frog, a Soufflé, and a Secret

Day four. Roger was still missing. Should Slimothy put up missing persons posters? Commandeer a milk carton? Send out a search party? Hire a private investigator who specialized in amphibians? Maybe enlist a squirrel with binoculars and questionable references?

Anyone could guess how that would go: a tardy squirrel, a heated acorn-payment discussion, and at least one acorn flung for authority. The "report" would be a crumpled leaf that read, *"Roger not in tree. Roger not in house. Roger not in Slimothy's lettuce."* Then, about five minutes into the stakeout, the squirrel would forget the case entirely, chase its own tail in circles, and declare the investigation closed due to lack of snacks. Some detective.

Or maybe none of that was necessary. Maybe Roger wasn't missing at all—just … prepping. Frogs had their own way of easing into winter, like shady-damp vacationers scoping out leaf-litter resorts. They noticed everything—the daylight stretching shorter, the ground cooling underfoot, the bug buffet thinning out. To Roger, it would be less disappearance and more seasonal Airbnb hunting.

The truth was frogs were survival experts—real MacGyvers of the mud. They could go weeks, even months, without eating a single bite, breathing only through their skin while they waited it out. Give a frog part of a puddle and a handful of leaves, and he could jury-rig a winter palace. If Roger had vanished into the mud, chances were he wasn't gone—just pulling his winter magic trick, biding his time until the garden warmed back up.

Slimothy, meanwhile, would simply die without eating. The frogs managed it. The bees managed it. Even the plants pulled off seasonal vanishings with a certain flair. Why was his species so different? Why hadn't slugs been given the gift of skipping meals without consequence? It felt unfair—cosmically rigged.

So while Slimothy was busy hypothesizing crime scenes and conspiracies, Roger was probably just laying low—eating less, sticking close to cover, and debating whether the mud pit or the mulch pile had better amenities. Or, far more chilling, maybe he had hopped off into the great big scary forest beyond the Bright Wild. Rumor had it creatures vanished out there—only to reappear three inches taller and oddly fond of jazz.

Slimothy could picture Roger not as a victim, but as the proprietor of some questionable establishment—a leaf-shack speakeasy with mossy stools, bark countertops, and a cocktail menu that featured nothing but swamp water and mosquito spritzers. Entry was by password only, whispered through a hollow reed. For the chosen few, there was a single item on the secret menu—a spinach soufflé, partially eaten before it ever hit the table. A pastry guarded like state secrets and mysteriously unavailable any time Slimothy asked for it.

Forget the missing frog—Slimothy was ready to stage an intervention.

No one kept a soufflé from him. No one.

CHAPTER FORTY

Mission Slimpossible

Slimothy had been reading about new inventions again—the kind meant for farmers with bigger problems than missing spinach and disappearing frogs. One particular contraption involved green beams sweeping across fields, making birds scatter like extras in a bad action movie. The article claimed it was more effective than cannons—or creepy balloons with eyes.

Slimothy squinted at the page, antennae curling, imagining such a thing in the Bright Wild. From somewhere within his satchel, he produced his trusty journal and scrawled:

Green sweeps = glow-in-the-dark "do-not-enter" lines.
Birds = expendable henchmen.
Field = high-security vault.
Footnote: only respected by slugs, snails, and occasionally polite aphids.

He doodled himself dangling from a thread of spider silk, acorn-cap goggles strapped on, weaving through emerald light. After a thought, he added:

Retrieve asset. Do not touch kale.
Deer = crime bosses. Possibly untouchable. Watch for hoofprints.

He sat with the revelation, the idea humming in his thoughts like classified intel. What he held in his metaphorical hands wasn't farm news. It wasn't pest-control literature. It was a mission dossier.

Classified file // [TOP SECRET]
Codename: "Slug Impossible"
Objective: infiltrate the Bright Wild produce vaults (blueberries, grapes, kale bed) with zero casualties, zero slime trails, and absolutely no triggering of the newly reported "laser scarecrow" defense system.

Intel // [RESTRICTED ACCESS]
50-milliwatt green beam. Field sweep.
Birds see instantly with 10x vision. Scatter. Repeat.
Results may include mass bird riots. Behavior escalates.
More sweeps = more panic. (Bird panic chart not included.)

Slimothy circled the phrase "50-milliwatt green beam" and muttered, "Naturally, spy tech always evolves when no one's looking," before glancing around the garden to make sure nothing was actually evolving right now.

Field notes // [EYES ONLY]
Blueberries, grapes: beams set just above canopy level. Sweeps cut across all cluster heights.
Slimothy note: clusters = crown jewels, guarded by emerald tripwires.
Additional note: tripwires non-negotiable.
Secondary note: tripwires possibly personal. (Beams may hold grudges.)

He briefly considered shin guards, then remembered the minor complication that slugs do not, in fact, possess shins.

Margin scribble: beams = tripwires. Clusters = vault contents. Annotation: retrieve asset. Do not touch kale.

Threat assessment // [CONFIDENTIAL]
Deer: unaffected. Mammals rely on scent and sound to sense threats, not light.
Translation: they stroll through laser beams like they're on a red carpet.
Additional threat: attitude problem.
Behavioral pattern: unbothered. Unimpressed. Unstoppable.
Recommended action: avoid eye contact. They will take it as a challenge.

Slimothy frowned. Naturally, the deer were immune. They already behaved like crime bosses—untouchable. He was fairly sure he heard them muttering, *"That's a nice grape cluster you got there ... shame if something happened to it."* He sketched a shady little scenario of them strolling through the beams, chomping blueberries like cigars, leaving hoofprints as calling cards.

Conclusion // [FOR INTERNAL USE ONLY]

The article claimed this was farm equipment—nothing more. Slimothy knew better. This was NASA for vegetables. This was agriculture with a grudge. This was espionage disguised as crop management.

[REDACTED]:  spinach

He closed the dossier and immediately checked if his lettuce was bugged. He even tapped one of the leaves and said, "this is a secure line," just in case. Satisfied it wasn't, he sighed. Breakfast would have to wait.

Mission status // [HUNGRY]

CHAPTER FORTY-ONE

Sunshine Protection Act

Slimothy's diet was not going well. Sure, he ate great during the day—salad for lunch, copious amounts of coffee, a banana chip snack here and there—but his garden was full of food that wasn't ready yet, stubborn little green things that refused to bloom, ripen, or otherwise present themselves as dinner. As usual, Slimothy was exhausted from waiting for the inevitability of things growing, blooming, and most importantly—harvesting and eating.

He had only a month before the time would change and drag his perfect afternoon garden soirées into darkness—mercilessly, joylessly. Perhaps the zoning board should hear about this.

#SaveTheSunshine. Posters practically started printing themselves.

The question kept gnawing at him, how did it even work anyway? If it were really called "daylight saving," why did everyone get less of it? Where did it even go? Was it siphoned off, invested at the First National Bank of Maybe? That was the real conspiracy—someone, somewhere, was hoarding daylight, keeping it locked away until spring.

Slimothy saw in his mind a vault under the Bright Wild, filled not with gold bars but long glowing beams of sunlight stacked neatly like baguettes. Clerks in tiny vests shuffled around with mason jars, carefully scooping up the afternoon and labeling each one "Property of Daylight Saving Time." The Chief Beam Officer checked each jar against the ledger, while the Senior Jar Technician adjusted them on the shelf with solemn precision. Every autumn, someone came by with a clipboard, crossed out an hour, and slid another jar into storage.

If that was the case, then he wanted receipts. He wanted his sunshine back with interest—neatly compounded, preferably in the late afternoon when the kale looked its best.

Of course, the zoning board probably wouldn't care. They'd say things like "standard practice," "federal guidelines," or "that's not how physics works." Slimothy knew better. Almost immediately, the whole meeting staged itself— gnomes trading paperwork, a mole nudging the agenda into alignment, and someone arguing about the legal boundaries of "afternoon." Noon to five? Noon to six? Could it, by statute, extend past dinner?

Slimothy would rise, antennae high, and demand action. A Sunshine Protection Act. Posters. Petitions. Hashtags. Possibly a march—assuming the crickets would agree to percussion duty and the fireflies handled lighting. He assembled a little internal demonstration of himself chanting slogans outside city hall, waving banners that read, *"Bring Back My Hour,"* and, *"Daylight Belongs to the People."*

The only thing worse than spinach debt, Slimothy decided, was daylight debt. Knowing his luck, there was already a collections agency for lost hours—shady moths in trench coats knocking at dusk and demanding payment in porch light bulbs. Slimothy envisioned himself frantically unscrewing every bulb in the Bright Wild, stuffing them under leaves, and pretending he wasn't home while the moths tapped politely on the window.

CHAPTER FORTY-TWO

Unsubscribe

It had been an awful, terrible, no-good week. Overstimulated and underslimed, Slimothy ended his mayoral duties promptly at 5 p.m. and marched outside to photosynthesize.

His pond was still algae-fied, Roger was still missing, and weeds were running rampant—along with the grass, which also refused to get the end-of-summer memo.

Stress oozed out of Slimothy in every direction—but his slime reserves were already in the red. He'd overspent the budget weeks ago. What little remained was reserved for true emergencies: escaping an overhanging eggplant, patching a crack in his favorite flowerpot, or figuring out where to rehome the lemon tree currently adrift in a sea of mulch.

Clearly, it was time for a full cortisol detox. Slimothy stretched his feelers to the sky, easing into Upward Slug—a pose best described as Downward Dog but with less dignity and more goo. He exhaled dramatically, transitioned into Slime Salutation, and declared the garden his personal wellness retreat. No emails, no mayoral complaints, and absolutely no conversations about re-zoning the needle stonecrop. Last week it had annexed two flowerbeds, redrawn the county line with a marker, and was now demanding its own school district.

Slimothy needed a break.

This was spa time.

He arranged two cucumber slices over his eye stalks, which kept sliding off as if gravity had no idea how spa days were supposed to work. Undeterred, he slathered himself in his own limited-edition slime mask and settled onto a damp patch of moss. After the third slip he muttered, "Namaste," ate them, and accepted that cucumbers were destined to be snacks anyway. They weren't pickles—he was doing his best not to judge.

For good measure, Slimothy attempted Lotus Leaf Lunge by lining a few pebbles along his back for hot stone therapy. Unfortunately, they were just cold, lumpy rocks that immediately tumbled off and pelted his backside like a xylophone solo. He sighed, decided this was also part of the process, rebranded it in his head as "Rock Massage Deluxe™—exactly the same as regular rocks, but with an unnecessarily fancy label," then started to get itchy and decided to try again another day. After all, self-care had limits—even for a slug who once mistook fertilizer for a superfood smoothie.

Apparently, limits were optional in the animal kingdom. Take the woolly bear caterpillar, for instance. Those little insectoid popsicles could freeze solid for over a year, thaw out, grab a snack, and then do it again like it was just another Tuesday. Slimothy tried not to take it personally—but really, why did caterpillars get all the cool survival tricks? Meanwhile, every conversation seemed to circle back to bears.

In some corner of the Bright Wild, a caterpillar festival was no doubt in progress—racing lanes no wider than a leaf vein, ragged marching bands, fuzzy costumes, and cheering echoing through imaginary bleachers. Basically "Groundhog Day," but with less dignity. Slimothy wondered if anyone had ever tried betting on them. He would. Five lettuce leaves on the under-pillar every single time.

They even looked like his scarf—fluffy, orange in the middle, and completely squishy. Slimothy draped it dramatically around himself and whispered, "High fashion insect couture." For once, he felt like he belonged on the runway—albeit one very, very slimy runway.

Slimothy thought about the woolly bears. If they could spend 90-something percent of their lives just ... waiting—then maybe he was doing life exactly right.

Maybe spa days that ended in itchy rocks and snack-sized cucumbers weren't failures at all. They were training. Perfecting the fine art of doing absolutely nothing—and calling it wellness.

He liked the sound of that. It made him feel less like a lazy slug on a moss patch and more like a visionary. A guru. The kind of enlightened creature who might one day open a retreat called Slug Stillness™, where the main event was lying around until something edible walked past.

CHAPTER FORTY-THREE

Horoscopes, Hubris, and Other Bright Ideas

Slimothy looked up at the night sky. It was vast, heroic, beautiful—and also looked suspiciously like sprinkles scattered across a zucchini pancake. There was so much more beyond the Bright Wild, and even the possibility felt edible (though he was always hungry for something).

Without the threat of hurricanes, yellow blight, rain, or the menacing red glare of crosswalk lights, the moon's embrace felt downright peaceful. This was Slimothy's favorite time to be outside. When the world hovered between sleep and morning, he thrived. No matter how many melatonin gummies he licked or chamomile leaves he steeped, he was a night owl through and through—though technically he was a night slug, which sounded less dignified.

So many things happened after dark. The mystery of the disappearing spinach was still unsolved—but honestly, the midnight hours were when the magic happened. Slimothy had stayed awake night after night, determined to catch the exact moment a new leaf unfurled or a flower bloomed. He wanted to witness the sparkle of dew drops in the predawn, to see the tiniest creatures sneak across the neighborhood under the safety of shadows. He wanted to be there for it all.

The problem was ... slug eyes weren't built for the job. No color. No sharp images. No focus. Just vague blobs in the dark. Which meant Slimothy's big stargazing, midnight-watching lifestyle basically amounted to staring into the void and whispering, "Wow," at shapes that might've been leaves. Or rocks. Or, once, a sleeping toad's behind.

Slimothy decided he wasn't about to let bad eyesight stop him from chasing cosmic wonder. If the universe wasn't going to hand him a telescope—he'd improvise.

First, he tried dew drops. He perched next to them and peered through like they were tiny lenses. Everything was magnified—just sideways, upside down, and occasionally distorted into what looked like cosmic tadpoles doing cartwheels.

Then he upgraded to the gnome's forgotten reading glasses. They slid right off his slime trail, of course—but not before giving him 10 glorious seconds of "clarity." He wasn't sure if it was Orion's Belt or the reflection of a porch light, but either way, it was breathtaking.

Finally, the pièce de résistance: Slimothy stacked two old snail shells and stared through them as if they were binoculars. Technically, they just made everything darker—but he felt astronomically important. Like a slug with a mission. A slug who saw things.

Once he had his "binoculars," Slimothy decided it was time to name the stars properly. Humans had their bears and hunters and dippers—but what good was any of that to a slug?

That tiny crooked cluster over the pond? Obviously The Lettuce Leaf.

The long glittery line near the hedge? The Great Slime Trail, shimmering eternally across the heavens.

A jagged triangle above Allison's house? Clearly Orion's Compost Bin, where the heroic hunter presumably dumped his carrot tops.

He kept going until the heavens were crowded with his own constellations: The Escargot Spiral. The Sacred Wheelbarrow. The Cosmic Kale.

Slimothy sighed with satisfaction. Finally, the universe made sense—not in bear-shaped stories, but in the unmistakable language of salad and slime.

Naming constellations wasn't enough. The humans had zodiacs, whole calendars of personality and fate pinned to the stars. Why shouldn't slugs have the same? Slimothy got to work.

The Lettuce Leaf: those born under this sign were destined to be soft, crunchy on the inside, and constantly devoured by their responsibilities.

The Great Slime Trail: bold pioneers, always leaving their mark—a little sticky in relationships, but unforgettable.

Orion's Compost Bin: natural leaders, often found at the center of garden drama; their lives smell faintly of melon rinds.

The Escargot Spiral: slow, yes—but also wise. Masters of spiraling both shells and emotions.

The Cosmic Kale: resilient, slightly bitter, but trendy with health nuts.

Slimothy squinted at the stars (or possibly the neighbor's porch light) and whispered, "Yes … it's all here."

"Dear Lettuce Leaf, don't trust the wheelbarrow today. Great Slime Trails, avoid dry mulch. Cosmic Kales, your week looks crunchy."

He nodded sagely to himself. The sky had spoken. Slimothy slithered back to his moss patch, inspired. If the stars had gifted him the Slug Zodiac, then it was his solemn duty to share their wisdom with the garden. He started small:

For Roger the frog (a clear Great Slime Trail if there ever was one):

"Beware sudden splashes. Your confidence may leap ahead of your landing."

For his prize rose bush (Cosmic Kale all the way):

"You will be admired today, but remember—beauty attracts both bees and beetles. Stay thorny."

For the gnome with the chipped hat (Orion's Compost Bin):

"An old secret will be unearthed near your feet. Also, don't move."

As for himself—naturally a Lettuce Leaf:

"Snack opportunities abound. Don't be afraid to chew through obstacles, literally."

He felt powerful. A mystic. A slimy fortune-teller cloaked in a fuzzy orange scarf and starlight. Maybe tomorrow he'd set up a little booth: *"Horoscopes: One Leaf Per Reading."*

Slimothy. A visionary. A slug with a line of clients and a business model based entirely on lettuce. Each reading landed like a thunderclap.

"Great Slime Trail, beware shallow puddles—your reflection is not your friend today. Expect drama among the aphids. Choose your side wisely."

By the time the gnome shuffled over (he didn't—but Slimothy liked to imagine he did), Slimothy was convinced he wasn't just a slug anymore. He was the Bright Wild's first astrologer.

Trouble was, prophecies had a habit of coming true in this garden.

By dusk, Slimothy's moss patch had been upgraded from "slug nap zone" to "sacred omen ground." A moth left him a leaf offering. A cricket bowed before hopping away. Even the roses leaned in—prickly but attentive.

Slimothy tried to look humble. Inside, he was already planning the next big thing: "The Slug Zodiac Almanac," now in leaf-back edition.

The success went straight to his feelers. Slimothy had gone from a humble everyday slug to a full-blown oracle practically overnight—and it felt good. Too good.

By the second day, he wasn't just predicting puddles and aphids—he was making things up to see how far the garden would follow.

To the cricket:

"Cosmic Kale. Your future holds romance ... and possibly a banjo."

To the moth:

"Escargot Spiral. Beware bright lights—they are not as warm and inviting as they seem."

(The moth gasped. Revolutionary.)

To a confused earthworm:

"Orion's Compost Bin. Big changes are coming. Literally. You'll be cut in two and both halves will go on to live fulfilling lives."

The worm wriggled away in existential horror.

Each outrageous prediction only deepened the garden's awe. By sundown, there was a waiting list. Someone left a head of lettuce as advance payment. A beetle offered him a shiny bottle cap, insisting it was "for the mystic fund."

Slimothy perched higher on his moss patch, scarf flapping dramatically, eye stalks tilted toward the heavens. He was no longer just Slimothy the slug. He was Slimothy the Seer. Slimothy the Sage. Slimothy, Visionary of the Bright Wild.

He had no idea what tomorrow's readings would be—but if everyone kept believing, he'd think of something.

That night, as Slimothy basked in his growing fame, the neighbor's porch light flickered. Once. Twice. Then it went out completely.

Slimothy froze. A sign.

Of course it was. The universe wasn't content with him sitting around the moss patch, whispering lettuce-flavored horoscopes. No—this was clearly bigger. This was cosmic. The stars weren't twinkling; they were communicating. They wanted proof. They wanted action. A cosmic test.

He looked skyward and thought, *"I hear you."* He didn't actually say it out loud (there were gnats nearby, and they loved drama), but the sentiment was there. *"I, Slimothy the Seer, accept your divine mission."*

The trouble was—he had no idea what the mission was.

So, naturally, he invented one. The stars wanted him to journey beyond the Bright Wild—to map new constellations, to bring back enlightenment, or possibly spinach. Yes, that sounded right. Maybe the two were connected.

He could see it all with startling clarity—himself gliding into the moonlight, scarf billowing like a hero's banner, embarking on his first great expedition, the air shimmering with destiny (and pollen). Every blade of grass grew monumental; every sound carried meaning.

To his left, the garden hose coiled across the path like a cosmic serpent—keeper of riddles and questionable puddles. Ah yes, Slimothy thought, the Serpent of Eternity. One must face it to be deemed worthy. He saw himself conquering it, inching over its mighty ridges, victorious, cheered on by unseen celestial beings who admired his slime trail of courage.

The cracked paving stones became The Path of Forgotten Giants, fractured remnants of some long-lost civilization. He sensed ancient voices murmuring beneath his foot ... well, his lower surface.

Up above, the bleeding-heart vine stood sentinel—The Watcher, guardian of stars and seeker of truths. Slimothy bowed in his mind, humbly, reverently, as any enlightened explorer would.

It was as if the universe whispered: *"You were made for this."*

A rush of purpose filled him. He cast himself as the hero conquering horizons, naming constellations after produce, solving the mystery of the disappearing spinach—and perhaps even getting his own statue one day (made of something waterproof).

In the theater of his thoughts, he looked up to the stars and declared, *"I will not fail you."*

Then reality blinked back in. The stars were silent. The hose was just a hose, and his stomach made a very unheroic sound.

Maybe it was just gas.

CHAPTER FORTY-FOUR

The Fountain of Youth (Probably)

Slimothy had heard of holy relics, excavations, and treasure hunts—but none were as fascinating as the fabled Fountain of Youth. Eternal youth, they said. A forever-young guarantee. As an optimist with trust issues, Slimothy was certain something would go wrong.

He wanted to read the fine print. Did you keep the wisdom of your older self in your younger body, or did you just get a fresh start and repeat all the same mistakes—only faster? Did you get to choose your preferred "youth age," or was it random, like a bad raffle? Was it a one-time dip or a subscription-based model with hidden fees? Most importantly—did it come with instructions for future generations, or at least a note for the time capsule?

Life, he decided, had far too many questions and not nearly enough customer support.

He sighed, scanning the garden for signs of mythical rejuvenation. Nothing. Not even a discount fountain. Just the lemon tree—still without a home and growing recklessly out of a random patch of mulch like it had given up on real estate altogether.

A quick, deliberate buzz sliced through the still air. Slimothy stalled for one alarming second. It could have been an apparition, a lettuce leaf, or a particularly judgmental horoscope. Possibly all three.

Or worse—members of Concrete Layers Anonymous, the underground movement threatening to walk off the job again.

If it was them, Slimothy had a bone to pick. Their chronic overpouring and chaotic infrastructure had caused nothing but turmoil whenever groundskeeping brought out the leaf blowers. Equal parts existential philosophers and gravel relocation specialists, they were a nightmare union to negotiate with.

Their full manifesto started ringing through his brain: *"We don't pour paths; we define destinies."* Classic.

Still, if anyone knew where to find the Fountain of Youth, it would be them—or at least wherever they'd most recently left the hose running. Slimothy followed the sound of trickling water, feelers lifted and clipboard at the ready, just in case divine immortality required documentation. The air grew damp, dense, and suspiciously chlorinated.

It was then that every sensible part of him filed for a brief pause while the rest debated panic. The humidity thickened, curling around Slimothy like a spa treatment gone rogue. The trickle grew louder, grander—the unmistakable rush of destiny disguised as faulty plumbing. A light mist dusted his face, cool and invigorating, like the universe itself had switched to exfoliating mode.

He squinted into the haze, heart pounding somewhere in his midsection. The air did its best impression of being magical. The mulch glistened. Something magnificent (or mildly unsanitary) awaited.

There it was—the legendary Fountain of Youth. Or possibly a broken irrigation pipe gushing beside the compost heap. Hard to tell. Still, it had a certain sparkle—the kind of shimmer that promised better skin, lower electric bills, and absolutely no refund policy in the fine print.

He considered his options. The stories all said "bathe in it" or "drink from it"— but he wasn't sure which was less dignified. Did a slug bathe? Not exactly. As for drinking? Well, he technically absorbed. How much youth could one really gain through osmosis?

Still, the water glowed invitingly, whispering of renewal and better posture.

Slimothy leaned closer, picturing himself young again: fewer creaks, faster slime production, the kind of bounce that didn't come from caffeine or questionable life choices. It was as if the years were peeling away, like old wallpaper revealing something fresher underneath.

Then a toad yelled, *"Hey! That's the sprinkler line!"*—and the illusion shattered.

The Fountain of Youth sputtered once, coughed up a pebble, and went silent. Slimothy stared at the puddle. The air smelled faintly of chlorine and disappointment.

Maybe immortality wasn't about eternal youth after all. Maybe it was about knowing when to stop chasing magic—and start appreciating the damp little miracles you already had.

He lingered a moment longer, watching the ripples fade before turning back toward the garden—older, perhaps, but not entirely unchanged. He'd call it personal growth. Just … a bit moist around the edges.

CHAPTER FORTY-FIVE

Things That Go Bump in the Night

Slimothy had spent the night tormented by horrible dreams. Killer snakes. Bathrooms that didn't exist. Floating castles in the sky packed with screaming souls. Libraries built not on books but on suffering and overdue fines. Rooms with no end. Entire universes locked away in an above-ground underworld that made no architectural sense whatsoever.

At one point, he'd found himself dragging a suitcase that wasn't his, using a pillowcase as a ruck-sack. He unzipped the bag, pulled out a T-shirt with a mysterious stain on the back and a cheery flower shop printed on the front, frowned, and immediately stuffed it back in. The stain might've been coffee, ketchup, or the ghostly handprint of someone with unfinished business in floral retail. For a moment Slimothy swore the shop's printed window display winked at him and tried to upsell carnations. That was enough. He abandoned the suitcase on the spot and slithered away at turbo-slug speed—which is to say . . . slightly faster than usual, but with purpose. By the time he woke, he was more tired than when he'd gone to sleep.

"What was in that salad last night?" he muttered. Had he accidentally dipped into the catmint? Again?

The worst part was how real it all felt. Were these just bad dreams—or legitimate premonitions? Warnings that he might one day be forced to trek through the Great Forest and beyond, into lands with absolutely no bathrooms whatsoever?

Should he name his fear? Would it shrink down to size if he slapped a jaunty label on it? Maybe it wasn't doom at all. Maybe it just needed a better marketing department.

Rebranded into something less nightmare and more epic adventure, the whole thing suddenly sounded tolerable. A noble quest! A bold expedition! Complete with his trusty ruck-sack and, naturally, a shiny treasure chest at the end. (Or at the very least—a complimentary tote bag.)

Slimothy swirled his morning coffee, trying to shake off the bizarre collage of lingering images—but the idea had taken root. Maybe the nightmares weren't warnings … maybe they were an itinerary.

Yes, he decided. If fear could be named, it could be charted. Which meant, obviously, it was time for a full-scale cartographic overreaction. Thus commenced:

The Forests of Slimothy's Imagination

The Great Forest was only one of many—stretching through his imagination like an overwatered backyard left to its own devices. Each region had its own hazards, currencies, and Yelp-level complaints.

Briarwood
Locals call it Briarwood—but Slimothy knew it as "the scratchy snack aisle." Every path is lined with thorny vines that look suspiciously like they're plotting against ankles. Legend says if you trip here, the roses laugh first—then bloom out of pity.

Brackenwood
Less forest, more all-you-can-eat salad bar that forgot it was supposed to have paths. Ferns, ferns, and more ferns—so many that Slimothy once held a naming

contest and still lost to his own slime trail.

Stickburg
Population: too many twigs.
Currency: snap sounds.
Tourist warning: you will leave with a stick in your slipper.

Stickburg isn't a forest—it's a lumber conspiracy. Every step Slimothy took, a twig materialized directly underfoot, grinning in victory. Some say sticks migrated here from other parts of the garden just to ambush passersby. Nobody had ever entered Stickburg and come out stick-free.

Leafington
Population: distinguished leaves only.
Currency: polite rustling.
Local law: absolutely no composting the residents.

Leafington was the Bright Wild's poshest suburb. Here, the leaves don't fall— they descend gracefully, like aristocrats fainting on velvet couches. Slimothy once tried to blend in, but the residents whispered that his slime trail was "terribly gauche." He's still on the waitlist for guest privileges.

Weedminster
"Welcome to Weedminster: population, uninvited." Every dandelion here insists it owns the block, and every crabgrass tuft is running for mayor. Slimothy once tried to evict them—now they've doubled their borders and started charging rent in socks full of seeds.

Stonewood
Population: stubborn rocks.
Currency: pebble taxes.
Tourist tip: don't bother bringing shoes—you'll stub your toe anyway.

Stonewood isn't trees at all, just endless rocks pretending to be important.

Boulders sit around like retired generals, pebbles roll underfoot purely to trip you, and moss clings to everything as if trying to soften the insult. Slimothy once asked for directions here and got nothing but stony silence from a granite slab.

Slimothy's Travel Guide to the Great Forests

Briarwood
★★ (2/5 slime trails)
Amenities: free snacks with built-in toothpicks.
Hazards: thorn ambushes, sarcastic roses.
Best for: slugs who enjoy cardio and bleeding.
Slimothy's note: pack extra slime for bandages. The roses will mock you anyway.

Brackenwood
★★★ (3/5 slime trails)
Amenities: infinite ferns, occasional shade.
Hazards: zero signage. Every direction looks like "fern."
Best for: salad enthusiasts who like to feel lost in their own buffet.
Slimothy's note: held a naming contest here once. Lost to myself. Still bitter.

Stickburg
★ (1/5 slime trails)
Amenities: none, unless you count splinters.
Hazards: every twig in existence, all of them with grudges.
Best for: masochists.
Slimothy's note: don't go. If you do, don't say I didn't warn you.

Leafington
★★★★ (4/5 slime trails)
Amenities: polished leaf piles, excellent rustling ambiance.
Hazards: snobbery. Compost is strictly forbidden.

Best for: fancy types with scarves that aren't fuzzy or orange.
Slimothy's note: tried to visit once. Was told my trail was "far too pedestrian." Still on the waitlist.

Weedminster
★★★.5 (3.5/5 slime trails)
Amenities: endless parties, free seed confetti.
Hazards: dandelions with power complexes, crabgrass politicians.
Best for: loud extroverts who like unsolicited debates.
Slimothy's note: eviction attempts only make them stronger. Trust him.

Stonewood
★★ (2/5 slime trails)
Amenities: moss cushions (lumpy).
Hazards: pebble taxes, complacent boulders.
Best for: geologists—or people who want to feel judged by rocks.
Slimothy's note: once asked for directions. Granite just stared. Rude.

Slimothy's Survival Tips for the Great Forests

Packing Essentials
~ One sturdy ruck-snack (pillowcase optional).
~ Extra slime for first aid, sealing leaks, or dramatic effect.
~ A scarf—because quests always look more official if you're accessorized.

General Rules
~ If it crunches underfoot in Brackenwood, it's probably a fern. Eat it anyway.
~ If it crunches underfoot in Stickburg, it's probably a twig. Cry about it later.
~ Never look smug in Leafington. They can smell insecurity.

~ In Weedminster, don't make eye contact with a dandelion unless you're prepared to debate tax reform.

Emergency Procedures
~ Briarwood thorns? Pretend you meant to exfoliate.
~ Stonewood toe-stubbing? Call it a "pilgrimage injury" and limp with pride.
~ Lost? Follow the sound of Roger snoring. You'll eventually circle back to the pond.

By this point, his "field manual" was less of a survival guide and more of a cry for help in list form. Still, every expedition needed a moral—or at least a closing statement that sounded profound.

Final Wisdom
Above all, remember: confidence keeps you going—snacks make it worthwhile.

Slimothy set down his questionably functional quill, closed the battered "journal" he'd been scribbling in (technically an old seed catalog), and sighed with satisfaction. The Great Forest that surrounded the Bright Wild was mapped, rated, and conquered—on paper, at least.

In reality, salvation came in a much simpler form: his beloved cucumber patch. His "pickles in training," lumpy green bodies nearly ready to pluck, lifted his spirits at once. They looked exactly like Roger had once on a hungover morning—puffy, uneven, and swearing off flies forever.

Slimothy smiled. That was comfort enough.

CHAPTER FORTY-SIX

Sail, Not Drift

S limothy had had a pretty amazing day. He'd enjoyed his favorite coffee, snacks, and a full tour of the garden. He'd fortified the cucumber battalion, discovered that carrots have shoulders too, and tried to count the days since he'd planted his inaugural batch—only to run out of things to count them on.

As the rain began its fifth encore in as many days, he tucked himself beneath a tree—grateful for its canopy and the illusion of dryness. From his little perch, he began to dream again of a greenhouse: a sanctuary where he could sit outside in the rain, the snow, or even the lightest breeze—cocooned in comfort and contentment.

Rain was always complicated. Too much for some, not enough for others. The peas had taken up striking positions, standing yellow-leafed and sullen, though Slimothy couldn't tell whether they were suffering from drought or drowning. Either way, they looked dramatic about it.

His mind drifted to umbrellas and parasols—humanity's noble effort to battle drizzle in style. He'd read that there was even a hybrid version called an *en tout cas,* French for "in any case." Somewhere in the archives of human absurdity also lurked the bumbershoot, a rare and fanciful Americanism from ages past.

Slimothy cast himself as a damp Victorian duke, strolling through the Bright Wild with one.

A newsflash interrupted his daydreaming: for the first time in 10 years, no hurricane had made landfall in the United States in September. Slimothy wasn't sure whether that meant the coming winter would be merciful—or that something enormous was simply waiting offshore, gathering snacks of its own.

Two months of hurricane season still lay ahead. He sighed, watching the drizzle blur the horizon. That meant one thing: time to restock the lettuce, reinforce the cucumbers, and remind the peas, sternly, that now was not the moment for theatrics.

A leaf loosened from the branch above, and Slimothy caught it before it hit the ground. He examined it thoughtfully, then balanced it over his head like an umbrella. It immediately folded, dumped a gallon of water on him, and floated away looking far too pleased with itself.

Slimothy sighed. Sail, not drift, he thought—though mostly, he was thinking about towels.

CHAPTER FORTY-SEVEN

Rogerpalooza

S limothy was over the moon to see his lump-covered companion back in his rightful place atop his terracotta throne. Where had he been? A luxury pond resort? A family reunion for frogs who pretended not to know him? A brief stint in witness protection? A hop-a-bout? Filming an episode of "Naked and Afraid: Bright Wild Edition"?

Whatever the reason, Roger's triumphant return filled Slimothy with joy. He immediately began planning a parade—complete with leaf floats, a marching aphid band, and fireworks made from questionable kitchen spices. He even drafted a proposal for a national holiday: Rogerpalooza, to be celebrated annually with naps, snacks, and absolutely no sudden movements.

Unfortunately, the plan derailed when Slimothy got distracted by the cactus next door, which had started leaning into everyone's sunlight like it was auditioning for Villain of the Year.

Later, while trying to hang the first Rogerpalooza banner, Slimothy accidentally glued himself to it. Roger blinked twice, unimpressed, and resumed his throne. Slimothy considered that as good as applause.

At the bottom of the banner, written in uneven letters and far too much glitter glue, it read: *"Rogerpalooza: Live, Laugh, Leap."*

Determined to make it official, Slimothy set off that very afternoon to get Rogerpalooza recognized by the city. He brought an application form (scribbled on a leaf), three pebbles as "filing fees," and a salad sandwich for the clerk.

Unfortunately, he got distracted by the cucumber bush—it looked exactly like a conductor, arms raised and confidently leading an orchestra that didn't exist. Slimothy stared for a good 12 minutes, waiting for the overture to begin.

By the time he remembered why he was there, the leaf had disintegrated, the pebbles were gone, and only a fraction of his sandwich remained. Slimothy sighed. Bureaucracy was exhausting. He decided to celebrate anyway.

Rogerpalooza would live on—if not in law, then at least in legend.

CHAPTER FORTY-EIGHT

The Peckening

A woodpecker pecked angrily—and in vain—on something that sounded vaguely hollow at the edge of the Bright Wild.

Slimothy read the directions on the bottle of algaecide, trying not to be thrown off by the bird's aggressively offbeat percussion. The rhythm was terrible. The persistence, however, was impressive.

He squinted toward the trees. Where had he put his binoculars, and what, exactly, was that bird hitting its beak on? Whatever it was, it sounded like it was losing.

If house drilling was an option, Slimothy thought, he had several outdoor decorations that could use hanging. Maybe he could hire the bird: *"Woodpecker Home Installations: Fast. Loud. Questionably Effective."*

He adjusted his gaze toward the far side of the street, where the sound was coming from—sharp, rhythmic, and increasingly unhinged. Whatever the woodpecker had found, it clearly had a personal grudge against it.

He squinted harder. Was it a mailbox? A drainpipe? A long-forgotten garden gnome, hollowed by time and regret? The bird hammered on, feathers puffed, determination unwavering.

A sudden *CRACK!* echoed through the air, startling Slimothy so badly that he accidentally dumped an entire capful of algaecide into the pond. He watched the ripples spread, sighed, and decided that was probably fine.

Some mysteries, he concluded, were meant to remain unsolved—at least until the bird gave up or achieved enlightenment through blunt force trauma.

Then, silence.

Slimothy blinked. No pecking. No rhythm. No noise at all.

He wasn't sure what had happened, but somehow, he felt like he'd just won something.

Slimothy woke the next morning feeling accomplished, though he wasn't entirely sure why. The air was still, the garden calm, and somewhere deep in his slug brain, a faint trumpet sounded.

He had, he decided, won.

What exactly he'd won was unclear—possibly an endurance contest against an unseen adversary, possibly *Best Reaction to a Startling Noise.* Either way, it felt like an achievement worth recognizing.

He crafted a makeshift award out of a bottle cap, two dandelion stems, and one slightly suspicious pebble. It read, in smudged ink:

"THE FIRST ANNUAL PECK PREVENTION PRIZE
Awarded to Slimothy, for Outstanding Performance in Startled Dumping."

He placed it proudly beside the pond, where it gleamed in the morning light like a monument to overreaction.

Roger blinked slowly, unimpressed, and returned to basking on his sun-warmed clay throne.

Slimothy smiled. Not everyone could appreciate greatness in its purest, most confusing form.

CHAPTER FORTY-NINE

White Lies and Yellow Flowers

When Slimothy first started gardening, he wanted a pristine white-flowered oasis—rows of angelic blooms glowing like laundry detergent commercials, untouched by chaos, color, or reality.

He soon discovered that his cotton-ball-colored dream was doomed. There simply weren't enough white-flowering plants in his area, at least not without taking out a second mortgage or smuggling seeds across county lines. Still, he tried valiantly. White asters. Echinacea. Gaura. Mexican heather. Heck, even the peas were blooming white. He started seeing white everywhere: paint chips, clouds, the neighbor's laundry. Did it count that the tops of the shrimp plants had white tendril bits? He decided it did. Desperation had no shame.

Nature, as it turned out, had other ideas—and zero respect for his design vision.

First came pink. Then blue, purple, orange, yellow, and reds, until his garden looked like a leprechaun had thrown up a rainbow and forgotten to clean it up. It was less "oasis of tranquility" and more "crime scene at a paint factory."

Colors had meaning, apparently. Important, ancient, probably spiritual meanings that Slimothy was definitely not following. His garden looked far from enlightened—closer to a motivational poster that had exploded.

Orange meant enthusiasm, success, and the color his slime became that one time he "cleaned up" spilled Cheeto dust with his whole body. Also, the exact shade of the aphids currently ruining his enthusiasm and hard-earned progress.

Blue stood for serenity, peace, and pretending he hadn't just overwatered everything, again.

Purple meant luxury, power, and the ability to make every other flower feel underdressed.

Red was passion, desire, and strong emotions—mostly rage—directed at the orange aphids.

Pink stood for admiration, gratitude, and love: feelings Slimothy had plenty of for his plants until they started wilting dramatically for attention.

The lavender, for instance, had very strong emotions. (Living up to its reputation as the noble flower that refused to bloom.) It complained bitterly about everything—the sun, the soil, its general state of existence—until Slimothy struck it from the color spectrum in sheer exasperation. It had graduated to its own category: "difficult."

Roger resided beneath a foamy sea of white blossoms, nestled among the scorpion's-tail. Slimothy only hoped the frog wasn't allergic to pollen. Just beyond grew the dwarf peanut—yellow for friendship, pride, and lightheartedness—little bursts of sunshine between green. Behind that, reds; in front, purples and lilacs, assuming the scorpion's-tail hadn't already conquered the society garlic.

Slimothy found himself wondering why nearly every vegetable had yellow flowers. Squash, pumpkins, cucumbers, tomatoes, mustard greens, brassicas— all the same sunny shade. Was that the bees' favorite color? Some kind of evolutionary marketing strategy?

At least yellow meant something bright: joy, optimism, maybe survival. Unlike white, it never betrayed you with stains. The plant-feeding insects seemed to agree, gravitating toward yellow as if it promised something better.

White however, remained his favorite—innocence, purity, and new beginnings. A color—or lack thereof—that promised calm in a world intent on overwhelming it. It went with everything, clashed with nothing, and, unlike most of his plants, didn't require daily pep talks to thrive.

He decided to make it official.

A garden map. Color-coded, labeled, and ideally symmetrical. Or at least legible. Preferably drawn before the third glass of wine—though history suggested otherwise.

He dragged out a stack of paper, a stubby pencil, and a glass of red hovering somewhere between sip and spill (which, he reasoned, counted as a straightedge in emergencies). Within minutes, the map had devolved into an abstract masterpiece—geometry having a nervous breakdown in public. Circles where squares were supposed to go. Squash vines merging with the society garlic. A pale red streak of wine where he'd gestured too dramatically.

By the end of the night, he had several versions of his plan: *The Refined Edition, The Realistic Revision,* and *The One Where I Gave Up and Just Doodled Bees.*

He stared at them proudly. They didn't look like blueprints, exactly. More like confessions.

Still, Slimothy had faith (well, optimism) that it would all come together. He raised his glass to the mess before him. *"To design,"* he toasted, *"and to color coordination, wherever it may be hiding."*

Somewhere outside, the wind rustled through the garden.

The white flowers didn't answer—but he took that as agreement.

The next morning, Slimothy stood in his miniature kingdom, holding his color-coded "plan" like a sacred text. None of it made sense. The white asters were pink, the pink cosmos had self-seeded into the yellow patch, and the yellow squash had launched an aggressive campaign toward the fence. As if not to be outdone, the scorpion's-tail had doubled in size overnight.

Slimothy decided it was a joint project with Mother Nature. His contribution was mostly supervision and commentary.

He squinted down at his wine-stained map, then back at the chaos before him. "Abstract expressionism," he declared. "Very in this season."

CHAPTER FIFTY

Zoning Board of Cucumbers

Slimothy was feeling old. He'd spent the evening sliming through the Bright Wild, checking on the new "developments" sprouting up around the neighborhood. Apparently, everyone had decided to become a contractor overnight.

A precarious cliff-town subdivision leaned at a 45-degree angle, proudly "grandfathered in" despite being held together by one plank and a prayer. Down by the pond, a flock of self-appointed architects debated the placement of "authentic" driftwood that looked suspiciously recently imported. Slimothy was fairly certain the gulls had opened a permitting office—possibly in the shallows.

He wasn't sure if the water looked clearer because of some secret avian filtration system or simply from the gulls doing unspeakable things in it. Either way, the pond seemed happier. Probably best not to question that.

He tried to enjoy the view, but relaxation was impossible. A friend had offhandedly mentioned that his cucumbers were "growing weird," and Slimothy hadn't stopped thinking about pickle proportions since. The words haunted him. Were they too short? Too lumpy? Socially unacceptable by gourd standards? He didn't know the first thing about male or female flowers, cross-pollination, or whatever dark science governed overwintering vegetables. He was just trying to keep his salad alive—and apparently, even that was an uphill battle.

Determined to restore some order, he launched a late-night inspection. Clipboard? Check. Wine glass? Also check. He slimed toward Cliff Town, muttering about load-bearing sticks and subterranean drainage requirements— terms he barely understood but found deeply reassuring to repeat. The path up was littered with sawdust, discarded feathers, and at least one sign that read, *"Future Home of Cliffview Villas (Pending Approval),"* which did not fill him with confidence.

At the precise moment he started feeling confident about the incline, a plank gave way beneath him. For one horrifying moment, he dangled—slug, clipboard, and a slow drip of Cabernet—before collapsing into the papyrus, which was being dramatic again and definitely wasn't up to code. Somewhere above, construction resumed as if nothing had happened—which, in Slimothy's opinion, said everything about their safety standards.

He reasserted his authority by scribbling something unintelligible on the clipboard and slapping a leaf on a nearby wall as a "Stop Work" notice. The wall immediately collapsed. So much for regulation.

By the time he dragged himself back to the pond, the renovation racket had escalated into what sounded like a full-blown avian HOA meeting. The gulls were squawking over waterfront access, the frogs demanded quiet-hours rules, and someone—probably the heron—was pitching a luxury timeshare development.

Slimothy took one look at the scene, decided none of it fell under his jurisdiction, and retreated into the cattails to stress-eat a kale leaf. It was one of his favorite coping mechanisms—high in iron and low in conversation.

When he finally reached the last stretch of moss-lined path, his feelers drooped under the weight of existential and horticultural fatigue. The Bright Wild was changing faster than his slime trail could dry. New neighborhoods. New residents. New arguments about zoning setbacks. He used to know everyone by their leaf choice—who grew bougainvilleas just for show, who overwatered their mint and called it "lush"—but now he couldn't even keep track of which puddles were public access and which required a permit.

He paused to watch the pond's ripples catch the moonlight. Maybe it wasn't age so much as overexposure to municipal drama. Maybe he'd just seen one too many *Under Construction* signs. Or maybe the truth lay with the baby pickles—small and uncertain, shaped like commas in a sentence that refused to end.

Enough adulting for one night. He'd earned his glass of something fermented and the right to stare at cucumbers like they'd skipped out on their lease. The Bright Wild could regulate itself for a few hours.

Tomorrow's crisis would arrive on schedule—freshly zoned, slightly crooked, and inevitably his problem again.

CHAPTER FIFTY-ONE

Three Minutes of Happiness (Give or Take a Cabbage)

Slimothy's appetite had staged a full-blown rebellion. He couldn't stop snacking. No matter which way he turned, everything made him hungry. Brussels sprouts? Delicious. He'd inhale 20 without blinking. Kale? An entire field wouldn't stand a chance. Lettuce, parsley, marigolds—if it grew, it was fair game. Everything was a salad bar, even if it wasn't.

He was starting to worry. Had he caught worms? Or worse, a case of seasonal snacking disorder? His posterior was expanding at a rate that deserved its own postal code. Something had to be done.

Meditation? He tried. He kept eating the moss. Hypnosis? Waste of money. The hypnotist was a praying mantis who only took payment in aphids. Yoga? He got stuck midway through Slug Pose.

Slowing down with the change of seasons wasn't helping either. Boredom made him hungry. Hunger made him stressed. Stress made him hungrier. It was a perfect, self-sliming circle.

Everything led back to snacks. Travel? Snacks. Destinations? Snacks. Happy? Snacks. Time to celebrate? Double snacks. He needed someone to follow him around and slap the food out of his mouth—gently, but firmly, and ideally with excellent reflexes.

The self-help brochures were no use. *"Manage stress by spending time in nature,"* they said. That was literally his full-time job. Yet nature led to weeds, weeds led to panic, and panic led directly to eating his way through the decorative edging.

He fancied himself a stress-eating specialist, but not in a good way.

According to one pamphlet, peeling citrus fruit was a *"mini-meditation."* If fruit wasn't available, it suggested breathing instead: *inhale for five seconds, hold for seven, exhale for eight.* Slimothy tried both at once. The orange exploded. The smell was delightful, the floor sticky, and for a fleeting moment, he actually felt calm—until he accidentally ate the peel, mistook the rind for enlightenment, and immediately questioned every life choice that led him there.

He'd read that the joy from comfort food only lasted three minutes. *Three minutes!* That was barely enough time to regret it properly. There had to be better uses for 180 seconds.

~ He could alphabetize his seed packets.

~ He could file another zoning complaint against the heron.

~ He could write a haiku about lettuce and immediately eat the subject.

~ He could check if the lemon tree was still judging him.

~ He could even take a quick power nap and wake up feeling only slightly more confused.

Maybe he didn't need a self-care sprig of parsley. Maybe he just needed structured chaos.

Spinach and kale, they claimed, were rich in magnesium and could reduce stress. Slimothy wouldn't know; his spinach vanished months ago in The Spinach Thief Incident. Only a few shaken survivors remained, spirited away into witness protection and relocated to an unnamed planter in Zone C, living discreetly and declining interviews.

The cabbage, meanwhile, was thriving, stretching skyward like it had just been promoted. Slimothy made a note to congratulate it later—then eat it out of principle.

He wondered if eating the cabbage out of revenge still counted as impulse eating, and whether he could do it in under three minutes.

He could start a podcast: "Three Minutes or Less: Regrettable Decisions in

Real Time."

He could meditate, fail, and still have a minute left to snack.

He'd call it mindfulness—if he ever managed to keep his mouth empty long enough to use his brain for something other than menu planning.

CHAPTER FIFTY-TWO

Certified Moment of Personal Development

S limothy had been thinking about the three-minute thing all afternoon. He drank water, took notes about drinking water, rewarded himself with a snack, and then felt guilty enough to write about the guilt. He followed it up with coffee for clarity and more water for balance. By the time he'd documented it all, he'd accidentally created a hydration-based food pyramid. Nothing was helping.

After the nutritional breakdown and zoning fatigue, his systems were collapsing. Everything he'd tried to control had either sprouted overnight, sunk mysteriously, or filed for independence and joined a self-governing micronation. Even his to-do list had unionized.

Now there was talk of a district expansion. The armadillos and squirrels were pushing for the annexation of the northern hedge, and as self-appointed inspector, Slimothy was apparently expected to assess this "new territory." He wasn't sure whether that meant exploration, paperwork, or mortal peril—but it definitely meant stress.

There was only one option left: find answers elsewhere. The current location had clearly stopped cooperating.

If the garden had become his primary source of anxiety, then perhaps leaving it would provide perspective—or at least better snacks. If, along the way, he happened to stumble upon his missing spinach, that would be a convenient bonus for his legacy.

The birds and butterflies were already flying south for the winter, their migration schedules far more organized than any zoning plan he'd ever approved. Slimothy watched them vanish over the hedge, wondering if they'd filed the proper paperwork—or if freedom really was just a matter of wings and timing.

Maybe it was time for a change for Slimothy too. Something drastic. Something inspiring. Or at the very least, something that didn't involve minutes, meetings, or spinach.

About the only things not migrating were the gnats, who seemed determined to make a full-time career out of biting him. They had no schedule, no purpose, and infinite enthusiasm for his misery.

Another of the self-help pamphlets had suggested exercise—something slimy creatures generally avoided on principle—but maybe that was the only way to escape the doldrums he'd found himself mired in. The brochures promised "increased vitality" and "mental clarity." He doubted either would survive the first stretch.

The ominous zoning board meeting loomed just one week away. The ducks were still battling over waterfront rights, the pigeons had drafted a proposal, and someone had started a rumor about imposing term limits. Slimothy wasn't sure for what—but it sounded threatening.

He wondered what life might look like after the meeting—if there would even be an after. Maybe he'd finally resign. Or maybe, like most crises in the Bright Wild, it would end with a vote, an argument about bylaws, and someone eating all the snacks out of stress before the minutes were even approved.

He tried to shake the thought, but something in the air felt different—unsettled, expectant. The kind of stillness that came before a rainstorm, a coup, or Roger deciding to "improve" the pond for the very first time.

Then he saw it: the blazing star, standing tall and luminous near the edge of the garden. Its tightly grouped flower buds glowed in a swirl of red and purple—

like a sunset that had forgotten how to quit—radiating calmly against the chaos. It was a botanical headliner, a beacon of beauty amid bureaucracy—so striking that Slimothy momentarily forgot about snacks, land-use debates, and the possibility of sudden leadership changes.

He watched it for a long time, the way one watches a thought they're not quite ready to have. Something about it felt important, though he couldn't say why—just a quiet nudge that the world might be bigger than his clipboard, and woefully underregulated.

For the first time in weeks, there was light at the end of his downward-spiral tunnel—faint, flickering, and almost certainly not up to code. He made a note to schedule an inspection. Then a gnat flew up his nose, and that was the end of self-improvement for the day.

CHAPTER FIFTY-THREE

Bright Wild, Inc.

Slimothy's stomach rumbled. Still, he woke up refreshed for once—with something to look forward to. It wasn't just the fact that he'd eaten his body weight in carbs for dinner. The cabbage was living its best leafy life, the cucumbers looked *less weird*, and he had a plan to, as he put it, "turn that frown upside down."

If he couldn't fix it, he was going to change it. If he couldn't beat them, he'd join them. For Slimothy, that meant only one thing—a full-scale rebranding.

Welcome, Bright Wild, Inc.

He wasn't entirely sure what that meant yet, but it sounded impressive enough to write on stationery.

Slimothy decided the first step of any proper organization was settling on a public persona—a logo, a motto, maybe even a corporate philosophy that didn't immediately collapse under humidity.

He gathered his supplies: one leaf (stationery), one stick (pen), and one dew droplet (coffee). At the top, he scrawled:

"Bright Wild, Inc.: Growth You Can Trip Over."

Below it, he began his mission statement:

"To bring unity, structure, and visionary leadership to an ecosystem that has consistently ignored memos."

That sounded good. Maybe even great. He underlined *visionary* three times.

Next came his team. Every company needed a team. The frogs were loud but reliable. The gulls were technically qualified but had terrible PR. The cabbage was an obvious choice for Head of Growth. The lemon tree could handle public relations—it already had charisma and opinions.

That left Roger.

Chief Operating Frog. Naturally.

Slimothy, of course, would serve as Acting Interim Permanent Director.

He wasn't entirely sure what that title meant, but it sounded powerful—and vaguely impossible to fire.

The first official meeting of Bright Wild, Inc. was, in truth, taking place entirely in his head. That didn't make it any less stressful. With the real zoning board meeting coming up next week—a bureaucratic nightmare involving pond permits, gnat population density, and the legality of keeping ornamental flamingos—Slimothy needed practice.

If he could handle this imaginary board, he reasoned, he could take on anything.

He mentally assembled them all around a damp conference table made from an upturned planter lid: frogs in business attire, the lemon tree in a corner glaring at everyone, and the cabbage acting like it chaired three other committees and had an MBA in chlorophyll management.

The meeting began exactly as expected: in complete chaos.

The frogs croaked over the agenda, arguing about whether flies should be considered "refreshments." The cabbage kept photosynthesizing loudly just for attention. The lemon tree refused to participate without proper catering— "something citrus-forward," naturally. The gulls demanded profit-sharing in leftover compost. Roger just blinked—radiating the quiet energy of someone who'd attended the wrong conference entirely but was too polite to leave.

Slimothy surveyed the scene and tried to take comfort in the chaos. This was how leadership worked, wasn't it? Herding opinions, maintaining composure, pretending everyone knew what the agenda meant.

It wasn't much—but for the first time in weeks, he felt almost ready. Or at least prepared to appear ready. Which, in the end, was often all that mattered.

He adjourned the meeting with a solemn nod to no one in particular and decided he might just be getting the hang of authority—or at least the illusion of it.

CHAPTER FIFTY-FOUR

A Very Marketable Slug

Slimothy had been out shopping when he discovered Gary—sitting there like fate with a price tag. Gary was a wonderful creature: soft, fluffy, and brimming with personality, the whole nine yards. Impressive feather structure, suspiciously realistic beady eyes, and the kind of posture that screamed "retired pirate" more than "home décor." They locked what passed for eyes in Slimothy's world, and he knew—instantly—that Gary had to come home with him.

Come hell or one of those inconvenient 9.9-foot tides that turned the road into a temporary island—Slimothy was getting Gary home, even if it meant commandeering an abandoned boogie board and calling it a daring maritime operation.

Slimothy wasn't entirely sure what species Gary belonged to, but he looked aerodynamic and slightly judgmental—two qualities Slimothy deeply respected.

Gary was a seagull.

Which, for no particular reason at all, got Slimothy thinking about his legacy again—and a possible plaster-cast statue of himself in the town square. Something tasteful, dignified, and only slightly larger than life. Maybe mid-slime, with excellent lighting and a plaque that read: *"Visionary. Slug. Occasional*

Menace."

Ultimately, he decided he wanted something more. He wanted to be immortalized in a soft green cloud—one of those irresistibly squishy, immediately cuddly creations that made you forget what personal space was. The kind of thing children adored, adults side-eyed, and safety labels politely warned against. It was likely a choking hazard, had absolutely no market research behind it, and possessed perfect branding in his mind. Green cloud was the vision; orange scarf was the artistic flourish no one asked for but everyone would discuss in interviews.

How did one immortalize oneself in something grander than fabric? Something rare, ambiguous, and gloriously unnecessary? Maybe it wasn't fabric at all but some exotic hybrid of velvet, moss, and delusion—the kind of minty-green material you could only find at the intersection of genius and poor decision-making. Who could he trust with his likeness? He set to work on a search.

This was a complicated world—overwhelming, even—much like anything involving overwintering or the shape of his vegetables. He realized he would need professional help. Not just to make himself forever-squishable, but also to manage the growing list of questionable life choices that had somehow led him here. Preferably someone licensed in both fabric procurement and feelings management.

Commitment was hard for a slug, and pursuing one tiny green bouncy creature through the Bright Wild was no exception. There were contracts to sign, NDAs to misunderstand, and legal jargon that made his feelers twitch. What he really needed was a savvy youngster with opposable thumbs—someone who could navigate paperwork, wield a glue gun responsibly, and resist the urge to turn him into a keychain.

Still, it got him thinking about materials. If he were to be mass-produced, what exactly would he be made of? Fleece? That would certainly be a choice—cozy, but dangerously close to bathrobe territory.

Memory foam? Intriguing. It could remember him forever, though that seemed like an unreasonable existential assignment for a pillow.

Velour? Now that was a statement—luxurious, impractical, and guaranteed to attract lint from three counties over.

The vision arrived uninvited and fully accessorized: a plastic green lawn-flamingo version of himself, proudly upright, gleaming in the sun, balancing on stilts so disproportionately large they looked like they'd been borrowed from a giraffe doing community theater. It was bold. It was marketable. It was deeply concerning.

Brilliant, he thought. He could sell himself next National Kale Day and call it *"art meets agriculture."*

He was becoming both calmer and more excited the more he overthought his tchotchke empire. The possibilities multiplied like aphids on a warm day—stationery, slug-approved decals, maybe even a limited-edition slime-scented candle. World domination was suddenly within reach, provided he could fit it all on a shelf at the garden center.

Water bottles plastered with green Slimothys and witty slogans like *"Save the Slugs"* and *"All Hail Kale."* Branded tote bags, possibly scented stickers. Maybe even a *"Slime Responsibly"* mug line for the ethically hydrated. He was going to bring a whole new meaning to grassroots.

Snow globes filled with tiny plants and eternal drizzle—the kind that rained just enough to look profound. Slimothy was going big. He was not going home.

Fame and grandeur were absolutely going to his head, but he decided that was part of the creative process. It was time for Slimothy to become an unofficial work of art—preferably one available in multiple sizes with optional glitter.

His imagination sprinted ahead: adoring fans, brand deals, maybe a stadium or two bearing his name.

Welcome to SlugLife Arena, he mused, modestly.

Reality, however, reminded him he was still a limited edition. One of a kind. Collectible, certainly—but not yet in circulation.

CHAPTER FIFTY-FIVE

Masked Intentions

Halloween was right around the corner, and Slimothy had been invited to a very swanky party where everyone would be wearing a mask. A relief, really—since his face had never quite decided on an expression. He practiced in a puddle for good measure, tilting his eye stalks at different angles to see if "mysterious" looked any different from "mildly congested." It didn't—but he decided to go with it anyway.

In theory, it sounded like a fabulous soirée. In reality, due to the height of Slimothy's eye stalks, masks had to be ordered from Above Average Outfitters—which was laughable, given his minute stature everywhere else. It took two fittings, three glue sticks, and one minor philosophical detour, but in the end, the mask fit … sort of.

Open bar. Heavy hors d'oeuvres. Fire entertainment. Slimothy could hardly contain himself trying to figure out what to wear. The possibilities were endless—dramatic, thematic, or just confusing enough to make people question if he'd been invited on purpose.

The host's home was breathtaking. Towering balustrades, staircases for days—an architectural Everest Slimothy couldn't hope to climb in a millennium. She'd once mentioned installing an elevator system, and Slimothy reasoned she should probably finish that project before expecting him to get his annual aerobic workout in a single evening. Regardless of stair tread or common sense, he was going anyway.

Her art collection was equally intimidating—original pieces, intricate sculptures, and a complete equine gallery of distinguished fabulousness, every hoof posed in a tiny gilded frame. Slimothy fancied himself a collector too—mostly of birdhouses, decorative pebbles, and snail-themed knickknacks—but even he had to admit, this was a different league of fancy.

Then there was the wine. Oh, the wine. She always had *that* kind—the one that made Slimothy's feelers tingle and his slime sparkle. Then there were her snacks. Impeccable. Delicious. Possibly enchanted.

Her home overlooked a park that stretched for miles, dotted with trees older than time—ancient giants so perfectly manicured they clearly had standing weekly appointments and preferred not to be kept waiting. The kind of towering elders that whispered secrets about the universe, soil, and which squirrels were late on rent again.

For the evening's culinary theatrics, she was making ice cream from scratch—using a seasonal cookbook that arranged recipes by holiday and occasional identity crisis. The planned selection was a Halloween special featuring black cocoa, pig's blood, and something optimistically labeled "optional protein." Slimothy was intrigued but quietly hoped it didn't come with a side of introspection he absolutely did not order.

The last time he'd been over, the garden had no flowers. It was all hedge and structure—stately and intentional—the kind of space that made you lower your voice out of respect. She simply wasn't a flower person, and Slimothy could appreciate that, even if it had made him want to sneak in a few seeds and later blame divine intervention. Though just as he'd been ready to write the place off as a horticultural monastery, he'd seen it: the bleeding-heart vine.

A white-and-red trailing beauty—delicate as gossip and twice as captivating. She'd imported it from far beyond the forest, a mysterious place Slimothy immediately decided sounded expensive. Within a week, imitation being the sincerest form of flattery (and impulse buying definitely ranking in his top five love languages), he had purchased the exact same plant.

For a slug, Slimothy was surprisingly competitive. He took great pride in measuring the length of his blooms against hers—sometimes with a tape measure, sometimes with whatever chaotic metric he invented on the spot. She had twin vines circling a marble fountain, white, imported, with an elegantly gurgling system. His own pond, of course, wasn't so grand, but it had heart—and significantly fewer shipping fees.

Still, it comforted him to know that her water was just as cloudy as his. They traded algaecide recipes, barley tricks, and copper-penny hacks like collectible playing cards, each pretending they weren't secretly keeping score. Nothing worked. Still, that was part of the charm—two horticultural gladiators locked in an eternal, mildly damp duel.

She did, however, have magnificent lawn flamingos—black ones—elegant and vaguely sinister, the kind that looked like they hosted secret meetings after dark. Slimothy decided she needed one more.

A green plastic version of himself, perched proudly on stilts between them. Nestled there, he thought, he'd look perfectly at home. Or perfectly creepy. Either way, it would really tie the yard together.

He couldn't wait to see it all—the costumes, the chaos, the inevitable spell-casting with ice cream that was sure to leave most of the guests enchanted and the rest pleasantly baffled by dairy-based magic. Easing through the crowd, he would try to look casual, mysterious, and only moderately flammable—which was harder than it sounded.

CHAPTER FIFTY-SIX

The Jar of Questionable Intentions

S limothy had seen those jars people used—little glass containers of possibility—where they'd write down things to do and pull one out on a random afternoon, pretending fate had a sense of organization.

He decided this was a brilliant idea.

He rinsed out an old jam jar—mostly with rainwater and hope—and set it proudly on the potting bench. The glass still smelled faintly of strawberries and wildly misplaced ambition. Perfect.

First slip of paper: "Take swimming lessons." A bold choice, considering the whole slug anatomy situation, but Slimothy was an optimist. He folded it carefully, dropped it into the jar, and gave it a ceremonious tap.

Next: "Start a slug support group." Lofty. Maybe someday. Probably with snacks. That one went in too.

Then came, "learn Italian," "grow an actual straight cucumber," "read that book about compost he'd been pretending to understand," and—if he was feeling particularly brave—"confront the mysterious hole near the kale bed." Each one folded with the kind of reverence usually reserved for lottery tickets and dramatic resignations.

He was on a roll now—purposeful, driven, slightly delusional.

A few entries got more personal: "Establish better work-life-slime balance." "Stop doomscrolling aphid news at 2 a.m." "Apologize to the basil for last year's accidental pruning incident."

He hesitated over one that sounded peaceful in theory and logistically impossible in practice: "Visit a silent monastery by a lake."

The idea filled him with a deep, if slightly confused, sense of peace. What did one even do at a silent monastery? Meditate? Reflect? Moisturize?

Still, a serene little daydream took shape—the still water, the quiet air, the faint sound of lily pads whispering secrets they definitely weren't qualified to keep. Maybe they'd let a small slug attend a mindfulness workshop between the tea ceremonies and the required silence.

He folded that one too, dropped it in the jar, and gave it a gentle swirl. The papers fluttered like sleepy moths—tiny, crumpled dreams waiting for their turn to ruin his schedule.

Slimothy considered adding "stop overcommitting to personal growth," but that felt counterproductive.

Instead, he just smiled, pleased with himself.

He was going to call it The Jar of Questionable Intentions.

Just like that, fate had a new co-pilot—and he had one more item to add to tomorrow's to-do list: "Actually follow through on something."

CHAPTER FIFTY-SEVEN

Hope, Weeds, and Other Cash Crops

Slimothy had had another awful nightmare.

He'd been forced to sell his house—the Bright Wild—and everything in it.

When he went back to visit his former garden refuge in his dream, it was a disaster. The air smelled wrong, like sadness and overwatered mulch. The kale beds were barren. The pond was nothing but a muddy crater, dimly reflecting, as if it were trying to remember happier times. His trellises were twisted in the weeds, reaching out as if ghostly arms were begging for one last cucumber.

Most of it was gone. Torn out, trampled, or left dramatically wilting for effect. Even in dreams, the Bright Wild had a flair for the theatrical. Somehow, there had been pajamas—apparently very important sleepwear—though their exact symbolism was tragically lost upon waking.

He lay there blinking at the ceiling, trying to decide if this counted as an omen, a metaphor, or just his subconscious being rude again. It felt a bit like that time he'd woken up from a medical procedure and started talking about his garden. Dramatic, confusing, and oddly specific.

Of course, it had to happen on National Mental Health Day. Perfect timing.

To make matters worse, his cucumbers—his pride, joy, and full-time babysitting project—had gone yellow, overripe, and filled with swollen seeds plotting some sort of uprising. The peas weren't any better: one lonely green pod clung for dear life to a wilted vine. So much for "easy to grow."

Even his prized papyruses were leaning dangerously toward the pond again, top-heavy and dramatic. "Do not recommend," he muttered.

Maybe domestic vegetables just didn't get the Bright Wild.

They wanted tidy rows, measured watering schedules, and predictable outcomes—things that had no place in a garden where chaos was practically a design principle. The Bright Wild demanded character, flair, and a little unhinged ambition.

That's when he remembered something he'd read in a horticultural forum at three in the morning, something called forest farming. Apparently, people grew rare and exotic plants beneath leafy canopies, doubling their land's use and earning all kinds of bragging rights for creativity. Non-timber Forest Products (NTFPs), as the experts called them—because even sustainability needed its acronyms.

He mulled it over. Technically, he wouldn't even have to go deep into the woods; the eastern side of the Bright Wild was already so overgrown it might qualify as a forest. He could just plant something there and call it a day.

According to his late-night research (and one very suspicious PDF), forest farming was all about cultivating plants under the shade of trees instead of foraging them from the wild. These plants weren't your typical crops. They could be mushrooms, herbs, medicinals, or fancy orchids—the kind people used in spa teas and overpriced lotions.

The best part? Hardly anyone was doing it. That meant untapped potential, conservation bragging rights, and, of course, the possibility of selling carbon credits. Whatever those were.

"*Small-scale forest landowners,*" the article had said—which to Slimothy felt like a personal invitation.

Small-scale was his entire brand.

Slimothy styled himself as a quinoa pioneer, tending imaginary rows of the stuff beneath moss-draped branches as if he were founding a tiny agricultural empire. The weeds were practically begging for a career change anyway—most of them already looked managerial. He could call it Bright Wild: Forest Division (BWFD). Maybe even apply for an ecosystem grant, if someone could explain to him what an ecosystem or a grant actually was.

Slimothy spent an unreasonable amount of time envisioning the future headquarters of BWFD—maybe a leaf-canopy office, or a moss conference room. He was fairly sure he heard the rustle of productivity. All he needed now was the right container to start his empire.

Although that, as always, was where the trouble began.

Finding the right pot was less "errand" and more "epic quest." Too shallow, too shiny, too judgmental. None of them ever felt quite right. He wanted something with presence—something that said: *"Yes, this slug means business."*

The air was soggy with ambition as he slid through the garden center, eyes scanning for the perfect vessel—the eternal shopping struggle for a slug.

He searched high, low, and moderately damp, but every pot seemed to mock him in its own special way.

He went home empty-handed, which, technically, was his default state. Still, it felt symbolic.

Some time (and several muttered complaints) later, with his slightly collapsed papyruses and overripe cucumbers behind him, Slimothy felt something he hadn't in weeks: possibility.

If others could grow goldenseal, ginseng, and orchids in the woods, then surely he could grow a little hope there too. Maybe even sell it at a premium, organic, artisanal price.

If nothing else, the weeds could fund the entire operation.

He took a deep breath, squared his nonexistent shoulders, and declared to no one in particular, "The forest won't know what hit it."

CHAPTER FIFTY-EIGHT

The Unholy Incident

A sudden break in the endless, soul-dampening rain had Slimothy moving faster than anything without feet had any right to move. He oozed across the patio at top speed, which, in slug terms, was roughly the pace of an indecisive cloud, eager to check on his beloved Bright Wild.

The blazing star was, for the first time ever, actually blazing. Life was good. Hope was in the air. He plucked his one perfect pea pod, munched it with a crunch of triumph, and sighed with genuine contentment.

He'd planned to tackle some weeding that morning, but that plan went out the window the moment he found himself mired in ... *poop*.

Not just any poop. Not an acceptable, garden-variety, fertilizer-adjacent deposit. No. This was a statement piece, a crime against nature, reason, and olfactory decency. It sat there like an alien artifact, faintly steaming, the color of despair. Slimothy halted, stunned into silence. His feelers twitched. Somewhere, a worm fainted.

He inched closer, horrified. The texture—unspeakable. The smell—an act of war. It radiated malevolence, as though whoever made it had unfinished business with the universe. Slimothy gagged dramatically, recoiling with all the elegance of someone clutching at imaginary pearls.

He stared at the scene, appalled. What kind of deranged beast would desecrate the Bright Wild like this? A raccoon with no conscience? A feral cat with an artistic streak? Some rogue toad with gastrointestinal vengeance? Whoever it was, they had crossed a line. This wasn't just a mess; it was a hate crime against beauty itself, and personally, against him.

He looked for something, anything, to scoop the abomination away. A leaf was too thin. A stick, too short. A trowel? He didn't own one—tools were for creatures with thumbs. At last he grabbed a cracked shell fragment and immediately regretted every life choice that had led him here. The smell clung to his being. His pores, his soul, his entire ancestral lineage felt it—past lives included. His spiritual slime whispered, *"Fix this."*

It was time for purification. Possibly divine intervention. Maybe both.

He couldn't swim, as a general rule, even though he had put "take swimming lessons" on the list in his Jar of Questionable Intentions. This required cleansing of an otherworldly nature. He feared he would never feel clean again.

He turned toward the pond for salvation, but it was no help. What should have been a tranquil oasis now looked like an unruly chlorophyll stew, algae gone feral and staging a full-scale *coup d'état*. Green scum sprawled across every surface, draping its wet, mossy garb over everything in its path, ignoring every known rule of pond etiquette. The little bee-watering stations he'd placed around the garden were far too deep after the relentless rain—potential drowning traps for the innocent. His birdbath was a crime of its own.

Slimothy stared at the waterlogged mess, briefly debating whether to declare the garden a disaster zone or a new aquatic feature.

Then, as if summoned by pity itself, the rain started in earnest again, a wall of water sweeping in from the south so fast he briefly considered drafting blueprints for an ark. It came at him sideways, powerful enough to flatten dandelions and his remaining sense of dignity. A downpour so sudden, so fierce, it felt biblical. Slimothy sprawled flat, letting it pelt him like nature's own power wash as mud splattered across his back in perfect irony. The rain poured harder, rearranging the garden's priorities and most of its topsoil.

He let it happen. It felt glorious. He soaked in nitrogen like some kind of nutrient-hungry spa guest. He still had a bone to pick with rain about "watering best practices," but at that moment he was too busy being reborn.

He lay there, letting the storm erase the morning's horror one blessed drop at a time, both in despair and in bliss, water cascading down his back like a redemption arc. Maybe he didn't need the Fountain of Youth after all. Maybe youth was just what happened when the sky blasted you with cold water and a second chance. Maybe the secret had been under his nose—or technically above it—all along.

Still … he'd never trust that patch of soil again. Probably cursed. Definitely suspicious. Which meant, surely, the guilty party was out there somewhere—cleaner than he deserved to be.

CHAPTER FIFTY-NINE

Bright Wild Security Protocols, Vol. 1

B y morning, the rain had scrubbed the world clean—or at least made everything look freshly rinsed and morally ambiguous. Slimothy felt … different. Not cleaner, exactly, just vigilant. You didn't survive a poopocalypse and return to business as usual. No, this was the beginning of something larger. Something organized.

He began with reconnaissance. The crime scene had been flattened, rinsed, and generally oversteeped by the storm, leaving behind nothing but suspicion and a faint smell of fertilizer. Convenient. Suspiciously orchestrated. Someone—or something—had used the chaos to cover their tracks.

It wasn't just an accident; it was an escalation. The Bright Wild had been compromised. In short, a systems failure, and where there was failure, there needed to be paperwork.

That was when he decided the Bright Wild needed a perimeter plan.

Slimothy spent the better part of the morning drafting blueprints in damp dirt, drawing circles, arrows, and a suspicious number of exclamation points. "Operation Containment" took shape before him. Bee patrol routes, snail checkpoint zones, and what he optimistically labeled "Restricted Compost Area."

Within hours, the Bright Wild was transformed. Fallen sticks became barricades. Bottle caps marked hazard zones. A small fence of twigs and bravado encircled the site of the "incident area." He even installed a makeshift warning sign crafted from a leaf that read, in very uneven slime script, *"ABSOLUTELY NOT HERE."*

He didn't stop there. Every corner of the garden was subject to inspection. The creeping Jenny received border control, its suspiciously enthusiastic sprawl flagged for future containment. The prickly pear was declared a high-risk zone—uncooperative, armed, and known for harboring trouble.

By midday, the Bright Wild resembled a cross between a construction site and a nature documentary gone wrong. Slimothy was everywhere at once: repositioning bark fragments for optimal visibility, filing mental reports, and glaring at anything that looked even remotely defiant.

A soggy pebble became the command post. A cluster of mushrooms served as temporary headquarters for Intelligence Operations. He even created a filing system—mostly damp napkin scraps and labeled dirt piles—for incident documentation and future investigations.

It was, he decided, a model of efficiency. Almost inspiring. *Almost.*

Protocol alone wasn't enough. A system untested was a system untrusted. There needed to be an emergency drill.

At noon sharp (give or take 45 damp minutes), Slimothy blew an imaginary whistle and began the first Bright Wild Emergency Response Simulation. He slithered purposefully across the garden, issuing silent mental alerts. All units, report! Sector Kale, secure! Bee division, buzz twice if compromised!

The kale didn't respond, which was typical, but the basil waved in light agreement. A lone bee zipped past, possibly in acknowledgment, possibly in pursuit of a dandelion bribe. Either way, morale was high.

Until the drill began to unravel.

A sudden breeze knocked over the Restricted Compost Area sign, sending it spiraling into the creeping Jenny district, which immediately went to DEFCON 2. The bee division misinterpreted the signal and launched a coordinated buzz attack on the watering can, which Slimothy had designated as Base of Operations—also known as the "Big Can." Meanwhile, a passing earthworm, entirely uninformed about the exercise, panicked and burrowed directly through the communications trench (also known as Slimothy's slime trail), cutting off contact between the Kale Sector and Basil Outpost.

Within minutes, chaos reigned. The emergency response protocol fell apart spectacularly. The scorpion's-tail zone seized the moment to expand its territory, declaring itself interim management of the pathway and enforcing new prickly zoning laws.

By the time order was restored (and the bees were coaxed down from high alert), Slimothy was both exhilarated and mortified. He called an immediate debrief—which in practice meant pacing in circles and updating the official Bright Wild Emergency Binder (a wet napkin) with critical, high-level strategy like *"bee diplomacy?"* and *"worm communication network needs training."*

By dusk, the Bright Wild had officially achieved Prepared Status, complete with contingency plans for everything from cat incursions to gnome relocation efforts. Slimothy, exhausted but proud, looked over his kingdom and felt the faint, slippery glow of satisfaction.

That's when Roger appeared, unamused. He loomed at the edge of the path like an auditor materializing at tax season, eyes narrowed, posture disapproving. He surveyed the so-called defense budget—a pile of twigs, two pebbles, and what might have been a button—and radiated judgment so potent it didn't need words.

Slimothy could practically hear the critique forming: *"excessive spending, unnecessary use of resources, zero measurable outcomes."* He refused to be rattled. Instead, he mentally filed a full report titled "Public Safety Justifications and Pond Security Initiatives, Volume I." It had charts. Possibly.

Roger stared for a long, slow moment, then turned back toward his castle without a word—which, to Slimothy, was practically an endorsement.

He made a final note in his binder: *"Next drill: fewer bees, more signage."*

He still didn't know who had done it. Next time, though, they wouldn't get away so easily.

Should they dare try again, there'd be protocol. Forms. A task force. A logo. Maybe even matching vests.

CHAPTER SIXTY

Caterpillar Drama and Other Lemon-Based Tragedies

Summer was having a late hot flash, fanning herself with heatwaves and regret. The papyrus, ever the drama queen, was attempting another public drowning in the pond, swaying, gasping, and sinking just enough to make sure everyone was watching. Meanwhile, some mysterious chomping creature had set up camp at the very top of Slimothy's lemon tree, turning it into an all-you-can-eat lemon leaf buffet with excellent reviews—courtesy of a diner who ate like a tiny outlaw with no regard for etiquette or property lines.

Roger had even emerged at dusk—an event rarer than a polite aphid—given his tendency to lounge dramatically and gripe about humidity. Maybe the commotion drew him out—or, more realistically, he'd caught wind of Slimothy's French red and decided the night demanded supervision and a glass (or three).

Slimothy watched, equal parts admiration and secondhand embarrassment, as Roger crossed the stepping stones like someone late for a meeting with destiny, each one 14 times his size. He refused to hop like a normal amphibian, of course. No, Roger strode, taking exaggerated leaps, pausing between each as if waiting for applause or an omen. It was less "frog in nature" and more "tiny thespian rehearsing an action sequence."

He was, Slimothy admitted, a handsome fellow in that lumpy, vaguely menacing, probably-has-a-tragic-backstory kind of way. A real pond-side heartthrob, if you squinted. Right now, that mysterious aura of brooding charm was advancing straight toward the wild coffee plant like it owed him money.

Was he out hunting for an evening aperitif, Slimothy wondered, or perhaps conducting a routine inspection of the holes nature kept digging without permission? He might have been tending to his summer estate on the other side of town—shuttering windows, polishing toadstools, and issuing orders to imaginary staff before the next storm rolled in.

Eight concrete steps and a long, mossy causeway led to that grand summer town, perched dramatically in the arms of an ancient tree—a location so exclusive even the snails needed an appointment to visit. Or maybe Roger was headed for the same destination as their newest tenant—the all-you-can-eat lemon leaf buffet. The newcomer, parts of his cocoon still dangling like a youngster with his pants around his ankles, munched away with the kind of carefree enthusiasm reserved for those who have never been told "that's enough."

Slimothy pulled out his trusty search engine, antennae twitching with purpose. "Orange dog caterpillar," the results declared. Great. He'd just finished dealing with the yellow dog-vomit slime mold, and now something in his second-favorite color palette was eating his third-favorite color palette's leaves. When did it end? Also, why were there so many "dogs" in nature that weren't even remotely dog-like? He was starting to suspect a conspiracy.

Apparently, the orange dog caterpillar would one day blossom into a giant yellow-and-black swallowtail butterfly—glamorous, dramatic, and probably radiating unearned confidence in the process. For now, though, it looked exactly like fresh bird droppings, which Slimothy had to admit was both repulsive and genius. Nature really did have a flair for chaotic disguise.

Since the other day's unfortunate poop incident, he wasn't taking any chances. Once you've mistaken actual droppings for emerging wildlife, you learn to approach all "mysteries of nature" with a healthy mix of skepticism and bleach.

He shuddered, but research demanded bravery. According to the Great Oracle of Bug Drama, the latest recorded sighting of a giant swallowtail in the state was October 20th. This big baby was then only days away from setting a record.

Slimothy was impressed, albeit unwilling to host a champion. He would've applauded if it weren't currently eating his property.

The caterpillar's favorite food? Lemon leaves. Naturally. Slimothy kicked himself for not re-homing the tree sooner. Now he was stuck on nursery duty with a hatchling under his proverbial wing—one that ate nonstop, required zero supervision, and still managed to be high maintenance.

If startled, the caterpillar could apparently extend a pair of reddish, horn-like glands behind its head called an osmeterium, releasing a foul-smelling chemical to ward off predators. Slimothy stared at an example photo, deeply envious. Why couldn't he evolve something like that? Something dignified, powerful, aromatically assertive. Instead, his default stress response remained the same as ever: excess slime, panic edition, usually followed by snacks and regret.

He wondered what life would be like with an osmeterium—marching through the garden, diffusing drama one stinky puff at a time. HOA meetings, solved. Roger's unsolicited pond maintenance advice? Handled. Even the neighborhood's overenthusiastic crickets would think twice. Alas, nature had dealt him the short, slimy straw. His only real weapon was passive-aggressive glistening.

He sent a silent apology to the lemon tree and slimed off toward the cut-and-come-again salad bar, passing through the spinach sector. Still missing, still suspicious. Locally known as The Leaf Triangle, it was infamous for its paranormal produce activity: disappearing greens, suspicious bite marks, and now a mysterious new flower that had taken up residence right in the graveyard of what should have been "Savoy's finest crinkled leaves."

A mystery for another day, perhaps. For now, Slimothy decided, it was best not to question cosmic gardening events before dinner. Last time he tried, he ended up overly invested in a compost heap and slightly tipsy on fertilizer fumes.

CHAPTER SIXTY-ONE

Soggy Wings and Other Existential Problems

S limothy was quite enjoying watching the lily put down water roots every few inches, like it was plotting world domination in dots. It was a small, slow kind of drama—one he could respect. A fascinating plant, really, just floating there, literally coasting through life, growing when it felt like it, no deadlines, no meetings, no "am I growing correctly?" panic attacks. Every few nodes it sent out a new shoot, as if to say, *"Look at me, thriving without trying."* It clearly had a five-year plan and the audacity to be following it.

Slimothy, on the other hand, was about as zen as a squirrel on espresso. He willed the lily to grow faster, to *"photosynthesize with a bit more enthusiasm"* as he liked to say. He needed at least three quarters of the pond covered in something green and respectable before the algae formed another committee. It was a long game, a noble ecological pursuit, but mostly an exercise in patience, and Slimothy was running dangerously low on that particular resource.

While he waited for the lily to do something, *anything,* Slimothy's mind wandered to the fairy folk of the Bright Wild. Rarely seen, barely mentioned, but somehow always loitering in the background like unpaid interns of the magical realm. They supposedly lived in that hazy twilight gap between waking and dreaming, conducting a quiet, sparkly sort of commerce: trading dew for moonlight, gossip for pollen, and whatever chaotic nonsense fairies tended to invent when there were no witnesses. Slimothy liked to think he kept a casual eye on them, though at the moment that eye was firmly trained on the lemon bush buffet, making sure the one shameless freeloader didn't upgrade to the basil course. Fairies were fine, but basil was sacred.

Their presence, he mused, had a way of tugging at memory, a nostalgia for the days when reality still had bendy edges and common sense hadn't yet ruined everything. Come to think of it, there was reportedly an old belief that dipping your face into a Scottish stream and making a wish could summon the fair folk. Maybe that's what the papyrus had been attempting with its daily swan dives into the pond, trying to slip into the magical realm via enthusiastic self-submersion. Wrong continent, right level of commitment.

Of course, there were rules. You weren't supposed to tell a fae your name; it gave them power over you. Knowing your true name let them twist it, track it, or file metaphysical paperwork in your soul's name for eternity. Slimothy gave a tiny, world-weary nod—as if his soul had already filled out form 47-B. He'd seen this tactic before, mostly from insurance companies and once from a very persistent gym membership. Bureaucracy, it seemed, was the one true universal constant.

Apparently, fairies couldn't fly in the rain because soggy wings made them visible to humans. Slimothy wasn't sure whether that made them tragic, relatable, or just poorly designed. He, too, became highly visible when damp and cranky, usually leaving a trail of regret and mild inconvenience behind him.

Still, there was something oddly comforting about it all, the idea that the magical world ran on mood swings and loopholes. Maybe that's why Slimothy found himself drawn to the so-called Tinkerbell Effect, the notion that belief itself made things real. The Bright Wild certainly thrived on that logic. If he believed the papyrus wasn't plotting a slow-motion drowning and the lemon bush wasn't being eaten alive by produce pirates, maybe, just maybe, they'd cooperate. Belief was notoriously invasive.

As the evening light melted into gold across the pond, Slimothy stared at his reflection and sighed. Somewhere out there, the fair folk were probably clocking in for their night shift, granting poorly thought-out wishes, meddling in mortal nonsense, and, unlike him, staying perfectly dry and conveniently unphotographable.

CHAPTER SIXTY-TWO

Blue Sky Thinking

Slimothy had been awake since 4:15 a.m. He'd already alphabetized his worries, adjusted his moss twice, and conducted a full audit of his pebble arrangement. Counting sheep did nothing. Counting leaves only made him hungry.

If he couldn't sleep, he might as well panic productively. So he did what any slug would do: he started thinking about everything. From the mysteries of the universe to whether his life had peaked when he found that perfectly symmetrical leaf last spring.

Somewhere between cosmic purpose and leaf geometry, he decided he was due for an epiphany. *"You get out what you put in."* Unless you're compost, in which case you just hope someone's grateful.

Or was it *"you get out what you put out?"* He wasn't sure, but it sounded fair. Fairness counted for something at four in the morning.

Then again, maybe this was why slugs shouldn't be allowed unsupervised philosophy hours. The last time that happened, he nearly wrote a manifesto on the moral ambiguity of lettuce. Still, thoughts had a way of wandering off without permission, like toddlers or tax returns.

"The perfect time to start was never." At least, that's what the wine bottle had

said last night. Honestly, the evening's pour had made some strong points. It had also made him sing to a fern, but that was beside the point. Maybe that was the problem: too much input, not enough chlorophyll-based wisdom. He wasn't sure if it was enlightenment or fermentation talking, but it had sounded convincing enough at the time, and the fern hadn't disagreed.

Now, as the early morning brain fog rolled in, his thoughts upgraded from "tipsy life advice" to "executive meeting nonsense." *"Blue-sky thinking,"* he mused, *"required blue-sky answers."* Though at this hour, the only blue sky was the one inside his imagination, currently scheduling thunderstorms and mild regret.

By the time the sun peeked over the horizon, Slimothy had achieved absolutely nothing except a few new overly dramatic life hypotheses, a lingering sense that the wine bottle should have been promoted to management, and a powerful urge to fire the concept of morning altogether.

He made a slow, determined exit to check on his lemon tree, only to find the orange dog caterpillar had eaten the top row of leaves and was moving confidently into the second, embarking on course two of its all-you-can-eat experience, judging each bite like a food critic with tenure.

The sunlight was offensively bright for someone who hadn't slept, rude and overenthusiastic, clearly showing off. Slimothy glared at it like it had personally scheduled the morning to spite him, and accepted that this would be a long, aggressively well-lit day. His slime caught every beam like an unwilling solar panel in desperate need of shade. Somewhere, the wine bottle was probably laughing from the recycling bin, empty, triumphant, and right.

Around noon, Slimothy decided that blue-sky thinking meant exactly what it sounded like: stop pretending to be productive and go sit under the actual blue sky. He wasn't sure what problems he was supposed to solve out there, but at least they'd look smaller from a horizontal position. Besides, perspective was everything, and lying very still was technically a kind of meditation, especially if you ignored the ants. Eventually, the ants would get bored, and Slimothy could achieve what could only be described as a state of enlightened loafing.

The afternoon was suspiciously warm for late October, the kind of weather that made one question every career choice that didn't involve lying in the sun. Bees droned like background music, and 27 yellow and orange butterflies of various professional affiliations flitted through the air like living confetti at a very polite parade. He'd counted, of course, sometimes self-care required spreadsheets.

The orange ones had overtaken the echinacea blooms, posing like couture shuttlecocks at a high-society badminton match. It wasn't pollination anymore; it was theater. They flitted, twirled, and made a spectacle of it, and Slimothy, ever the critic, gave them a solid nine for form and a 10 for commitment.

Meanwhile, the sun-colored ones were doing their own thing, graceful and chaotic, impossible to identify without a minor in lepidopterology. Cloudless Sulphurs, or possibly Little Yellows. Maybe even a rogue Large Orange Sulphur or two, which, of course, were also bright yellow. The naming department, he decided, had clearly gone on strike sometime around the invention of irony.

At least this batch of names had moved on from all things dog-related. The actually orange ones—Monarchs, maybe Fritillaries—floated through like royalty, far too glamorous to bother with identification. They knew exactly who they were.

Funnily enough, the Cloudless Sulphurs were also yellow, not opaque, a shocking twist he would've appreciated more if he hadn't been awake since four. They fluttered through the garden like tiny highlighters on wings, bright enough to annotate the afternoon. With Slimothy's limited vision, though, they could've been anything from flying gold coins to particularly ambitious Post-its.

Eventually, the butterflies flitted off to wherever beautiful distractions file their timesheets, leaving the garden calm and sun-dappled again. Slimothy stretched, or at least elongated dramatically, and took in the view with something dangerously close to contentment, which he immediately distrusted. Mental stability never ended well in his experience; it usually meant something nearby was preparing to turn his hard work into salad.

He loved seeing the garden in daylight. Marty McFly the pineapple was nearly ripe, and there was still a glimmer of hope that he'd finally get a cauliflower, or perhaps even a cabbage, though that, like sleep, remained elusive.

Still, optimism was a crop worth tending, even if it hadn't sprouted yet. He gave Marty an approving nod and decided that if nothing else, he'd mastered the art of doing nothing beautifully. The garden hummed around him in quiet agreement, sunlight pooling between the leaves. It wasn't the most productive day, but it was arguably his most successful one.

Enlightenment, he reasoned, came easier when you didn't have bones to ache or deadlines to meet. As the sun dipped lower and the garden hummed with leftover warmth, Slimothy realized that sometimes the best kind of progress was simply not moving at all. Inner peace, he decided, was just boredom with better branding, and for today, that was good enough.

At least, it was until a suspicious rustle came from behind the lemon tree. Slimothy sighed. The universe had a way of scheduling interruptions right after he'd finally gotten comfortable.

CHAPTER SIXTY-THREE

The Great Gnat Massacre

No fewer than nine gnats had drowned themselves in Slimothy's glass of Cab the moment he turned his back, apparently mistaking it for an infinity pool. He'd spent the past hour alternating between rescue operations and strategic sipping, neither approach particularly dignified, each option equally inconvenient, equally disgusting. Each tiny floater stared up at him like it regretted nothing. It was hard to decide which was worse: the faint crunch of a survivor or the creeping suspicion that he'd just added protein to the vintage.

What a way to go, though, punch-drunk, marinating in Cabernet, doing the backstroke of bad decisions. Maybe they couldn't swim. Or maybe they could and just decided life was no longer worth buzzing about. A chosen exit strategy, served room temperature with notes of regret.

He looked over his wine at the pond, built with all the precision of a tiny civil engineer—ramps, stone stairs, pebble bridges, even a section he proudly called "amphibian ADA-compliant." Yet he'd never accounted for the gnats.

Maybe they, like the fae, lost all magic once damp, he thought, watching another one spiral dramatically into the shallows of his glass. Or maybe they were just idiots.

He scooped it out with a sigh. *Honestly, if you can't handle a little humidity, maybe outdoor living isn't for you.*

They shouldn't even be out right now. If Mother Nature could just get her thermostat under control and stop these end-of-year hot flashes, the gnats would've been long gone. No, she'd clearly mislabeled the remote and was panic-mashing "reheat" instead of "autumn." Now the whole world was stuck in her sweaty encore tour.

Just as Slimothy sighed into his glass, something larger, winged, and wildly dramatic dive-bombed his face like it was auditioning for a soap opera titled "Days of Our Pollen."

"What's a slug gotta do to get a little peace?" he thought, flailing so violently he almost turned the wine into a one-slug fountain.

At least his allergies were better. Probably because he hadn't touched dirt in ages. Still, he missed summer already, even though currently she—stubborn thing—refused to leave the party.

"Go home, Summer. You're sticky, overconfident, and your entourage can't handle open beverages."

Slimothy was restless. Not just from the humidity thick enough to butter toast, but from the looming date on his calendar. Tomorrow was the zoning meeting.

He shuddered. The words alone carried the dramatic heft of a root canal performed by committee. What would become of his beloved Bright Wild? More rules? Fewer cabbages? A total ban on ornamental puddles? Anything felt possible, and none of it good.

He was starting to feel like the main character in one of those tragic garden dramas where "progress" bulldozes everything wholesome and leafy, forcing the locals to relocate "far, far away."

The only problem was, the only place Slimothy could go that counted as far away involved crossing into the forest. Which was about as appealing as a salt bath during allergy season. Between the thorns, frogs, and suspiciously judgmental mushrooms, he decided that, for now, staying put and catastrophizing locally would do just fine.

He wondered if he'd get any sleep tonight either. Probably not. Between the humidity, the politics, and the faint hum of gnat ghosts circling his wine, peace and quiet had officially gone extinct.

He sighed, drained the glass, and stared out across the pond, his tiny kingdom blurred into a soft, gold haze. Tomorrow, the zoning board. Tonight, one last toast to the chaos.

CHAPTER SIXTY-FOUR

Bright Wild Zoning Proposal #42B: Sanctuary Request (Urgent)

Slimothy surfaced from the kind of sleep where you don't immediately know where you are upon waking. Drool on the pillow, eyelids glued shut, and a neck that had apparently signed a separate lease during the night. His dreams? Gone. Vanished. Probably in witness protection.

Did he feel refreshed? Not really. Rested? Maybe a little. Ready to conquer the zoning meeting? Absolutely not.

First thing on the agenda: coffee.

He took one tentative sip, shuddered, and muttered, "Perfect."

It wasn't. Not even close. Pretending it was felt safer than admitting he'd need something stronger, like courage, or maybe fertilizer.

Today was going to require fortitude, questionable decision-making, and possibly divine intervention. Fortunately, he had at least two of the three on standby.

Slimothy stared at the zoning map like it was a crime scene photo. West? No one went west. Not since the Great Compost Spill of '19. That way lay chaos, drainage issues, and an alarming number of squirrels—feral, wide-eyed things with the energy of unpaid interns and nothing left to lose.

The room buzzed with bureaucratic words that sounded both important and personally offensive: "displacement," "sewage management," "public benefit." He felt like he was being gently bulldozed in spirit long before the real land-moving machines arrived.

Somewhere in the chaos, he'd probably said too much. Admittedly, he didn't actually know where the Bright Wild's official boundaries were. The gasps had been audible, the judgment immediate. An alarming percentage of the room now regarded him as some kind of unlicensed garden drifter, freeloading on municipal soil. A rookie mistake, and one he'd be replaying in his head right up until the bulldozers flattened both his reputation and his compost heap.

They were going to take everything he'd optimistically labeled "unusable terrain" in a direction he'd never even considered. Wider roads. Pedestrian pathways. The excavators were basically already at his door.

He wondered if it was too early in the day for a nervous breakdown, or too late to move to the pond and declare independence.

He needed to protest. Chain himself to a tree. Write his local arborist. Petition to save the Bright Wild from development—the kind that promised "green spaces" and then installed two ferns, one trash can, and a bench that burst into flames at the first hint of sunlight.

As if fate wanted to drive the point home, 14 ants bit him mid-thought, each one a tiny, vengeful punctuation mark on his misery. By the time the last bite landed, his sanity levels had reached critical moss. He needed a plan. Something dramatic. Something televised. Something that would make future generations of slugs whisper, *"That's the one who tried,"* and then, inevitably, add, *"... and immediately regretted it."*

His Director of Slug Sanity had been maddeningly calm about it all. *"It's almost the weekend,"* she'd said, in the same tone one might use to announce a royal birth or the discovery of indoor plumbing. *"My SunPatiens just bloomed,"* she added, like someone casually dropping world peace into conversation.

He wasn't sure what SunPatiens were, but they sounded like something recovering from too much optimism. Still, she had a point. If her flowers could bloom through chaos, heat exhaustion, and the mental gymnastics of living next to a wind chime, maybe he could too.

The question remained: what next? A survey? A settlement? A new easement? More shrubs? Maybe a hedge to hide the impending horror of progress. What would become of his wildflower patch, his beloved cut-and-come-again salad bar, the crown jewel of moderately edible chaos?

His DOSS swore she'd chain herself beside him in solidarity (which was heartening), but he needed something bigger. Bolder. Slimier. Something that would leave a mark, preferably one that wasn't just from ant bites.

That's when inspiration struck: sanctuary status. *The Bright Wild Wildlife Refuge—a haven for endangered species, misunderstood invertebrates, and overly dramatic roses.* The list of qualifications was endless, and he, heroically, fulfilled them all.

He knew exactly how the headlines would read: *"Local Slug Chains Self to Shrub in Heroic Act of Mild Resistance." "Tiny Protest, Big Feelings,"* and *"Experts Confirm: Slime Not Crime."*

It was perfect. Noble. Slightly damp. Perhaps, at last, his moment had come, preferably before the metal beasts did.

He spun up a guided-tour fantasy with whispered commentary: *"Here we see Slimothy, the last known slug of questionable stability, spotted near the compost heap doing paperwork."* There would be plaques for the late-blooming butterfly, the overachieving moss, and the rose currently in therapy. Maybe even a gift shop—assuming anyone was brave enough to manage inventory in a humidity zone.

Yes, this could work. Bureaucracy might have maps and permits, but he had vision, and a clipboard, assuming he hadn't accidentally composted it.

He sat a little taller—or as tall as a slug reasonably could. The future of the Bright Wild was uncertain, but for the first time all day, he felt something dangerously close to hope.

If the world wanted paperwork, he'd give them paperwork. Forms. Declarations. Possibly a mission statement with tasteful clip art.

After all, revolutions didn't always start with fireworks. Sometimes they started with a slug, a dream, and a slightly sticky to-do list.

CHAPTER SIXTY-FIVE

Love (and Other Pond Complications)

O ut of the corner of his eye, Slimothy spotted it: a suspiciously wet patch glistening on the flagstone beside the faerie statue in her perpetually damp wedding dress. For a moment, he assumed it was just Roger's latest plumbing disaster.

Then it blinked.

Something extraordinary had infiltrated the Bright Wild's fragile ecosystem—a new frog, glossy, improbable, and looking suspiciously like it had been delivered by enchanted overnight courier.

Was she a visitor? A prophecy? Roger's next romantic cliffhanger? His theories multiplied like panicked tadpoles—maybe the faeries summoned her, maybe she was a mirage with elite posture, maybe even a rogue deity in frog form.

The air sparkled with magic, scandal, and swamp-tinted humidity. Absolutely anything felt possible—and all of it felt deliciously dramatic.

Either way, he was beside himself with excitement—buzzing, pacing, already drafting the press release: "Local Frog Sparks Diplomatic Incident," and "Love

(Possibly) Comes to the Pond," plus a limited-edition commemorative sticker for good measure.

To his delight, the new terrestrial creature hadn't required a single one of Slimothy's painstakingly drafted easement plans for pond access. Not one ramp, bridge, or moss-covered walkway consulted. Just one giant, reckless hop from the top straight to the ground. It was both insulting and impressive, proof perhaps that some species thrived on chaos while others, like Slimothy, preferred a well-documented detour.

After the week he'd endured, he needed a win, and naming the newcomer absolutely qualified. Nora—practical with dramatic leanings? Beatrice—advice-heavy, pearl-obsessed? Or maybe not a she. Maybe a Kevin—bold, unhinged, and seconds away from starting a beetle turf dispute. June had quiet authority. Flora sounded like the kind of frog who composed lyrical odes to her own reflection.

Slimothy lit from within. Whoever this frog was, they were living proof the pond was waking up—his dream finally gaining legs (literally).

The new frog was strikingly good-looking, in that glossy, freshly-hopped-into-town sort of fashion—like an express delivery he'd already opened, admired, and pretended to be surprised by.

Slimothy immediately began sketching out a celebration worthy of legend—the sort that made butterflies sigh and rearrange their plans. There would be gentle fanfare, leaf garlands, maybe even synchronized fireflies if pollen could be negotiated. A warm "Welcome to the Pond" gathering with all the trimmings: a leaf-raft parade, a sprinkle of firefly glow, Roger offering a heartfelt speech, and refreshments curated by Slimothy himself. Dewdrop cocktails, compost bites, and his newest invention: a signature drink called The Muddled Lily.

He'd need decorations too, of course. Streamers made of pondweed, lily-pad confetti, and maybe a banner that read, "Congratulations on Being Ambiguously Important!" Classy, inclusive, and just vague enough to suit any occasion—from hello to heartbreak.

Yes, this was exactly the kind of event the Bright Wild needed: a distraction wrapped in chaos with a side of moral purpose. "Local Slug Hosts Gala, Accidentally Invents Festival." After all, it wasn't every day you got to celebrate the arrival of potential romance, questionable gossip, and one extremely photogenic amphibian.

Whatever the occasion truly was—arrival, romance, or an unregulated public-relations experiment—one thing was certain: the Bright Wild was alive, thriving, and Slimothy was going to make absolutely sure everyone knew it. Preferably with music, snacks, and at least one regrettable speech.

By the time he'd perfected the menu, re-engineered the guest list, and forced the fireflies to undergo high-stakes glow tests, Slimothy had arrived at the only conclusion with enough dramatic heft: the newcomer had to be a love interest. Anything less felt tragically unmarketable. The pond needed a love story—mysterious, alluring, and supported by a tasteful line of limited-edition tote bags.

He weighed names as though selecting titles for royalty, eventually landing on Lilibet—a soft, regal nickname once bestowed on Queen Elizabeth II when her own family couldn't manage the full version. It fit the frog beautifully: elegant, slightly bewildered, and exactly the sort of amphibian Roger would become smitten with in under eight seconds.

Better still, it gave Slimothy a new purpose. The Bright Wild ought to be a sanctuary for amphibian love. If zoning laws couldn't protect romance, what good were they? Surely a clause existed about safeguarding therapeutically important ecosystems. If not, Slimothy would simply draft one himself.

CHAPTER SIXTY-SIX

The Beret Offensive

There were only 40 to 58 days left until the first frost—and even less time than that before the appraisers arrived. Stakes weren't just *going* to be planted, they *were* being planted. Slimothy could feel it in the soil, in the tension humming through every root and rock. Borders were shifting, and the phrase "pending appraisal" hung over the Bright Wild like an ominous cloud with a checklist. Something was coming, and for once it wasn't compost tea.

If the frost didn't reach them first, the appraisers would. Slimothy needed a plan. He needed to protect Roger and Lilibet. This was war.

Operation: "Itch and Run" (Top Secret)
Phase one: release the gnats.
Phase two: release the ants.

A two-pronged assault guaranteed to get under the skin—literally and metaphysically. It wasn't elegant warfare, but it was effective. The gnats would target morale, deploying high-frequency irritation and airborne confusion tactics. The ants would manage logistics, specializing in infiltration, petty sabotage, and maximum distraction with optional histamine reactions. Together, they were nature's answer to bureaucracy—itchy, unstoppable, and impossible to reason with.

That wasn't enough. Annoyance alone couldn't win a war—at least not one with appraisers involved. He needed to strike while the iron was hot (or at least before it rusted again).

First on the list: establish some structure. Even rebellions required it. So, like any self-respecting revolutionary slug, Slimothy began outlining his master plan.

Step one: petitions.

The cornerstone of any respectable uprising. The more signatures, the better. Public support was everything, even if a suspicious number of the signatures came from worms who couldn't technically read and one from a very enthusiastic beetle who signed in mulch. Optics mattered. So did the illusion of democracy. It was, admittedly, a one-slug campaign, but Slimothy had range.

Step two: remove any suspicious stakes that might mark property boundaries.

A preemptive strike, really. If no one could find the lines, no one could cross them. He called it strategic landscaping. Others might call it tampering with evidence. Either way, it looked great on paper.

Step three: figure out what a property boundary actually was.

Minor detail. Tactical ignorance had its perks—it made deniability not just possible, but downright convincing. Besides, how could one trespass on land they didn't technically understand?

Step four: drink some French red.

Every revolution needed morale boosters, and his came in a repurposed bottle cap labeled Pinot Noir, probably. He wasn't sure what made it French—maybe the attitude—yet it proved effective. *Vive la révolution!*

Step five: buy a beret for undercover work.

Style and stealth could coexist, and Slimothy intended to prove it. After all, nothing said "don't mind me, just a regular citizen" quite like a slug in a beret.

Step six: infiltrate the enemy camp.

Subtlety would be key, or at least that was the goal. His plan involved a carefully timed nighttime approach, a makeshift disguise made of mulch, and an emergency ration of cucumber slices in case diplomacy failed. Snacks, after all, were the backbone of any successful mission. If he couldn't outwit them, he'd simply out-snack them.

Step seven: find out what female frogs ate and order it in bulk.

This was, of course, entirely for Roger's new love interest. Morale extended to allies too—especially beautiful amphibians with good posture. Was it flies? Crickets? Some kind of trendy pond-to-table diet? Whatever it was, he'd buy enough to qualify for wholesale pricing. A well-fed Lilibet was a happy Lilibet, and a happy Lilibet meant Roger stayed loyal to the cause.

Slimothy's list was shaping up nicely. Revolutionary, even. All he needed now was a slogan, a dramatic speech, and maybe a flag made of damp lettuce. Something that said, *"Justice, unity, and please don't bulldoze my salad bar."*

The mental movie started immediately: the crowd (mostly insects) roaring in approval, Roger wiping away a proud tear, and Lilibet posing heroically atop a lily pad as the Bright Wild anthem played on a leaf flute someone had definitely made five minutes ago. Yes, this was history in the making—slimy, slightly ridiculous nonsense of great importance, but legendary nonetheless.

Let them come.

The appraisers, the developers, the clipboard brigade—he was ready. The Bright Wild would not go quietly. Not while there was slime in his trail, Pinot in his system, and just enough chaos in his heart to call it strategy.

They could take his land, his dignity, even his compost heap, but they'd never take his snacks. If they did manage to find him, good luck. The beret made him practically invisible. Very French. Very mysterious. Possibly wanted in three gardens.

CHAPTER SIXTY-SEVEN

The Amphibian Affair

L ilibet was back.

Slimothy had only seen her once before, the night prior—a fleeting, moonlit vision gliding across the gravel like a fever dream in grey and brown. She'd vanished almost instantly, leaving behind nothing but the shimmer of spots, the faint scent of mystery, and a general feeling that taxes were due.

Now she'd returned, radiant and real, and Slimothy—ever the self-appointed scholar of chaos—was ready. Form-adjacent documentation in hand, notes compiled, heart doing Jazzercise. Whatever this was, it was science. Or destiny. Or possibly indigestion.

He'd spent the entire day researching, consulting the Bright Wild Archives and several highly unreliable garden blogs. The results were astonishing. Lilibet was a Southern leopard frog, *Lithobates sphenocephalus* to those who liked their gossip Latin. Slimothy read it aloud a few times, rolling the syllables like fine compost. It sounded almost royal—*Lithobates* ... Lilibet. Close enough to confirm what he already knew: destiny had a sense of humor.

She was native to the southern regions and apparently "common throughout the southeastern United States." *Common!* As if anyone who looked like that could be common.

Grey or light brown—the classic shade of "approach with caution"—her sides were patterned with dark, designer-camouflage spots, and a golden stripe raced down her back like it had somewhere important to be, somewhere between high fashion and hazard signage. Her eyes, wide and unblinking, offered nearly 360 degrees of judgment, capable of spotting predators, rivals, and any nearby slugs who didn't know when to look away.

The real revelation came moments later under "diet." She was an invertivore—*an eater of insects, spiders, worms,* and, Slimothy's breath caught, *slugs.*

He reread the line three times, hoping it would change. It didn't. It just sat there on the page, bold and unrepentant, like a menu with his name on it.

He blinked again in disbelief, rapidly and without improvement, as if repetition might soften it. Carnivorous. Elegant. Merciless. Roger's supposed sweetheart wasn't just a frog; she was a glamorous apex predator with the vibe of a Bond villain and a mating call like a balloon losing a slow argument with gravity.

He looked up from his notes, equal parts terrified and impressed. Lilibet wasn't just back—she was a force of nature. Nocturnal, strategic, beautifully spotted, and absolutely lethal. The kind of creature that made you question the food chain and your place on it.

He wrote carefully in his notebook:

Avoid eye contact. Compliment her from a safe distance. Under no circumstances volunteer as bait.

Then, after a pause, added another line:

Still ... impeccable posture. Uncomfortably charismatic.

Her arrival was almost imperceptible, the way most of Slimothy's memorable disasters tended to be—no fanfare, no warning, just a flicker of movement at the corner of his eye. A ripple where there shouldn't have been one. That was how it began. The moment the Bright Wild changed forever, and Slimothy's peace (and possibly food-chain position) took a sharp turn for the worse.

She liked the water, living predominantly in or around it—a true aquatic sophisticate. Slimothy was ecstatic; his pond dreams had worked. After exactly 33 days of strategic muck rearranging, algae negotiations, and passionately worded zoning memos, his grand vision had paid off.

Though where was she hopping off to on her mysterious dusk dry-land rendezvous? Last night and again today—no sign of Roger anywhere. It was suspicious. According to Slimothy's research, Southern leopard frogs preferred to mate in water, which made her land excursions highly irregular. Unless, of course, there was a hidden fjord or waterfall somewhere in the Bright Wild—a secret romantic getaway tucked behind the compost bins. Or did Roger owe back child support? The possibilities were endless and equally scandalous. Slimothy made a note to investigate immediately, for science. Not because he was curious, of course, but because someone had to update the Bright Wild topographical records. It was, after all, simply good civic duty.

Slimothy closed his notebook with the satisfaction of someone who believed, against all odds, that he was in control of the situation. The pond glimmered quietly behind him, suspiciously peaceful once more. Somewhere out there, Lilibet was probably plotting dinner or destiny. Either way, he decided, tomorrow he'd bring binoculars. Possibly a helmet, too.

CHAPTER SIXTY-EIGHT

Slimothy, Esq. (Pending Bar Approval)

The property lawyers were no good. They'd informed Slimothy that there were only two firms in town, both proudly serving the city—and by "serving," they meant ignoring everyone else. You couldn't get them to answer a phone, email, or carrier pigeon; even smoke signals went unacknowledged. Slimothy had tried it all. Disheartened didn't quite cover it. He was teetering somewhere between mild despair and the urge to start his own law firm out of spite.

What were his options? Put spike strips on the road? Pull out all the flags? Sabotage the concrete? Push the light pole over for dramatic effect? All excellent ideas—tragically incompatible with being the approximate size of a dinner roll and possessing neither bones nor upper-body strength. He sighed and accepted the only plan he could reasonably execute: the ancient art of hurry up and wait.

Ever the entrepreneur, Slimothy began to wonder if this looming disaster could at least turn a profit. Maybe he could start charging admission to the garden—*See it before it's paved!*—or sell tickets for *authentic pre-construction experiences*. Maybe, just maybe, he could finally commission that long-overdue statue of himself right in the middle of the new driveway. A permanent Slimothy landmark, gazed upon reverently by sweaty joggers and confused mail carriers alike. His legacy, preserved in something tasteful, slightly shiny, and impossible to ignore.

Sabotage still had its charm. There was something satisfying about the mental image of chaos in a reflective vest. Deep down though, Slimothy knew he wouldn't last a day in jail. He needed the wide sky, his salad patch, and the freedom to dramatically sigh whenever inspiration struck. Confinement, structure, and schedules weren't for him. He'd wither faster than unwatered lettuce.

He forced himself back onto the positivity bandwagon, mostly because despair was terrible for his slime quality. Fewer square feet meant less mowing, less weeding, and far fewer zoning-induced panic attacks. Maybe this was the universe's way of giving him a break. A smaller plot. A simpler life. A walled-off secret garden actually started to sound rather lovely.

Slimothy oscillated between bursts of optimism and soul-shattering stress—a metaphorical seesaw powered by caffeine and bad ideas. Maybe it was time to visit that silent monastery, preferably one with good snacks and no paperwork. Or perhaps the real answer was obvious: become a lawyer and litigate his own chaos. How hard could it be? Lots of talking, some pointing, and the occasional dramatic, *"Your Honor, I object!"* He added "attend law school" to his ever-expanding Jar of Questionable Intentions, right between "build your own irrigation system," and "invest in decorative snails."

Slimothy, Esq. had a ring to it. Authority. Gravitas. Possibly even its own letterhead. Maybe the real battle was just having intimidating stationery—thick, embossed, and smelling faintly of victory, or at least mildew. A small, damp stack of business cards had been drafted in the privacy of his imagination: elegant serif font, tasteful slime-trail border, and maybe a tiny disclaimer at the bottom—*Not licensed anywhere, technically.*

He still had the card from the man who'd laughed at him for not having a property survey. A small, glossy rectangle of smugness. It had once oozed importance; now it reeked mostly of pond scum. Slimothy had used it to scrape gull excrement off the rocks, a task it performed admirably. In fairness, the man would've made a phenomenal sleazy lawyer. He already had the qualifications:

the tan of someone allergic to honesty, a handshake that felt like a contract you didn't remember signing, and a voice that made "market value" sound like a threat.

If Slimothy's allergies could handle it, maybe he could turn the front yard into a certified pollinator refuge. Butterflies, bees, perhaps even a motivational beetle or two. Surely the city wouldn't dare bulldoze that. Who in their right mind would want to be known as the villain who paved paradise and murdered the Monarchs? He made a note to look into it tomorrow, right after "figure out what zoning actually means."

Who was even paying for all this nonsense? He'd overheard something about "SPLOST," which sounded less like a funding source and more like something you'd need an ointment for, and made another note: "unravel the mystery of how to vote it down—or at least stall it creatively." 84 ant bites made the whole ordeal even more aggravating; it was hard to focus on civic sabotage when his entire underside felt like it was sizzling on a skillet.

Ideas began percolating—slow, slightly unhinged, and just dangerous enough to be satisfying. Startle-activated noise boxes. Dramatic surprise tactics. Maybe even a wicked-witch setup with a suspiciously well-timed oven, because nothing says private property like the faint smell of gingerbread and terror. Yes, that would teach them.

Alternatively, a motion-activated sprinkler system had real promise. Equal parts deterrent and entertainment. The solution was simple: funnel it directly into the sewage line they were so desperate to tear up—poetic justice with plumbing.

Maybe, for good measure, he could employ a team of porcupines for perimeter defense. The thought calmed him. Now only 83 bites itched, and one of them almost felt like satisfaction.

A deliciously petty idea slithered into his mind, bringing with it the face of that conceited survey man—Randall, the human embodiment of a parking ticket. *You love concrete, don't you, Randall? Probably whisper sweet nothings to fresh pavement, too.* Slimothy's eye stalks narrowed. *Let's see how you like a concrete apron, you overcaffeinated traffic cone.*

Revenge, he decided, didn't need to be fast—just properly cured.

CHAPTER SIXTY-NINE

The Drawer of Infinite Possibility

There was a drawer in the potting bench that Slimothy had never opened. He toyed with the notion that it might hold all the mysteries of the universe—or none at all. Perhaps a single spare screw, the one its previous owner had searched for in vain. Over time, Slimothy had decided the drawer wasn't meant to be opened at all. It was a sacred artifact. A structural cornerstone. A shrine to procrastination and curiosity. A relic best admired from afar for its quiet, locked-up wisdom. Slimothy, ever the romantic, loved a good mystery almost as much as he loved pretending he'd get around to solving one.

His affection for the potting bench grew daily. He watched it like a secret admirer—longing glances, wistful sighs, and the occasional internal sonnet. He missed the summer days when he'd loiter there constantly, rearranging pots, giving motivational speeches to seedlings, and pretending to understand soil pH. Now, wrapped in layers of scarves and questionable fashion choices from the Bright Wild Winter Collection, he contemplated how best to insulate his 267 potted treasures before the frost came. There would be tears shed by spring, he knew—but also triumph, resilience, and new life bursting forth. He just had to survive 154 more days and approximately 300 mental breakdowns in the meantime.

Then—the backyard bash of the century.

The Bright Wild's first birthday.

Slimothy could hardly believe it—one whole year of questionable gardening decisions, character development, and mild pest infestations. A miracle, really. Or a warning.

So much life had unfolded in so little time. He thought about his first great loss: the glorious, fiery Mrs. Bradshaw Geum, taken too soon. Overwatering, they said. Really—how could something that loves rain hate commitment?

Then came lavender—predictably dramatic, of course. Always the actress, Slimothy could still hear her fainting sighs, the whispered, *"Tell my seedlings I love them,"* as she withered into compostable tragedy.

Most recently, the phlox twins. Reliable. Dependable. Until they weren't. They'd left him only a cryptic note: *"It's not you, it's the drainage."* He'd tried to be strong about it, but every time it rained, he felt personally attacked.

The pepper plants were thriving. Of course they were. Give them a bit of adversity—say, run a concrete obstruction over everything but the roots and bend them into avant-garde shapes—and instead of dying, they throw a festival.

He stared at them in disbelief. *Oh, sure, must be nice to photosynthesize under pressure. Some of us crumble under lichen-level anxiety.*

Even Spaulding, the original pineapple—long exiled to the forgotten corner where plants went to reflect on their failures—had somehow sprouted an entirely new set of shoots in the middle of his already plucked crown.

Slimothy blinked at it. Reincarnation? Desperation? Mid-life crisis? Whatever it was, he respected the audacity.

Maybe that was the secret—pretend you're thriving until it confuses everyone into believing it.

He wondered if he could do that. A little self-propagation. Therapeutic cuttings, he thought. Take a snip of optimism here, a clipping of patience there, root them in denial, and see what happens.

The idea had merit. Therapeutic horticulture, he'd call it. A personal growth experiment disguised as gardening. Worst-case scenario, he'd end up with another plant; best case, inner peace ... and maybe a biodegradable pot.

Slimothy's brain, ever the opportunist, shifted gears. Therapeutic horticulture was one thing, but profitable growing? That had potential.

He could be a fill-in farmer for troubled plants—or even a rehabilitative botanical life coach. People could drop off their struggling fruits and vegetables, and he'd nurse them back to health like a plant whisperer with trust issues. Or, if that failed, he'd swap in a new one and swear it just *"had a growth spurt."* Customer satisfaction guaranteed, ethics negotiable.

This could work. Probably.

Suddenly it had a name—The Bright Wild Nursery. A thriving enterprise built on empathy, compost, and mild delusion. Maybe this was how empires began— one slightly suspicious zucchini at a time. Finally, a reason to wear his *World's Okayest Gardener* sash with conviction.

Slimothy sat back, quite pleased with himself. The Bright Wild was growing with suspicious enthusiasm—mostly—and for once he wasn't just keeping things alive; he was building something. Progress, purpose, and a legacy of questionable morals paired with excellent branding.

There were still 153 days until the Bright Wild's first birthday, but he was already planning. The theme, the guest list, the tearful speeches. Maybe even matching party hats for the succulents. Nothing said "celebration" like coordinated foliage and mild panic that had absolutely no respect for the calendar.

CHAPTER SEVENTY

The Jersey Wall Project

A fine day had finally arrived. Slimothy had hosed out every birdbath, bathtub, and suspiciously repurposed decorative basin in the Bright Wild. By midmorning, every mosquito within three feet had either evacuated, filed a complaint, or waved a tiny white flag made of despair.

Feeling productive, he turned his attention to the pond—a noble but doomed endeavor. He tried to stir up the algae, give it a run for its money, but the old water dug in its heels. It sloshed around like a guest who'd unpacked, claimed a side of the fridge, and started referring to the pond as *our place.*

After several failed attempts and one near-death experience with the hose, Slimothy decided he'd done enough for one day—or at least enough to file under "character building."

Then came the real excitement: new plants. Some collards—steady, dependable, the beige slacks of the vegetable world—and something far more thrilling, a weird-colored kale he'd never seen nor tried before. Jersey kale, to be exact. Also known as walking stick kale, tall jacks, or cow cabbage. It sounded less like a vegetable and more like a 19th-century pub band that only played songs about crop rotation.

Apparently, its stems were so tough and tall that humans used to dry and varnish them into walking sticks, fence posts, and even small roof rafters. Because naturally, when life gives you salad greens, you build architecture.

It could grow up to 12 feet tall—20 under optimal conditions—which Slimothy assumed meant supervised by the city planning department. He wasn't entirely sure how to eat something that could technically apply for its own mailing address.

Then there was the bit about sheep. Supposedly, those that ate Jersey kale grew silky wool coats up to 25 inches long. Slimothy had no immediate plans for livestock, but the mental image of himself draped in kale-powered luxury—glowing, glamorous, possibly flammable—was almost enough to justify the purchase. Almost.

He stared at the seedling tray, wondering where on earth he was going to put these monolithic greens. Maybe next to the lemon tree? Or better yet, let them form a privacy hedge to hide the evidence of his previous gardening experiments.

Or perhaps a fence for the proposed bike path—something so absurdly tall it would spook joggers, require aviation lights, and make Jersey proud.

Yes. That was it. Visionary urban planning—powered entirely by kale.

CHAPTER SEVENTY-ONE

The Wedding of the Century (Pending Confirmation)

Slimothy worried he may have thrown the pond's delicate equilibrium into chaos—and possibly sabotaged an interspecies love story—during the morning's overly ambitious hose work. What if Lilibet had babies in there? Did he need to get Roger a bigger house? Could the two of them even cohabitate? Lilibet was technically an aquatic frog, and Roger was emphatically not. How did that even work in the amphibian world? Was there a zoning variance for that?

Technically, he had never actually seen them together, but that felt like a minor detail. In his mind, theirs was an epic romance, a pondside union destined to culminate in the wedding of the century. There would be mosquito choirs, algae garlands, and lavender glaring from the back row, clutching a gift receipt.

It was a nice thought—love blooming in unlikely places. Though in Slimothy's experience, most things in the garden only thrived when mildly threatened. Perfect, when he came to think of it, since he may have just vacuumed an uncomfortably large section of their honeymoon suite out of the water earlier.

Still, he reasoned, things in the garden tended to do better with a little stress. Make it too easy and they got complacent. The ones that weathered near-death experiences and passive-aggressive watering schedules were the ones that flourished. Threaten rehoming, and suddenly everyone was photosynthesizing like it was the Garden Olympics. He wasn't saying fear was a fertilizer, but the results spoke for themselves.

Maybe that was what Roger and Lilibet needed to make it official—some daring encounter to bond over. A little shared peril. Perhaps he'd rescue her from a falling leaf, or she'd mistake him for a noble savior after he heroically retrieved a mosquito. Or maybe Roger just needed to catch a snack midair in a suave, slow-motion way—something cinematic enough to spark true amphibian passion.

Slimothy made a mental note to leave extra gnats out. He was practically running a matchmaking service at this point. If things went well, he might even print pamphlets: "How to Find Love and Lose Excess Algae—Lessons from the Bright Wild."

Of course, there was always the chance he was meddling in forces far beyond his pay grade and powers he didn't fully understand. Nature operated on a delicate balance, and Slimothy's version of helping tended to result in ecosystem-wide identity crises. His track record of "minor improvements" usually ended with something taking over a small biome—often through invasive species or mild flooding.

This was different. Slimothy could feel it in his lack of bone structure, in the majestic slosh of his internal water reservoir. He was practically one of them: honorary frog, part-time pond consultant, full-time nuisance. Naturally, that made him both guest of honor and emcee at the wedding.

As emcee, he had certain responsibilities—serious ones. The kind that required poise, professionalism, and, thankfully, his ever-present clipboard. No major life event in the Bright Wild had ever been executed without it.

He'd need to curate the guest list, of course. Roger's side of the pond was notorious for showing up uninvited and bringing questionable snacks. He suspected Lilibet's family had high standards—maybe even four-legged connections. He'd seen two cats the day before, gliding through the Bright Wild with the quiet confidence of landlords collecting rent in fish. Fitting, really, considering she was a leopard frog.

Music would be crucial. Something timeless yet appropriately sentimental—tender enough for tears, but waterproof just in case. Maybe a cricket ensemble for rhythm, a bullfrog solo for drama, and a tasteful splash or two for ambiance.

Seating was another matter entirely. Lily pads were the obvious choice, but he'd need the wide, non-sinking variety—preferably the ones that didn't panic under pressure. He envisioned the seating chart: frogs up front, insects in the back (for safety reasons), and Roger somewhere in the middle, pretending not to sweat through his vows. A few dramatic dunkings were inevitable, but honestly, it would add to the aquatic charm.

Then there were the speeches. He'd been workshopping lines in his head for days. *"Love, like algae, thrives under pressure"* was a timeless classic, but *"May your union be as stable as a properly chlorinated ecosystem"* had undeniable flair. He'd probably cry midway through. It would be powerful. Historic, even. The kind of speech that made tadpoles believe in romance.

A certainty pooled in his slime. The ceremony, the emotions, the inevitable standing ovation—it was all coming together. Finally, recognition for a lifetime of unsolicited project management. Everything began unfolding in slow motion—vows echoing across the pond, sunlight behaving like special effects, Roger looking heroically damp. It was going to be his "Titanic"—but with more frogs and less sinking.

There was only one small problem. He had absolutely no idea when the wedding was—or if the happy couple had even met yet. Minor details. Every great event needed a visionary, and he was already mentally typesetting the programs in triumph.

CHAPTER SEVENTY-TWO

The Curious Case of Lilibet

Lilibet hopped her way toward the pond, gracefully navigating the formation of slate staircases that Slimothy had painstakingly arranged. Frogs, he'd observed, were hopelessly by-the-book creatures when it came to stepping stones. Precision leapers. Very rule-oriented.

Though at the last second, she turned and diverted south. A plot twist. Was she secretly planning a rendezvous with Roger all along? Or were the step arrangements not up to code? Perhaps she simply wanted to investigate the latest Bright Wild décor—a limited-edition mushroom-encased "Alice in Wonderland" sculpture, open to a page about … well, he couldn't quite remember. Something deeply profound about tea and tumbling through metaphorical rabbit holes, probably.

Slimothy stayed motionless. He didn't dare move, didn't dare blink. What if this was the moment—the grand, cinematic first encounter of Roger's love story? He couldn't risk ruining it with his usual sniffly presence, which tended to be described as energetically inconvenient.

Still, he worried. What if he'd miscalculated the pond access scale? Were the stairs too steep? The south side was a long way from the water, and any frog that vanished over there had made a deliberate choice to go. There was

nothing over there except a forgotten patch of dill that had long since gone
to seed and a broken concrete mushroom dropped mid-unboxing, now living
permanently in its unfinished era. Unless, of course, one counted the citronella
plant—undecided on the whole life thing but fully committed to being dramatic.
Slimothy suspected it was related to the lavender. The constant bickering
between the two could power a soap opera.

Maddeningly, Lilibet had turned again, now determined to reach the pond
after all. She perched herself on a piece of driftwood, eyeing the next level with
military precision.

Then, once more, she retreated—back toward Lewis Carroll and the teacup crowd. Maybe she didn't want Roger. Maybe she just had a thing for
mushrooms and slightly unhinged literature.

Slimothy watched her go, his hopes sagging slightly—metaphorically, though
given his anatomy, there was some literal sagging involved too.

Maybe she was playing hard to get. That seemed plausible. Or maybe it was a
test, one of those elaborate courting rituals nature documentaries were always
talking about. He really should have been filming this. The footage alone could
fund a new birdbath.

Still, something nagged at him—like a thought he'd misplaced behind
a flowerpot. Maybe this was part of a 12-part ritual involving patience,
observation, and absolutely no sudden movements. He was already failing step
three.

Slimothy adjusted slightly, pretending to look casual—an impossible feat when
one's entire body operated like a sentient stress ball. What if she wasn't playing
hard to get? What if this was a territorial inspection? Or worse, a Yelp review?
He suddenly felt self-conscious about the pond's murk level. He should have
skimmed again. Or added more duckweed. Or maybe he should've gone with
water lilies—the universally adored celebrities of floating plants. They practically
advertised romance and low-maintenance upkeep.

He made mental notes for next time. If there was a next time. Assuming
Lilibet didn't rate the pond three stars and hop off to a more exclusive wetland.

He'd always known the Bright Wild had its critics, but it stung to think one
of them might be amphibious. Maybe she was judging the layout—too many
ferns, not enough shade. Or maybe she was one of those frogs who preferred

minimalist landscapes. The kind who said things like *"less is more"* while sitting on a log that looked like it came with a mortgage.

He glanced toward the far edge of the pond. Maybe he should've added signage—something simple, like *"Welcome Future Newlyweds."* No, too forward. *"Open for Courtship,"* maybe? Still too desperate.

He sighed. Romance was complicated. Especially when you weren't in it but somehow running logistics for it.

CHAPTER SEVENTY-THREE

Unscheduled Plot Development

Slimothy had had a lovely day. He'd treated himself to a stone massage—premium pebble selection—and a bit of pampering, followed by some light cultural enrichment at the Bright Wild Ballet Company. The troupe, composed entirely of leggy society garlic and blue fescue, was performing "Cinderella." Or at least something inspired by it. The plot was a little unclear, mostly because he'd arrived late after mediating a heated dispute between the foxtail ferns and the perpetually offended lavender.

The performance was elegant, if slightly itchy. Lots of twirling, rustling, and interpretive wilting. Slimothy gave an approving wiggle. He appreciated the arts, even when they were photosynthetic.

As the curtain of dusk fell, the forest began to hum with activity. Crickets tuning up, leaves gossiping, something large and unseen stomping in the distance. There were a lot of noises afoot in the Bright Wild that night—none of which sounded like they came with a glass slipper, a prince, or a princess.

Slimothy listened carefully. The rustling was getting louder—dramatic, even. Perhaps the royal entourage had arrived early. It wouldn't be the first time someone got lost trying to find the Bright Wild; his signage situation was, admittedly, a work in progress.

He straightened up, trying to look presentable, though there was only so much one could do without bones or formalwear. Maybe this was it—the grand finale, the royal ball, the afterparty for the "Cinderella" cast. He glanced toward the pond, expecting a pumpkin carriage to roll up or at least a frog in a tuxedo.

Instead, something small and suspicious darted across the mulch, followed by a sound that could only be described as crunchy chaos. Definitely not regal.

Not a prince, he thought. *Unless the monarchy's taken a turn.* He squinted into the shadows. Could still be a royal messenger. Or an understudy. Or ... something carnivorous.

Slimothy stayed perfectly still. No sudden movements. *If it's friendly, I'll wave. If it's not, I'll pretend to be decorative.*

Maybe it's fine, he told himself. Maybe Lilibet just hired security. Perfectly normal for a frog of her social standing.

Yes—that made sense. Pond attendants, probably. A few personal guards, perhaps even a stage manager. She had seemed theatrical. They were likely just here to guide her safely through the labyrinthine maze that he'd generously attempted to reorganize earlier in a frantic three-minute burst of urban renewal.

Yes, that had to be it. A full entourage. Possibly a production crew. Maybe even press coverage. This could be the start of something big—"The Pond Chronicles: A Tale of Love and Algae." He really should've worn something less ... slug-colored.

Slimothy tried to recall the last time he'd hosted distinguished guests. Never, technically, but how hard could it be? He'd just need to project confidence. Smile. No—impossible. Maintain good posture then. Also impossible.

All right, posture optional, he reasoned. Confidence it is. He tried to look authoritative, which mostly resulted in a slow, uncertain lean to the left. Hopefully they'd interpret that as charm.

Maybe he should offer refreshments. That was what good hosts did, right? The question was what one served to frog security. He didn't have any spare gnats on hand—he'd left them out for Roger and Lilibet's date rehearsal. Maybe some damp bark? A tasteful puddle? Too casual, he decided. Needs more oomph.

He straightened again—or tried to. His reflection in the pond wobbled back at him, equally unconvinced. *This is fine,* he thought. *They'll appreciate authenticity. Everyone loves authenticity.*

A new sound came from the shadows—heavier this time. An Unidentified Rustling (UIR, as he'd later log it). *Oh no,* he thought. *That's not press. That's plot development.*

He nervously plucked an unripe grape tomato—and stopped cold. The tang hit him first: sharp, electric, vaguely forbidden. Divine. The tomato thief had been right all along. Only then came the chill—the creeping suspicion settling where certainty used to live.

What if there wasn't a thief?

What if it had always been him—some shadow-self slipping out under the guise of moonlight and Merlot, a nocturnal produce bandit powered by chaotic instincts and digestive bravado?

What if, after one particularly spirited glass of Cabernet, he'd wandered the garden in a fugue state, declaring himself "Keeper of the Nightshade" and helping himself to whatever looked emotionally vulnerable?

He replayed the clues: the half-eaten tomatoes; the trail of slime leading nowhere; the faint basil smell on his breath every morning; the hunger window between 11:58 p.m. and 12:07 a.m.; and the sticky note reading, "Do not question the cravings," in handwriting suspiciously like his own. Each bite blurred the line further. Memory wobbled. Reality rippled.

Had he even planted these tomatoes? Or had they simply ... appeared?

Was this a harvest, or an alibi?

The Bright Wild tilted. Guilt settled on him like damp mulch.

If he'd been moonlight-munching this whole time, he'd need legal counsel.

The only thing worse than chasing a criminal was realizing you might have to interview yourself—under leaf-lamp lighting, which made everyone look guilty. The idea short-circuited his entire system, leaving him frozen like a startled garden ornament—poised, damp, and in no way emotionally prepared for whatever came next.

CHAPTER SEVENTY-FOUR

"Don't Stop Beleafing"

Slimothy decided today was the day to pluck a piece of paper from the Jar of Questionable Intentions. He wasn't sure why—only that the air had that "do something" feeling again, the kind that usually started with optimism and ended with mild chaos. The big ideas kind.

The jar sat beside the potting bench, dusted with pure, unearned optimism and the faint scent of mint tea. Unfortunately, it also had a lid. Slimothy, despite years of self-improvement, remained tragically handless. He leaned into it. He nudged. He even tried strategic wiggling, followed by what could only be described as a slow-motion body slam. Nothing. The jar didn't budge.

Maybe this was symbolic, he thought. A metaphor about limitations. Or laziness. Or how gravity was just plain rude.

Still, he felt creative today—charged, even. Maybe he didn't need paper. Maybe he'd channel that energy into something grander: a Bright Wild motivational song. Something to stir the mulch, inspire the seedlings, and remind everyone that even wilted things could stage a comeback.

The soundtrack was already assembling itself: a ballad for the basil, a chorus for the compost, maybe even a heartfelt bridge about overcoming mildew—if he could get through it without crying. Verse two would have to wait for personal equilibrium. He'd call it "Don't Stop Beleafing," the first and possibly only slug anthem in garden history.

Slimothy hummed softly to himself, still riding the creative high. It wasn't finished—nothing this legendary ever was—but he felt the Bright Wild needed something hopeful, something to stir even the most jaded leaf.

He dabbed a bit of dew off his notebook and decided to balance his musical genius with a touch of poetic restraint.

Petal to petal,
hope hums where the wind forgets me—
compost, be kind now.

He sat back, satisfied. It was equal parts breakup song and fertilizer prayer—truly, a masterpiece in two confused genres.

For one brief golden moment, he felt like a true artist: visionary, vulnerable, possibly misunderstood. He basked in the glow of his own brilliance for a full 45 seconds before curiosity elbowed in, demanding equal attention. Reality slithered in right after, as it always did. Inspiration never stuck around for long.

As often happened, art gave way to analytics. If art was food for the soul, surely science was dessert. Paperwork, however, always came first—because dessert never simply appeared; it had steps, structure, rules.

As luck would have it, he'd found a note tucked under a petal that morning—probably from the Assassin Bug Society again.

The assassin bug, as far as he could tell, was nature's overachiever: part hunter, part fashion statement, with legs like stilts and the resting posture of someone who charged by the hour. They skewered their prey with alarming efficiency and a downright audacious sense of confidence. Slimothy both admired and deeply distrusted them.

"Preferred dining zones: umbels, solitaries, and the occasional raceme."

Honestly, Slimothy didn't even know what a raceme was, but it sounded like something that required a permit and at least one safety briefing. He stitched together a tiny café vignette: a bug with a monocle, consulting a menu, *"Hmm, yes, I'll take the simple spike with a side of pollen, please."*

The note intrigued him—not because he cared what the assassin bugs were eating, but because it suggested they had meetings. Committees. Possibly bylaws. If there was one thing Slimothy loved more than leafy rumor-mill chatter, it was organized chaos with minutes. So naturally, he decided this warranted a field guide entry. Because science, unlike gossip, sounded respectable when written in a notebook.

Research demanded follow-through, and Slimothy, tragically, had both time and stationery to spare.

He fashioned a disguise—or what he believed passed for undercover attire. An acorn beret, a dandelion for cover, and 90% confidence that he looked like natural foliage. The remaining 10% was loudly humming the Indiana Jones theme song, ready for nonsense.

After several days of covert surveillance (and one regrettable incident involving a thistle and misplaced confidence), his findings were clear-ish—at least by the standards of the Bright Wild's Plant Naming Committee, who hadn't made a logical decision since midsummer.

Umbels topped the menu: tall, poofy, shaped like nature's own cocktail umbrellas. Solitary blooms came next—dramatic, self-important, the kind that looked like they'd post motivational quotes if given Wi-Fi. Racemes followed, tall and awkward, like floral coat racks that never quite grew into their potential. Simple spikes and heads were beneath consideration—too plain, too predictable. Compound cymes had been blacklisted for crimes against flavor, and compound racemes were the culinary equivalent of a side salad: acknowledged, but only to make the main course look better.

It was all so confusing, he'd been forced—professionally compelled, really—to make detailed field notes.

Field notes: "Assassin Bug Flower-Shape Preferences" (compiled with rigorous focus and an unnecessary amount of confusion)

Umbels: large, poofy, dramatically social—floral chandeliers for insects who enjoy a crowd. 10/10 ambiance.
Solitary blooms: tall, confident, and slightly self-important. The kind of flower that hums its own theme music.
Racemes: long and awkward, clearly still figuring themselves out.

Acceptable, but only if you're into vertical dining.
Simple spikes: thin, uptight, stingy with space. Possibly on a cleanse.
Heads: squat, round, trying too hard to be symmetrical. Not fooling
anyone.
Compound cymes: overcomplicated architecture. Tastes like regret
and paperwork.
Compound racemes: decorative at best—the garnish of the floral
world. Bugs pretend to care, but no one actually eats them.

By the end, Slimothy wasn't sure if he'd documented the eating habits of assassin bugs or accidentally written a personality profile of himself. Either way, he decided it was publishable material.

He tapped his pen against the page, thoughtful. "Even predators," he murmured, "have standards."

Then, after a moment of deep scientific reflection—or possibly boredom—he added a final note for posterity:

Conclusion: would not date an assassin bug.

He let out a contented sigh. Another groundbreaking discovery completed, peer-reviewed by absolutely no one and destined for an audience of exactly himself.

Research, as it turned out, was mostly about confidence, legible handwriting, and knowing when to stop pretending you knew what you were doing.

With a solemn nod, he closed the notebook. Science, he thought, is just drama with citations.

Somewhere in the garden, a leaf rustled. Or applauded. He chose to believe it was the latter.

With that, Slimothy resumed humming "Don't Stop Beleafing"—because in the Bright Wild, even the dirt knew a good performance when it heard one.

CHAPTER SEVENTY-FIVE

37 Days to Doom (Give or Take)

It was currently 62 degrees. Correction: 60. "Temperature falling faster than morale." 55 when he woke up, and 37 days until the unofficial official first freeze.

Slimothy checked the math twice, just to be sure it was wrong. It wasn't. He stared into the middle distance like a slug in a weather documentary. He was not ready—physically, mentally, spiritually, or in terms of available blankets—to face a season of frozen optimism.

He knew the basics: 32 degrees meant trouble, 28 meant drama. At that point, the water inside plants turned to ice, expanded, and—*poof*—instant horticultural heartbreak. The scientists called it "cell rupture." Slimothy called it rude.

A light frost was one thing—a chilly warning, a polite nibble at the edges. A killing frost though? That was personal.

This called for a meeting. With himself.

He needed a plan. A real one this time—not just panic-snuggling the kale at midnight. Kale which apparently tasted better after a frost. A cruel twist of fate if there ever was one.

First, insulation. Every respectable plant parent in the Bright Wild would soon be hauling out blankets, tarps, and the occasional repurposed bath towel.

Slimothy had none of those things, but he did have imagination, a questionable poncho, and an arguably codependent bond to a mostly depleted bag of mulch. In an emergency, the plan was simple: vibe at the cold until something gave.

It had snowed the year before—a rare Bright Wild event that happened roughly once every seven years and immediately got added to Slimothy's list of things never to repeat, right between "leaf blower season" and "Roger's karaoke phase." Statistically, it wasn't due again for a while. In protest, he still wasn't speaking to the sky about it. Everyone else had called it beautiful. Slimothy called it trauma with good lighting and sincerely hoped the sequel had been canceled.

He scribbled a final note in his weather log:

Frost defense strategy—pending bravery, available blankets, and one motivational speech.

He stared at the page for a long moment, then underlined *"bravery"* twice. It seemed easier to find blankets.

All right, he told himself. *Keep it short, sound confident, try not to cry.*

He took a deep, entirely symbolic breath—purely for effect, since respiration wasn't exactly in his skill set—and composed the speech in his head:

Stay calm. Stay covered. Nobody lick the ice.

He reread it silently, nodded to himself. Brief, inspiring, and only slightly desperate. Exactly what the situation required.

The air was crisp, the kind of sharp clarity better suited for wine than worry.

No one applauded, but no one froze to death either—so, statistically speaking, it was his most successful meeting yet.

CHAPTER SEVENTY-SIX

Bright Wild Technologies: Proudly Nonfunctional

Slimothy's Director of Slug Sanity had given him something to chew on the other day—figuratively, thankfully. She'd fandangled a system that could summon help for all sorts of civic crises: downed branches, flooded gutters, even the tragic case of a squirrel named Linda, who, according to neighborhood gossip, *"just didn't look both ways."* It was, in Slimothy's view, nothing short of modern magic. Push a button, and poof—Linda disappears, order restored, personal closure achieved.

If creatures with opposable thumbs could make squirrels vanish with a single tap, imagine what he could do. Pond assistance requests for residents who needed "gentle encouragement." Pollen alerts that triggered tissue deliveries. Feline border patrol notifications. Aphid invasion tracking. Weather warnings. Maybe even a neighborhood-watch portal to log suspicious activity—like Roger's late-night "compost inspections," which he swore were routine, but strangely, every "inspection" coincided with produce mysteriously vanishing.

If fate, Wi-Fi, and divine programming aligned, The Great Disappearing Spinach Mystery might finally get its ending. It was time.

The possibilities were endless. The user interface, however, was still entirely theoretical. Naturally, he needed more features. A good app had depth.

Maybe a slug speed tracker for fitness accountability. A mood log that correlated mental stability with rainfall. Automatic alerts whenever someone overwatered the mint again. A find my marigold function for when things went missing during storms or zoning disputes.

He scribbled faster, ideas multiplying like aphids. A built-in pollen index, soil gossip chatrooms, fern emergency hotlines, a random compliment generator for seedlings in crisis.

By the time he paused, his notepad resembled less an app plan and more the frantic scrawl of a caffeine-buzzed mollusk.

Still, he admired it. Innovation, he told himself. Chaotic, unhinged ingenuity.

Naturally, he moved straight into the Prototype Phase. Easy. How hard could app development be?

He gathered his materials: one cracked acorn shell for hardware, a leaf fragment for the screen, and a stick for his stylus, wand, and magic conductor to the cucumbers, which were still so wildly sprawled they needed constant orchestrating. Their original conductor, he suspected, had migrated south for the winter along with Slimothy's motivation. A few pebbles for aesthetics—because every good startup needed atmosphere, or at least something to trip over dramatically. Launch sequence engaged. Time to make history—or at the very least, a small mess.

Slimothy pressed a tiny dent in the acorn. Nothing. Perfect. Stable. No premature crashes. He poked the leaf. Booting system, he told himself. The only thing booting was a beetle passing by. Excellent. Beta user detected.

He dragged a pine needle across the dirt in what could only generously be described as "code." Look at that syntax, he marveled. Genius-level gibberish. Then a drop of dew landed squarely on the acorn. Ah. First bug. Classic. He watched it soak in and sighed. Every visionary faced setbacks. Edison, Newton, me. He made a note in his log:

Version 1. 0, waterproofing required. Investor confidence: low but determined.

He stared proudly at the soggy mess, a wet acorn surrounded by ambition, and nodded with quiet conviction that greatness often began damp and confused. *We're revolutionizing tech,* he thought. *Just very, very slowly.*

This was how empires started.

The Bright Wild App: still in beta, perpetually buffering. The future was calling—it just needed better Wi-Fi and fewer cucumbers.

CHAPTER SEVENTY-SEVEN

The Waiting Room Trials

S limothy's head hurt. He was in the doctor's waiting room, enduring what could only be described as aural warfare—a wayward phone blaring at full volume as though someone had mistaken the clinic for a concert venue. Slimothy had tried to glare, but without eyelids, it was hard to convey the full gravity of his disapproval. Still, he gave it his best glossy stare. It accomplished absolutely nothing.

He wasn't looking for trouble. Not today. He was just trying to live his best, law-abiding, adequately hydrated, leafy-green-consuming life. Between the fluorescent lighting, the outdated magazines, and the musical stylings of *Who Even Is That?* drifting from the corner, his patience was thinning faster than mulch in a drought.

He flipped open his notebook, ready to document the chaos.

Waiting room: environment—hostile; air—medicinal; chairs—designed by sadists. One loud phone, its obnoxious owner, and a sniffing frequency approaching level 1,000 ... an atmosphere so cursed it deserves its own medical code.

Slimothy adjusted his posture, exhaled through imaginary nostrils, and prepared to achieve inner peace—or at least survive until his name was called. Enlightenment felt unlikely, but the phone battery finally dying? Now that felt like salvation within reach.

He did, admittedly, have a bone to pick with his doctor—metaphorically, of course. His CT scan had raised questions. Big ones, like: *Why does my head feel like a marching band set up camp behind my eyes?* Maybe this was karma for something he'd done in a past life—trampling a prized daisy, perhaps, or cutting in line at compost day.

"Disorders of the upper airway," the report had said. Could be turbinates—though he'd always thought turbinado was sugar—or maybe *"salute syndrome,"* which was ironic, considering his lack of hands. Apparently, Slimothy had one or more of these issues. Not that there was a real fix, because no one actually knew what was officially wrong. The latest suggestion was to see a neurologist, which felt excessive for someone whose nerves were already on the edge.

He sighed. It was exhausting living with a brain that treated thinking like a recreational activity. Some days it felt less like a skull and more like a small, poorly managed weather system.

He stared at the report again, hoping the words might rearrange themselves into something useful. They didn't. He wasn't sure what a neurologist could do for a slug. Maybe untangle his overthinking? Maybe confirm that his brain had been running on low power mode since 2019?

If this was part of his healing journey, Slimothy decided, then healing was wildly overrated. He wanted a refund, a snack, and maybe a small plaque that read: *"Tried My Best, Got Headache Instead."*

He mentally hung it proudly above the potting bench—right between *World's Okayest Gardener* and the calendar he'd given up updating in June.

CHAPTER SEVENTY-EIGHT

Bread, Bugs, and Big Ideas

S limothy had had a rough day. Between the aural nightmare of the morning, the wishy-washy doctor, and the horrifying discovery that his "healthy in a pinch" bagged salad had more calories than a casserole with confidence issues, he'd officially quit calorie counting and declared nutritional bankruptcy. In protest, he ate an entire platter of artisan bread.

He told himself he should do better, then immediately told himself the bread was divine and carbs were basically therapy you could butter. The regret wouldn't hit until the next day—right around the time the scale screamed and tried to file for psychological damages.

Come to think of it, Slimothy realized he did most things in binge mode. Kale, hobbies, period love stories, gardening—he didn't dabble; he fully relocated his feelings. By the second episode of whatever he was bingeing at the moment, he was usually weeping into a lettuce leaf and whispering, *"Don't do it, Mildred, he's not worth your harvest."*

As dusk settled in, he surveyed the day's small-scale devastation: several seedling casualties in the name of progress. The fallen had made way for his newest pride and joy, "championship limbo division" kale.

Then there were the mustard greens: an enigma—leafy, confident, and clearly in charge. They looked like the kind of vegetables that owned property and corrected your grammar.

He wondered if they were friends with the Swiss chard he'd be harvesting soon, and if they all met up at night to laugh about his cooking skills. Probably. Nothing bonded garden plants faster than shared disappointment in their owner.

He really needed to check on the radishes, too. The carrots were probably due for a poke to see if any had grown shoulders yet, not that he'd remember which day that was supposed to happen. Everything had started to blur together in a fog of dirt and delusion. Was it 55 days to harvest? Or 75? Did he have 287 varietals or 294? Hard to say. Math wasn't Slimothy's strong suit, especially when performed under the influence of bread.

Maybe he needed a new hobby. Something cultural. The next town over was apparently accepting submissions for Phase 2 of a storm drain art project—whatever that meant. It sounded thrillingly official, like "community service but with paint." He wasn't exactly clear on storm drains or art, but he *was* an optimistic slug with a generous imagination and catastrophically little self-control.

Plus, Roger and Lilibet were taking forever to meet and fall in love. Honestly, he'd seen moss grow faster. At this rate, he'd have grand-slugs before they even exchanged eye contact. If they didn't hurry up, he was going to start writing fanfiction just to move things along.

Apparently, the project aimed to raise awareness about local waterways, reduce pollution, and protect ecosystems through art, which sounded suspiciously like giving paintbrushes to people who couldn't be trusted with recycling bins.

Slimothy was intrigued. Maybe this was destiny, or at least mildly subsidized nonsense. Maybe the solution was a moat—suspicious water, a few decorative twigs, and a bold label reading "modern eco-expressionism."

He'd been hanging on to a special name for just such an auspicious occasion: Arthropod-Mediated Ecosystem Services (AMES)—known to locals (mostly Slimothy) as *"bugs doing all the work while humans take the credit."* It had everything: science, flair, and the faint smell of dirt-based prestige.

In short, insects, spiders, and mites were holding civilization together with six legs and no benefits. Not unlike Slimothy's own matchmaking services, they quietly kept the world running—pollinating crops, eating pests, and recycling dead stuff into fresh dirt. Altogether, they were worth about $8 billion a year, which was impressive for creatures with zero marketing budget and even less workplace morale.

Slimothy figured it was time he got in on that kind of action. If bugs could accidentally save the planet and rack up $8 billion in the process, surely he could contribute something, preferably with snacks involved. Maybe art, maybe a moat, maybe a bold new form of performance gardening that confused everyone but looked incredible on grant paperwork.

Whatever it turned out to be, the Bright Wild was due for a comeback—a revival, a renaissance, a slightly damp rebrand. Who knew? In a rare alignment of miracles, he might even stop the bulldozers while he was at it. If not, at least the debris would make excellent mulch.

CHAPTER SEVENTY-NINE

Bright Wild and Company

Today was an historic day in the Bright Wild, a big, limited-liability kind of day. The kind that began with optimism, a borrowed notary stamp, and at least one misunderstanding about what "articles of organization" actually meant.

Slimothy had woken with conviction and the faint aftertaste of a plan to save his patch of paradise. It tasted suspiciously like overconfidence. Somewhere between midnight inspiration and mild indigestion, he decided the only way to protect the Bright Wild was through paperwork. Real, official, government-acknowledged bureaucratic glory.

The Bright Wild Company, LLC, was born out of this burst of purpose, a rebranding effort so ambitious it practically required a mission statement, a logo, and several unnecessary meetings about font choice. All in the name of saving his patch of paradise from eminent domain.

The sentry cats approved, mostly for the pageantry, and the poor collards—planted after one too many glasses of red in the dark—were too wilted to object. Wine, as it turned out, made for excellent confidence but terrible crop placement.

He got to work immediately, fueled by purpose and a mild hangover. Filing paperwork without opposable thumbs was an uphill battle. The pen kept sliding, the ink ran, and the "LLC" came out looking more like "LCCCCC." However, persistence was the cornerstone of any respectable paperwork fiasco, he reasoned, and illegibility had never stopped progress before.

By midafternoon, he'd declared victory. The BWCLLC was registered, signed, sealed, and soon to receive its commemorative plaque, which, according to the fine print, would arrive in "six-to-eight business months."

That didn't stop Slimothy from preparing a spot for it: a flat rock near the pond, perfectly lit for admiration and future photo ops. Until the plaque's arrival, he marked the area with a single leaf labeled *"Reserved for Greatness."*

Naturally, every great company needed a founding document. Slimothy dipped a stick in mud and began to draft.

The Articles of Organization (and Occasional Inspiration)

Article I: the purpose of this entity shall be to preserve, protect, and occasionally water the Bright Wild.

Article II: all members are entitled to equal sunlight, reasonable hydration, and at least one emotional support fern.

Article III: profit shall be measured in vibes, not currency. Exceptions may be made for limited-edition sticker sales.

Article IV: slogan: "Where Every Leaf Counts, Even the Weird Ones."

Article V: all disputes shall be settled via interpretive sliding or leaf toss. Decisions are final unless overturned by a passing breeze.

Article VI: meetings shall include snacks. Failure to provide snacks automatically nullifies all decisions made therein.

Article VII: executive power shall rest with Slimothy, pending any future coup, hostile takeover by squirrels, or divine intervention via rainstorm.

Article VIII: any errors, omissions, or accidental wine stains on this document shall be considered stylistic choices and therefore legally binding.

Slimothy added a final flourish—a slime seal that glistened in the afternoon light—and leaned back, figuratively of course, pleased with himself. The paperwork was official, the mission was noble, and the plaque (eventually) would be stunning.

Bureaucracy, he decided, was just gardening with extra paperwork.

CHAPTER EIGHTY

In Memoriam, Sort of

S limothy had come home from an adventurous day and was immediately struck with sorrow at the sight before him. There, perched delicately on the blazing star, was the biggest bumblebee he had ever seen—roughly the size of a floral arrangement with a past, its fuzz catching the last light of day.

He'd read somewhere that some bees, in their final moments, simply fall asleep on flowers as the sun sets, never to rise again. Their life's work complete, their final act a quiet offering to the world they helped keep alive.

Slimothy immediately burst into tears.

It wasn't fair that such beautiful, tireless creatures were given so little time under the sun, while others—like Zoning Board Randall—seemed destined to live forever in mediocrity. *"What has he ever done for nature?"* Slimothy muttered bitterly, glaring toward the fence as if Randall might appear just to file another complaint about mulch.

His heart ached for the bee. He didn't see the garden much in daylight, so he'd been largely spared from witnessing nature's gentle heartbreaks. Yet, standing there now, he couldn't look away. Without bees, none of his favorite vegetables would exist—the eggplants, the tomatoes, the pickles-in-training. Even the cut-and-come-again salad bar, which technically didn't need pollinators, still looked better when bees zipped by, like regulars checking in for lunch.

He didn't want to go back to that side of the garden. The grief felt personal. He barely knew this bee, and yet he felt wholly responsible for her. A creature should never pass alone, he thought. At the very least, she deserved a eulogy.

Slimothy sat in the damp earth, trying to steady his thoughts. He'd recently learned that worker bees lived for only six to eight weeks and, in that short time, managed to fly the equivalent of one and a half times around the Earth. That was roughly 37,000—*37 thousand*—miles.

He paused, letting that sink in. His entire garden was maybe 35 feet across on a generous day—40 if you counted the overflow kale and the annex fern.

So: 37,351 miles ÷ 49 days = 762 miles per day.
That's about 31.7 miles per hour if they never stopped (which they did).
Or roughly 134,000 crossings of the Bright Wild per day, assuming an average span of 30 feet.

In bee math, that's:
1 bee = 37,351 miles = 1.5 Earths = 1 Bright Wild × 6.6 million laps.

Slimothy stared at the numbers, horrified. "Imagine the cardio," he thought to himself. "Or the existential dread."

He decided, then and there, that any creature capable of that much productivity in under two months should absolutely not be trusted.

Still, he couldn't help but admire them. Much like Slimothy, bees communicated through a series of dance moves like "the waggle dance." Slimothy found this profoundly relatable. He too had been known to convey complex feelings through interpretive wiggling—especially after two cups of coffee.

As it turned out, bees also loved caffeine. That explained a lot—the frantic energy, the questionable decision-making, the tendency to buzz around productivity but never quite land on anything. That practically made them family: frenetic, overcaffeinated workaholics with boundary issues.

He was also jealous that bees had two stomachs—clearly a sign of strong internal infrastructure. *One for snacks,* he mused, *and one for backup snacks. That's just good management.*

Slimothy gazed at the still bumblebee resting on the blazing star, the gold and black fuzz glowing faintly, like a sunset in miniature.

He wasn't sure what the proper etiquette was for a bee funeral. He didn't have flowers—the situation seemed to come pre-furnished with those—and he doubted a formal statement would reach the hive. Still, it felt wrong to just walk (well, slide) away.

So he cleared his throat and said softly, "Thank you for your service, your pollination, and your questionable work-life balance." Then, after a pause, he added, "You were excellent at your job. Maybe too excellent."

He placed a single petal beside the base of the very tall flower, partly ceremonial and partly because it felt like something dramatic people did in movies. Then he bowed his head.

"Rest well," he whispered. "You've earned your time off."

With that, he turned to leave—quietly resolving to add "Employee Wellness Program" to the next Bright Wild board agenda.

The next morning, Slimothy returned to the blazing star, ready to pay his respects again—or at least check on his floral graveyard etiquette.

The bee was gone. The petal he'd left had been nudged aside, and the air smelled faintly of motion and pollen.

He blinked, stunned. "Back to work?" he murmured. "Typical."

A low hum drifted through the garden, and for a moment a flash of yellow slipped between the tomato blossoms—alive, unstoppable, clearly late for something important.

Slimothy smiled. Hope, he decided, had wings—and absolutely no concept of paid time off.

CHAPTER EIGHTY-ONE

Pond and Circumstance

S limothy picked the 97th leaf out of the pond that week and immediately regretted every landscaping decision he'd ever made. Who, he wondered, puts a pond directly under a fruitless pear tree (the messy kind)? A fool. A sentimental, well-intentioned, moisture-obsessed dreamer.

One of his codependent lilies had developed a suspicious red splotch disease, and the papyrus (already testing the limits of vertical and horizontal space) had produced yet another stem, apparently out of spite.

He'd been searching for weeks for a pot big enough to rehome the overgrown green fluffy cloud hedge, but it wasn't pot season, and every decent vessel within a 30-foot radius was already occupied or not accepting new plants at this time. Inspirational water vessels that could also be used for plants were, as always, a rare breed.

Still, he pressed on. Roger and Lilibet's forever-ish home had to be maintained. If not pristine, then at least vaguely interesting. He wasn't sure if it was love, fate, or a poorly timed science experiment, but he was determined to give them the best shot possible. After all, if frogs couldn't find romance in the Bright Wild, what hope did anyone have?

A rooster crowed. It was 7:32 p.m. The world was upside down. Somewhere, the moon was probably late for work, and the basil had already started its nightly gossip hour. Slimothy sighed.

He adjusted another pebble that didn't need adjusting, then the one beside it, for balance. Then, because balance was a slippery slope, he redid the first one.

He knew how these things started. First, you add a rock. Then a frog. Then a bridge. Then a solar-powered waterfall and a questionable sense of authority. Before long, there were committee meetings about algae management and passive-aggressive cattails filing complaints.

He wasn't falling for it again. Not after the pond plant zoning debacle of recent memory. Chaos was the default setting here. Lately, though, it had gotten bold enough to make announcements. In the Bright Wild, the only real rule was that there were no time zones—only moods.

Slimothy smiled despite himself. The Bright Wild was a mess. Most of the plants freeloaded, the insects ran their own economy, and the water features required near-constant supervision. Still, it was *his* mess.

A bubble rose to the surface and popped. He took it as a sign that this little chaos had chosen him back.

CHAPTER EIGHTY-TWO

Failure to Bulb

I t was somewhere between garlic season and the great tulip countdown: roughly 60 days until the planting of flower bulbs, 30 until onions, and one very confused slug trying to keep a calendar with no hands.

Slimothy had long suspected that the people who named fruits and vegetables met once a year in a dimly lit room to compete for the most misleading title possible. "Short-day onions" were clearly the reigning champions.

Apparently, these "short-day" varieties started putting in bulb work when daylight lasted 10 to 12 hours. By Slimothy's math, that was practically a full-time job. Wouldn't that technically make them long-day onions? Or at least salaried-day onions? The naming committee had clearly gone rogue—or possibly just gone outside too long without a hat.

He wasn't sure whose day they were measuring, but it clearly wasn't his. If 12 hours counted as "short," then the review board must have been working government hours. That wasn't a short day, he thought. That was a medium crisis. The committee had no sense of proportion and even less sunlight exposure.

There were, of course, other varieties—intermediate-day and long-day onions—each with their own sunlight demands like divas with lighting riders.

Short-day onions wanted 10 to 12 hours, intermediates insisted on 12 to 14, and long-day onions refused to perform without a full 16. *16 hours!* Where exactly was that happening? Probably wherever the sun had tenure, union benefits, and a strong sense of self-importance.

The warning at the bottom of the guide struck him like a prophecy: *Planting the wrong type can lead to small bulbs or failure to bulb at all.*

He stared at it for a while, reflective. "Failure to bulb," he murmured. "Relatable."

He flipped through the handbook again, as if the pages might whisper encouragement. They didn't. The diagrams were cheerful in a way that felt condescending. He'd seen happier warnings on pesticide bottles.

He was beginning to suspect the planting manual was written by someone who had never met an actual bulb. The instructions were all so vague: *ensure adequate sunlight, provide consistent moisture, avoid emotional instability in the soil.* How much moisture? What counted as adequate? Who decided dirt couldn't have feelings?

He turned to look back toward the Bright Wild. Most of his plants thrived primarily out of spite. It was a high-performance ecosystem fueled entirely by defiance and caffeine runoff.

Still, maybe this would be the season he finally figured it out—or at least produced something vaguely bulb-shaped. Failure, he reasoned, was just photosynthesis with better storytelling. Of course, he'd probably plant the wrong ones anyway. Tradition was important.

Slimothy tried to picture the coming months: tiny green shoots breaking through the soil, the kind of delicate hope that made even failure look poetic. Or, more realistically, the same stubborn patch of dirt staring back at him with judgment. Either outcome seemed equally likely.

Did the ones you planted face down really grow down first, then up? He wasn't sure. The diagrams made it look easy, but the images also assumed a basic grasp of gravity and opposable thumbs he simply did not possess.

He stared at one of the bulbs, unsure which end was supposed to be optimistic. It didn't help that they all looked vaguely like eggs with trust issues. Still, he was determined. Progress, he told himself, was nonlinear—and possibly sideways, depending on bulb orientation.

Slimothy didn't even really like onions, but he did like garlic, and he loved a good tulip. There were 62 days left until tulip planting season, which he mentioned casually to anyone who hadn't asked. His calendar was annotated, laminated, and possibly cursed. Statistically speaking, no one had ever prepared for tulips harder.

He glanced at the sky, calculating nothing in particular, then tucked the planting guide beneath a hopeful leaf. Maybe this year he'd finally bulb. Maybe he'd get it right.

Or maybe he'd panic-buy more garlic and call it productivity. Either way, he decided, that still counted as growth.

CHAPTER EIGHTY-THREE

Buzzed, Bruised, and Botanically Confused

Slimothy was thoroughly enjoying Mother Nature's current perimenopausal hot flash, another late-October day threatening to hit a number higher than an interstate speed limit.

He had, rather unceremoniously, plucked Marty McFly the pineapple from his pot the night before—a split-second decision fueled by overconfidence, bad lighting, and what he could only describe as "premature harvest syndrome." Now, with wine replaced by coffee and his conscience a little scuffed, Slimothy stared at the empty pot like it was waiting for an apology he wasn't ready to give. The timing, of course, was tragic: one day too late for "Back to the Future Day," honoring the very movie that inspired Marty's name. Typical. Even his fruit had better scheduling skills.

Slimothy took a slow sip of his coffee and wondered if regret was an acceptable creamer, feeling the kind of quiet sadness usually reserved for tragic movie endings and the slow, theatrical demise of a basil plant that had simply decided life was too much photosynthesis. It was only his second pineapple to reach full ripeness—the first that wouldn't grow again. There'd be no baby pineapples, no head to replant, no proud lineage of spiky botanical heirs. Just a wordless farewell and the grim absurdity of being carried around like a decapitated tropical trophy.

He stared at the empty pot, heavy with regret and a touch of daylight-induced eye-stalk ache. Maybe this was growth. Or maybe it was just grief with better lighting. Still, Slimothy thought, that sort of morbid sentimentality probably meant he'd crossed the line from hobbyist to horticultural tragic. If feeling this much guilt over fruit wasn't the mark of a true gardener, it was at least solid evidence he needed a support group.

Slimothy blinked away the sunlight stabbing his eye stalks and decided it was best to focus on life's small victories—preferably ones that hadn't just been decapitated. He'd, after all, managed to harvest a single, glorious tomato, a feat achieved only once before the Tomato Thief's reign of terror began. Eight eggplants still hung on the vine too, waiting patiently for their turn to be celebrated, sautéed, or ignored. Slimothy eyed them warily. He was, by this stage of the season, what some might call "eggplanted out."

He poked at one, gleaming purple-black and inky with the kind of suspicion usually reserved for unsolicited advice, then decided to let the bees handle the productivity for the day. They were still out there, buzzing away at 200 to 400 hertz, blissfully unaware of his personal produce crisis. Slimothy watched them work with mild envy. They had focus. Purpose. Legs.

He wondered if "buzz pollination" was something he could learn—maybe an evening class, or a certification program with a very forgiving attendance policy. Bumblebees and their solitary cousins made it look easy. Since waggle-dancing was within his skill set—or at least within his imagination, how hard could it be?

He made a mental note to add "become certified pollinator" to the Jar of Questionable Intentions, slotted neatly between "teach yoga to earthworms" and "initiate feelings-based decomposition."

Slimothy sat back, feeling oddly accomplished for someone who had achieved absolutely nothing. The garden murmured around him, and Slimothy chose to interpret it as applause. Maybe tomorrow he'd do something productive, like begin his pollination certification—or maybe he'd just pencil in another meeting with himself called Buzz Practice. Either way, he decided, progress was progress, even if it occasionally involved holding staff meetings with vegetables.

CHAPTER EIGHTY-FOUR

The Glug Hypothesis

Slimothy had drunk more wine this past weekend than his entire little lifetime had budgeted for. It was one of those rare weekends with nothing pressing on the social calendar—just some much-needed rest and rehydration of the grape-based variety.

He wasn't proud of it, exactly, but after the second bottle, he started thinking in numbers again. It was his coping mechanism. Some creatures journaled; Slimothy charted. By the third glug, he'd entered what scientists might call "the data collection phase." It was only natural, he thought, to quantify the experience for future reference.

The quiet made his thoughts louder, and by Saturday afternoon he was already doing what he did best—turning feelings into spreadsheets.

Volume: Glugs
One glug = the sound of wine leaving the bottle, approximately three ounces.
A tasting pour = one glug.
Slimothy's pour = four glugs.

A "how did I finish this?!" night = 25 glugs.

The numbers told one story, but the recovery told another. By Sunday morning, he'd realized data alone couldn't explain gravity's personal vendetta against him. Quantitative analysis had its limits, especially when horizontal felt like the only viable position.

That's when he introduced a new metric. Enter: The Huff System.

Energy: Huffs
One huff = the effort it takes to move from one patch of shade to another.
Finding motivation after three glugs = seven huffs.
Answering Roger's texts out of principle = 12 huffs.
Standing up too fast and regretting existence = 45 huffs.
Attempting productivity on a Sunday = immeasurable huffs.

According to his calculations, balance was theoretically possible—just unlikely in this lifetime.

Slimothy considered adding a third metric to the chart: Social Energy (Rogers). One Roger would represent the mental effort required to hold a conversation longer than three sentences without faking a tunnel connection. Unfortunately, the unit wasn't testable at the moment.

Roger was probably off brumating again, indulging in his annual vanishing act. Could be weeks, could be months—depending entirely on how dramatic he felt the weather was. Not that Slimothy blamed him; "cold" these days felt more like a rumor started by someone nostalgic for sweaters. The afternoons were still warm enough to make even a slug question his life choices, the calendar, and whether hibernation was just an elaborate excuse to ignore emails.

Maybe hibernation wasn't about cold at all. Maybe it was about boundaries— about having the courage to say, *"I'm unavailable,"* and then burying yourself under a leaf for six to eight weeks. The idea had merit. Peace, quiet, no unexpected visitors asking about compost ratios or psychological breakthroughs.

The vision came easily: a tidy burrow, dim light, the faint sound of pond water in the distance. A to-do list with exactly one item: *no.* Maybe a blanket of damp moss, perhaps a single motivational poster that read, *"Minimalism Starts With Me."*

He couldn't help but smile. Roger wasn't lazy—he was enlightened. His seasonal disappearing act wasn't avoidance; it was strategy.

He took another small glug (purely for research purposes) and added one final line to his chart:

Existential boundaries = pending.

CHAPTER EIGHTY-FIVE

The Tomato Situation: A Study in Seasonal Denial and Festive Delusion

S limothy had found a new tomato bush. It appeared suddenly, as if grown out of sheer audacity, nestled between the forbidden zucchini and the glowingly self-congratulatory shoulders of the radishes. Its leaves were green and full, its fruit blushing red around the edges, as if caught doing something scandalous in daylight.

He stared in disbelief. Slimothy had a vague memory of tomatoes reaching ripeness once, long ago, but it could've been a dream or a hallucination brought on by kale. The Bright Wild's mysterious tomato thief had seen to that—always striking early, leaving only semi-eaten remains and juice-stained evidence. Never a proper picking. Never a celebration. Never the simple joy of a caprese salad done right.

This, he thought, could be the one.

He picked it (and its quiet companion) without pomp or circumstance, just to prove he could. No fanfare, no audience—just the soft snap of victory. The first bite was revelation. Somehow salty, somehow tangy, somehow everything all at once. It was one of the most heavenly flavors imaginable, like the universe had finally conspired in his favor.

In an instant, the world made sense. The sun hit just right, the soil smelled like promise, and Slimothy decided that if enlightenment had a taste, it would be fresh tomato—preferably with basil and minimal drama.

For a fleeting, perfect moment, Slimothy was untouchable. A tomato champion. The stuff of gardening legends. He even considered drafting a thank-you speech to the sun, the soil, and whichever worm had handled irrigation duty this season.

He knew it wouldn't last. His tomato-gathering days were numbered.

Apparently, one could protect tomato plants from the cold with plastic sheeting or by wrapping them in incandescent Christmas lights—a cozy illusion of hope for plants destined to perish anyway. The guides all agreed: they wouldn't survive the winter, but at least they could go out shining.

Too much water this late in the season, however, meant tragedy. *Watery, flavorless fruit. Characterless tomatoes.* The horror. According to his research, one had to stop—or at least dramatically reduce—watering in late summer or early autumn, stressing the plants just enough to encourage their final, desperate ripening.

Slimothy found that oddly relatable. He'd spent weeks fretting over watering schedules, toggling between drought and deluge like a tiny weather god with poor impulse control. Now he wasn't sure if the plants were thriving or just too polite to die in front of him.

He wondered how many more warm evenings he had left—nights to lounge luxuriously under the moon's glow and pretend the season wasn't turning. The days were thinning out, the chill arriving a little earlier each dusk, as if sneaking in before he could protest. The air had shifted, softer now, carrying the faint hum of change. Even the crickets sounded tired, and the gnats had taken to nostalgia. He respected that. Sentimentality was an underrated survival tactic.

He watched the tomato bush sway slightly in the evening breeze. It looked calm, but he knew better. Every leaf was already negotiating with the cold to come.

"Hang in there," he whispered. "We'll go out twinkling."

It wasn't much of a strategy, but sparkle was still better than surrender. When the frost finally came, at least the tomatoes would look festive.

If anyone asked, he'd just say it was all part of the plan—a controlled seasonal collapse with excellent lighting.

CHAPTER EIGHTY-SIX

How to Get the Ladies (Entomologically Speaking)

In his downtime—of which there was, lately, a generous and concerning amount—Slimothy had been re-reading a stack of old garden books. He told himself it was research, though most of it read more like survival literature for plants.

One book in particular, "Habitat Management for the Thoughtful Gardener," had caught his eye. It claimed that a *"well-balanced garden intentionally attracts beneficial insects."* Slimothy wasn't sure what counted as intentional anymore.

Most of his insect-attracting efforts were accidental. Some days it felt less like a garden and more like an all-inclusive resort for bugs with questionable ethics.

Still, the idea of structure appealed to him—rules, ratios, measurable effort. Finally, a system that rewarded overthinking. Somewhere, buried between the compost and the chaos, he landed on something called the 70/30 Rule: 70% native plants for the local wildlife, 30% non-native for decoration and aesthetic balance.

It sounded less like gardening advice and more like life philosophy: part native, part chaos—roughly a 70/30 split that felt suspiciously like a personality test in disguise. He liked those odds; they were about the same as his ratio of good intentions to small, containable fires.

He glanced toward Roger's empty abode and could already see the look he'd give: that slow blink of amphibian disapproval that said, *"percentages are for creatures with spreadsheets, not swamps."* Still, Slimothy was intrigued. Maybe what the garden needed wasn't more plants, but better representation.

The more he read, the more complicated the idea became. Apparently, proper habitat management didn't end with planting ratios. A true gardener was also expected to provide suitable zones for overwintering, storm protection, and something described as "overnight staging," which sounded suspiciously like a theater term. His imagination launched straight into rehearsal mode—butterflies delivering moonlit soliloquies, wings shimmering like velvet curtains parting for a tragic hero.

There was also the matter of salt sources, resting areas, and roaming zones— an entire insect suburb with infrastructure demands. It was less gardening and more small-town governance. Slimothy wasn't sure if he was cultivating a habitat or accidentally running for mayor again.

Yet even with all his reading and reorganizing, there was one resident he'd yet to attract—his most elusive, and most desired.

The ladybug.

Every source he consulted (and even his own wishful thinking) agreed on one thing: no garden was truly complete without her. This scarlet speck, the crown jewel of any thriving habitat—the red-dotted enforcer who kept aphids trembling and gardeners feeling quietly superior.

He'd even started a section in his notes titled "How to Get the Ladies," which, in hindsight, sounded more like a self-help manual than a gardening log. From what he'd gathered, ladybugs preferred healthy plants, mild humidity, and a steady buffet of aphids—all things Slimothy technically had, though maybe not in the confidence or charisma department.

He wasn't sure what else to offer. He'd tried everything: leaving out fresh dew in tiny droplets like hors d'oeuvres, arranging petals artfully in concentric circles, even playing soft pond noises at dusk to set the mood. Nothing. Not one polka-dotted Coccinellid.

He'd checked under leaves, behind stems, near aphid buffets—everywhere a lady beetle with a sliver of a conscience might loiter. Still no sign. It was starting to feel personal. Maybe they'd launched a leaf-rights movement—or perhaps they'd simply heard about his overwatering reputation.

He sighed, staring at an empty stem where salvation should have landed—six legs, red shell, punctual. The garden didn't need more mulch; it needed management. At this rate, he thought, he'd have to start posting job listings: *Wanted: one reliable lady beetle. Benefits include pollen access and moral superiority.*

Slimothy stared out at the Bright Wild, partially convinced the ladybugs were holding out just to test him. "Maybe they don't like committees," he muttered, thinking back to the 70/30 Rule. "Or maybe they just know a desperate gardener when they see one."

Still, he left a small patch untouched—a messy sprawl of dill, fennel, and mildly feral parsley—just in case word got around. Hope, he decided, was a lot like compost: you had to keep turning it over and pretending the smell meant progress.

CHAPTER EIGHTY-SEVEN

The Day the Wi-Fi Died

T he internet had vanished with the arrival of rain that came out of nowhere. One minute the Bright Wild was basking in sunshine, the next it was as if the sky had accidentally opened a group chat and everyone replied "storm."

At first, Slimothy assumed it was just his own connection acting up again. He tried refreshing the Bright Wild App, then the weather site, then the frog meme page—each one spinning endlessly like a doomed "Wheel of Fortune." The rain grew heavier, as though the clouds had taken personal offense to his troubleshooting.

It wasn't just him this time, though. Reports—well, pre-outage summaries— had said the last collapse had "crippled most of the continent," which sounded dramatic until you realized how many of those parts overlapped. No weather alerts, no garden forums, no Roger sending passive-aggressive GIFs about pond maintenance. Civilization, as far as Slimothy could tell, was hanging by a single damp router somewhere in the stratosphere, probably guarded by a raccoon with poor life choices.

He stared out into the storm, watching the rain blur the edges of everything familiar. It struck him how fragile the whole operation really was—this grand system of "progress" held together by spending sprees, stubbornness, and whatever strange magic kept technology alive past midnight. All their networks, notifications, blue-light assurances, and backup plans—just one lightning strike from reverting to carrier pigeons and uncomfortably honest letters, one tangled extension cord from the horrifying return of eye contact.

The silence that followed felt enormous. It wasn't just quiet; it was expectant—the kind of hush that made you aware of every drip, every sigh, every unflattering internal thought. Even the ferns seemed to be listening for a ping that would never come, their fronds tilted upward like anxious little antennas waiting for a signal from a world that had gone offline.

The more Slimothy thought about it, the stranger it became. What if the invisible fibers in the heavens really did stop? Would the clouds still get their updates? Would the worms still clock in for their night shifts without the push notifications? How would the bees coordinate their routes without GPS pollen tracking?

It would be chaos. Beautiful, muddy, analog chaos.

Old-school gardening, that's what would happen. No apps, no syncing, no digital dashboards tallying sunlight exposure. Just intuition and mud, compost and guesswork, faith in the weather, and the occasional bribe to the local butterfly union.

Thankfully, the only thing he didn't need Wi-Fi for was his watering system—mainly because it was him. No app, no automation, just one determined slug with a questionable hydration schedule.

While everyone else relied on smart sprinklers and weather integrations, Slimothy relied on instinct, enthusiasm, and a body composition that was roughly 80% moisture. He didn't need Bluetooth to drip dramatically across the garden beds; he was the original low-tech irrigation operation.

If anything, he thought proudly, he *was* the backup plan. Proof that even in the digital age, some systems still ran perfectly fine on slime and stubbornness.

A steady drizzle of dedication and mild panic kept the Bright Wild alive, even on days when the sky refused to cooperate.

The Bright Wild App (pre-production version) wasn't so fortunate. It relied on those magic sky boxes to measure humidity, track soil nutrients, and send him important alerts like, *"Congratulations, your mint is once again attempting world domination.*" Without it, Slimothy was adrift—a gardener without a compass, or worse, a slug without a signal.

He tried to be rational about it. Bandwidth would come back eventually. It always did. Yet the longer the little loading wheel spun on his cracked tablet screen, the more Slimothy himself began buffering.

What if this was permanent? What if the garden went offline forever? Would his data sync with the dirt automatically? Would his progress bar just … decompose? Could he file a ticket with Mother Nature's help desk, or was that system down too?

The thoughts made him queasy. His brain was starting to overheat—too many tabs open, none of them helpful. Anxiety crept in like a slow-loading page, and before he knew it, he was unraveling in every direction: mentally, existentially, and, when the thunder rolled, physically. The potting bench gave a dramatic shudder, the storm voiced its displeasure, and a raindrop the size of a small berry smacked him square in the face—baptizing him in panic, perspective, and at least three forms of self-pity.

When the storm finally eased, he realized it had been the longest 47 minutes of his life. The calendar hadn't changed, but he was fairly certain the century had.

CHAPTER EIGHTY-EIGHT

In the Name of Frog-gress: Radio Pants and Other Ethical Dilemmas

A fter the chaos of the last few days, the sudden quiet felt suspiciously luxurious. In the unexpected absence of drama, something strange happened: peace. Slimothy found he had enjoyed his lack-of-technology tranquility to such a degree that he began to wonder what it would be like to turn off the world on command. Not forever, just on speed dial—a quick tap to silence the chaos.

He glanced at his pond's remote control and concocted new settings—*Mild Contact, Absolutely No Contact,* and *Post-Apocalyptic Times.* Maybe even a bonus feature: *Selective Interaction,* where only well-adjusted plants could reach him.

It was a tempting fantasy. After all, he mused, if Roger could vanish for an entire season, surely he deserved at least a weekend of professional avoidance.

The idea wouldn't leave him alone. By midafternoon, Slimothy had gathered an alarming amount of equipment for someone with no technical skills: a timer, a broken sprinkler sensor, two decorative rocks, and what he optimistically labeled "circuitry"—a repurposed string of fairy lights.

He wired them together (or, more accurately, near each other) and declared it his prototype: "The Pond Peace Protocol (Beta)." One button to dim the noise, mute unsolicited advice from passing dragonflies, and block out the existential hum of the compost pile.

For a glorious 12 seconds, it worked. The pond lit up briefly, the air went still, and Slimothy was certain serenity itself had just hummed his name. Then the system rebooted, fired the sprinkler, and soaked him from scarf to slime.

He blinked, dripping, mildly electrocuted but oddly satisfied.

Damp, dramatic, and full of misplaced confidence, Slimothy wondered if the logic he'd just applied to the Pond Peace Protocol could work on other parts of his life. Maybe there was a button for that—something between *System Reboot* and *Selective Memory Wipe.*

The idea hadn't even finished assembling itself before it was abruptly dismantled.

Roger!

He hadn't realized how much he missed his sometime-silent companion until now. The frog's absence had carved a strange quiet into the Bright Wild. When Roger finally reappeared, hopping in that maddeningly precise way along the concrete flagstones, Slimothy felt a surge of relief, and, uncomfortably, curiosity. Where had he been spending his days? He liked to think it was with Lilibet, but there was no real way to know. Or was there?

Slimothy glanced at the remnants of his latest invention and felt a spark of mischief. Could he engineer a tracker? Something subtle, discreet, amphibian-compatible—and finally solve the mystery of Roger's disappearing act?

It was, he decided, only mildly invasive in the name of science. The real question was, how would he affix it? Roger wasn't exactly cooperative on a good day. The idea of placing a tracker on the surly amphibian who likely slept less than Slimothy himself was ambitious at best, delusional at worst.

A discreet, frog-approved tracking system: lightweight, waterproof, morally flexible. Slimothy entertained the idea with the confidence of a scientist and the résumé of a damp leaf.

Passive Integrated Transponder Tags, his brain announced. Maybe even tiny custom radio-pants (patent pending, naturally). To complete the suite, he'd need a receiver—a "Frog Logger," obviously—something sleek, sophisticated, and completely unnecessary.

It all sounded perfectly reasonable until he considered explaining it to anyone else. He sighed. Genius, he realized, often sounded suspiciously like obsession, especially when your blueprints included radio-pants and a surveillance system for frogs. Still, history would thank him. Or at least quietly delete his emails.

CHAPTER EIGHTY-NINE

The Ping

The tracking project was, by all accounts, a success—if you defined "success" as "no one was arrested and Roger remained blissfully untracked." Exhausted and only slightly electrocuted, Slimothy called it a night. The garden settled around him in that peculiar stillness that always followed his ideas, quiet, thoughtful, and vaguely concerned.

By morning, the quiet had changed. Slimothy awoke to the faint rustle of leaves that didn't belong to the usual morning gossip. It was sharper, deliberate, like the garden itself had cleared its throat. Probably just Roger, he thought, or the wind being theatrical again.

Then it happened—a soft ping. Not a sound, exactly, but something that felt like one: a vibration through the soil, a ripple across the moss. Slimothy went perfectly motionless, like the world had just pressed pause on him. *It couldn't be.* His partway-fried contraption, the prototype of the "Frog Logger," wasn't even on. He hadn't meant for it to do ... well, anything, really.

He looked toward the pond, where the device sat partially submerged, fairy lights dimmed but faintly flickering like they knew something he didn't. If the universe had push notifications—and Slimothy strongly suspected it did—this would've been one:

"Bright Wild App Notification: Activity Detected Beyond Registered Perimeter."

Slimothy blinked. *That's impossible,* he thought. *The app doesn't even exist yet.* He waited for logic to step in and explain itself, but it didn't. Instead, curiosity did what logic never could—it shoved him forward. Maybe it was a sign. A push notification from destiny, or potential investors.

He peered past the pond's edge toward the tangle of overgrown stems and weeds that marked the start of the forest. Something in the space beyond had shifted—subtle, watchful, like the garden itself had leaned in to listen.

The leaves trembled, then stilled, and the soft rattle of unseen things brushed faintly through the undergrowth. Even the bottlebrush had gone still, its red bristles frozen mid-rustle, as if holding its breath. It looked quiet, but the kind of quiet that had opinions. The sort that waited for you to say something foolish first.

"Well," he said, "I come in peace and possibly with snacks."

Nothing answered, which he decided was either a good sign or the beginning of a bad one. The pond behind him gurgled softly, as if to remind him where the sensible creatures stayed. Ahead, the forest loomed like a thought he wasn't ready to finish. Probably nothing, he reasoned. Probably everything.

Either way, he decided, he'd have to check. Slimothy adjusted his posture, which in practice meant thinking very hard about looking brave. If the forest wanted to be dramatic, it should at least file a report through proper channels.

He stayed perfectly still for a long moment, as if courage might arrive if he didn't move too quickly and scare it off. The garden seemed to hold its breath with him. Even the pond gurgled quieter, waiting to see if he'd actually do it.

Finally, he moved. One slow slide forward, then another. He was somewhere between confident and clueless and a full mile from prepared. The ground felt different here—denser, as though even the dirt had opinions about his life choices.

The sago palm came first, standing proud-as-a-peacock and spiny like a bouncer guarding the unknown. Slimothy gave it a wide berth, because nothing about that plant said friendly. He slipped past it with all the stealth of a damp potato and reached the bottlebrush, its bristles crowding like disapproving spectators.

Beyond it lay the forest—dark, tangled, humming faintly, as if aware of his arrival. Slimothy hesitated. He had, technically, wanted to start forest farming: an ambitious expansion that had so far consisted mostly of daydreaming and soil-related overthinking. Still, this could count as progress. Technically, it qualified as field research, if by field you meant mild panic in a shaded area. Forestry, after all, was just gardening with commitment issues and better PR.

He pulled out his notebook and steadied his trusty twig pen, the official instrument of great discoveries and mild regret. If this went horribly wrong, at least future generations (or nosy squirrels) would find a detailed account of his final moments and think, *"Wow. He really committed to the bit."*

Field notes: "Forest Border Assessment"
Bottlebrush acting defensive, like it owns the place. Sago palm clearly designed by someone with trust issues. Beyond them lies uncharted foliage, radiating the kind of energy that says, "Proceed if you hate your current life expectancy."

Then it came again—the ping. Not a sound, but a pulse rippling up from the soil, low and persuasive, like the earth itself whispering, *"Free kale samples … limited time only."* It was louder this time, impossible to ignore, and frankly a little too confident for something without a marketing department.

It's fine, he told himself. *Just the wind. Or destiny.* Hard to tell which has the worse Yelp reviews.

He glanced toward the forest, where the shadows lounged like they paid rent, then back to the garden, the last known location of his dignity and reliable Wi-Fi.

Another ping.

Louder. Closer.

The moss at his feet shivered like it suddenly remembered an unpaid debt. It wasn't technically alive enough to panic, but it was giving it a solid try.

He scribbled a final entry in his trusty notebook:

Field notes: "Operation Absolutely Not"
Forest entry postponed indefinitely due to suspicious vibrations,

questionable mental stability, and a general shortage of survival-based enthusiasm. Further observation to continue from a safe, well-snacked distance.

Slimothy's heart thudded somewhere in the general chest area, probably. The forest could wait, but whatever was calling him clearly had no respect for personal space, psychological cooldown periods, or lunch breaks.

If destiny wanted him, it could send an email like everyone else. Until then, he had snacks to defend and a reputation for cautious cowardice to uphold.

He turned to leave, satisfied that retreat absolutely counted as strategy when properly documented. The pond burbled approvingly, the bottlebrush relaxed, and for a glorious 12 seconds, the Bright Wild felt normal again.

Then, *ping*

Softer this time, like the forest was just checking if he was still there.

Slimothy halted. "No," he whispered to the trees. "We're not doing this."

He began a slow, dignified retreat that quickly escalated into a full-scale, panic-powered evacuation drill—equal parts chaos and questionable physics. Behind him, the moss wobbled, clearly impressed by his commitment to fleeing heroically from absolutely nothing.

CHAPTER NINETY

The "Chonk Scale Initiative"

After a night of dramatic reflection and two supportive carbohydrate snacks, Slimothy decided everything was under control. Mostly. Probably. *In theory.* The forest, he reasoned, could wait; what the Bright Wild really needed was community engagement, culminating in the founding of the "Bright Wild Garden Club," membership: one slug, one suspicious fern, and whatever breeze signed up first.

The inaugural meeting began at 8:07 a.m. sharp with a moment of silence for "recent pings," followed by light refreshments and a heated debate over mulch distribution (he lost). The motion to increase snack funding, however, passed unanimously.

He took attendance anyway, because that's what leaders did. The woodland pinkroot abstained on moral grounds, the sedum left early for light-based obligations, and the moss pretended to be neutral but was clearly gossiping. The minutes were duly recorded, laminated, and filed in the Progress Binder, a three-ring symbol of his fragile authority.

To commemorate the occasion, he even designed an official motto: *"Unity Through Compost."* It looked excellent screen-printed across a limited-edition Garden Club sweatband—handmade, slightly damp, and available exclusively in "soil tone." He wore it proudly for 10 minutes before it slid dramatically over one eye stalk and refused to come off.

It wasn't the most dignified look, but Slimothy decided it sent the right message: commitment, perspiration, and mild confusion.

Every successful organization, he reasoned, needed a wellness program. Something uplifting. Grounded. Slightly delusional. Thus was born the "Chonk Scale Initiative," a fitness and morale endeavor designed to *"celebrate diverse body structures and snack-based lifestyles."*

Slimothy had long argued that wellness couldn't be measured by traditional means. Calorie charts and BMI didn't apply to gastropods. What mattered, he insisted, was vibe density.

Enter: the "Chonk Scale."

Developed in partnership with the "Bright Wild Garden Club" (membership still one), it ranked all local wildlife on a sliding scale from "ethereal leaf whisper" to "Chunkosaurus-level majesty." Participants were encouraged to "embrace their natural circumference" through light movement, attitude adjustments, and responsible grazing.

The classes focused on small isometric movements—small being Slimothy's unofficial middle name, in both theory and waistline. They involved more mud than balance, and the constant temptation of nearby lettuce. Classes met twice a week under a single guiding motto: *"Lengthen, Strengthen, Snacken."* Attendance was optional but highly encouraged by Slimothy's clipboard-based guilt tactics. Signature moves included The Motivated Pause, Hydration Reach, and Snack-Oriented Leap of Faith.

As part of the Garden Club's ambitious expansion into "wellness infrastructure," Slimothy launched what he called a "limited-edition wellness drop." The collection featured resistance bands and motivational tote bags proudly emblazoned with his custom slogan, *"Embrace the Circumference."* Both were handcrafted, questionably tested, and immediately available to anyone who hadn't asked for them.

The tote bags arrived damp (a printing mishap, allegedly), and the resistance bands immediately snapped under even mild psychological strain. Still, he called it a success. "Early prototypes," he assured the moss, who looked unconvinced. The fern refused comment, citing burnout.

It wasn't about perfection, he reasoned—it was about morale, movement, and tasteful accessories.

Naturally, Slimothy credited the movement's inspiration to "Fat Squirrel Week," where legends like Chunkosaurus Rex and his rival, Chunk Norris, had redefined what it meant to be both heroic and spherical. "If they could celebrate circumference," he reasoned, "so could we."

The program was, predictably, controversial.

He spent the afternoon enforcing new garden ordinances while incorporating "intentional movement," a "Bright Wild Wellness Club" principle that turned even basic clipboard work into low-impact cardio. Among the new rules: no unintentional rustling after sunset, no unapproved vines crossing into neighboring jurisdictions, and, all mysterious activity must now be reported directly to the Garden Club, preferably in triplicate. He even drafted a "Code of Conduct for Photosynthesis," which he planned to laminate once he found the good tape.

By dusk, the Bright Wild had never looked more official. Everything had labels, minutes, bylaws, and the faint smell of overconfidence. The forest remained politely unresponsive, the pond gurgled with what he chose to interpret as respect, and Slimothy finally exhaled. Maybe, just maybe, bureaucracy had triumphed over chaos.

He adjusted his sweatband, straightened his clipboard, and gave a small, self-satisfied nod. Peace at last, he thought. Order restored.

For the first time in days, the garden was finally following instructions—or at least pretending to. Everything sat upright, photosynthesizing politely, the air itself on its best behavior, like chaos holding its breath until roll call was over. Slimothy basked in the illusion of stability, letting his mind wander toward smaller, safer concerns: how to color-code his soil charts, whether the lavender required psychological fencing, and if it was time to design Garden Club membership cards.

Yes, things were finally back under control. Predictable. Regulated. Comfortably mundane—the holy trinity of mediocrity.

Then, just as the air began to settle into that soft evening hush, something shifted. A sound came again—faint, deliberate—the rustle of leaves parting like someone opening a suspense novel too close to him.

Slimothy paused—mid-thought, mid-slime, mid-hope. Every optimistic thought instantly fled, replaced by its older, more reliable sibling: dread.

Paperwork, he thought. *I need more paperwork.*

CHAPTER NINETY-ONE

Slimothy and the Art of Interpretive Sliding

S limothy gazed into the reflection of the pond, chomping thoughtfully—8,000 tiny teeth working overtime to look suave. Somewhere between nibble and gnash, he wondered if this was what charisma looked like, or if he just resembled a nervous salad spinner.

Recently, he'd learned several facts that had sent him spiraling through an existential compost heap. The first: a distant cousin on his great-great-grand-slug's side apparently had a rather dramatic set of chompers too. In fact, an entire legend had been based on them. Count Dracula—known in slug folklore as Count Draculeaf, Vlad the Impaleaf, Baron von Slugula, or simply The Overly Moist One—had been a love story all along. Who knew romance could involve that many capes, so little sunlight, and a frankly irresponsible amount of biting?

The second revelation was even more confusing. This one had bunnies. "Dracula" hadn't, and he was beginning to see the wisdom in that creative choice. One of Slimothy's lifelong heroes, Peter Rabbit, turned out to be based on a real bunny—a genuine fluffy hare, meticulously documented by her owner with pages of delicate fungus notes and garden sketches, his every hop recorded like a nature documentary filmed inside a gilded cage. It was oddly tragic—much like Dracula's brides, though technically that had been a love story ... ish. Everywhere Slimothy looked now, he saw bunnies in tiny epaulettes teaching moral lessons nobody asked for. Nothing was making sense anymore.

So when the Bright Wild Theater Company announced a one-off moderately suggestive garden ballet (with mulch) of "Dracula," Slimothy went. Culture, he reasoned, was a balm for confusion—plus, tickets were two-for-one if you brought your own leaf.

He arrived early, dressed in his finest scarf and an air of artistic seriousness. The program promised *"a haunting reimagining of love, loss, and limited chlorophyll."* Slimothy wasn't entirely sure what that meant, but he was prepared to be mentally flattened.

The ushers—two beetles in bow ties—led him to his seat, technically a patch of moss with *"reserved"* written in dew, and the lights dimmed. Somewhere in the orchestra pit, a grasshopper cleared its throat.

This was it. Real culture. High art. Possibly even interpretive biting.

Truly, what culture it was. The stage—a repurposed mulch tarp—came alive with swirling petals, synchronized moths, and one particularly committed praying mantis in a tulle cape. Music fluttered through the air (or maybe that was the wine). It was the most beautiful thing Slimothy had ever seen—high praise from someone whose previous top three were:

His pickles in training,

one quarter of a tomato that had smiled at him once,

and literally anything that photosynthesized on cue.

When the curtain fell—a repurposed bedsheet from the Garden Lost & Found—Slimothy felt changed. Enlightened. Possibly even worldly, like someone who had witnessed greatness and immediately wanted a souvenir cup shaped like a fang.

The reality of garden life felt painfully ordinary after such high drama—but the merchandise softened the blow. He looked down at his new prize: a glow-in-the-dark enamel pin that read "I ♥ **Bite Ballet**" and, when tilted, briefly flashed tiny fangs. He nodded, deeply moved.

Art changed lives, he decided—and occasionally came with limited-edition accessories.

The glow of the enamel pin still gleamed faintly on his leaf shelf that night, a tiny reminder of culture, chaos, and questionable choreography. He went to bed humming the overture, certain he'd never be the same again.

By morning, he wasn't.

Slimothy awoke with purpose—grand, glittering intent. Inspiration had struck sometime between dreams about capes, suspiciously romantic fog, and a very aggressive *pas de deux*.

If a bunch of bugs in capes could make "Dracula" work in a mulch pile, matching that level of tragedy was hardly a stretch. Something with meaning. Emotion. Fewer fatalities. Teeth optional, of course.

He began with a title: "The Slug Who Loved Too Mulch."

It had drama. It had range. It had at least one pun so moving it nearly earned a standing ovation from his own reflection. Slimothy dabbed at an imaginary tear, convinced he'd just written the "Swan Lake" of slugs—only slimier, and with better wordplay.

He positioned himself by the pond, the same reflective surface where he'd first practiced looking mysterious, and, on a few occasions, taller. He took a deep breath—or the slug equivalent of one—and launched into what he believed was a graceful spin.

For a brief, glorious moment, it was. Then he realized he'd accidentally glued himself to a wet leaf and was now performing an unplanned duet titled "Help."

Art, he told himself solemnly, always requires sacrifice. Preferably not adhesive-related, but still—sacrifice.

He pressed on, spinning, swaying, occasionally performing what could only be described as interpretive sliding. A beetle passing by paused mid-stride, torn between applause and filing a safety report.

Halfway through "Act Two (Unrequited Compost)," Slimothy attempted a daring lift—forgetting he was both the lifter and the liftee. The result was less "Swan Lake" and more "Moss Slide: A Tragedy in Three Squeaks," featuring one dramatic gasp and an unscheduled intermission.

Still, the performance had heart—and possibly a minor concussion. He gave himself a standing ovation afterward, which for a slug meant sitting slightly taller and nodding at his reflection like a director who'd just witnessed genius.

The critics—a trio of skeptical ants—gave it mixed reviews, citing *"excessive glistening"* and *"confusing narrative moisture."* Still, Slimothy didn't mind. He'd discovered something profound: passion could move even the smallest creature, and with proper lighting, he could finally pass for avant-garde.

As the sun dipped below the fence line, Slimothy took one final bow—slightly off balance, moderately sticky, and profoundly pleased with himself. The leaf stage was in ruins, his audience had wandered off, and his scarf had somehow become part of the set design. It was, he decided, his most successful performance to date.

Despite everything, he smiled. Art had been made. History, possibly rewritten.

"Note to self," he murmured, gazing at the pond's rippling reflection. "Next time ... fewer spins, more snacks, and someone remind me why there were bunnies at all."

With that, the curtain of night fell—quite literally, as a moth crash-landed on his head, declared itself the understudy, and refused to leave.

Before Slimothy could protest, the final act arrived: a mosquito, buzzing with overconfidence, seemingly unpaid for this role, and determined to make it a tragedy bit him squarely on the neck. Slimothy gasped in horror as the insect took its bow, exited stage left, and stole the spotlight.

He'd seen "Dracula" just once—he just hadn't expected audience participation.

CHAPTER NINETY-TWO

Lettuce Pray

Slimothy's lettuce had bolted.

Not the good kind—like a spooked horse fleeing a bad plot twist. Not the other kind either—like a bride who suddenly remembers she left the oven on, or worse, that her fiancé collects decorative gourds.

Come to think of it, there were no good boltings. Only fast exits and expensive lessons in commitment.

His lettuce was no exception.

He had, for weeks, followed the sacred cut-and-come-again doctrine: *"harvest the outer leaves, leave the center to thrive."* A salad bar of virtue. A buffet of restraint.

"Yes," he thought to no one in particular. "Thank you, garden annals, for this valuably useless advice."

He glared up at what could only be described as a lettuce skyscraper—easily two feet tall—towering where his second-favorite plant once lived a humble, leafy life.

"Cut leaves frequently," the guidebooks had said. *"Encourage leaf production. Prevent seed formation."* His lettuce was likely bolting early due to heat and light stress. "Me too," thought Slimothy. "Relatable."

Apparently, he had not harvested frequently enough. The entire bed had read the same book—then decided to interpret it as a threat. Overnight, it shot upward in defiance, a green monument to misunderstanding. A plant possessed, determined to prove a point no one had made.

Everywhere he looked, lettuce legs towered. They hadn't even bothered to shut the garden gate in their hasty escape. It wasn't cut-and-come-again—it was *cut and see you later.*

Maybe they'd finally joined forces with the Union of Lavender—chalk another one up to the "Too Moist, Too Dry, Too Hot, Too Cold Coalition."

The rain had been relentless all week. Between the downpours and the ballet distraction, Slimothy hadn't made it to the garden nearly as much as planned.

Warm one day, wet the next, cold by morning, hot by lunch—like dating someone with too many weather apps and no temperament control.

Now came the reckoning. The kind you can't compost your way out of. Very expensive lettuce leaves. Premium heartbreak. Locally sourced, non-refundable.

All the love and care in the world, and not even a farewell crunch. Bolted lettuce didn't grow back—it just quit the workforce entirely, bitter, dramatic, and convinced it deserved better benefits. He blamed Mother Nature again.

Slimothy looked at the stretched-out tangle of greens where his prize salad once stood and sighed. Another victim of climate drama. Another heartbreak the Bright Wild had filed under "natural consequences."

At this point, he was starting to suspect his garden wasn't growing plants at all—just elaborate lessons in psychological fortitude.

Maybe next season, he decided, he'd stick to root vegetables. At least they couldn't abandon you vertically.

CHAPTER NINETY-THREE

The Great Seasonal Sulk

S limothy wasn't ready to give up on summer just yet. He had precisely one radish, two eggplants, and a possibly sentient summer squash in the fridge drawer—his entire remaining harvest, marinating in the slow funk of denial. It wasn't hoarding, he told himself. It was sentimentality with vitamins.

He knew the season was closing. The bees were fewer, the days were darker and damper. The sunlight was slipping away far too fast. The sun itself, clearly on unapproved leave, had clocked out early without so much as a two-week notice.

He'd read about faraway lands where daylight lingered for months, and others where night refused to leave. He wondered what that would be like. Slimothy couldn't decide which sounded better—eternal sunshine or permanent pajamas.

Either way, both sounded like a blessed escape from bolting lettuce, browning leaves, and mosquitoes who had clearly missed every cease-and-desist memo Slimothy had circulated—repeatedly, and with excellent stationery. They remained maddeningly meddlesome, a winged public relations disaster he simply couldn't shake. Slimothy had the summertime blues and was in quite a state: melancholy, mildly moldy, and monumentally mopey.

A post-summer slump. Vitamin D on backorder. Desperate, dismal, delightfully dramatic. Dirt levels: definitely depleted. He was one compost crumble away from writing poetry in the mulch, emotionally waterlogged, and overanalyzing adjectives. Far too many bleak descriptors for a creature whose name started with "S."

Still, a respectable set of words starting with proper letters—unlike the strange slang of the modern age. The latest craze wasn't even a word but a number: 6-7. Not "sixty-seven," but *six seven*—uttered separately, sometimes with a hand motion like weighing invisible produce. It could mean "so-so," "mid," or perhaps "we understand something you never will."

It could also mean pure nonsensical gibberish—a meaningless interjection whose entire purpose was to mean absolutely nothing. Its lack of meaning was, apparently, the point. Modern slang, he decided, was mostly performance art for people who enjoyed exclusion. Or, more simply put: "we get it and you don't."

Slimothy didn't get it at all. Youngsters these days. Shibboleth.

He only hoped future generations would use their slang powers for good—like inventing a word for whatever this feeling was. Something between "meh" and "send help." If this was the height of human communication, no wonder the sun had packed up and left.

Back to the matter—or lack thereof—at hand. Daylight saving time was looming again, that annual conspiracy against productivity and slugs everywhere. Dark mornings, dreary evenings, and the unsettling sense that the sun had taken indefinite leave—all clearly designed to test him personally.

He decided the only logical cure was action. Not productive action, of course— just the kind that made you feel like you were accomplishing something while actively avoiding meaning.

Slimothy began by rearranging his seed packets alphabetically, then seasonally, then according to feelings. "Kale," he muttered, "you're definitely a winter soul. Peas, you peaked too early. As for zucchini ... I'm still waiting on you."

When that failed to lift his spirits, he brewed tea from questionable mint leaves and drafted a list.

"Ways to Reignite Summer Energy (Without Photosynthesis): Essential Supplies for the Mildly Unmotivated"

~ Basking under artificial sunshine until optimism returns.
~ Rewatching the weather forecast like a tragic love story.
~ Writing to the sun directly ("Dear Sir or Madam, please reconsider your retreat").
~ Starting a podcast called "Partly Cloudy with a Chance of Tears."
~ Standing in front of the fridge pretending it is a tropical breeze.

By mid-afternoon, he was wrapped in a towel like a chlorophyll-challenged burrito, humming something that might've been hopeful if it hadn't sounded like a tired harmonica slowly losing air. He was chilled to his lack of bones and couldn't shake the feeling that something was … off. Possibly the weather. Possibly the wine. Possibly the mosquito bite from the other night that now felt suspiciously like the work of a reanimated hemoglobin enthusiast—a nocturnal nectar fiend rumored to haunt compost heaps under full moons.

Somewhere in the distance, a single bee buzzed weakly past—the final note in summer's dying symphony, a faint echo of pollen-rich days gone by. Slimothy raised his glass in solemn tribute. "Respect the fallen," he whispered heroically, then immediately sneezed into it, ending the ceremony with more sincerity than accuracy.

The Bright Wild was slipping into shadow, and Slimothy could feel it in his slime. Most other creatures were hibernating, but he, however, was just getting started—delusional, determined, and dramatically defiant in the face of perfectly reasonable rest—charged with misplaced ambition, questionable caffeine levels, and the unshakable conviction that something, somewhere, still needed organizing.

CHAPTER NINETY-FOUR

Welcome to the Woods: Population, *Oh No*

It was All Hallows Eve, and Slimothy was feeling slightly jumpy. All day long, the Bright Wild had been conspiring to rattle him.

The garden gate creaked twice, like it had gossip to share but wanted him to ask first. Then the compost pile burped, long and dramatic, as if auditioning for a haunted-house sound effects reel. Slimothy adjusted his slime trail politely, deciding that whatever was happening clearly required a witness, not a participant.

A pumpkin rolled three quarters of an inch without wind assistance. Even the kale rustled dramatically, as though rehearsing for its big break in a horror movie titled "The Leaves That Knew Too Much."

At one point, a crow cawed from the fence, and Slimothy nearly flung his scarf in self-defense—as though a well-aimed accessory might scare off evil itself. He wasn't sure why; perhaps deep down he believed ghosts feared good fashion choices.

By evening, he'd convinced himself it was all nonsense. The Bright Wild was safe, cozy, and entirely spirit-free—or at least adequately insured. Still, when a shadow twitched at the edge of his limited eye-stalk vision, he stalled mid-slide, suddenly aware that bravery was a daytime activity.

Something was beckoning again. Not shouting, not calling—just politely suggesting—a whisper from the damp undergrowth, the kind of invitation that started as curiosity and ended as a cautionary tale. The kind written in fine print and possibly blood.

Slimothy squinted toward the trees lining the forest. Maybe it was just the wind. Maybe Roger. Maybe the universe sending him a final notice about bravery. The trees didn't answer, just swayed in that suspiciously choreographed way plants do when they're pretending to be casual.

Something shifted deeper in the brush. Not loudly, just enough to send a chill through his slime and briefly pause circulation in all three of his blue blood cells.

Slimothy flinched, executed what could only be described as a defensive wiggle, and in the scramble to look brave, managed to trip over a stick that definitely hadn't been there five seconds ago—and, judging by its self-assured angle, knew exactly what it was doing.

That's when he remembered ... the mosquito.

Not *a* mosquito. *The* mosquito—the one that bit like it meant it.

He went still. The bite. The chills. The sudden craving for shade. It all lined up far too neatly. Maybe this wasn't just All Hallows Eve mischief after all. Maybe that overzealous nocturnal phlebotomist who'd taken biting commentary a little too literally had done something to him. Slimothy swallowed hard. No pulse, no problem, sure—but he drew the line at undeath. He wasn't nearly dramatic enough to start brooding by moonlight.

Before his brain could file a complaint, the ground made a faint *glorp*. Not the kind of *glorp* moss should make. Not the kind of *glorp* anything should make. He poked it experimentally, and it rippled—once, twice, like water trying to remember how to behave.

Slimothy stared. "That's ... new," he declared in a voice small but sincere, the kind one might use upon discovering a second sun or an unexpected in-law.

The ground pulsed faintly blue (of course it matched his blood), casting a ghostly glow across the moss. Slimothy leaned closer, entranced by his reflection—shimmering, slightly distorted, but undeniably distinguished. His scarf caught the light beautifully; if this was the underworld, at least he looked fantastic for it. The reflection blinked back at him, which was both flattering and deeply concerning.

Before he had a single alternative thought, the ground gave a slippery sigh, and he plunged—scarf first—straight through his own poor decision.

For a moment, everything spun. His life flashed before his eyes—not dramatically, just inconveniently. Mostly images of wilted lettuce, missed weather reports, and that one time he accidentally declared war on the snails' book club. There was also an uncomfortable amount of kale.

The fall was slow, silent, and absurdly well-organized. He drifted past streaks of glowing soil, pockets of suspended raindrops, and a dandelion seed that waved politely on its way up. For a moment, he was sure he saw the reflection of his reflection, whispering something superior about hydration.

Colors smeared like wet paint. The world stretched and folded, then folded again just to be thorough. His scarf streamed behind him like a heroic ribbon in a story he did not sign up for.

When the spinning stopped, Slimothy lay very still, trying to decide whether he was alive, dead, or in some middle management position between the two. The earth beneath him felt wrong—too soft, too echoey—and the air hummed faintly, like it was thinking.

It smelled different here too—older, stranger. Everything dripped: trees, leaves, possibly time itself. Somewhere nearby, something hooted in a tone that suggested it wasn't impressed.

He blinked once, twice, and the realization crept in with all the subtlety of a watering can to the head. He wasn't in the garden anymore.

Slimothy peeled himself off a fern and took stock. His slime was mildly fluorescent. His scarf was smoking, and to make matters worse, a single, inexplicably glowing acorn had attached itself to his back like it was hitching a ride.

He blinked, dazed. Where was he? The Deep Drip? The Forbidden Fernery? The Slightly Off-Putting Arboretum? The Gloom Grove? The Dreadful Drizzle? The Bureau of Unfinished Compost Affairs? The Moist Unknown? The Regional Bog of Poor Decisions?

He looked around, mumbling the possibilities as if saying them might make them less alarming. The words drifted upward and hung there for a moment before fading into the mist, as though the air itself was filing them alphabetically.

It was damp, of course. Damp in a way that defied physics, logic, and personal boundaries. Drops hovered without falling, moss pulsed softly underfoot, and a nearby mushroom appeared to be exhaling. Slimothy was beginning to suspect that the humidity, wherever this was, had opinions.

He was certain time itself had disappeared, then sheepishly returned with an apology note and a wilted fern. He straightened up, attempting to look composed for the nearby bushes—who seemed deeply invested in the drama— and noticed a crooked wooden sign just ahead. It was planted upside down in a puddle, its letters wobbling and rearranging like they were mid-argument about grammar.

"LEFT → RIGHT ← BACK ↑ DOWN ↑," it offered helpfully, then sighed and added, *"Probably."*

Slimothy frowned. "Terrific. A map made by optimism."

Before picking a direction, something darted across the path—a warm blur of chestnut and light, like sunset given legs.

It paused just long enough to shake out its tail, the white tip catching what little glow the forest offered. For a heartbeat, the world went very still.

Slimothy stared. It couldn't be. The fox. *That* fox. The one from his waking dreams—the beautiful, radiant blur he'd seen only once, somewhere between a thunderstorm nap and an identity crisis. Calm. Knowing. Entirely out of his league.

Now here she was, breathing, real, and entirely uninterested in explaining herself.

"Wait—what?" Slimothy whispered.

The fox's ear twitched, as if she'd heard but decided not to dignify the question. Then she turned, elegant as a sigh, and slipped into the dripping dark.

"Right," Slimothy said softly, flinging his scarf behind as though it mattered. "Haunted forest. Obviously fine."

The forest didn't answer. A single leaf flipped itself over in polite swooning, and somewhere beyond the canopy, the stars seemed to lean in—winking like a group chat that had opinions about his chances.

He hesitated only a moment before sliding after her—because if there was one thing worse than being lost in a haunted forest, it was letting the fox of his dreams ghost him twice.

CHAPTER NINETY-FIVE

An Agenda Would've Been Nice

S limothy glanced up, but the sky had vanished, swallowed by branches that had clearly conspired against daylight. Whatever time it was, it wasn't his anymore. The thicket had decided on night and hadn't told him. He really needed to get on that email chain. It was, after all, his first forest trip, and he would've appreciated an agenda.

A glade opened before him, a sea of kale the color of bruised twilight, glimmering faintly as if moonlit from within. The general vibe smelled faintly of dirt and poor decisions. Beautiful, yes, but unsettling, like the kind of salad that knows too much about your search history.

A bee buzzed by his head, brilliant and iridescent green, as if someone had over-polished spring itself. The light came from nowhere in particular, his sense of direction had resigned mid-shift, and morale among his remaining thoughts was noticeably low.

Slimothy pulled out his journal to take notes and began rummaging for a pen, only to find two earthworms, a suspicious pebble, and what might've once been optimism. One of the worms looked eager, like it was about to volunteer for writing duty. Everything was different here, and the office supplies were apparently alive and plotting administrative overthrow.

Naturally, Slimothy had brought the wrong tools to the right problem: charts, lists, gadgets, even a soil pH reader he'd borrowed and never returned. Somewhere between the kale and the unknown, he decided to make sense of it all the only way he knew how—metrics.

Up to now, the Bright Wild had been his entire world, a self-contained garden-kingdom where every leaf, rule, and complaint was familiar.

This forest, with foliar textures ranging from fine to coarse and colors shifting from chartreuse to deep, unsettling purple, felt alive in a way that defied cataloging. He tried to file a field report, but the paper went soggy and a beetle ate his pen. He sighed. Data collection was never easy in the wild.

Still, for the sake of scientific integrity (and his own sanity), Slimothy began developing a new measurement system, one better suited to this magical forest.

Distance: Slimes
One slime = the average length of Slimothy's nightly slime trail before he got distracted (about eight feet).
A garden bed = three slimes.
To the fence = six slimes.
To enlightenment = infinity slimes.

Time: Blinks
One blink = the time it took Roger to deliver a sigh and judge Slimothy silently (about three seconds).
A conversation with Roger = five blinks.
A bottle of wine disappearing = 400 blinks.
Kale to sprout = 30,000 blinks and counting.

Now that he had that sorted, Slimothy decided the best way out was through.

So, with his notebook clutched like a manifesto for bad ideas and logic trailing somewhere in protest, he slimed ahead for bureaucratic reasons best left unexamined into the violet clouds of kale.

CHAPTER NINETY-SIX

Pickles, Frogs, and Balloon-Based Mysteries

S omewhere between one blink and the next, the kale began to speak. Not in words exactly—more in riddles, like a dream trying to explain itself before evaporating.

What grows where nothing listens, yet hears all the same?

It didn't sound like a question meant to be solved—only survived. Slimothy didn't know the answer, but he had a creeping suspicion it was about him.

He looked around, hoping for context, or at least subtitles, but the clearing had already gone quiet again—except for the faint, glittering sound of kale pretending not to watch him.

He pondered as he slid, noting he might have to adjust his slime-trail metric measurements, as things seemed somewhat lengthened here. Possibly by magic. Or humidity.

Either way, it was a terrible time to be scientifically inconsistent.

Moments later, the kale thinned into a small rise, tiny by most standards, but for Slimothy, a full-scale expedition complete with altitude sickness and mental rumination. Something stood waiting at the top, or slouching really, as if it had been exhausted by centuries of indecision.

A signpost. Its arrows pointed toward places that almost certainly didn't exist: Sideways, Near Enough, Emotional North, and one that simply read Tuesday.

Slimothy stared. He'd encountered many confusing things in the garden—philosophical crickets, judgmental mushrooms, a mirror that gave unsolicited advice—but never signage having an identity crisis.

He tried to make sense of it. The arrows flickered faintly, rearranging themselves when he wasn't looking. One briefly flashed Exit-ish, which somehow felt both encouraging and threatening.

"Of course," he said flatly. "A sign that can't commit." He tapped the post with one cautious feeler. "Alright, forest—show me the way. Preferably one that doesn't end in therapy or paperwork."

The arrowpost twitched, then rotated with the weary precision of a bureaucrat on their third coffee and last nerve. Every arrow spun dramatically before snapping to a stop—each one pointing directly at him.

Slimothy stared. "Oh good," he said. "Finally, a map that's cognitively cooperative." Then, softer, like he'd just solved the world's most obvious mystery: "Ah. A metaphor."

He waited for clarification, or applause, or divine intervention, but the sign just creaked like it was pretending to be mysterious on purpose. So he did the only reasonable thing: picked a direction at random and inched heroically onward.

Toward Emotional North.

He didn't know what that meant exactly—it just sounded purposeful. Adventurous. The kind of direction one takes when one is in search of meaning, or at least a snack. He expected enlightenment, or at least a playlist. Maybe a nice booming inner voice to guide him on the path. Something with a bit of echo.

No voice came—only the soft squelch of his own determination, expressed through what could technically be described as forward motion. That was fine, he decided. Independent slugs forged their own destinies. Probably.

He hadn't gone far when the forest made another attempt at drama. The reeds rustled like someone had just yelled *act natural!*, the moss exhaled tragedy, and the ground gave an ominous little shimmy that clearly meant plot development. Slimothy took attendance of his courage, trying to look unbothered. Emotional North, he decided, was auditioning for something—and absolutely nailing it.

Before his next thought even formed, four enormous seed packets flickered into existence before him—glowing softly, their labels fractionally legible in the gloom: Mystery Mix, Soulful Development, Second Chances, and Do Not Water After Midnight.

They hovered just above the moss, humming like very confident salad ingredients. The general ambiance was equal parts divine revelation and farmers-market fever dream. Each packet rustled faintly, as though aware it was about to ruin someone's day in a metaphorical sense.

He began listing possibilities. Portals? Bureaucratic installations? Possibly a horticultural art exhibit he hadn't RSVP'd to. He glanced around for a sign-up sheet, because surely something this official came with a filing system and a waiting period. When none appeared, he did the next most sensible thing— took out his field notebook, labeled the sighting "Unscheduled Germination Phenomenon," and began to measure absolutely nothing with great confidence.

His slime scale was unhelpful, his pencil kept slipping, and one of the packets made a faint crinkling noise every time he got too close—as if mocking his methodology. A small insect wandered past, gave him a once-over, and clicked its mandibles in the universal language of "amateur."

Slimothy doubled down, adding a few dramatic underlines to his notes for emphasis. It all felt very scientific, in the way pretending to understand a wine label feels like expertise.

The first packet was emblazoned with a partially-eaten tomato—oozing faint regret and a hint of unresolved salad trauma. The second, a tidy cluster of spinach leaves, looked judgmental but well-intentioned—like it had read "Boundaries for Beginners" and now thought it was better than everyone. The third was labeled with a bottle of red wine—open, naturally, and three-quarters empty in a way that felt deeply personal, as if it had already formed opinions about his life choices.

The fourth ... the fourth was unmarked. Plain, humming softly, smugly—the way something does when it already knows it's the wrong choice and can't wait for you to prove it right.

Slimothy stared at them, unsure whether he'd stumbled into a test, a metaphor, or just Tuesday's mental audit—a recurring event he was never fully prepared for.

The tomato packet glowed faintly, its printed fruit glistening in the dim light. It smelled of nostalgia, bad decisions, and the kind of confidence that only comes before disaster. The spinach packet straightened the moment he looked at it, radiating the composure of something that journaled regularly and had strong opinions about boundaries. It practically glowed with moral superiority. The wine packet sighed—long, luxurious, and enabling. It was the kind of sigh that promised clarity, delivered naps, and came with the faintest undertone of *"you deserve this."*

As for the unmarked packet ... it just hummed. Not ominously, not kindly—just in that specific frequency reserved for Slimothy's worst ideas, the ones that always began with, "how hard could it be?"

Then he heard it again—faint but unmistakable—threaded through the air like a secret trying to sound casual:

What grows where nothing listens, yet hears all the same?

The words slinked through his mind, curling around his thoughts like ivy.

What grows ... he echoed silently, staring at the lineup of existential produce before him. Not the tomato—it had already grown, peaked, and retired into a life of semi-eaten regret. Not the spinach—it grew, sure, but with the obedient energy of something that color-codes its own planner. The wine—well, that had once grown, but it had clearly moved on to a different phase of personal development.

That left the unmarked packet. It trembled faintly, vibrating with the same reckless promise that made slugs sign up for adventure without reading the waiver. The light deepened, pulsing in sync with his questionable curiosity.

Slimothy exhaled dramatically. *"Fine,"* he muttered, adjusting his posture like someone about to make a terrible but narratively satisfying decision. *"Mystery it is."*

The packet fluttered open—not politely, but with the self-importance of something that had been waiting all season to make an entrance. Its paper edges curled outward, releasing a glimmering puff of light and the faint smell of cosmic fertilizer. Every leaf, every tuft of moss, every judgmental fern went still.

Then, a final whisper drifted through the air—soft, knowing, almost quietly pleased:

At last, something listens.

There was a delicate *pop!*—the kind usually reserved for soap bubbles or bad decisions—and a cloud of iridescent pollen erupted through the clearing.

When it finally dispersed, something small and slightly dented lay in the moss—a package wrapped in twine, stamped with three question marks, and humming faintly like it was barely resisting the urge to say, *"took you long enough."*

Slimothy blinked once, then again, just to make sure his eye stalks weren't fabricating closure. Inside were his long-lost tomato cages—wayward supports returning at last.

He gasped—the way only a slug can—silently, with devastating personal subtlety. His long-lost tomato fortifications. The very same ones he'd accused Roger of "borrowing indefinitely" during last season's Great Trellis Debacle.

A rush of regret washed over him, followed by the sharper sting of administrative horror. It unfolded before him like prophecy: the passive-aggressive garden notes, the carefully rolled scrolls of accusation, the annotated diagrams. There had even been a pie chart labeled Tomato Cage Theft Probability, complete with gradient shading and footnotes.

"Well," he muttered, inspecting the package with the reverence of someone who'd just received a cosmic HR memo. "I suppose that's what grows where nothing listens."

The realization dawned slowly, as most of his important thoughts did—hesitant, slightly damp, and inconveniently profound. Maybe the forest hadn't been talking about plants at all. Maybe the thing that "grew" was him—metaphorically, which was frankly the worst kind of growth. The tomato cages weren't a gift. They were a lesson. A perfectly wrapped, gently mocking masterclass in patience, apology, and unnecessary chart formatting.

Growth, it seemed, sometimes arrived disguised as embarrassment and delivered via enchanted parcel service. Slimothy sighed. The universe had a strange sense of humor—and unfortunately, he was fluent in it.

Slimothy glanced back toward where the kale had been, fully bracing for the riddle to reprise itself—perhaps with a breeze and interpretive dance. The forest was quiet now, triumphantly so, as though satisfied the message had finally landed.

He slid the package behind his journal, humility (and mild mortification) settling in like damp moss. "Fine," he said at last. "I'll apologize to Roger. Probably."

He made to leave, dignity patched together with sheer optimism—but of course, the woods weren't done. The ground tilted just enough to make a point, the air rearranged itself into new intentions, and that familiar tug of unfinished narrative curled around his slime trail.

It wasn't much of a trail anymore—just a glistening mess looping in on itself, doodled confusion masquerading as direction. Around him, the grove had rearranged itself—quietly, efficiently, and with the satisfaction of something that already knew how this story would end.

The signpost was gone, of course. In its place hung a single leaf, suspended by dew and bad manners, with words scratched across it in what could only be described as rude cursive: *"Nice try."*

Slimothy stared. "Excellent," he muttered. "We've entered the feedback stage."

He squared his journal, straightened his posture (for morale, mostly), and declared to no one in particular, "Very well. We improvise."

So, clutching his recovered tomato cages and a slightly bruised ego, he pressed deeper into the underbrush. The air thickened, heavy with that telltale shimmer that meant the forest was preparing another round of "growth opportunities." Just beyond the canopy, blurred into the mist, something enormous shifted—slowly, silently, impossibly—as if the wood were exhaling a dream it had forgotten to finish.

It looked like the hot air balloon from the garden—those same faded orange and green stripes, rippling faintly in the haze. Only it wasn't flying—it was hovering, like a memory pretending to be solid. The ropes dangled lazily, brushing the mist, reaching down not as an invitation but as a dare.

Slimothy squinted up at it, trying to decide whether it was real, metaphorical, or a bureaucratic hallucination brought on by dehydration. The Bright Wild had a long history of blurring those distinctions, and frankly, he didn't have the paperwork for another cosmic incident.

Still, something in him stirred—that reckless tug between curiosity and bad judgment, humming louder than reason and twice as confident.

The balloon dipped lower, its striped glow scattering a faint shower of golden light, like someone shaking glitter out of a daydream. For one glorious second, Slimothy thought it might land—*finally, a straightforward development.* He straightened, tomato cages clutched like crisis management equipment.

Then, with the serene confidence of something that knew exactly how to be unhelpful, the balloon flickered, folded in on itself, and vanished behind a stand of trees. There was a soft *whoomp,* a flash of improbable light—and just like that, it was gone.

Not into the sky. Not into the mist.

Behind a seed rack.

Well—three seed packets.

They appeared with a polite *pop!*—not dramatic, not ominous, just the kind of sound reality makes when it gives up explaining itself. The air sparkled, and there they were, fluttering neatly in a row in the exact spot where the kale had once been (rest in leaves). Because clearly, what Slimothy needed right now was more choices.

Each packet gleamed faintly, perfectly aligned, as if arranged by someone with impeccable taste and a questionable sense of humor. Slimothy blinked, his sense of stability sliding sideways. Apparently, Emotional North had gone into sequel mode.

The first packet was a lush, mossy green and smelled faintly of ink, mildew, and misplaced paperwork—like a bureaucratic fern. The second shimmered like sunlight trapped in glass, glowing softly but refusing to cast a shadow—an act of botanical arrogance if ever there was one. The third—small, crooked, and clearly printed on discount cardstock—had a little gold label reading simply: "#3 (Good Luck?)."

Slimothy stared, his posture dangling somewhere between confusion and collapse. "Of course," he muttered. "Because one round of cryptic garden lessons wasn't enough."

He glanced upward, hoping for the balloon, or at least a sign that the universe was done improvising. Instead, the sky stared back blankly; the forest thrummed with held breath, and Slimothy sensed the next act had already slipped ahead without him.

Slimothy sighed. "Alright, fine. Round two."

The seed packets lit up, their designs reforming until vivid illustrations bloomed across the paper—bright, dramatic, and far too personal for comfort.

The first displayed a jar of perfect pickles, glistening like emeralds in brine. They radiated smug satisfaction—the kind that comes only from being both well-preserved and emotionally stable.

The second showed two frogs perched side by side on a lily pad, crowns slightly crooked, looking insufferably pleased with themselves. Above them, elegant gold script read: *"Hoppily Ever After."* Slimothy squinted. The scene reeked of sentimentality—and Roger's handwriting.

The third packet pulsed with faint orange and green stripes—the same pattern as the hot air balloon that had just ghosted him. Its paper seemed to breathe, expanding slightly, as if it were waiting for him to notice.

Slimothy's scarf rustled in the breeze, as if bracing itself for whatever fresh nonsense awaited. "Pickles, romance, or balloon-based mystery," he muttered. "The forest has really captured the full emotional range. Honestly, if I see one more symbolic packet, I'm filing a complaint with Reality Management."

He slid a cautious circle around them, each one humming with its own brand of temptation. The frogs smiled politely, like campaign posters. The pickles sparkled under an imaginary spotlight, radiating the confidence of snacks that had never made a mistake. The balloon packet exhaled a faint, sweet scent of ozone and adventure—inviting, comforting, and almost certainly untrustworthy.

He stared at them all, unsure whether he was meant to choose ... or be chosen.

Slimothy considered his options like a creature faced with destiny, responsibility, and fermented cucumbers.

The pickle packet was safe. Predictable. Possibly crunchy. The frog packet radiated romance and amphibian self-satisfaction—the kind of domestic bliss he'd always (begrudgingly) wished for Roger and Lilibet, though he still questioned their pond décor choices.

Bright, impossible, and vibrating faintly with the same mischievous pull he'd felt before, the balloon packet was calling him. Whispering adventure. Or chaos. Or both.

Slimothy hesitated. The pickles sparkled harder, aggressively cheerful. The frogs waved again, one of them blowing a kiss purely for dramatic effect. The balloon packet gave a faint sigh—the universal sound of opportunity running out of patience.

"Look," Slimothy said to no one in particular, "I am perfectly capable of making a bad decision on my own."

The forest, newly opinionated and unafraid to show it, disagreed. A sudden gust tore through the clearing, scattering leaves and glittering dust as the packets whirled in a frantic cyclone. Slimothy tried to cling to the soil itself, which, unhelpfully, tried to wriggle away, heart pounding as the air crackled with possibility.

Then—*snap!*—the packets froze mid-spin, their edges glowing softly. The balloon packet peeled itself open with the enthusiasm of something that had been waiting specifically to cause trouble. A coil of glowing twine shot outward like an eager vine, looping around him with unsettling precision.

Before Slimothy could even mutter a complaint or file a dignity preservation report, he was scooped up—swiftly, unceremoniously, and with all the grace of an unprepared raffle winner.

The forest fell away beneath him, shrinking into a patchwork of green and glitter. The seed packets folded back into nothing, like reality tidying up after itself. Slimothy tried to hang on for dear life as the world blurred into watercolor chaos.

He squinted up at the vast, spinning sky and muttered, as dry as a leaf in August, "Well … that's one way to measure elevation."

Somewhere above, the unseen balloon creaked approvingly, as if altitude and absurdity were the same thing.

CHAPTER NINETY-SEVEN

Up, Up, and Mildly Alarmed

S limothy had always assumed adventure would feel grand—wind in his nonexistent hair, heroic music swelling in the background, maybe a commemorative plaque someday. Instead, it mostly felt windy and poorly planned.

For a fleeting, glorious moment, he believed he was soaring. The wind rushed past (or maybe just around) him, the basket creaked heroically, and the ropes hummed with the tension of destiny. He dared a look down, ready to be humbled by the vast, breathtaking expanse of wherever-this-was below.

There it was—every leaf, every vine, every suspiciously opinionated fern— exactly three inches beneath him.

He stared long enough to qualify it as data collection, then longer out of disbelief.

The forest stretched out flat and indifferent, close enough to count as ground contact. A beetle waved as it strolled by at roughly the same speed as his "aircraft."

"Ah," Slimothy said, gripping the edge of the basket with unnecessary drama. "So not flying, then. More of a ... hovering situation."

The balloon gave a low, self-satisfied groan, as if to confirm it was indeed performing at maximum effort.

"Excellent," he muttered. "Truly, the very edge of innovation."

He straightened his journal—because if he wasn't in control of the flight, he could at least document its incompetence—and stared ahead as the balloon drifted lazily forward, scraping the "treetops" like a creature fully committed to the concept of flight but not the execution.

Green rolled out beside him, glowing with a calm, fluid brilliance. Everywhere he looked, tiny sprouts pushed through the soil, each one gleaming like a gem in a very enthusiastic jewelry commercial. They weren't ordinary seedlings; their pods glowed pale to deep green—bright, soft, argumentative—all of them far too pleased with themselves. Every few seconds one would *ping!* open, releasing a puff of luminescent flecks that hung in the air before drifting away like confetti with a sense of purpose.

Magic beans. Hundreds of them. Maybe thousands.

Slimothy's eyes widened—equal parts awe and imminent overanalysis. Wonder lasted all of three seconds before giving way to calculation, the inevitable slide from marvel of nature to potential spreadsheet. His expression sharpened into the look of someone preparing to audit wonder itself.

"Right," he murmured, reaching for his observational register. "If I can quantify sparkle output per square inch, we may be looking at a new era in legume-based innovation."

He flipped to a blank page, licked the tip of his pencil (for science), and prepared to record the first data point in agricultural history.

Ping!

A bean launched directly into his face, leaving a faint constellation of sparkles across his forehead.

Slimothy remained unimpressed. "Noted," he said flatly.

Aggressively interactive species.

Taking the hint, he stopped theorizing and started listening.

Wiping the bean residue from his face, he adjusted his composure—no small feat after being publicly assaulted by agriculture.

"All right," he muttered, adopting his best field-research tone. "Observation before participation."

Bean Behavior Log, Entry One:
Emits sparkle upon emergence.
Defies known soil composition.
May be sentient.
Aggressive when provoked.
Possibly armed with dubious performance energy.

He tapped the page thoughtfully. The beans pinged again in unison, like they were confirming the data—or mocking his handwriting.

Before he finished writing the next line, three beans sprouted beside him—fast, confident, and just a little showy about it. Their vines stretched upward, then sideways, then back again, like they were still negotiating choreography. One made an ambitious attempt at handing him another bean, though "handing" was generous. It flung the thing in his general direction with polite determination and questionable aim.

The bean bounced off his side, rolled to a stop, and began to pulse faintly, like it was trying to remember its lines. Then, with a delicate *bloop*, it projected a tiny holographic diagram of … another bean. This one came fully annotated with labels: "Altitude," "Mood," and "Potential for Mischief."

Slimothy blinked, then leaned closer, intrigued despite himself. "Finally," he murmured, "something measurable."

Above him, the balloon gave a low, creaky sound of approval and began to drift forward, its ropes tugging toward the horizon. Below, the vines mirrored the motion, all leaning in the same direction—like the entire forest had silently agreed on a new research initiative.

Slimothy watched them, feeling that distinct blend of awe and dread reserved for moments when nature got ideas. "Oh no," he said softly. "We're collaborating."

No one answered. Moments later, another bean pinged—the unmistakable sound of enthusiasm he didn't remember authorizing.

The vines didn't wait for input. They curled and crossed with the quiet authority of things that had already made up their minds, the kind of confidence usually reserved for doomed group projects. Light flowed through their green bodies, knotting into a path that seemed both inviting and slightly condescending.

Slimothy's expression caught somewhere between awe and administrative concern. "Ah. Relocation," he said dryly. "Classic escalation."

Before he had time to object—let alone file a formal complaint with the Department of Unexpected Motion—the vines scooped him up, graceful yet unyielding, like waitstaff trained in abduction etiquette. He drifted forward, wobbling majestically—equal parts research specimen and reluctant parade float.

Above, the balloon kept pace like a vibe-maintenance blimp, humming softly in unhelpful solidarity.

"Very efficient," Slimothy muttered, trying to sound like a man in charge of the situation. "If I survive, I'll recommend this method to the Garden Transit Committee."

The ecosystem around him blurred—microbes, moss, and herbaceous busybodies bending politely out of the way, like they'd received an all-staff memo marked "Slug in Transit." Bioluminescent spores winked to life across the soil, tracing constellations in his slime trail with unsettling precision. Every few inches, a bean *pinged!* and released a puff of glittering mist that smelled faintly of dill, ozone, and déjà vu—like the universe itself had opened a salad bar and immediately regretted it.

Slimothy craned his neck—or at least approximated it, which for a slug meant mostly widening his stare and leaning with conviction. *"Is this ... transport? Or abduction?"* he asked the air, which offered no clarification.

The vines didn't answer either, though they were clearly congratulating themselves on the execution. After a few minutes—or possibly 30 blinks, a subjective eternity in slug time—they began to decelerate with the self-satisfaction of a committee that had just concluded a wildly unnecessary meeting. Then, with exaggerated ceremony, they unfurled and deposited him onto a patch of moss so plush it practically whispered, *"Apologies for the inconvenience; this wasn't on the agenda."*

Slimothy looked around, adjusting to the new decor. The kale was gone—either erased, relocated, or promoted to middle management. As for the light ... it wasn't green anymore. It had gone lavender, cool and unexpected—the sort of luminescence that moved in without paying rent and immediately started rearranging the atmosphere.

Slimothy squinted. "Well," he said carefully, "that can't possibly be trouble."

The ground gave a satisfied little sigh and settled. The ancient plants—rooted, glowing, and unmistakably pleased with themselves—eased back into the moss, pretending they hadn't just staged an unsolicited transportation experiment. Their light faded to a polite shimmer, the kind that said, *"nothing happened here and we'd prefer no follow-up questions."*

The air stilled again—too still, a brand of calm that usually precedes either enlightenment or a strongly worded garden memo.

Then, with a crisp *pop!* three new seed packets appeared in midair, landing smartly in a row before Slimothy. Each one flickered faintly, edges glowing like bad decisions pressed flat and preserved.

He stared. "Perfect," he muttered. "Because what this story really needed was round three of magical horticulture and unresolved symbolism."

They weren't grand or theatrically lit this time—no pomp, no cosmic fanfare. Just expectant. Three enchanted pouches sitting quietly in the lilac light, radiating the unnerving confidence of things that already knew how the story would end. Each bore a tiny hand-painted label, the brushstrokes uneven but purposeful.

The first read: "A Proper Forest Agenda."

It smelled faintly of ink, damp wood, and the kind of authority that always loses its pen mid-meeting.

The second offered: "A Wish (Singular) To Be Granted."

It gave off a low hum of energy—hopeful, hesitant, and faintly self-aware—like it was bracing for the moment it inevitably disappointed someone.

The third—slightly crooked, a tuft of moss curling over one corner—stated: "Return To The Garden (But With a Twist)."

It looked casual. Maybe too casual. The sort of nonchalance that had seen things.

Slimothy regarded them for a long moment. "So ... three sachets of destiny instead of three wishes," he murmured. "Statistically consistent. Existentially annoying."

He looked between them, twitching in concentration. The first promised structure. The second, temptation. The third, home—perhaps, though with a twist sounded worryingly like a sequel no one had budgeted for.

"Right," he said at last, mostly to the moss, which rustled like an audience pretending not to pick favorites. "Round three."

He advanced at the speed of doubt, the air around him rippling in quiet anticipation. The packets waited—still, patient, unreadable.

Above, the balloon hovered soundlessly in the haze, swaying ever so slightly, as if taking notes for the universe—or worse, live-tweeting the whole thing.

CHAPTER NINETY-EIGHT

Minutes, Miracles, and Mild Panic

S limothy tried to calculate packet outcomes the way one might measure fog—ambitiously, pointlessly, and with growing suspicion that the mist was doing the same to him.

The Forest Agenda envelope caught his eye first, promising structure, order, and the sweet illusion of control. The scent of freshly printed minutes practically materialized, the tidy bullet points, the intoxicating whisper of accountability. Beautiful lies.

The Wish (Singular) packet thrummed louder, its glow deepening like it had just realized it was his weak spot. It pulsed with possibility, smelling faintly of risk and regret—the exact scent of things Slimothy historically could not resist.

The Return To The Garden (But With a Twist) compostable mystery mail didn't call at all. It simply waited—quiet, patient, familiar. It lit up in a mild, optimistic sort of way, like spring itself: warm, forgiving, and looking dangerously close to writing its own memoir.

Slimothy stared at them. "Right," he muttered. "Three packets, three chances, one slug who should really know better."

Naturally, he decided to start with the most dangerous option: overthinking.

He set to work on a wish list; if the universe intended to tempt him, he was at least bringing documentation.

Wishes:
~ For the garden road expansion to finally, mercifully, go away.
~ To uncover Roger and Lilibet's secret uptown hideout once and for all.
~ For an algae-free pond.
~ Unlimited daily calories with no consequences.
~ A lifetime supply of kale (obviously), and of course,
~ To expose the elusive, cold-leafed culprit known only as The Mysterious Spinach Thief.

The list mushroomed, spiraling somewhere between noble ambition and petty administrative vengeance.

Could he wish for more wishes? Or a clearer definition of singular? Or maybe just a copy of the terms and conditions before accidentally agreeing to enlightenment?

The possibilities tangled together until his reasoning folded in on itself like damp origami. Within moments, he was knee-deep in a cognitive casserole of doubt and imagination.

Eventually, even his mind went still. His thoughts—once bubbling and overcomplicated—settled into something small and steady. It took him a while to recognize it.

Homesickness.

He wasn't sure how long he'd been gone, but the ache of it sat heavy and oddly specific to slugs. He missed the garden—the gossiping insects, the overgrown leaves, the satisfying squelch of well-hydrated soil. He even missed the watering (or, more accurately, the rage of its inconsistency).

Were the plants still thriving without him? Had the zucchini finally fruited? Did anyone remember to whisper encouragement to the lavender by the fence?

A cold thought slithered in. Was time here different? Would seven years pass back home while, for him, only a blink? Or worse ... would nothing have changed at all?

For once, he didn't analyze. He just sat there—quiet, thoughtful, and very small.

The forest, ever punctual with personal disruptions, decided that was quite enough reflection for one slug. With a faint *pop,* a bottle of wine appeared beside him.

Slimothy blinked—not metaphorically, but audibly. Wine never just appeared in the Bright Wild. Someone had clearly upgraded the soul-soothing infrastructure.

He turned the bottle over, somewhat expecting the label to read *"Emergency Coping Mechanism."* No such luck. Still, it gleamed invitingly, that perfect deep red that promised both clarity and immediate regret.

"If this is a trap," he said, uncorking it anyway, "it's a very considerate one."

He hoped someone back home had noticed his absence—if only the sudden silence where his commentary used to echo. Though, knowing Roger, he'd already replaced him with a decorative rock and called it a leadership upgrade.

Still … maybe they missed him. *Maybe.*

Then again, he thought, pouring himself a cautious glug, the wine here was quite possibly worth the paperwork.

CHAPTER NINETY-NINE

The Art of Avoidance

After a few nice glasses of the earthy red, Slimothy eyed the seed packets warily.

They sat there a little too confidently, like they'd been briefed on the plot and were just waiting for him to catch up.

"Because apparently, personal growth comes with a planting guide."

If the forest could conjure wine, surely it could conjure answers, too—preferably in list form, with columns, headings, and at least one color-coded chart. Maybe he just needed to look around a bit longer. Or make a spreadsheet. Or take a short, reflective walk that accidentally lasted several hours. Besides, he reasoned, any realm sophisticated enough to provide wine probably stocked snacks somewhere nearby.

So, with the logic of a creature who had learned nothing and yet everything, Slimothy did what any responsible slug would do when faced with destiny—he postponed it.

He turned away from the seed packets and proceeded in dignified squelches toward the faintest glimmer between the trees, telling himself it was research. The light shifted softly, alive and watchful, almost playful, as if it were trying to lead him somewhere, or at least keep him mildly entertained. After all, destiny would still be there later. If it wasn't, well, that would be destiny's fault for poor scheduling.

He'd made it only a few slimes forward when something glinted between the trees. Not stepped, not approached—just appeared.

The fox stood there.

Sleek, narrow-faced, silver-white and brown, with fur that caught the light like liquid fire. Wisps of plum-colored veil coiled around her paws, the same hue that had trailed him all throughout the wood. Tucked behind her ear, she carried a single, radiant sprig of spinach.

"You seem troubled," she said, voice low and lilting, like laughter in disguise.

Slimothy blinked—or attempted to. "You talk."

The fox tilted her head, unimpressed. "You overthink."

He squinted. "That's called analysis."

"That's called denial." She dropped the spinach delicately at his side and sat back, curling her tail around her paws with the patience of someone who enjoyed being cryptic. "You seek direction."

"I was actually seeking snacks," Slimothy said.

The fox smiled, a small, knowing thing. "Most seekers confuse hunger for purpose."

Slimothy frowned. "Forest creatures always assume silence equals wisdom."

Her whiskers twitched, amused but not offended. "Perhaps. Though silence lasts longer."

Before any kale-based retort could leave his brain, the fox stood. The air wavered around her; the forest seemed to lean in, waiting. Then she took three graceful steps backward into the mist and, without ceremony, dissolved like smoke retreating with a secret.

Slimothy stared after her. "Of course," he muttered. "Philosophy and produce. Just what I needed."

The clearing went quiet again—too quiet, like the world was waiting for him to admit something profound.

Slimothy eyed the spinach on the ground suspiciously, then the space where the fox had been. "Nope," he said. "Not touching that metaphor."

The moss began to glow anyway. Slowly, deliberately, like it had been taking notes the whole time. Letters unfurled in the damp earth—neat, self-satisfied, and just pretentious enough to feel poetic.

He squinted. "Oh no," he whispered. "Homework."

It wasn't a note exactly, more like a riddle that had sprouted uninvited from the soil, humming faintly as if proud of itself:

To move ahead, you must go back.
To see the truth, stay off the track.
What you seek will never hide—
It simply waits where rules collide.

Slimothy groaned. "That's not even formatted properly."

He read it again. Then a third time, slower, as if punctuation might suddenly appear. The forest, unhelpfully, did not provide citations.

"Well," he sighed, "that's either philosophy or bad directions."

He stared at the glowing lines, feeling the familiar tug of the universe asking him to learn something he definitely didn't sign up for. It was the same feeling you get when you realize the lesson was optional but graded anyway.

"Fine. Back it is."

With that, Slimothy turned toward wherever "back" was supposed to be, fully prepared to misunderstand destiny all over again, and, if possible, take notes while doing it.

Reflections and Other Poor Decisions

S limothy pressed onward in what he assumed was the general direction of "back."

It wasn't a straight line—more of a purposeful wobble, a meander with conviction. After several heroic glides, two wrong turns, and one brief argument with a fern that refused to yield right of way, the faint glimmer of the seed packets appeared through the ultraviolet mist once more.

Something was off.

For one thing, there were only two packets now. The third, his presumed "safe" option, had vanished entirely. In its place sat a small puddle, perfectly round and rippling lazily, as though it had opinions it wasn't ready to share.

Slimothy frowned. "Oh, perfect. Budget cuts."

He crept closer, peering at the remaining packets. Their glossy surfaces weren't still anymore; they seemed to breathe and shift like wet ink, with faint silhouettes moving beneath the printed illustrations.

In one, he thought he saw the outline of his garden: the familiar paths, the tilting gnome, the basil that refused to cooperate. It glowed softly, warm, green, and painfully nostalgic.

In the other, he saw ... himself. Or rather, a version of himself, taller and shinier, with the confident glisten of a slug who never misplaced a chart. This Slimothy looked efficient, poised, and alarmingly well-hydrated.

Between them, the puddle gave a low, deliberate gurgle like a throat being cleared by destiny.

Slimothy stared. "Great," he muttered. "Now even the water's judging me."

He glanced down. *"You're not about to talk too, are you?"*

The puddle said nothing, which somehow made it worse. It just held a quiet gleam, the liquid equivalent of a poker face.

Slimothy sighed. "Right. So the riddle says go back. I went back." He leaned closer, and the puddle rippled once, twice, then flickered like a screen booting up. The third seed packet was suddenly back—its reflection joining the others, all of them casting faint ripples of light across the surface. Only now, their symbols had changed: one bore a swirling spiral, one a simple leaf, and the third, his missing one, displayed what was unmistakably a spork.

Slimothy squinted. "Three packets, a riddle, a puddle. Honestly, this forest needs an editor."

Then he paused, eyes narrowing. "Oh no. Snack destiny."

Folding his nonexistent arms, he studied the reflection. "I know this drill. Pick the safe packet, end up in mental disarray. Pick the mysterious one, get character development. Pick the snack one, gain five glugs and a moral I'll immediately ignore."

The spork symbol pulsed brighter, glinting like a cosmic inside joke.

"Don't you dare," Slimothy warned. "I'm not hungry for meaning, I'm just hungry."

The puddle gurgled ominously, low and deliberate, deeply judgmental.

Slimothy groaned. "Fantastic. I'm being peer-pressured by hydration."

In the space of a single blink, everything went sideways. Reality stretched, folded, and promptly gave up trying to make sense. For one glorious, centrifugally confusing second, Slimothy experienced life as a salad spinner. Colors blurred. Logic detached. Then, thunk.

He landed gracefully, if one were grading on a curve that included mid-scream somersaults, on something soft, warm, and faintly judgmental. The air smelled of thyme, chaos, and regret baked at 350 degrees. Before him sprawled a floating landscape of unfinished meals: garden feasts paused mid-bite. Salads missing dressing. Sandwiches missing purpose. Soups caught mid-simmer, like they'd frozen mid-argument about seasoning.

"Fantastic," Slimothy muttered, brushing off imaginary crumbs. "It's purgatory, but catered."

Then the tables began to tilt. Slowly at first, then all at once. Salads skidded off the edges in synchronized despair, soups spun into dramatic whirlpools, and one particularly confident quiche locked eyes with him as it twirled past, graceful, unbothered, and absolutely certain it had won whatever this was.

Light fractured: greens, golds, and the deep, theatrical purple of twilight having a meltdown. "The Sporking Room" folded inward with a sound like the universe trying to uncork itself and immediately regretting it. There was a faint *pop*, sharp and final, and just like that, the ground disappeared.

Then, because consistency was clearly optional, it reappeared underneath him again, softer this time, damp and humming faintly, as if politely asking whether he was done yet. Slimothy found himself back in the patch of purple kale where his journey had first begun.

He groaned softly. "Of course. Full circle. Very poetic. Very exhausting."

The scene was unnervingly familiar: the same trees, the same mist, the same kale looking far too pleased with itself. Except everything had that rearranged feel, like the forest had held a surprise inspection while he was gone and was now pretending it had always been this organized.

He tried to gauge distance, but his slime scale was useless again. Time and space here had clearly had a messy breakup and were refusing to speak to each other. "Is this the forest equivalent of daylight saving?" he muttered. "A chaos of clocks, all running late, early, and sideways at once?"

As if on cue, a soft ding echoed through the clearing. Slimothy turned. Nestled smugly between two kale leaves sat a tiny brass timer, its face glowing faintly as its hands ticked backward, slow and deliberate.

He leaned closer. The little mechanism whirred and clicked, spinning its hands in small, fussy circles, like it was trying to decide whether time was optional today.

"Alright," he sighed, straightening up. "So we've got kale, a countdown, and no idea what happens at zero. Classic Thursday."

Poof. A plate appeared in front of him, perfectly arranged kale chips, still warm and glistening, dotted with red tomatoes and an unapologetic mountain of spinach on the side.

Slimothy froze. "Oh no," he whispered. "It's reading my thoughts."

The timer gave another polite ding. The spinach lit up in a way he did not trust. The timer ticked louder. 7:22.

"Alright," Slimothy said slowly, in cautious diplomacy. "If this is some kind of truce, I accept."

He reached for a kale chip. The forest responded with a low hum, patient and ancient, and, if he wasn't mistaken, slightly condescending.

The chip crumbled into dust before it even touched his mouth. A whisper drifted through the leaves, soft but unmistakable, perfectly in rhythm with the timer's tick:

Name the forest, and you may go.

Slimothy squinted upward. "That's … that's a big ask. I barely remember my recycling schedule."

The forest rustled, unimpressed. The timer clicked down to 7:01.

"Right," he muttered. "So now I'm in a naming ceremony with vegetables. Fantastic."

He began to pace, small, anxious slimes back and forth, muttering options like a contestant on a very unhinged game show.

"Something dignified? Mysterious? Poetic? Fernando?"

Tick.

"Have it your way," he grumbled. "Not Fernando. What about The Bright Wilder Forest? Department of Unfinished Business? Nature, But Mean?"

Tock.

"Right," Slimothy said flatly. "Tough crowd. You know, if you wanted branding help, you could've just asked. I've chaired committees for less."

He glared upward. "Fine. You want a name? You get a name."

He raised his voice, channeling the authority of someone who once led the Garden Subcommittee on Compost Logistics. "I hereby dub thee The Kale of

Mystery."

Silence. Then, a single polite ding. The timer stopped. Everything held its breath.

Slimothy blinked. "Did ... did that work?"

The air flickered at the edges. A warm breeze swept through, and the kale patch glowed brighter, just enough to look unbearably pleased with itself.

He sighed. "Of course it worked. The forest is as dramatic as I am."

A wasp landed along his upper side, giving him a look that suggested it agreed. Slimothy turned, scanning the clearing. The vines pulsed gently. The puddle twinkled in the murk. The kale radiated the quiet confidence of something that had just been promoted to executive leafership.

"The Bright Wild," he began, then stopped. That was home. This was something else. Older. Wilder, and definitely more sarcastic.

He squinted, feeling the word rise before he could stop it, a truth crawling out from under the mulch of his thoughts.

Something in the air shifted—like the forest finally giving him permission to be dramatic.

"You're not bright," he murmured. "You're weird. You're unpredictable. You're ..." He hesitated, then delivered the title with due ceremony.

"The Wild Wood."

The forest exhaled, deep and ancient, utterly satisfied. Every leaf, every shadow, every breath of air seemed to lean toward him, acknowledging, accepting, like the whole forest had just signed off on a very important document.

The timer went silent at exactly 6:00, its light flickering out with a soft, self-congratulatory sigh.

The kale rustled approvingly. The puddle brightened. The ground rearranged itself, roots shifting, moss parting, paths unfurling through the undergrowth. Light threaded between the foliage like spun gold, soft and deliberate, pointing the way home.

He felt it before he understood it: that warm, magnetic pull of *there you are, finally.*

The way to the Bright Wild lay ahead, outlined in pale light, waiting.

He turned to the kale patch. "You're staying, I suppose?"

The kale did not deny it. Slimothy sighed, equal parts wistful and proud. "Fine. Hold down the fort. I'll send a watering schedule."

The path stretched out before him, beautiful and familiar. It looked safe. Comforting. Practically brochure-worthy.

He drifted forward, powered by curiosity and inertia. The light warmed beneath him. A second slide, steady and sure, like the music swelling at the end of a story. Then, naturally, a third.

"At this point," he muttered, "I'm starting to think the universe has a bulk discount on metaphors."

Of course, the third slide led straight to a puddle. The ground gave a polite *shloop*, the forest exhaled what sounded suspiciously like laughter, and Slimothy dropped straight through.

There was a flash of light, a single kale leaf spinning past his face like sarcastic applause, and the unmistakable sound of distant woodland giggling as gravity reclaimed him.

When he landed, it was on familiar dirt, the real kind. The home kind. The Bright Wild.

The air smelled normal again: dew, algae, faint regret. The regular kale was vain, as expected. The pond was gurgling, good. Reality, check one.

He sat up slowly, head buzzing with the faint static of too many metaphors. A thin ribbon of drool clung to the soil beneath him, an unflattering but conclusive sign that either he'd been unconscious or extremely contemplative. He chose the latter.

Slimothy began a slow, methodical reconnaissance slime around the Bright Wild, measured, deliberate, and mildly paranoid, at a speed best described as "technically movement."

Then, fully embracing his inner administrator, he pulled out his science binder—tabbed, over-labeled, and questionably waterproof—to begin what he proudly referred to as an existential audit.

"A full audit of existence"

Slime scale: appears to be functioning again and—shockingly—on the correct measurement system.

Birdbath and pond: the only things burbling. Acceptable.
Pond: still coated in algae. Somehow counts as progress.
Bees: normal color. Check.
Zucchini: still hasn't fruited, but several suspicious seedlings suggest
ambition. Check.
Roger: still absent. Check. Possibly intentional.

A giant leaf smacked him squarely across the face. Excellent. Gravity was operational.

He wiped the indignity off his front and kept going. Then he entered what his notes would later describe as "a momentary lapse of momentum due to feelings-based turbulence."

A frost-tipped patch of fur darted past, quick and deliberate. Slimothy and his slime came to a full and undignified stop, mid-trail, like a traffic jam with feelings.

For one glorious second, he caught a glimpse of a silver-tipped tail vanishing behind the zucchini bed.

He squinted into the greenery, almost expecting a sly voice to drift back, something cryptic about hunger, purpose, or hydration schedules. Instead the garden stayed silent, quietly satisfied, as though the Wild Wood itself had signed an NDA.

Slimothy eased back a cautious length, dignity wobbling like a loose rock. He scribbled furiously in his garden data log:

Fox—possibly sentient. Potential forest liaison or undercover
auditor.

Then, below that, in slightly shakier handwriting:

Prepare diplomatic snack options.

Finally, one last line, firm and professional:

Reality audit: inconclusive. Possible overlap. Recommend snacks before further investigation.

"If this is home," he murmured, "it's definitely under new management."

His vision wobbled faintly at the edges, either fatigue or an overdue eye exam. Possibly both.

A breeze drifted through the garden, warm and sweet, carrying a faint violet haze that curled lazily through the air before fading into nothing.

Slimothy watched it go, sighed, and jotted a final note:

Status: concussion or portal. Both plausible. Proceed with snacks.

Then, after a pause, one more line, just in case:

Schedule vision test. Possible residual shimmer.

The Mushrooms That Judge You

Slimothy was all out of whack. The sun had set before he'd even had a chance to wake up, he'd forgotten to turn the pond feature lights on, his wine was giving him heartburn, and he still had no idea whether the past few days had been reality or dream—or possibly a joint venture between the two.

The still-in-beta Bright Wild App had picked up bizarre data readings between 2 and 4 a.m. on All Hallows Eve. He wasn't sure if he'd gone walkabout, had an out-of-body experience for Día de los Muertos, or simply hit his head on that traitorous stick in the first place.

The moon—though full—was refusing to cooperate with the time-change command (and honestly, who could blame it). Slimothy's entire being felt backward, upside-down, and overstuffed with purple kale, launch-capacity beans, mysterious uncatalogued seeds, and the faint echo of talking animals.

Thankfully, his regular kale appeared unharmed and safely bolt-free. At least something in the Bright Wild still respected a schedule.

He stared toward the decorative hot-air balloon in the far corner of the garden. Definitely there—check. Still glowing—check. Weird vine-like tentacle ropes—none detected—good. Check. Still impossibly high up and unreachable due to his well-developed fear of height and common sense—double check.

He pulled out his usually trustworthy plant app (which had never gaslit him before, at least not on purpose) and began a cautious patrol of the garden, looking for suspects.

The app chirped to life in its aggressively cheerful tone.

"Did you know mass hallucinations from produce have been documented?"

Slimothy stopped mid-slime.

Apparently, somewhere called Australia, people had once eaten spinach so suspicious it made them see things. Over a hundred victims, the app bragged— like it had personally organized the event. The culprit? Some sneaky weed that had crashed the spinach party uninvited.

The app continued, utterly unbothered.

"Unripe tomatoes can also cause confusion and hallucinations."

"Of course they can," Slimothy reasoned. "They've always been dramatic."

"Salvia leaves may also induce visions," the interface announced brightly, as if suggesting a weekend hobby.

Slimothy looked at the mint patch where the salvia swayed like guilty backup dancers. "Visions of what, exactly?" he wondered.

Silence. The mint refused comment.

He sighed. So either his vegetables were out to get him, or his app had joined the conspiracy.

Then the screen flickered. Once. Twice. The cheerful display warped into static, and letters began rearranging themselves:

Field report: "Subject active. Anomaly detected. Location: The Bright Wild."

Slimothy blinked. The app buzzed, glitched again, then calmly resumed its usual home screen like nothing had happened.

"Oh," Slimothy said softly. "Good. Excellent. Definitely fine."

He closed the program—then immediately reopened it, because curiosity had never once gone well, but traditions were traditions.

Its warning was simple and foreboding: *"Enter the Agaric Abyss at your own risk."*

He hadn't eaten any mushrooms that he could recall. There weren't many that grew in the garden, but toxic fungi could still be responsible for whatever Slimothy had—or hadn't—seen in the last few days. Hard to say with confidence.

He decided, logically, that the shrooms were the place to start. His app agreed, practically buzzing with joy that he had finally asked it the correct question, like a long-bottled genie finally getting to grant a wish.

Slimothy found the first patch of suspicious organisms and leveled the identifier like a detective in a nature documentary no one had funded.

The display blinked obligingly, processing, spinning, then politely announced:

"Warning: Possible fungal presence. Or toast."

There was a long pause.

Slimothy stared at the screen, then at the moss. "Excellent," he said. "We're officially in the realm of interpretive science."

"Bright Wild Field Guide, Vol. III: The Mushrooms That Judge You"

Category: fungal (suspiciously so).
Habitat: anywhere moist enough to regret.
Last seen: under your compost bin, plotting.

⊘ DESCRIPTION: Agaricaceae
Status: ancient. Overconfident. Full of unearned swagger.
Reputation: cornerstone of the fungal realm (self-appointed).
Species count: 1,000+—each with its own questionable agenda.
Range of threat: some edible. Some existential threats. All confusing on purpose.
Behavior: tiny troublemakers to meaty enigmas. Evolving theatrics for ~20.44 million years—give or take a few dramatic centuries.
Conclusion: highly competent at confusion. Not to be trusted without snacks present.

☠ TOXICITY
General warning: many appear charming; few are trustworthy.
Yellow-staining mushroom (Agaricus xanthodermus):
Offers false hospitality.
Rewards visitors with digestive chaos.
Smells innocent. Is not.

Deadly dapperling (*Lepiota brunneoincarnata*):
Graceful. Polite. A liar.
Packs alpha-amanitin, a toxin with a 10-hour delay—just long enough
to lull victims into a false sense of security.
Fatal intentions arrive on a schedule it finds convenient.

① REPORTED SYMPTOMS
Nausea. Liver failure.
A sudden realization that takeout would have been the superior life
choice.

▸▸ CONCLUSION
Mushrooms are organized, dramatic, and possibly reading from an
outdated etiquette manual.

✗ HANDLING ADVISORY
Do not poke.
Do not taste.
Do not listen if it whispers.
If found: admire respectfully, document artistically, and retreat
slowly. Purchase edible mushrooms from reputable establishments
(preferably the ones with lighting and a cashier).

Then, as if proud of itself, the app eagerly added a new section titled *"Incident Report,"* which currently contained one entry:

"Report on Slimothy: uncertainty high. Situation remains ambiguous. Confidence level: 2% and slipping."

"Directive: should any organism glow, glare, or emit existential commentary, Slimothy must disengage and file no follow-up questions."

The night hummed softly around him—leaves whispering gossip, pond pretending to meditate, moon pretending it had better things to do. The app, meanwhile, was still glowing helpfully, like a waiter who refused to take the hint that dinner was over and enlightenment wasn't being served.

Slimothy ignored it and stared into the dark beyond the compost bin, where the Wild Wood pulsed faintly at its edges—quiet, watchful, and almost expectant.

The forest winked once—mockingly—as if penciling him into its sequel anyway.

Right. Another check. He logged it in his mental ledger:

Survived probable hallucination.
Field data: interpretive at best.
Confidence in reality: 37%.
Appetite: thriving against all odds.

The Committee For Mystical Inconveniences Will See You Now

After what he charitably classified as a good night's sleep—and that was saying a lot, considering the dream about kale filing its own tax returns—Slimothy decided there was only one responsible course of action: return to the Wild Wood, on purpose this time.

If it had all been a dream, fine. If it was an interdimensional vortex, also fine, though he did make a note to file a safety complaint later, preferably under "General Mystical Inconveniences." Either way, science demanded answers, and Slimothy, scientist, gardener, and occasional chaos magnet, was prepared to deliver them.

The expedition, he knew, would be perilous. It would require bravery, strategy, and at least one unnecessary gadget. So he began to pack with great ceremony, muttering like an explorer preparing for a televised special no one had requested, narrated by a disapproving British fern.

Into his ruck-sack went:

~ One partially-used notebook (for observations, self-reflection, and doodles of hypothetical conspirators).

~ Two sharpened pencils, one for documentation and one for self-defense.

~ A compact mirror (in case he needed to confirm his own existence).

~ A stale cracker labeled "rations," though it mostly served as emotional support.

~ A laminated list titled: "Things That Probably Were Hallucinations" (the kale, the fox with the spinach, mystical seed packets).

~ A magnifying glass for dramatically peering at clues and pretending to understand them, and,

~ A small bottle labeled "Emergency Confidence," which turned out to be olive oil but felt symbolically correct.

He paused, surveying his equipment with the dramatic weight of a creature about to deliver a deeply unnecessary PowerPoint presentation. Then, feeling inspired, he added one final item: a so-called "magic bean" he'd found a few days ago—labeled only with a question mark. "For luck," he said, or possibly for plausible deniability.

He considered briefly that most great expeditions began with better plans, sturdier maps, and fewer snack-related regrets. Naturally, this led him into a five-minute spiral about preparedness, destiny, and whether he should have packed a third pencil.

Ruck-sack secured around what could only generously be described as shoulders, Slimothy faced the misty edge of the Wild Wood. The trees swayed like hungry critics, ready to award his bravery two stars, a side of identity-level unease, and a complimentary bread roll of regret.

He hesitated, glancing back at his perpetual work-in-progress of a garden. The tulips and daffodils still waited for their pots—unplanted, unamused, and silently judging like a panel of horticultural reality show hosts. "I'll be home soon," he promised softly. "Probably. Maybe. Don't start without me."

He took one deep, unnecessarily dramatic breath—the kind reserved for mythic heroes ... or anyone about to reboot their Wi-Fi.

Then Slimothy pushed forward—defying his better judgment and a few local ordinances—into the possibly unknown. His gear: optimism, snacks, and the sort of reckless confidence only a slug hauling *"Notes on Unsolicited Miracles"* and a lifetime of unresolved psychological paperwork could muster.

Maybe, if the universe was feeling merciful, he'd even find the fox again. Or at least the truth. Whichever required less cardio.